THE PLEDGE

College Bound Series

Laura Ward & Christine Manzari

This is a work of fiction. Names, characters, places, brands, media, and incidents are either the product of the authors' imagination or are used fictiously. The authors acknowledge the trademarked status and trademark owners of various products, brands, and/or restaurants referenced in this work of fiction, which have been used without permission. The publication/use of these trademarks is not authorized, associated with, or sponsored by the trademark owners.

Copyright © 2015 by Laura Ward and Christine Manzari
Cover Design by: Sarah Hansen of Okay Creations
Cover Photo by: Vania Stoyanova
Cover Models: Jordan Verroi and Fawn Coba

All rights reserved. Without limiting the rights under copyright reserved above, no part of this publication may be reproduced, stored in or introduced into a retrieval system, or transmitted, in any form, or by any means (electronic, mechanical, photocopying, recording, or otherwise) without the prior written permission of both the copyright owner and the publisher of this book.

First Edition: July 2015
Library of Congress Cataloguing-in-Publication Data

Dedication

To Christine's Gymkana friends and Laura's Alpha Omicron Pi sisters for making our college experiences unforgettable. And to anyone who has ever felt unworthy or less than. Each of us is unique and the most important pledge we can make is to believe in ourselves.

Chapter 1

Taren

"Hello ladies!" A booming voice echoed down the dormitory hallway. Denton, an eight-story, concrete block of a building, would be my home-away-from-home for the next year.

Popping her head out of our minuscule closet, my roommate, Alexis, blew a strand of blonde hair away from her eyes. "What on earth?" She shot me a questioning look.

I shrugged and peeked out our door.

"Now this is what I'm talking about!" A guy with perfectly styled, gelled hair called out with a laugh. He opened up his arms and curled his fingers in a come-hither motion. "Come to Daddy!"

My mouth fell open. A group of guys strolled down the hall in their cargo shorts and trendy T-shirts as if they owned the place. They were definitely not freshman.

Their leader headed toward me with a cocky swagger. A whistle hung from his neck. I bit back a smile as Aunt Claire's departing words of wisdom popped into my head. *Have fun and get into trouble.* I chewed on my lower lip. I was clueless in those departments, but something told me I was about to be schooled in both of them.

Tweeeeeeetttt! The guy in front blew the whistle and then let it dangle from his lips. He pointed in my direction and waggled his eyebrows. For a split second, a warm blush touched my cheeks, but then reality dawned on me. Certain he wasn't singling me out, I looked over my shoulder to see if Alexis was behind me. She wasn't. I turned back around and gave him a coy smile, trying to play it cool.

"Party tonight." His eyes scanned my body from top to bottom. "I want YOU there." My stomach dropped to the floor, and my hand casually covered my gaping mouth. *Be cool Taren.*

He handed me a flyer with a picture of a rundown house and a handwritten address. Plastered all over the paper was the word: BEER.

I tilted my head to the side. Well, then.

"Me?" I questioned, pointing at my chest and looking around again.

Whistle-blower ran his finger down the side of my arm, causing goose bumps to rise to the surface. "Of course you, darlin'. I'm Doug." My heart raced in my chest. "Party tonight at my fraternity house. Bring your friends. I'll be looking for you." He pointed to the address on the paper and walked backward when his friend called his name. "Don't let me down. Be there."

What? My face flushed, and I stared at the paper in my trembling hands. Doug wanted me at his party. I lifted my eyes and watched the guys stalking down the hallway. A sense of excitement filled me. I couldn't help but think that maybe trouble would find me after all.

"Dorm storming." Gum snapped loudly to end the sentence. A petite pixie crossed the hall to me. Her dark brown bob swayed like she was a fashion model. "Julie." She extended her hand and snapped her gum again. "Nice to meet you."

"I'm Taren. Nice to meet you, too." I propped my foot on the wall behind me and looked down the hall. "What is dorm storming?"

Julie joined me on the wall. "My cousin is in a frat back home in Pennsylvania. The fraternity guys race to the freshman dorms on move-in day and recruit people to come to their parties. They want the best guys to come, party with them, and then rush their frat. They also need the hottest girls at their parties because, duh, the hot girls are where the guys want to be."

"Oh." I looked back down at the flyer, and my excitement evaporated. "So why did he give me this?" Frowning, I handed it to her. "Was he just messing with me?" Taren Richards did not get invited to parties.

Julie jerked her head up and narrowed her eyes. "Are you for real?" She leaned back and gestured at my body with her hand. "Um, because you're hawt."

I opened my mouth ready to argue with her, but before I uttered a word, I snapped it shut.

Fresh start. New beginning. No one knows me here. That was the promise I had made to myself during summer break.

I looked down at the flyer once again and nodded with a hesitant smile. College was my chance to start over. No more fear. No more stereotypes. I could be whoever I wanted to be, and for once, I wanted to be the hawt girl.

***

Julie bounced down on Alexis' bed and almost landed in her lap. "Drink up." She handed me the bottle of rum. Her words were a dare. "Liquid courage."

I hesitated, trying to decide if I had the nerve to be different, outgoing, or even fun.

Live a little, Taren. Aunt Claire's words on our ride to campus rang in my ears. *This is college. These will be the best four years of your life. Enjoy them.*

I sniffed the liquor in the bottle I clutched. Oh my god. The vapors burned my nostrils. There was no way it was going down the hatch easily. I closed my eyes and tipped my head back, hoping for the best. The sweet, yet fiery, liquid ran down my throat before I could chicken out. I swallowed a large gulp as tears formed in the corners of my eyes, and then I coughed.

"Holy shit, T. That was amazeballs!" Julie laughed, and I passed Alexis the bottle with a grimace.

"I need this tonight," Alexis murmured and gulped down a large swig like a champ.

I was surprised both by the way Alexis swallowed the rum and that she had even agreed to come to the party with us. She had mentioned a boyfriend back home. Closing her eyes, she sucked in a large breath, and a smile spread across her face. She seemed almost relieved that we would be leaving the dorm.

Julie had planned our entire night. She went online and found the campus bus schedule. After studying the map, she found the route that would get us close to fraternity row. Somehow she had also managed to find a hook up for our pre-gaming beverage. Donning a micro-mini skirt, wedge heels, and a tube top, Julie was more than ready to enter the Greek party scene.

She passed the half empty bottle back to me. A warm buzz was already coursing through me. I drank again.

Julie leaned back. "So, going out to a party on the first night of college is a big deal. I feel like we need to get to know each other better." Julie straightened up, mischief written all over her face. "Let's play a drinking game. We'll take turns asking questions. When you answer, you have to take a drink." We nodded, and my lips spread into a wide grin. I handed the bottle back to her. By that point, my thoughts were a bit scattered and fuzzy, but pleasant.

"What was it like the first time you had sex?" Julie held the bottle under my face like a microphone, and I could feel my voice lodging in my throat, refusing to play along. How could I possibly answer the question without embarrassing myself?

"Okay, I'll go first. Mine was bad. I gave it up to my boyfriend, now ex-boyfriend. I waited until my senior year to do the deed, and then it lasted all of two point five seconds. I didn't even have a chance to realize he was in before it was over. What a waste." She shook her head in disgust. Julie pressed the bottle to her lips and tilted it back, taking a large sip. She made a hissing sound through her teeth, wiped her mouth with the back of her hand, and then handed the bottle to Alexis.

Alexis bit her lip and studied the bottle. "I haven't actually had sex yet." She took a drink and then looked up at us, her face bright red. She straightened her shoulders. "I love Liam, but we've been through a lot together. I'm not ready to complicate things. Then there's the fact that my parents hate him." She looked at the picture of her and Liam on her dresser. They were shockingly different. Night and day. Good and bad. Not that I knew that with any certainty or anything, but they certainly looked the part. She was dressed all in white. White jeans, tiny white sweater, her long blonde hair in curls. He was in all black. Tight black T-shirt, black jeans, black metal studded cuffs on his wrists, black sunglasses, and dark spiky hair. They looked like polar opposites.

"What are you waiting for?" Julie snatched the picture off the dresser to study it. "He's some mean-looking eye candy, sister. I've heard the bad boys are a little rough, but in a good way." She elbowed

Alexis, and I laughed.

Alexis shrugged and drank again. "Long story for another time. I'm just not ready yet." She handed me the bottle.

I was glad we were in the same boat. I would have been embarrassed if I was the only virgin. "Same here. I'm still a virgin. I just haven't met the right guy, I guess." *Liar.* I hadn't met *any* guy. Not a single one who was interested. Whistle-blowing Doug was the first attention I'd ever garnered for anything other than ridicule. So yeah, I was a virgin, but not exactly by choice. I took a drink and thought of a question since it was my turn. I didn't want to be too heavy, but I was curious. "What are you most afraid of?"

Julie looked contemplative, so I handed the bottle to Alexis.

"Easy one for me. I'm terrified of a lot of things, but I'd say I'm most scared of letting my parents down. I'm an only child. They have high hopes for me. I don't want to fail them." She took a long pull from the bottle, shuddering as she handed it back to me.

The psychology geniuses who wrote the personality quiz used to match roommates in college were spot on. "I think we were meant to be roommates." I smiled at her and blew out a breath. "I'm most scared of regrets. I left high school with so many things I wish I'd done differently and chances I wish I'd been brave enough to take." I sipped the rum and cleared my throat, the alcohol burning on the way down. "No more. The next four years will be about taking the steps to be who I want to be. No excuses."

Julie yelled out, "Hell yeah!" She grabbed the bottle and leaned in close to us. "Listen girls, after I answer the question, we need to jet. We're just the right amount of tipsy, and we'll be right on time to be fashionably late." She lowered her voice and she waved us closer, as if she didn't want anyone to overhear her confession. "Want to know my biggest fear?"

Alexis and I both nodded.

"I have microphobia." Julie took a drink and closed her eyes like she'd just revealed a terrible secret.

I looked at Alexis, and she shrugged, so I asked, "What's microphobia?"

Julie opened her eyes, her expression grave. "The fear of tiny things. I'm terrified of miniature dogs, fun-sized candy bars, mini-muffins, those little nightmares known as micro machines my nephew always leaves lying around..."

"What about the mini skirt you're wearing?" I pointed out, sure that she was trying to be funny.

"No, no. Clothes are fine. It has to be something genuinely mini." Her eyes opened wide and in all seriousness she asked, "Do you want to know what mini thing I fear the most?"

Alexis and I nodded.

"Tiny dicks," she whispered.

I didn't know if it was the alcohol or the girl talk, but for the first time in my life, I couldn't stop laughing.

I never wanted to stop.

Chapter 2

Alec

The black Escalade pulled away from the curb, and my mother turned in her seat to wave to me through the back window. I expected the sight of my father's taillights to give me a sense of freedom, but the weight of his expectations was still heavy on my mind.

Prove yourself, Alec. Make me forget last year ever happened.

I took a deep breath, forcing his parting words out of my thoughts. Before the SUV was out of sight, I turned and made my way toward the dorm. Something about turning my back on him and his threats gave me a sense of victory.

I jogged up the steps to find a girl with a UMD T-shirt and hipster glasses struggling to get two suitcases through the back door.

I rushed over and grabbed one from her. "Need help?"

"Oh, thanks," she said. When she looked up and met my eyes, she blushed and gave me a shy smile. I was used to the effect my looks had on girls. Instead of offering her one of my flirty lines, I held the door open for her. I wasn't in the mood to be charming right now.

She pulled her suitcase through the entrance, bumping it into the doorjamb and almost falling over in her eagerness. Reaching out to steady her, I smiled for a moment, reminded of another shy, anxious girl. My smile disappeared when I remembered that same girl was the reason for my father's last warning.

I helped hipster girl get her stuff to the elevator. Before she could give me her name, I found a set of stairs and took them two at a time up to room 7220, my new home.

I slammed the door shut and then collapsed on my bed, kicking an unopened package of sheets to the floor.

I hadn't met my roommate yet, and he was stretched out on his bed, completely at ease. His side of the room was organized and unpacked as if he'd moved in months ago. My side was littered with piles of brand new things for my dorm room and boxes that were still taped shut.

My roommate looked up from the TV and raised an eyebrow at me. "Who pissed in your Cheerios, sunshine?" He had a spoon in one hand and a white can in the other as he nodded toward the door.

I put my hands behind my head and chuckled. "My parents." Mostly it was my old man. He spent the entire ride to campus detailing what lecture series he expected me to attend and the connections I needed to be making. Alexander Hart, Sr. had grand plans. He was raising a Senator, after all. "I'm Alec." I leaned up on my elbow and held out my hand.

My roommate shoved the spoon in his mouth and wiped his palm on his shirt before extending his hand to me. "Caz," he said around the spoon. He shook my hand and then sat back on his bed.

Caz? That wasn't the name of the guy on my room assignment. This guy had to be in the wrong room. I reached for my backpack and pulled out the stack of welcome-to-campus shit I'd been sent.

"They must have sent me the wrong paperwork." I found the paper

I was looking for and double-checked the name. "It says here my roommate is—"

Caz jumped up, darting across the space between our beds to rip the sheet out of my hand. "Forget you ever saw that." He shredded the paper. "Dude. If you ever tell anyone what my real name is, I will make your life a living hell." He pointed the spoon at me like a weapon.

I put my hands up in mock defense, laughing. "Caz it is." If I had his first name, I'd go by Caz, too.

He tossed the tiny pieces of paper into the trash and returned to his bed. "The 'rents gone?"

"Finally." I grabbed the pillow still wrapped in plastic and folded it under my head. I took a good look around at the mess on my side of the room. My mom would lose her shit if she saw it, but I kind of liked the clutter.

Caz's attention was back on some CrossFit competition he'd been watching on TV. "So what is it? Are they pushy or clingy?"

"Both." I stretched my legs and then crossed them at my ankles. "My dad is a hotshot lawyer. He likes being in control of everything. My mom is the one who has a hard time letting go." I took a deep breath, remembering how my father had to coerce her out of her goodbye hug. "The curse of being an only child, I guess."

"My mom's the same, and I'm the youngest of five. She totally broke down last year when she dropped me off." Caz's eyes remained rooted on the TV as he ate frosting out of a can.

"You're a sophomore?"

Caz nodded, swallowing.

"Why did you choose to stay in the dorms?" I was already looking forward to transferring into upperclassman housing on the other side of campus. I had wanted to get an off-campus apartment, but my father said the stigma of the freshman dorms would be good for me. Teach me humility.

"Why would I move? This dorm is prime real estate, man. It's close to the gym, and the dining hall is just one quad over."

I couldn't argue with that. I looked around the room. Caz had already finished unpacking, but some of the things he had laying around were unusual. "What's this?" I pointed to the strange wooden structure that was pushed up against the end of his bed.

"Parallettes." Caz grinned as if he knew a secret. "You can borrow it if you want."

"What's it for?" It looked like two wooden towel bars had been attached to one another.

Caz got up from his bed and pulled the apparatus into the middle of the room. He gripped the bars with his hands and then kicked his feet up over his head, holding a perfect handstand.

"Holy shit, dude! How'd you learn to do that?" I'd seen a lot of party tricks, but this was one I definitely wanted to learn.

He dropped his feet back to the floor with a shit-eating grin plastered on his face, and ran his hand through his hair, making it stand up all over the place. "A lot of practice."

"You must be a pro at keg stands." I sat up to get a better look at the parallettes.

Caz laughed. "Nah, Brah. No kegs for me. I'm part of the Acroletes. We have a no-drinking policy."

"The Acroletes?" I reached over to grab the lacrosse ball sitting in the pile of junk on my desk. Reclining back on my bed, I tossed it in the air, catching it in my fist.

"Yup. Best club on campus. Come with me to practice, and I'll show you around." Caz reached for the wooden contraption again and then slowly pressed his body into another handstand. This time, he made it look like he was moving in slow motion.

Shit. That was cool.

"I have lacrosse training every afternoon. Can't miss it."

"Lacrosse is in the spring." He talked normally as if it was natural to hold a conversation while upside down.

I kept my eyes on the ball as I tossed it in the air again. "Yeah, but I have year-round commitments because of my scholarship."

"Come after your training." Caz was still holding his handstand and dipped down into an inverted pushup before pressing back up again.

"Maybe." The idea of doing something that hadn't been pre-ordained by my father was tempting. I hadn't risked temptation like that in a long time.

Caz pressed back down and stood. Then he walked over to his bed and picked up the can of frosting and took another spoonful.

I laughed. "Dude. I can't believe you're eating that."

"Sorry, man." Caz leaned over to open his mini-fridge. "How rude of me. You want one?" At least eight cans of icing and a six pack of Mountain Dew lined the shelves.

"Christ. That's a lot of fucking sugar in one place. I'm getting diabetes just looking at that."

Caz shrugged. "More for me." He snapped the lid back on the can and shoved it into the mini-fridge. "First night of college, roomie. I don't feel like spending it in this cell, how about you?"

I looked around at my unmade bed and unpacked boxes. "I'm ready to get out of here. What do you want to do?"

Caz grabbed his phone off the desk and swiped his finger across the screen. "Ever seen *American Ninja*?"

"Yeah, a few times." I got up from my bed and stretched my arms over my head.

The maniacal grin on Caz's face was a sure sign that whatever he was planning was trouble.

"Ever tried any of that shit?" He slipped his phone into his back pocket.

"Thought about it, but never had the chance."

Caz slapped his hands together and rubbed his palms against one another. "An unspoiled, adrenaline virgin." He chuckled. "It's gonna be fun popping your cherry."

My head snapped up and I looked him right in the eyes as I shook my head. "Don't repeat that."

Caz opened the door to our room and stepped into the hallway before yelling, "Let it be known that I am claiming Alec Hart's V-card tonight!"

"Stop while you're ahead," I warned. I shoved my feet into my shoes and walked out the door to join him in the hallway. "I know your real name." Caz looked at me like I'd just shoved a knife between his shoulder blades. I raised my eyebrow in challenge.

"Damn. That's a fucked up threat."

"We're still going, though, right?"

He laughed. "Like I would miss the chance to hear you scream like a little bitch."

***

We stood in the woods, decked out in harnesses and carabiners. I stared at the series of cables and obstacles that connected the trees like a demented spider web. The sky was dark, but ropes of lights were strung in the trees, illuminating the intimidating course. I watched as a guy quickly climbed several stories in the air on a wooden ladder that was attached to a tree. He unhooked the pulley from his belt and fastened it over the zip line before tossing himself off the launching pad. His body plummeted down the cable until his feet touched a platform in another tree.

I couldn't wait to burn off some frustration.

Sandy Spring Adventure Park was a ropes and zip line course about half an hour from campus. Caz's friends Jon, Maureen, and Amanda came with us. I didn't know places like this existed, but I was itching to get started. The training session on how to use the equipment had already taken too fucking long.

I heard a whooping yell, and looked up as a girl used a rope to swing down from a tree. She landed in a cargo net that was suspended at least two stories off the ground.

"You look terrified," Caz said. "You do realize there are girls here. Don't act like a little ass hat and back out."

I turned to grin at him. "You worried I'm going to show you up?"

"Twenty bucks says you get stuck on those." Caz pointed to a series of mini trapezes that were hung between two trees. "And you'll need a guide to come rescue you."

I hooked my thumbs into my harness and glanced at the tree next to us. Colorful rock climbing holds were nailed to the side of it leading up to a platform. "Twenty bucks says I can get up to that platform faster than you."

Caz looked at me like I was insane and laughed. "Easy money, roomie. I hope you brought cash with you." He pulled his phone out and opened the stopwatch feature before waving Amanda over. "You can time us," he told her.

Amanda had a hot little body and a smile to match. She was wearing a skin-tight tank top and yoga pants that left nothing to the imagination. I was digging the way the harness fit snugly around her upper thighs and hugged her ass.

She licked her lips and looked at me. "I want in on this bet."

"Buy in is twenty," Caz told her, pointing his finger in her face. "You on my side?" He puffed out his chest. "Or Hart's?" He jerked his thumb over toward me.

Amanda's gaze raked over me as a smile teased along her lips. When her eyes reached mine, I winked.

"I think Alec can give you a run for your money, Caz," Amanda said, keeping her gaze fixed on me. "I'm in. If you win, I'll give you the money. If Alec wins," she twirled the end of her ponytail around her finger and bit her bottom lip, "I'll make it worth his while in other ways."

I didn't have to guess what she meant and I was ready to cash in on whatever she was offering.

"Jesus, Amanda. Why don't you just hump his leg and get it over with?" Jon took the phone out of her hand while shaking his head. "I got twenty bucks on Caz. Sorry, Hart. He's a sure thing."

"And so is Amanda!" Caz slung his arm over her shoulder. She shoved his chest and squealed in protest, but it was half-hearted. In the end, she laughed as he pulled her into a friendly headlock.

"What about you, Maureen?" Jon asked.

Maureen was built like a body builder. She wore a serious expression that made it clear she wasn't interested in flirting or bets. She pushed past Caz and clipped her carabiner onto the safety cable of the first obstacle. "I'm here to climb, not stroke your egos." She slid her fingers over one of the holds and tucked her toes into another one.

"I've got something you can stroke." Caz grabbed his crotch.

Maureen rolled her eyes and flipped him the bird. Soon she was shimmying up the side of the tree without hesitation. Less than a minute later she pulled herself up onto the platform. She leaned over the edge. "Are you gonna talk or you gonna climb, boys?"

"Well, Hart? You ready?" Caz nodded toward the tree.

I stepped back and motioned for him to go ahead. "You're the veteran. You go first. I'll let you enjoy success before I crush your time."

Caz huffed out a laugh. "You're awfully cocky for a virgin, my friend. I'm going to have to teach you how to respect your elders." He clipped into the safety cable and placed his hands and feet in the ready position. "Count me down, Jon."

"Three...Two...One...Go!" Jon shouted.

If I had blinked, I would have missed the first half of Caz's ascent. He scaled the tree as if he was born to climb. Maureen was quick, but Caz was faster—much faster than I'd expected. Each foot placement and handhold was confident and purposeful. He was like a goddamn squirrel.

"Seventeen seconds." Jon whistled before turning to me. "Think you can beat that, Hart?"

My smile was confident. "I got twenty bucks that says I can." I stood at the bottom of the tree mapping out my route before I clipped into the safety cable. My blood was surging through my veins, and my heart beat wildly. I'd always thrived on challenge. I was addicted to the sweet thrill of competition. That's what I loved most about lacrosse—the battle. This wasn't any different.

"Go!" Jon said.

I pushed off the ground, my arm muscles straining as I pulled myself up the side of the tree. Caz and Maureen had made it look easy, but Amanda's cheers were proof that I was holding my own.

"Eleven...Twelve..." Jon counted from below.

I was a little over halfway up, but if I wanted to win, I needed to hurry. Skipping over the closest grip, I reached for one higher up knowing I could use my arm strength to make up some time. My fingers curled around the edge of the plastic and I pushed off with my legs. My foot slipped and I ended up dangling by one arm, swinging around until my back hit the tree.

My breath caught in my throat as I glanced down at the ground twenty feet below. If I fell from this height, I could kiss my lacrosse scholarship goodbye. I knew the safety cable wouldn't let me fall, but knowing that and trusting it were two different things.

"Thirteen..."

"Hurry." Amanda had her hands cupped around her mouth. "You can still win."

She had no idea I'd been envisioning fractured bones and broken dreams. Sweat trickled down my neck as I swung myself around to face the tree. I reached up with my other arm and grabbed a handhold. I gritted my teeth as I yanked myself up the remaining part of the climb and over the edge of the platform.

When I finally pulled myself to a standing position, Caz was smiling. He held his fist out and I bumped it with mine as I breathed heavily.

"That was pretty awesome, dude, but you owe me twenty bucks."

"Double or nothing next obstacle?" I bounced on my feet, energy and life surging through my body.

He grinned. "You're on." Flipping his pulley over the zip line in front of him, he threw himself off the platform. He flew down the cable, howling like an animal.

I looked down to see Amanda climbing onto the platform behind me. I reached down to help her stand, and she sucked on her bottom lip before smiling.

"Sorry you lost," she said. "But it was still a worthy climb for a first timer. I think that deserves a little something." She ran her finger along my chest.

"Is that so?" I grinned back, my hand resting on her hip as we stood close to each other on the small platform. "What did you have in mind?"

Amanda reached up and wrapped her hand around my neck, pulling my face down to hers. When our lips touched, her tongue was immediately in my mouth. *Christ.* She certainly wasn't shy. I gripped the cable above me to steady myself as I kissed her back. With my other hand, I grabbed the harness at her waist and pulled her against me. She moaned into my mouth and I was so turned on I wanted to press her up against the tree and devour her.

I should lose more often.

"There's no kissing on the obstacle course!" Caz yelled.

I pulled back from Amanda and looked across the way to my roommate. "Jealous?"

"Let's go, Hart. You're not getting out of this by sucking face, you pansy ass. It's trapeze time. I'm ready to make another twenty," he yelled back.

I smiled at Amanda as I unhooked the pulley from my harness and attached it to the zip line cable. "Thanks for the reward."

"That wasn't a reward." Amanda tucked her tongue in her cheek. "That was a preview."

Fuck. Yes.

Without a thought to what I was about to do, I gripped the pulley and launched my body off the platform. I hurtled down the cable, suspended thirty feet in the air, the wind tearing at my clothes. My heart was crashing against my rib cage, as adrenaline surged through me.

I had no fear.

I felt alive.

For the first time in my life, I was free.

Chapter 3

Taren

Music blared out of each and every house on the row, their conflicting beats confusing my alcohol-muddled brain. Confused or not, my anticipation was on overdrive. The houses on Fraternity Row sat in a horseshoe. People stumbled in and out of the front doors. Strobe lights flashed from inside one house, while spotlights blazed on the front of another.

I looked down at the picture of the flyer I'd taken with my phone and pointed to the next house in line. "That one!" I shouted.

Julie clutched my right hand, and I held Alexis' hand in my left. Butterflies danced a mosh pit in my stomach. I was so scared and excited and nervous and ready—ready to break free and let loose. I took a deep breath and led my friends up the wooden stairs and through the open door. Inside I was hit by the overwhelming stench of beer. We squeezed by the worn leather couches. The walls were decorated with huge, glass-encased, composite pictures of the brothers of Delta Epsilon. Row after row, picture after picture, they all looked the same—handsome, smiling guys in blue blazers and matching ties. Only the hairstyles gave any indication of what year the pictures were taken.

We edged past a folding table and the wannabe DJ who was busy taking song requests from a line of scantily dressed, giggling girls. Julie tried to pull us into the middle of the room where a group was dancing, but I shook my head no. I had no ability to dance, whatsoever.

"Catch!" A clean-cut guy wearing a polo, collar popped up, yelled as a ping-pong ball headed right for Alexis.

"Got it!" Her reflexes were fast and she snagged the ball out of the air before it hit her. The guy who yelled out the warning waved us over and we walked to the other side of the room, where he stood next to another folding table that was set up with cups.

"Know how to play?" The preppy polo dude smiled at Alexis and nodded toward the cups.

"I've seen it done before." Alexis walked to the edge of the table and bounced a ping-pong ball across the table. The ball landed right into one of the beer-filled red Solos. The guy at that end of the table muttered a curse and chugged the beer, much of it sliding down his shirt on the process. Preppy polo cheered and wrapped an arm around Alexis' shoulders.

"I'm Asher. You've got to be my partner." He squeezed her closer and I noticed her body stiffen.

"No...I can't...I'm with friends...Bye," Alexis stammered, shrugging out of Asher's grip.

Tweeeeettttt!

"Oh snap. Here comes whistle boy," Julie said two notches too loud in my ear, and I turned in time to bump right into whistling Doug.

"You came! Denton girl came!" Doug picked me up and twirled me around before placing me back on my feet. "Let's get you ladies something to drink!"

Doug ushered us over to a large black trashcan filed with ice and beer. Another pearl of wisdom from Aunt Claire hit me. *If you remember anything I've taught you, remember this. Never drink anything that is served from a garbage can.*

The height of gentility, Doug pulled out three cans, popped the tabs, and handed each of us a National Bohemian. I studied the can and giggled. I was going to break Claire's rule my first night out. Then again, she did tell me to get into trouble.

"Natty Boh?" Julie took a sip. "Eh. Even after all that rum, this shit still tastes like piss water." She wrinkled her nose as she chugged her beer. "But it's free, and it's beer. So thank you whistle dude."

Doug saluted her and then tilted his head back and downed his entire beer in one shot. He belched and crushed the can on his forehead.

Julie rolled her eyes. "I think he just crushed his last remaining brain cells with that brilliant move. Time to get our groove on girls." She grabbed our hands to lead us to the dance floor.

"Wait! Denton, don't go!" Doug begged. I turned back around to see him on his knees, shuffling toward me with his hands pressed together in a gesture of prayer. "I wanted to get to know you better." I smiled, hoping that would keep my jaw from dropping open. This was a first. I looked between Julie and Alexis and threw caution to the wind. "You guys dance. No regrets, right?"

"Fine," Alexis stated with a look of disapproval. "But just so you know, we won't be going home without you. I'll check back in an hour. If you're not here, we'll come find you." She gave me a quick hug while Julie squealed and hurried out onto the dance floor. Without a second thought, she joined the sweating bodies and pulsing rhythms.

Doug stood up, leaning into me so I could hear him over the music. "Want to go somewhere quiet and talk?"

In the back of my mind, a small voice told me this wasn't a smart decision. I chose to ignore that voice and nodded.

"Come on, Denton." Doug took my hand and led me around the corner to a closed door covered in graffiti. "This is my room. No one will bother us here."

I followed Doug into the dark room, and my knee bumped into something. *Dang, that hurt.* My eyes took a minute to adjust. Doug had guided me around a pole. The pole was one of several used to hold up a high platform, like the top of a bunk bed. Doug ducked underneath and switched on a desk lamp. Instead of a bottom bunk, a desk, dresser, and a chair were in the space. An identical structure was set up across the room. I was assuming the areas on top were for beds, but they were hidden, covered in draped sheets and blankets to look like tents. What were they hiding in there?

Doug placed his hand on my back and walked me over to a small sofa. I stopped walking when realization hit me.

Oh...right.

Doug sat down, but I stood in front of him, a bit unsure what I should do next. This was so new to me, and I hadn't the slightest idea how to handle myself. I didn't want him to know I was inexperienced, but I didn't want him to think I was easy either.

Doug took my hands and pulled me down next to him. "Whaddya think of your first college party?"

My pulse raced, and I wanted to shake my head to clear the fog from my brain. "Um, it's great. Nice. I..."

My voice trailed off. I didn't know how to do this. What should I say? I couldn't even manage a coherent sentence right now. No, I could do this. *Fresh start. New beginning. No one knows me here.* "It was really nice of your frat to invite us." I smiled, proud of myself for not only putting more than two words together, but also speaking them aloud.

"Fraternity." Doug's voice sounded irritated, and my stomach plummeted to the floor.

"Excuse me?" I stuttered and tucked my hair behind my ear. I knew I would say something wrong.

"It's not a *frat*—it's a fraternity. You wouldn't call your country a cunt, now would ya, Denton?" He winked at me, and I relaxed. A little. Whistleblower Doug took this Greek stuff very seriously.

"No. And I wouldn't call a cocktail a cock," I said, eager to play along.

His head tilted to the side, and his eyebrows furrowed as he looked at me. "Right."

Oh crap. Did I seriously just say *cock*? How awkward could I possibly be? First night out and I said cock to the only guy interested in talking to me. *Abort. Abort.*

"I should probably get back to my friends," I said nervously, starting to stand. Doug's hand was quickly on my arm, pulling me back down to the couch and I fell even closer to him.

"Not yet, Denton. We're just getting to know each other." He grinned and brought his face closer to mine. I could smell the beer lingering on his breath. "You're so damn pretty." My body tensed as he continued to move in closer. I watched as he closed his eyes, tilted his head, and headed for my face. He was cute. Definitely not a hottie, but he was decent. Decent was good, right?

His lips were a breath away from mine.

Ohmygod! He was going to kiss me. I wasn't ready. I hadn't prepared for this. I needed to research the best kissing tips. I needed a mint. Hell, he needed a mint. *Quick, do something, Denton.* I tilted my head in the same direction as his and our foreheads knocked together.

"Sorry!" I whispered, pulling back quickly.

He smiled, leaned in again, and brought his lips to mine. His lips felt...nice. Only I wasn't sure what to do with mine. I kept my lips pressed together until something wet and warm pushed at them.

Mother Scratcher! His tongue. *Retreat! Retreat!* Wait. No. Tongue was normal. This was a good thing.

I opened my mouth, just a smidge, and allowed him access. Doug grunted his approval and moved closer still. He pressed his chest against mine while his hands dug into my hair. The thirty minutes I had spent perfecting my hair were wasted.

Never mind that, Denton, you're getting your first kiss.

Doug's tongue continued to flop around like a fish. I didn't have any other tongues to compare his to, but it felt huge in my mouth. Girls liked this sort of thing?

He pulled back, and his head cocked to the side. "You gonna participate here, Denton?"

"What do you mean?" Warmth crept up my neck and flushed my face. I was doing something wrong, and I didn't have a clue what it was.

He brought his mouth close to my ear and whispered, "You gotta move your tongue around, too. Kiss me back, you know?"

No, I didn't know, but I was a quick study. I licked the corner of my lips and took a good look at his. I could do this kissing thing. I would tongue wrestle with that big wet fish and show that whistle-blower just how good this good girl could be.

"Sorry. I've been drinking a bit tonight." I smiled and squared my shoulders. With liquid courage on my side, I was loose enough to let go a little and have some fun.

Doug leaned in again. This time, I tilted my head correctly, avoiding his nose and opening my lips as soon as we made contact. He shoved his tongue in, ready for round two, and I lifted mine in return. He grunted again, and I gave myself an imaginary fist pump. Apparently, grunts from boys were good.

I moved my tongue around his in a slippery kind of tango, and my confidence grew. I hadn't felt any of those tell-tale fireworks yet that everyone was always waxing poetic about, but maybe that was because I was concentrating so hard on not screwing up. Maybe all first kisses were like this.

"You find some fresh meat, Pickles?" A voice from above called out, and I jumped back.

"Shut it, Watson." Doug lifted his middle finger, and I followed the direction of his gesture to see a guy with shaggy brown hair poking his head out from the opening in one of the tent beds.

Sweet merciful crap. Had he been there the whole time? This was completely mortifying. My flushed face now burned with heat. Had he heard us? I wanted to die.

"Hiya, Dougy!" A female face appeared next to Watson and I wanted to hide in the other tent bed. This wasn't really happening, was it?

"Hi, Katie." Doug turned to me, apologetically. "I didn't know my roommate was up there with his girl. Sorry." He stood up and offered me his hand. "We'll give you all some privacy."

We walked into the hallway and he turned to face me, leaning against the wall with his arms crossed across his chest. "You ready to go back to the party or do you want to find someplace else to be alone?"

"Do you even want to know my name?" I wiped my sweaty palms on my jeans. I needed to calm the hell down.

He grinned. "Sure, Denton."

"Taren Richards. And you are Doug…" I stretched out his name, hoping he would fill in the blank. I had my first kiss with a guy whose last name I didn't know and he didn't seem to even care to know my name at all. Talk about a fresh start.

"Pickles." He beamed proudly. "Doug Pickles."

I bit my lip to keep from laughing. His last name was Pickles? I had my first kiss with a guy named Pickles?

"So you want to go talk some more, Denton?" Doug leaned in closer, still smiling, like he was going to kiss me right here in the hallway.

"I should probably check in with my friends." I just kissed a guy I barely knew while his roommate was hooking up with another girl not ten feet away in a tent bed. I was feeling a little unnerved.

"Sure thing, Denton. I need another beer anyway." Pickles grabbed my hand and led me back down the hall. His hand was clammy, but he held mine firmly. The possessive way he held on to me gave me a thrill. We entered the now out of control party. He cleared a path while I searched the room for Julie and Alexis. Alexis stood in a corner, tapping away on her iPhone. Julie, on the other hand, danced on a coffee table, sandwiched between two guys. I stood on my toes and waved to each of them. Julie hugged both guys before hopping down from the table. Alexis tucked her phone in her back pocket and made her way over to us, eyeing Doug's hand in mine.

She rubbed her temples. "You guys ready to go? I'm exhausted."

I nodded. The combination of loud music and alcohol had my head begging for a break. I squeezed Doug's arm. "Thanks for inviting us. We have to go, but I had a good time."

"Need your digits, Denton." Doug waved his phone at me. I took it and typed in my number under "Denton" because I wasn't actually sure he remembered my name even though I had told him less than five minutes ago. I handed his phone back, and he tucked it into his pocket.

"Catch you later!" He winked and headed straight for the trash can of beer.

"I'm sorry if I'm cutting your night short," Alexis frowned.

"I'm ready to go back, too," I admitted, slipping my hands into my friends' arms so we wouldn't get separated as we navigated our way back outside.

"Me too." Julie exhaled loudly. "Next time maybe we shouldn't do so much prep work beforehand. That bottle of rum is cashing in right about now."

Once we were out of the stuffy house and enjoying the cool August night, we started the walk to the campus bus stop.

"What were you up to with Whistler?" Julie bumped my arm with her elbow.

"Not much. Just a kiss." I would not, could not, tell them that it was my first kiss. I was already embarrassed to be a college freshman who hadn't been kissed before. Confessing that I had my first kiss with a guy I had just met could put me in the skank category. I breathed in the warm summer air and walked with a skip in my step. I felt alive. Exhilarated. Being wanted by a guy felt incredible.

"You kissed him?" Julie squealed, as I nodded.

"Did you even bother to ask Whistler for his name?" She questioned with narrowed eyes. We sat on the bench to wait for the next bus.

His name. Oh, hell. I was never going to live this down. I knew it. Might as well own it.

"Yup. I kissed Mr. Doug Pickles."

We all paused before laughing. Of all the guys on campus, I had to hook up with one who was named Pickles.

Julie finally calmed down long enough to speak. "Please tell me you didn't tickle that pickle; you hardly know the guy!" Then she laughed so hard she snorted.

Alexis dissolved in a fit of giggles. She fell off the bench and knocked over a newspaper vending machine. "Oh my god. Stop it. I'm going to pee."

Between the uncontrollable laughter and clumsiness, we were creating quite a racket, making it more difficult to be serious. Two campus police officers approached us as Alexis stumbled around, trying to get the machine upright again.

"We're going to need you to calm down, ladies." The shorter officer had his thumbs tucked into his belt loops as he glared at us. Even that wasn't enough to sober us up. We tried to get the giggling under control, but it was damn near impossible.

"Destruction of property and underage public intoxication are both very serious offenses," warned the bigger officer. He didn't look much older than us, but he was wearing an official looking uniform and an expression that wasn't quite as severe as his partner's.

"Shit," Julie whispered loudly to us. "He's gorgeous! I might have to do something indecent just to get arrested. Junior Officer Hotpants can handcuff me any time."

"Julie!" Alexis and I blurted out at the same time. God. I hoped Hotpants hadn't heard her. One look at the smirk on his face was proof that he probably had. Which made the goody-two-shoes in me so nervous that I hiccupped. I did not want to go to jail no matter how hot the arresting officer might be. Could campus police arrest you? I wasn't willing to risk it.

"I think you ladies need to get on the next bus, go home, and sleep it off," Hotpants suggested.

"Yes, sir." Alexis politely answered him as she finally got the newspaper stand back to where it should be.

Luckily, a campus shuttle pulled up. The three of us shuffled onto it before Hotpants could change his mind. We found three empty seats and collapsed into them, trying not to laugh at our idiocy, but failing miserably. Or wonderfully. I couldn't decide which. I was feeling pretty incredible at the moment.

I had my fresh start.

Chapter 4

Alec

I had hit the jackpot when it came to roommates, but Caz had his asshole moments. Like this morning when he threw a sneaker at my chest at 7:00 am and then demanded we go for a run. When he made up his mind, I had no chance of changing it.

We were almost back to the dorm when Caz led me to a building right across the street from our dorm. "I want to show you something."

"I hope it's a big plate of pancakes and hash browns because I'm fucking starved." We slowed down to a walk, and I took deep breaths, wiping the sweat off my forehead with the bottom of my shirt.

"Hey, I offered you a can of Betty's best this morning. It's not my fault you declined." He drained the rest of his water before tossing it into a nearby recycling can. When we reached the entrance, he pulled open the door and I followed him inside.

"I don't know who told you icing was a meal, but they were yanking your dick, compadré." I followed Caz down the hall. Despite how early it was, we weren't the only ones finishing up a workout. The building was filled with people carrying racquets and gym bags.

"Don't hate on Betty, man. Our friendship has limits," Caz retaliated.

My roommate was a fucking weirdo, but at least he was interesting. We jogged up a flight of stairs, and Caz led me to a wall of windows. "This is where the Acroletes train."

The room was more like an arena, the ceiling several stories high. Inside I could see gymnastics equipment and trampolines of all different sizes. I thought he'd said the Acroletes was a club.

"What do you guys do in there?" I leaned closer to the window so I could see more clearly. In the dark corners of the massive room, ladders were tied to the ceiling and ropes hung from rafters. For the life of me, I couldn't figure this shit out.

"Badass stuff. You take gymnastics, mix it with the circus, add in a little extreme sports, and you have the Acroletes. Oh, and don't forget flipping through fire. That's the best part."

"That sounds insane." Memories of zip lines and obstacles flashed through my mind. I needed to come back and check this out later.

"You mean awesome. Come to practice, you won't be sorry." Caz walked backward toward the main entrance, and I turned to follow him.

"It depends how training goes." I looked back over my shoulder for one more peek. Who was I kidding? I wouldn't be able to stay away.

"We have the hottest chicks on campus, Hart. You haven't seen anything as fine as girls in spandex bouncing on trampolines." He tilted his head. "Amanda will be there."

I laughed and considered what he said. Girls, spandex, and trampolines. You couldn't go wrong with that combo. Besides, if Amanda's kiss the other night was a preview, I was ready to catch up with her again for another viewing. "I guess I have no choice then."

***

People think that the life of a university athlete is all fortune and glory. That's because they don't see all the hours we spend getting abused on the field or working our asses off in the gym. There was a lot of grunt work that went into the actual playing of the game. That part sucked.

My muscles screamed as I pushed the bar up, and Jeremy, who was spotting, helped me guide it back to the support. I never liked lifting weights, but now I hated it. Caz and his ropes course had ruined my idea of working out.

"Nice," Jeremy said. "Spot me?"

I traded places with him, glancing at the clock. If training ended on time, I'd be able to make it to the Acroletes practice, if I hurried.

Jeremy reached up, adjusting his grip around the bar. "This is not what I thought training was going to be like. I can't wait to get on the field and do actual drills." He lifted the bar off the supports and lowered it to his chest. "This shit sucks." He growled through his teeth. His breath hissed out of his mouth as he pushed the weight up.

"Tomorrow we have interval training," I reminded him. "You'll be missing this place when you're puking up your guts after the sprint drills and burpees."

Jeremy grunted as he forced the bar up in another rep. He did a few more before finishing his set and then sat up. He grabbed the towel and wiped his face. "Any interest in getting together before weight training to do some stick drills? Toss the ball around a bit?"

I shrugged. "Sure. I don't have a class beforehand. I'm free."

"Cool. Meet me tomorrow at two on the practice field."

"Time to hit the showers boys!" Coach called. The sound of weights crashing back into place filled the room as we headed for the locker room.

"Hart. Hold up a minute," Coach barked out.

"See you tomorrow," I told Jeremy as I tossed my towel into the bin and headed for Coach. I stretched my neck from side to side and rolled my shoulders, wondering what I'd done to deserve a lecture.

He leaned a shoulder against the wall and watched with a serious expression as my teammates left. When we were alone, he said, "Your father called me yesterday to check in on your progress."

Fuck. I'd been at college for less than a goddamn week and the man was already breathing down my neck.

"Yes, sir." I nodded, trying to appear unfazed.

"He asked me to give you some extra sets in the weight room to make sure you maintained your focus. He's concerned you'll lose your way here on campus before the season starts. Is there something going on that I need to know about?"

Other than the fact that my father is a prick? "No, sir. My father is…" I paused, searching for the right words but all I could think of was *an asshole.*

Coach cut me off. "I get it. I meet guys like him all the time." He crossed his arms and pushed off the wall to stand in front of me like a brick wall. "Listen, Hart. I treat my players like adults. I have no interest in being your daddy, but you need to keep on the straight and narrow. Don't make this harder on yourself by giving him reason to interfere. I don't have time for it and neither do you. Prove him wrong."

Nodding, I turned to head to the locker room, and Coach slapped me on the back. *Prove him wrong.* I'd spent most of my life trying to show my old man I wasn't a fuckup.

***

The double doors to the Acroletes gym were swung wide open, but through the windows I could already see bodies flipping through the air. No wonder they needed such high ceilings.

I entered the lobby and my pulse kicked up a notch as I stared at the surrounding activity. A guy right in front of me was spinning around a high bar like he was going to rip it right off its supports. The rest of the gym was a gymnastic free-for-all. Orderly chaos was the only way to describe it. I wanted to try it all.

"I knew you'd come." Caz jogged up to me, a self-satisfied grin on his face. "Come check out the trampolines."

Off to the left, and what I hadn't been able to see through the front window earlier, was another huge room filled with five trampolines.

My eyes widened, and energy surged through me like a raging tsunami. "Fuck yeah. Where can I put my stuff?"

"Over there." Caz motioned to a wall of lockers against the wall. "Oh, and keep your eyes open. Double mini trampoline and vault do their runs over there by the carpet. People get pissed if you get in their way." He pointed to the other side where people were running, jumping, and spinning into the air. "Plus, it sucks to take a donkey kick to the face if someone flips on top of you."

"Got it."

Caz slapped me on the back. "Let me know if you need anything." He headed for the room of trampolines and yelled something that sounded like, "Move over bitches, my turn!"

As I was tossing my stuff into one of the free lockers, I felt a tap on my shoulder. I turned to find Amanda standing behind me in tight, tiny shorts and an even smaller sports bra. I grinned to myself. Two minutes into Acroletes' practice, and it was already more interesting than weight training.

"Did you come to play?" Amanda tilted her head. I couldn't help but notice that her words weren't so much a question as they were an offer—and not just about the gym. The kiss and promise she'd made at the ropes course were still fresh in my mind.

"Yeah, Caz invited me. I'm gonna check out the trampolines." I hooked my thumb over my shoulder, but Amanda reached out to grab my free hand.

"No, you have to come balance with me." She pulled me toward the carpeted floor on the other side of the gym. "It'd be a shame to waste all this muscle. I've been looking for a new partner since my old one graduated last year."

I allowed her to pull me along. I didn't know what the hell balancing was, but with Amanda's hands on me, it wasn't something I was going to turn down. "I'm not planning to join," I warned her. "I'm just here for today."

She shrugged. "That's okay. We can just play around. You never know, you might change your mind."

I chuckled. "Caz seems to think so, too. He doesn't know how to take no for an answer."

We reached the carpeted area, and she turned to face me. "Funny. People say the same thing about me." A wicked gleam danced in her eye and...goddamn, she was hot.

A thousand inappropriate things battled to come out of my mouth. I rubbed my palms together, looking at the people around us. "I've never done anything like this before."

Amanda reached up to tighten her ponytail, putting her sleek body on display and drawing my gaze back to her. "Don't worry, I'll tell you where to put your hands."

"Are we still talking about balancing?" I grinned at her.

"For now. Later you can tell me where to put my hands." The corner of her mouth pulled up into a smile as she arched an eyebrow. Before I could respond, she pointed to the floor. "Lie down, arms up."

I did as I was told and Amanda moved so that she was standing over top of me, a foot on either side of my hip.

"There you are. What the fuck happened to you? I thought you were coming to the trampoline room?" Caz glared down at me.

"I got sidetracked." I grinned up at him, and Amanda leaned over, putting her shoulders into my outstretched hands before gripping my elbows.

"I'm teaching him how to do an arm-to-arm," Amanda said. She pressed her body into a tuck before extending her legs straight into the air. Her body snapped into the pose with ease, and I was surprised at how easy it was to balance her.

"More like giving him a free show," Caz muttered. "That sports bra is begging for a wardrobe malfunction."

Instead of being offended, Amanda giggled as she came out of the pose. She straddled my hips as she stood above me—all soft curves and tight muscles.

"Coach wants you over at beam," he told her, nodding toward the area where all the different apparatus were set up. "I'm stealing Alec."

Amanda rolled her eyes at Caz before turning her attention to me and lifting her mouth into a smile. "Next time I'll teach you a hand-to-hand."

I laughed and shook my head at her assumption that my return was a foregone conclusion.

"Come on, let me show you how to vault." Caz waved his hand for me to follow him. "I want to watch you crash and burn."

"What makes you think I'll crash?" I got up, and we walked toward the area where people were using mini trampolines to flip over a wooden box. I swallowed past the apprehension lodged in my throat. Nervous energy flowed through me. I stretched my fingers and shook out my hands as we stood in line waiting our turn.

"You're getting pretty friendly with Amanda." Caz stood with his hands on his hips, but he didn't meet my eyes.

"Are you calling Bro Code on her?" I didn't steal other guys' girls if that's what he was worried about. Besides, he was the one who told me she'd be here.

Caz whipped around. His lip curled in disgust and his eyebrows pinched low. "Fuck no. If you want Amanda, she's all yours, dude." He stepped forward as the line moved. "Just don't be surprised if you see her hanging all over someone else later on. That's just how she is."

"Noted." I wasn't looking for a girlfriend. I had too much going on with training and classes as it was. If Amanda wanted no-strings-attached fun, I was the right guy for the job.

"So, have you ever flipped before?" Caz asked, abandoning the topic of Amanda.

I shrugged. "Off a diving board." Only two people waited in front of us. I rolled my shoulders, excitement racing through me as we got closer. I felt like I was about to run into a burning building to rescue a baby or something.

"Okay. Let's start small." Caz pointed toward the trampoline and box. "Run hard, jump on the mini tramp, and just try to clear the box. No rotation. Get used to the flight before you start flipping."

I nodded, bouncing on my toes as the girl in front of me took off in a run. When she landed safely on the other side of the vaulting box, Caz pushed me forward. I ran toward the trampoline, my heart thudding with each step. When I hit the small round bed and my body shot into the air and over the box, adrenaline surged through my chest, lighting my entire body on fire. In that moment, right before my feet landed back on the mat, I knew it was too late. The Acroletes had gotten under my skin. I was addicted.

Chapter 5

Taren

"I'm sorry." Julie stood in front of my closet, holding a plaid tunic that was bedazzled with sequins. "You own this? Like you've actually walked over to your closet and put it on your body? Willingly?"

"I have the fashion judgment of a blind nun. I get it. That's why I asked you for help, Jules." I reclined on my bed with my forearm pressed against my eyes. I didn't need to look at the atrocity in her hands. I knew how heinous my wardrobe was. Unfortunately, my high school years had been more focused on rocking the bell curve than rocking any fashion sense. Sadly, my closet had suffered greatly.

"You don't own skinny jeans. Not one pair. But you own a shit-ton of corduroy. Why?"

I groaned in shame. I wore whatever was comfortable. Evidently, corduroy and plaid had crept into the rotation, and to be honest, I had no explanation for how that happened. Even I knew wearing corduroy was akin to giving myself social leprosy.

"Alexis, look at this. This is so tacky!" Julie held up a floral sweater twinset. "I didn't know twinsets still existed!"

Alexis raised her head from her iPad, eyebrows arched. "Hey, that's mine."

"Oh, I, uh, sorry, Lex. I didn't mean to..." Julie stammered, a pink flush warming her cheeks.

Alexis put her iPad down next to her and sat cross-legged on her bed. "It's fine, Jules. You know I need help, too. My clothes basically have *virgin* stamped across the chest." Alexis laughed at herself. I was once again reminded how lucky I was to have her as a roommate.

She and I both wanted a fresh start, and the first step was shedding our old, boring styles. We were trusting Julie with our makeovers. Goodbye sheltered, mundane wallflowers. Hello confident, gorgeous, social butterflies. At least that was the plan. First, we needed updated wardrobes.

Once Alexis' attention was back on the iPad, Julie tossed the offending twinset into the donation pile...or burning pile if Jules had her way. She turned back to the closets of shame to continue the weeding process.

"Did Whistler ever call you?" she asked, weighing the fate of yet another fashion fail.

My stomach twisted until it felt like it was in a knot. Nearly a week had passed since he asked for my number. After the third day of no calls, I had to resign myself to the fact that Doug Pickles had come to his senses once he took off his beer goggles.

"No, he didn't." I shrugged and stared at the text book in front of me. I tried to play it off like it was nothing, but deep down the pain of dismissal was as acute as it had been in high school. Rejection never got easier to bear. At least this time, the rejection wasn't broadcast in front of the entire school, leaving me with permanent loser status.

"His loss. You can do better than him anyway. Okay. Clean out is complete." She tossed a few more offending items into the donation pile. "Time to replenish these closets." Julie sat down at my desk and clicked the keys on my laptop, navigating to her favorite online store. She was eager to use the money we'd given her to purchase new outfits for us.

I read from my textbook while Julie shopped. She was quiet for several minutes as she searched. That didn't last long, though.

"Yes." *Click.* "Yes." *Click.* "Oh hell yes." *Click.* "Need it." *Click.* "Want it." *Click.* "*Mother father*, that one is sweet!"

"Jules! We have limited budgets. Don't go crazy." Alexis sat up straight and attempted to sound strict. The smile she couldn't hold back gave her away. Neither of us looked to see what Julie was choosing for us. Our friendship was still brand new, but we already trusted one another completely. I'd never trusted anyone with such devoted friendship before.

Being friends with these girls felt good.

Having friends at all felt incredible.

"Done. There were three bucks left, so I bought myself a neon thong. Consider it my commission." Julie snapped the laptop shut and headed for the door. "I've got some reading to do for class, but don't forget about the rush informational meeting. It's Thursday at five o' clock."

Alexis groaned and fell back against her pillows. "Are you really making us go? I am so not sorority girl material."

"Neither am I. I can't imagine fitting in with a sorority." The truth was, I wasn't afraid that I wouldn't find one that I liked. I was afraid of being excluded. I knew all too well what it was like to be the last pick in schoolyard selections. I wasn't looking forward to the reminder of that humiliation at the college level.

"Stop it. The Greek system will embrace you." Julie threw her arms open wide. "Besides, you promised." She air kissed us and closed the door behind her.

"Are you sure about this?" Alexis lay sideways on her bed, facing me.

"No, but I love Julie, and I promised to reinvent myself in college. No regrets, right?" Alexis nodded. "Let's go together, and if we find out all the sorority houses suck, we don't have to pledge."

"Can we also make a promise to do it together? I mean, choose a house we like and hope they like us both? Alexis flopped onto her back and stared at the ceiling. "I don't want to do this without you." Her face pinched, and she closed her eyes. "I have a lot going on back home."

She'd hinted before that her home life was not the best. I could only hope that she would trust me enough to confide in me one day. "Of course. I feel the same way." I smiled at her, but deep down the violent thrashing of my high school insecurity reared its ugly head.

Alexis was beautiful, and with a few wardrobe changes, she'd have no problem pledging a sorority. I, on the other hand, was another story. I couldn't see how I could possibly be converted from geek to Greek. My nerdy roots might run too deep.

"I'm so glad you're my roommate, Taren." Alexis spoke softly, her voice strained. "I didn't have many close friends in high school."

"I didn't have any." I pulled at the end of my pillowcase, avoiding the look of pity I was sure to see in her eyes.

"What do you mean? You can't be serious." Alexis sat up and pulled her knees to her chest.

"My Aunt Claire has always been my closest friend." I swallowed against the lump in my throat, guilty at the thought of my aunt. She was my only family, and she had sacrificed for me in more ways than I could count.

"What about your parents?" Alexis tilted her head to the side, biting her lip as if bracing herself for my answer.

"My mom died years ago. I never met my dad." I wiped at the brimming tears in my eyes. My tears weren't for my parents. Sure I missed having them in my life, but it was more. Talking to Alexis about my lack of friends back home brought back so many memories. Not many that were good. In fact, a few that were awful. More than anything, I realized how lonely I'd been. I hadn't known how much I needed a friend until I met her.

She jumped off her bed and hopped up next to me on mine. Slinging an arm around my shoulder, she hugged me to her. "Well, you and I are just going to have to become sisters then, aren't we? We both really need that."

Sniffing, I rested my head on her shoulder and nodded. "Yeah, I really do need that."

***

"Jules, you just inhaled that pizza, and you have room for more?" I teased. Julie was attempting to conquer a mountain of FroYo sitting on top of a small cone. Contrary to popular belief, the dining hall food wasn't all bad. I mostly stuck to turkey sandwiches or the salad bar. Tonight, however, we had decided we needed real, homemade pizza and frozen yogurt, so we ventured off campus to Route One.

"Shopping burns calories for me. Then I get hungry. Shut it." She glared at me before grinning. Then she went right back to her conquest.

Alexis stopped walking in front of a coffee shop filled with students. "The coffee smells so good. Hold on a sec, I'm going to buy a cup." Alexis walked into the shop, having claimed she was too full from pizza for frozen yogurt.

"Ooooh! I think I need that dress over there." Julie pointed to the boutique window next door and walked over, peering through the glass at a hot pink dress.

I looked around Route One, the main road that ran along campus, as I ate small bites of my chocolate FroYo. The street was filled with funky stores, as well as the typical college-town bars, restaurants, and take-out places. Small wrought iron tables sat clustered in front of a café, where students lingered, eating and talking. I smiled at the peaceful image, but then my grin vanished.

Alec Hart. I'd recognize him anywhere.

He leaned back and laughed, tagging a blond guy on the arm. The guy smacked the back of Alec's head and a tiny brunette leaned close to Alec and spoke into his ear. His grin grew bigger, and his head turned in my direction as he spoke to her.

I plastered my back against the brick wall of the coffee shop. *Don't let him see me. Don't let him see me.* My heart stopped beating. I was sure it did.

After a few moments, I ventured another look to where he sat. Thankfully, he hadn't noticed me. God, he looked so hot. Why did jerks like him get to be hot? It made hating them that much harder. The small girl next to him ran her fingers up his leg, resting them high on his thigh. My face burned. They were a couple. Of course, they were together. She was beautiful. He was gorgeous. Pretty people paired up. That was how it worked in life. Everything was easy for pretty people.

The bells on the door of the coffee shop jingled as Alexis came out, sipping a large cup of steaming coffee. "That place is so cute. They even have live music on Tuesday nights."

Noticing that Alexis had returned, Julie joined us and we crossed the street to head back to campus. Alexis was chatting away about the coffee shop, but I barely heard a word.

Alec Hart.

I couldn't believe he was here at my college. I didn't want anyone here knowing about the old Taren, and Alec knew it all. Those painful memories needed to stay away. Fuck it. I would just leave Alec Hart and my ridiculous crush where it belonged. In my past.

As we passed by the upperclassmen dormitories, a guy called out to us from where he stood in front of one of the buildings.

"Hey girls! Looking good!"

"I'm pretty sure he's referencing the oral skills Julie's demonstrating as she works over that yogurt," Alexis whispered, her nose wrinkled.

"No one has ever complained about my oral skills." Julie ran her tongue along the edge of the cone in a way that made me blush.

"Hey," the guy yelled, clearly not discouraged by the fact that we never answered his first catcall. "Need a ride?"

I looked back over my shoulder because, well hell, it was a long walk back to the dorms. If he had a car, that might be worth a "hello."

The guy smirked when he caught my eye. "I've been told I'm a great ride."

I didn't see any car, only a loser palming his junk. I whipped my head back around. "Jesus. I thought guys were only that douchey in movies."

"Nope, that there is a real, live jackass." Julie rolled her eyes.

"You know what they say?" The guy followed us, hoping to get another reaction. We ignored him and continued walking. "Need a date? Try a Gamma. You three gotta be Tri-Gams for sure."

I looked at Alexis and shook my head. Ah. A fraternity dude classifying us by a sorority house. How wonderfully judgmental of him. We picked up our pace, refusing to respond, and he stopped stalking us.

"It just goes to prove that what I've been telling you since last week is true." Julie walked with her chin held high and chest puffed out.

"What?" I threw my cup and spoon in the trash can.

"Have you heard of Tri-Gam?" she asked. Alexis and I shook our heads. "He's talking about Gamma Gamma Gamma. It's the *hottest* sorority on campus. They only take beautiful girls who have daddies with fat wallets."

I smiled to myself. I didn't even know my daddy, let alone a relative with a fat wallet, but I'd gladly take a compliment about being beautiful, even if it did come from a douche waffle making catcalls.

***

"There! Perfecto!" Julie stood back to admire her handiwork. "Working at mom's beauty shop every summer finally paid off." Evidently, she was not only a fashion guru, but a genius with hair, too.

She turned me to face the mirror, and I gasped. "That's me?"

Julie rested her chin on my shoulder. "You've looked like this all along little nugget. I just shaped you up."

Shaped up my ass. Julie had worked a freaking makeover miracle. I ran my fingers through my hair. She cut several inches off my long brown locks, added a ton of blonde highlights, and plucked my eyebrows into graceful arches.

I took a moment and studied my reflection. I didn't just look good. I looked like I'd walked off a runway. I didn't recognize myself, and that was a damn good thing. I may have been queen of my nerdom in high school, but today I was ruling my makeover.

Alexis stood next to me with her mouth hung open, staring into the mirror. Her face was pale, and her eyes wide with shock. "Liam's going to be so pissed." Those were her first words since Julie had finished with her. Gone were the barrettes that held back Alexis' thick hair, followed by a few inches off the length. Now her hair hung down to her shoulders with flattering layers that made her look at least five years older.

I moved behind her, wrapping my arms around her shoulders. "Why? You look amazing." She was stunning, and I was surprised she sounded more wary than ecstatic.

"Oh, it's just different. I'm not sure he'll like the change." Alexis' brow furrowed, and she played with a strand of her hair.

"How do *you* feel, Alexis?" Julie planted her hands on her hips.

Alexis met my eyes in the mirror and spoke in a shaky voice. "I feel...I feel...renewed." *Renewed?* What an odd choice of words. Her eyes were full of tears as she turned to face Julie. "And pretty. I do feel very pretty, so thank you."

"No tears! We want to make a good impression tonight." Julie blew air in Alexis' face and waved her hands manically in front of her. "Let's do your makeup and get dressed, okay?"

The rush informational meeting started in one hour. With altered looks and attitudes, we were almost ready to unveil the brand new Alexis and Taren.

***

Julie yanked my arm, steering me toward the sorority section on the mall. The "mall" at the University of Maryland was really a long stretch of grass with a reflecting pool in the middle. It was housed in between several of the largest and oldest academic buildings on campus. Today all the fraternities and sororities, along with other clubs, were participating in the First Look Fair in an attempt to get freshmen to join.

Julie was currently explaining the rush process and that "rushing" meant different things if you were a female than if you were a male.

"Guys stop by fraternity houses during parties. They make the decision to pledge based on several factors." Julie held up one finger. "Amount and quality of available beer." She added a second finger. "Amount and quality of available girls." She held up a third finger. "And amount and quality of interest in sports." Julie rolled her eyes, and we giggled.

"Girls have a formal rush. We'll visit each sorority house on campus in rounds until we're left with our top three houses. Then the Preference Ceremonies occur." Julie talked like a cruise director. While Alexis and I studied for our classes at night, Jules studied the Greek system. "That's when the rushees and the sororities rank each other and final matches are made."

After hearing the lengthy details, my brain hurt. Calculus was easier to understand than the complex, social algorithm that was the sorority rush process.

"Denton! Over here!" I glanced toward the sound of my nickname to see Doug waving his hand over his head.

"Keep walking. Head down. Avoid eye contact," Julie whispered. "Don't you dare give him the time of day."

As Julie tried to lead me away, I looked over my shoulder at Pickles. He sat at the Delta Epsilon table and was still trying to get my attention. I smiled, flattered that he remembered me. Despite Julie's warning, I wanted to talk to him again.

"I'm going to say hi to him. Just for a second. I'll meet you in a minute."

Julie shook her head in disapproval. "Just so you know, I think he's a bad idea." She and Alexis walked away as I turned and headed for Doug.

"How are you, Denton-now-Taren?" Doug came around from behind his table and hugged me.

"You remembered my name. Nice. You also lost your whistle. Nicer." I did my best impression of a flirty smile, and Doug laughed.

"You look different." His eyes took a leisurely stroll along my curves, and I resisted the urge to cover my body from his appreciative gaze. I wasn't quite used to the fitted, revealing clothes that Julie had picked for me, but it was clear that Doug liked them.

I shrugged and moved a strand of hair behind my ear. "I got a haircut." *Be cool, Denton.*

"You rushing?" He crossed his arms over his chest and surveyed the crowd.

"I guess. My friends are trying to talk me into it. I'll check it out and see if I like it."

"Stop by my house tomorrow after round one." Doug continued to look at the crowd as he spoke. "We're having a party. Bring your girls." His friend smacked him on the back of the head and Doug cursed. "Gotta go. See you tomorrow, right?"

And just like that, I forgave him for the fact that he hadn't called me after the last party. I smiled and nodded before hurrying over to find Julie and Alexis. Sassy hair, new clothes, a guy interested in me, and rushing a sorority? Every day I found it easier to forget the girl I used to be. I liked this new Taren very much.

***

"Here you go, ladies. You're all registered." Alexis, Julie, and I were all placed in different small groups. We would see each sorority house tomorrow evening, but not at the same time. We took our paperwork and walked away from the Greek section of the fair.

"Do you want to check out anything else? Lots of clubs have tables set up," Alexis said as we meandered along the mall. She was right; a club existed for every possible interest. We saw signs for acapella, comedy improv, various bands, the campus newspaper, and the school radio station. The university had over 800 clubs on campus, and the First Look Fair was their chance to recruit members.

"My schedule is full. Boys, parties, shopping, and, if I can squeeze it in, studying." Julie winked and accepted a brochure from the campus police. She stopped midstride and turned to face the officer who had given her the paper. "Hey! I remember you...you're Junior Officer Hotpants!"

Sure enough, it was the officer-in-training who had warned us about our obnoxious, intoxicated behavior a few nights past.

Hotpants blushed. "Hello, ladies. Any interest in joining our program?" Hotpants was cute. His hair was shaved in a close crop, and he was stacked, muscles bulging out from his short-sleeved uniform. Perhaps it was my drunken haze or the darkness, but my memory hadn't done Junior Officer Hotpants justice. He was certainly worth a second look.

Julie gave him a wide smile. "I'm interested in joining *your* program." Her fingers danced along his bicep.

Hotpants leaned closer to her, lips pursed. "Is that so? Maybe you can give me your number then."

Alexis and I turned away to avoid the discomfort of watching Julie flirt with yet another guy.

"Look!" Alexis nudged me with her elbow. "That is so badass."

Across the way, a guy was bouncing, spinning, and contorting his body on a huge trampoline. We watched as he gained more height before throwing his body into multiple flips.

My mouth hung open in awe. "Did you see that? I think he flipped three times!"

Alexis nodded. "That is wicked."

"Their banner says *Acroletes*." I read the motto out loud, "Sober Minds, Strong Bodies." I glanced around at some of the other people near the trampoline. "Look at her!" A girl was balanced on a tower of chairs, pressing her body into a handstand. Other students were standing on each other's shoulders or balancing like human pyramids. My eyes couldn't seem to decide where to settle.

Then, at a nearby table I noticed a guy who looked familiar. Leaning past Alexis, I tried to get a closer look. He glanced up at the same time and our eyes met. He looked confused, as if he couldn't remember how he knew me. My eyes widened and then narrowed in anger.

That fucknut didn't even know who I was. He was too good to even recognize or remember me. What an asshole.

"Hey," Alexis nudged my arm with her elbow. "That guy over there is totally staring at you. Do you know him?"

Know him? I hate him. I hate Alec Hart.

Chapter 6

Alec

Jeremy elbowed me in the ribs. "Who's the hot girl? Looks like she wants to rip your fucking nuts off."

"I don't know." She was really pretty. "If I'd met her, I'd definitely remember her." I racked my brain, trying to figure out why she looked so familiar, but I couldn't place her. I tried to move from behind the lacrosse table so that I could get a better look, but within seconds, she'd blended into the crowd and disappeared.

"Here you go." Jeremy shoved a game schedule into the hands of a girl who'd slowed down in front of our table to see what we were giving away. Her eyebrows creased as she looked at the paper in her hand, and then she gave us a small forced smile before walking away. Two tables down I saw her toss the schedule into a recycling bin. She wasn't the first.

"This is such a fucking waste of time," Jeremy growled.

"You're telling me." I stood up, stretching my arms overhead. I tossed my stack of schedules on the table in front of him. "I'm going for a walk." I was bored out of my fucking mind. If anyone was interested in picking up a schedule, Jeremy could handle it on his own. Besides, my shift only lasted for another ten minutes.

"You coming back?" Jeremy asked.

"Nah. Consider this my gift. The lacrosse babes are all yours."

"You're an asshole, Hart," he yelled after me. "You better not be late to training."

I turned and nodded to him with a smile to let him know I heard him. Then I made my way through the crowd to the Acroletes table.

"I was wondering when you'd grow some balls and show up." Caz jumped down from the trampoline, catching my hand mid-air before pulling me in for a chest bump. "Did you put in your time at the LAX table?"

I shrugged. "Yeah. Are you guys getting many recruits?"

"We always do. Nobody can resist the lure of the trampoline." He waggled his eyebrows like a super villain. "My milkshake brings all the girls to the yard." Caz pulled the hem of his shirt up while dancing.

"Cut it out, Caz," Jon yelled from his stack of chairs. "You're scaring people off." As usual, Jon was upside down and high off the ground.

"Is that so?" Caz's smile was big as he stalked over to look up at his friend. "I guess I need to rectify that then."

Jon came out of his handstand and climbed down the precariously stacked tower of chairs. He grinned and joined me along the side of the trampoline. Caz had jumped back up and was already in the center of the white webbing, launching himself high into the air.

I grabbed one of the unused chairs. "He doesn't have any fear." I flipped the chair around to sit backward on it and folded my arms across the back.

"Not that we've discovered." Jon sat down and crossed his arms across his chest. "We also haven't found a trick he can't do or won't try. He's so fucking talented it's not fair." Jon shook his head in disbelief. "But don't tell him I said that."

"Don't worry." I watched Caz throw his body into a laid out, twisting flip. "If his head gets any bigger, it'll throw off his rotation."

Jon threw his head back and laughed. "When are you going to pledge, Hart?"

I shook my head and sighed in frustration. "I can't make the commitment because of lacrosse."

"That doesn't seem to be stopping you from coming into practice every day."

"Yeah, well once our season starts, I won't have time for the Acroletes." The words tasted wrong in my mouth, and I wanted to swallow them down.

We watched in silence as Caz defied death a few more times, flipping and spinning like he was born to do it.

"Well, flipping through the fire hoop is sick. You gotta try that at least once before your season starts."

"We'll see." I cocked my head to the side and watched the people passing the tables.

Jon turned to smile at me knowingly. "Yes we will."

As Caz got down off the trampoline, a familiar voice caught my attention. My mouth went dry and my body tensed. That was a voice I hoped I'd never hear again. I stood up and searched the area, immediately finding the source—the girl from earlier who, as Jeremy put it, looked like she wanted to rip my balls off. She was walking past the Acroletes table, deep in conversation with her friend. She hadn't noticed me this time, but her voice tugged at memories I'd buried months ago. She might have ditched the glasses, and gotten a new hairstyle and clothes, but I'd never forget her voice or how she ruined my senior year.

College Park was a big university, but seeing her just a few feet away, a campus of thirty thousand students didn't feel big enough for the both of us. I wanted that self-righteous prude to stay in my past where she belonged.

Taren Richards was a fucking snitch.

Chapter 7

Taren

"Why were you shooting a death glare at that hot guy at the lacrosse table?" Alexis asked as she stuffed flyers into her messenger bag. She'd taken a pamphlet from every table we passed. She could barely fit anything else in her overflowing bag. "It looked like you wanted to claw his eyes out."

I pointedly ignored her question, gesturing instead, to her bag. "Why are you keeping those things, Lex? It's like a fire hazard in there."

She shrugged. "Just keeping my options open in case we don't get into a sorority. I want to join something while in college." She adjusted the strap of her purse and reached for yet another pamphlet. "And good try, but you didn't answer my question. What was that look for?"

I sighed. I was hoping she hadn't noticed that. Reliving my history with Alec was the last thing I wanted to do. "We went to high school together. I guess I don't want to be reminded of my past. I don't want to be the girl I was back then."

Alexis finished storing her flyers in her bag and then slipped her arm through mine. "I get that, but why do you seem to *hate* him?"

I stiffened, and she pressed closer to me. I took a deep breath. Trusting Alexis was easy, but reliving my past was painful. "Because I do hate him. He pretended to be my friend, and then he ripped out my heart and stomped all over it." I cleared my throat. I wanted to rid myself of any sign of emotion that lingered when I thought of Alec.

"You dated?"

My laugh was bitter. "No. We were paired up together to be debate team partners for Model Congress. He was Mr. Popularity, and I was Little Miss Geek. We had nothing in common except that we both wanted to win the award for the top orator of the competition. Who wouldn't want to win a full scholarship to college?"

"So what happened?" She motioned to a bench, and we sat down.

I blew out a long breath, shaking my head. "His name is Alec, and I had the biggest crush on him. He was amazing—gorgeous, athletic, smart. We worked together every day for weeks. He supported my idea to write our bill on anti-bullying and surprisingly, we got along really well. I thought we were friends. He even told me I was unique…" I shook my head, memories of my stupidity overwhelming me.

"You are unique, Taren," Alexis added with a small smile.

I rolled my eyes. "He was just being polite. He was the first person who was ever nice to me in high school. The fact that I had a crush on him didn't help." I stood up and picked at piece of imaginary lint on my shirt. "Can we head back to the dorms?"

Alexis nodded, and I led us away from the fair, desperately wanting to put distance between me and Alec.

"I fail to see why you hate him. He sounds like a pretty decent guy."

"Yeah, well, one day we were talking about how we couldn't meet up to work on our project because of the Homecoming Dance. When he asked if I was going, I said no. He told me he didn't have a date but that he was going, so I should too. That I'd have fun." My steps became more hurried, the urge to flee too strong to ignore.

"Did you go?" Alexis panted as she jogged to keep up with me.

I stopped walking and turned to face her. "Lex, I was such an idiot. I thought that because he was nice to me it meant he liked me. When I told my aunt Claire that Alec was going to the dance alone and that he suggested I come too, she thought that it was an invitation. She encouraged me to ask him to go with me."

"Oh." Alexis' eyes and lips were rounded in understanding.

I don't know if my aunt was oblivious to the extent of my awkwardness, but I should have known better. Claire, even as she aged, was beautiful, young, and confident. She never had to deal with rejection. Rejection was my entire existence in high school. No matter how nice Alec was to me in private, I should have known that when it came down to it, his reputation was important in public. He was popular, and I was a nerd.

"I showed up at our high school's homecoming bonfire. Everyone was there. I asked him to go to the dance with me in front of the entire school because I thought he liked me." We walked in silence for a moment. The crushing pain I'd buried a year ago slammed back into me. "Actually, you know what? I'm not sure I really thought he did like me. At least like that. I just wanted him to so badly that I let my aunt convince me it could happen."

"What happened?" Alexis' voice was little more than a whisper.

"He was the popular jock. I was the nerd that was constantly bullied." I swallowed loudly against the lump in my throat. "What do you think happened? It was a recipe for disaster."

"He said no?"

"Worse. He told me we weren't in the same league." I huffed and shook my head. "I can't believe I was stupid enough to ask him in front of everyone like that. I set myself up to be humiliated, and I was." I blinked back my tears. "I trusted him. At the very least, I thought he was my friend. But when I became everyone's favorite joke, he didn't even stand up for me." I crossed my arms over my chest, gripping myself as if I could keep all the broken parts of my heart together if I just held on tightly enough. "I was so clueless back then."

Alexis put her hand on my arm. "Taren, you're in a league of your own, and that's a good thing. You're awesome, and he's an ass for not being able to see that." She put her arm around me, and we walked in silence back to the dorm. My mind was anything but silent. It relentlessly replayed that night in my thoughts until the hurt was just as acute as ever.

***

"Taren, is your Instagram account under a different name?" Julie barged into our room while Alexis and I were applying makeup for today's rush events. "I just realized we aren't following each other. I'm posting a picture of us, and I want to tag you and Alexis."

Pulling the mascara wand away from my eye, I blinked before looking at her. "I don't do social media."

"What the holy hell? Even my Nana has an account. She posts pics of everything from her freshly baked banana nut bread to half naked pictures of men from her favorite romance novels. Why in the world don't you have one?" Julie tilted her head to the side, foot tapping in irritation.

"I used to, but I deleted it." Hoping to end the conversation, I applied mascara methodically to my other eyelashes.

"Why?" Alexis asked, moving to stand next to Julie. I told her I didn't have any friends in high school, but I never gave any details other than the bonfire disaster. I didn't want them to know how bad it had been.

"You are such a loser, Taren."

"Get a life."

"That outfit wasn't even in style when the tags were still on it."

"I hope you choke on all the shit that comes out of your mouth."

"How often do you have to shave your back?"

"I didn't know being a slut was genetic."

"Lesbian."

"Shouldn't you have a license for being that ugly?"

"A face even a mother couldn't love. Is that why you're adopted?"

Those were just some of the comments I got on my Instagram photos. My lunch had been dumped in the trash, insults whispered in my ear, and when I walked into a classroom, books were moved onto empty seats in hopes that I wouldn't try to sit there. Not to mention that time Jesse Blevins pantsed me in gym in ninth grade. Damn those loose shorts and my "I love bacon" underwear. People called me Bacon Bits for the rest of high school. Other kids had it worse, no doubt, but still—some days were an emotional battlefield.

A sigh escaped before I could hide it. "Look. I've let the past go. Let's just say there was some cyber-bullying stuff, and I deleted my account. No biggie." My thick voice betrayed me. All I wanted was to start over and I felt like my past was coming back to haunt me.

Julie shook her head. "Fuck them."

Alexis squeezed my shoulders. "Fuck them."

Standing up, I took a deep breath, blinking back the painful tears. I was done with the past. I was moving on once and for all. "Fuck them! Now, let's do this."

***

"Groups D through G, line up!" President Perky, of the Pan-Hellenic organization, coordinated all the freshman and sophomore girls for the start of Rush. We huddled in groups along Route One, ready to split up and visit the sorority houses. We'd be heading to Fraternity Row as well as the houses along the Graham Cracker. The Graham Cracker was an area between two streets that housed seven sororities. The nickname was given because the area looked like a graham cracker. I thought it just looked like a regular old rectangle, but referencing a cookie cracker made for a much better nickname.

Julie leaned toward me. "Doesn't it feel like we're a herd of cattle?"

"Yes." I shifted nervously. "We are meeting at Danny's Sub Shop after this, right?" This process was supposed to take three hours. I was ready for this to be over, and it hadn't even started yet.

Julie nodded. "Then we'll head over to Whistler's party."

"Wait, I thought you had a date with Hotpants?"

She had gone on several dates with Junior Officer Hotpants. I thought things were going well with her flirtationship, as she called it.

"We were eating lunch in the Union. When I looked at him closely, I realized his head was shaped like an eggplant." Julie grimaced and scrunched up her nose. "That was it. We're over. I can't date a vegetable."

"An eggplant? You're ridiculous." I laughed. Glancing two groups over, Alexis stood alone, looking as if she might bolt at any minute. I waved, and she gave me a lopsided grin and a half-hearted wave in return. I empathized with her.

I had my share of embarrassments in high school, but this? This was weirdly worse. Excited and nervous girls, dressed in "dressy-casual" as we were mandated for round one, were huddled in groups according to letter. We each wore a badge, pinned to our shirt, with a number assignment. We were cataloged, organized, lined up, and ready to be paraded in front of the sororities like cows at a farm fair.

We crossed the street en masse, cars honking impatiently, and then split into our groups. My group was starting at the first house on the Graham Cracker. Gamma Gamma Gamma. My stomach rolled. I stared at my feet and toyed with the end of my tiny jean skirt. This was it.

I steeled myself for judgment as the front door opened and fifty girls in matching red shirts ran out onto the lawn in front of us, lining up in rows. Music from a nearby stereo played as Taylor Swift's "Shake it Off" blared out. Except, I couldn't hear Taylor, since the girls shouted their own perfectly rhymed lyrics to the song, "Cause our sisters gonna play, play, play, play, play and the brothers gonna say, say, say, say, say. Baby, we just gonna hey, hey, hey, hey, hey. Rush with Gamma. Rush with Gamma. Wooo hooo." They danced, bright smiles plastered on their gorgeous, magazine-worthy faces. Then they wrapped their arms around each other, demonstrating their love and devotion to their sisterhood. I supposed, anyway.

What in the ever-loving-hell was going on?

I turned my head to look down the Graham Cracker. Every house was exactly the same. Girls in matching ensembles sang and danced to choreographed routines as music rang out in the air.

When the performance ended, several girls hollered out and the rest clapped, as a thin redhead stepped forward from the crowd. "Welcome to Gamma Gamma Gamma, ladies. My name is Tiffany, and I'm Rush Chair for Tri-Gam. Please come inside for refreshments and to meet some of our sisters."

As she spoke, the sisters of Tri-Gam lined up on the staircase.

When we walked in, they descended one by one, pairing off with the next rushee in line. Taking us by the arm, they led us into other rooms for our informal chats.

This was definitely weird. I was feeling a little cynical about the whole process, but I was also feeling the strongest desire to fit in. For once, I just wanted to be able to belong.

Chapter 8

Alec

I could feel Caz breathing down my neck as he chased me. He might be a powerhouse in the Acroletes gym, but out here on the football stadium steps, I was king again.

Twenty bucks said I could finish running every set of stairs in the stadium before he could. Knowing he was fading with each set only made me push harder.

"What's your hurry, Hart?" Caz taunted from below. "Got a hot date?"

"Yeah," I yelled over my shoulder. "With your money."

He cursed behind me, and I grimaced with effort as I scaled the stairs two at a time.

I thrived on the sound of Caz's footsteps behind me. I welcomed the burn in my chest from sucking in the air. I needed the scream of my muscles as I forced my body to go just a little faster.

My foot barely touched the top step before I spun around and charged down the stairs I'd just climbed. I flashed Caz my middle finger and a flippant grin as I passed him.

"You're slowing down, boss."

"Fuck you, Hart." His words were hardly understandable through his labored breathing.

I finished the last set just as Caz was starting his. Grabbing my water, I leaned against the half wall at the bottom of the stairs and emptied the entire bottle in seconds. Pushing off the wall, I paced along the front row of seats as the numbing haze of the race faded, and the thoughts crept back in my head.

Seeing Taren at the First Look Fair dredged up shit from my past that I didn't want to think about. I didn't want to remember my senior year, or how big of an asshole I'd been.

When Caz finished, he grabbed his duffle bag, water, and towel as we headed for the dining hall.

"Don't get used to this." Caz growled as he threw a crumpled up bill at my chest.

I caught the money and shoved it into my pocket. Sweat dripped down my forehead, and I snatched Caz's towel, wiping my face and neck with it.

He tried to grab his towel from me, and I stepped out of his range. "What? No comeback? What crawled up your ass, sunshine?"

"You really want to know?" I tilted my head side to side, stretching the tightness in my shoulders. We walked through the gate of the stadium, and I slung the towel over my shoulder.

"Not really. I want my fucking money back. Double or nothing? This time blindfolded." He turned to face me, and his eyebrows raised in challenge.

We stopped at the intersection, waiting for a break in traffic so we could head over to the dining hall. "I'll save you the pain and humiliation. You can just buy me lunch." I threw his towel at him, and he stuffed it into his duffle.

A flash of blonde hair passed me just as a blue car came careening around the corner. The girl's face was buried in a textbook and earbuds were stuffed in her ears as she stepped off the curb. I grabbed her and pulled her against my chest. The blue car sped by, accompanied by the blare of a horn.

My heart pounded against my rib cage, and my arms were wrapped protectively around her small shaking body. *Jesus.* The asshole missed hitting her by inches.

"Oh my Lord. I almost died," she whispered, yanking on the cord to pull her earphones out. She didn't try to move away from me. Cars continued to speed by. Her book lay on the road with a dirty smudge of tire tracks across the ripped pages.

"You're lucky my boy has quick reflexes, sweetheart." Caz shook his head. "You almost activated your medical plan." He leaned over to pick up her book and closed it to peek at the cover. "*Introduction to Probability,*" he read. He chuckled and looked up at her. "Here's some homework for you. What would your chance of survival have been if Hart hadn't been here?"

She stiffened in my arms, and I realized I was still holding on to her but I hadn't said anything. "Are you all right?" I loosened my grip, and she slowly turned to look at me.

Brown eyes that used to be hidden behind glasses peered up at me, frightened and vulnerable. The terrified look on her face made me forget the anger from the other day. I wanted to reassure her I wasn't going to hurt her. Not this time.

"Alec?" She said my name like it caused her pain. The way her mouth wrapped around those four letters was something I hadn't realized I missed until I heard it again. My hands hung loosely around her back, and I had the urge to pull her close again. I don't know why, but

I wanted to protect her and make her forget the suffering I'd caused her in high school.

"Are you okay, Taren?" Her mouth hung slightly open as her eyes searched my face. When she didn't answer, I moved my hands to her shoulders to comfort her. "Do you need to sit down? It was a close call." My fingertips tingled where they touched her bare shoulders, and my thumbs rubbed the smooth skin next to the strap of her tank top.

Taren blinked and then pulled away, nearly falling into the street again. I reached for her, but she took two steps to the side, shaking her head. Before she turned away, her eyes flashed angrily, a silent reminder about our past. She snatched her book from Caz and took off running without another word.

Caz watched her and laughed. "What the hell? You save a girl's life, and she runs away scared." He turned to face me, a crooked grin splitting his face in two. "Probably doesn't help that you smell like a dirty jock strap."

I reached up and ran my hand through my hair as I watched Taren disappear in the crowd of students. "I haven't seen her since high school. We worked on a project together."

Caz adjusted the strap of his duffle across his chest as we crossed the road. "Looks like she was hating on you pretty hard. What did you do, leave her to do all the work alone?"

"No, worse. I think I broke her heart." I rubbed my hands on the legs of my shorts as if I could wash away the shame of my actions.

Caz's head dropped and he groaned in disgust. "Do I look like Dr. Drew? This isn't *Loveline*, Hart. I'm not the guy you have a fucking heart to heart with about your love life. That's Jon's gig."

"Who said I wanted to talk about it anyway?" I pressed my mouth in a tight line.

He sighed and rolled his eyes, motioning with his hand for me to continue. "Okay fine. You called my bluff. What's the deal? Was she a butterface back then?" Caz took a drink of water and grinned at my confused look. "Everything is hot but her face."

"Jesus. It's no wonder you're single." I shook my head, thinking back to all the time Taren and I had spent together on our project. "Nah. It wasn't like that. She was actually kind of cute. In a hot librarian kind of way."

"I fail to see the problem." Caz pulled out a can of Mountain Dew from his bag, popped the top, and chugged the contents.

My stomach revolted at the sight, and I turned away. "She was a geek. Bottom of the social ladder." I huffed a laugh, staring ahead. "Fuck. She was so far down, she couldn't even see the bottom rung."

"So? Did you like her?"

I reached up and scratched the back of my head. I had no easy way to answer that question. "Doesn't matter. I humiliated her in front of the entire school."

Caz stopped in his tracks. "That's a dick move, Hart." I turned, but couldn't meet his eyes. "I'd fucking kick a guy's ass if he did that to one of my sisters."

I shoved my hands in my pockets and turned to walk back to the dining hall. "Yeah, well she got her revenge. We're even."

***

I set my phone down on the desk with the speaker on so I could re-tape my lacrosse stick while my dad spoke.

"How's practice going?" he asked.

"Fine." I ran the utility knife down the handle of my stick.

"And classes?"

"Good." I laid the blade aside and started peeling the tape away.

He grunted. "Are you getting along with your teammates?"

"Sure." Giving him short answers was best. When I gave him detailed responses, it only gave him more fuel for criticism.

"What do you think the team will be like? Are they any good?" he pressed. I glanced over at Caz to see if the noise was bothering him. He had his headphones on as he leaned over his desk, doing homework, while eating a plate of brownies.

"Hard to say, Dad. Right now we're just doing a lot of weight training and cardio workouts." I paused as I tried to peel away a portion of the tape which was about as pliant as my father. I grunted with the effort. "Formal practices don't start for a few months." He knew all this. He'd been talking to Coach regularly, and it was like having a goddamn nanny cam installed in my life.

"But you're still working on your stick skills, right?" His voice was deliberate and tight. It was less a question and more a threat.

"Of course."

"Did you sign up for the Distinguished Lecture Series?" His rapid fire questions were like a list of demands by a terrorist in a hostage crisis. He probably had a checklist drawn up by his secretary on official letterhead to keep track of my accomplishments and shortcomings.

"Not yet."

He breathed heavily into the phone as if he was trying to control his frustration. "You need to do that, Alec. You need to show the faculty that you're serious about your major. That will help you when you decide to apply for internships."

"Okay." Shit. I didn't want to attend the lectures. They looked boring as fuck.

"What about internships? Have you started researching one for the summer?"

"The semester just started, Dad." I twisted my hand with a vicious yank, tearing off a piece of tape and throwing it on the desk.

"It's never too early to prepare. If you want an internship, you need to start working toward it now. Connect with prominent members of the faculty and network with people who can help you get a decent internship in D.C."

I tore my attention away from where my fingers gripped the handle of my lacrosse stick, and I glared at the phone. *If I wanted an internship?*

I tossed my lacrosse stick on the bed and then snatched the phone. Standing up, I took a few steps before turning on my heel and stalking across the small room like a caged animal. I gripped the front of my hair, yanking my head down until my chin touched my chest.

"That's just it, Dad." I squeezed my phone so hard I expected it to shatter into pieces. "I don't want an internship in D.C."

"Have you been listening to a word I've said, Alec?" His words snapped out like the crack of a whip. "You'll never be a senator if you don't start laying the groundwork now. An internship is the first step."

I took a deep breath. "An internship would be a waste of time since I'm planning to change my major next semester. I want to study Exercise Science."

"Like hell you will!" Even with the tiny speaker on my phone, my father's rage echoed through the room. I glanced over to Caz again, but he didn't even flinch. "Your major is Political Science." My father's voice was flat and hard as if my statement wasn't even worth consideration.

"I'm not interested in politics, Dad." My voice was strong and steady as I spoke. "I'm not going to waste my time on internships or networking. I'm planning to go into Physical Therapy. Politics isn't my passion."

"Who cares what your passion is?" he scoffed. "Passion doesn't put food on the table or a roof over your head. The law is in our blood. That's where your future lies."

My "lawyerly" blood was boiling that I even had to have this conversation with him. Why was I continuing this argument? I was an adult, and I could make my own fucking choices. He'd just have to get over it. "That's not a future I want."

"Really?" His voice dropped dangerously low. "You blew your chance at the full scholarship at Model Congress last year when you let that girl out-debate you. That means I have to pay for the expenses your lacrosse scholarship doesn't cover. You need my help, and I'm not paying for my son to be a lousy therapist. If you wanted to be a doctor, we could discuss that, but a therapist? Not on my dime."

He allowed his words to hang in the silence between us, and I clenched my hand into a fist.

"Have I made myself clear?" my father asked in a clipped voice.

"Yes, sir." I hated the way the words sounded coming out of my mouth, almost like I was sacrificing myself. If I had any chance of winning my father over to my side, I was going to have to ace all my classes this semester. I'd just have to spend the next few months preparing my argument and come back at him with good grades and a plan for my future that he couldn't refuse.

"Good. Call me next week and let me know when you've signed up for that lecture."

He hung up without saying goodbye, and I tossed my phone on the bed next to the lacrosse stick. I collapsed into my chair, leaning my elbows onto my knees.

Caz pulled off his headphones and hung them around his neck. He turned in his chair to glare at me. "Why do you let your dad talk to you like that?"

"You were eavesdropping?" I sighed and leaned back in my chair, stretching my legs in front of me.

"That was a hell of a lot more interesting than my Biology homework."

"Dude, does Betty know you're cheating on her?" I asked, nodding toward the plate of brownies. I didn't want to rehash my conversation with my dad.

"Don't be ridiculous, Hart. These are Betty's brand." Caz opened his mouth and shoved an entire brownie inside. He chewed and then swallowed.

"How has your body not revolted on you?" I felt physically sick watching him eat sometimes.

"I'm like a luxury car. I need special fuel. My diet is very important to me. I make sure it's well balanced between the four food groups: Betty's best, brownies, Mountain Dew, and steak." He reached for another brownie.

Shaking my head, I reached behind me to grab the lacrosse stick. I leaned it against my knee, tearing at the shreds of tape still clinging to the handle. My chest was still filled with the indignation only my father could inspire. All I could hear were his words repeating on a loop. *You blew your chance.*

"You didn't answer my question," Caz said.

"I don't remember you asking one. You were too busy going all Buddy Elf on me and explaining the four food groups. Although yours was seriously lacking in candy corn."

"I asked why you let your dad talk to you like that."

I shrugged. "That's how all dads talk." Discussing how stubborn and uncompromising my father could be wasn't going to change anything.

"No. That's how jackasses talk. My dad doesn't talk like that."

I watched my fingers rip the grip tape away from the lacrosse stick. A sticky residue clung to the metal. "It's just how he is."

"You want to change your major, and I know you don't like lacrosse. Why are you doing what your dad wants you to do?"

"I like lacrosse."

Caz huffed. "Yeah, that's why you rush out of there every day so you can make it to Acroletes practice on time. I can't believe you haven't signed the pledge yet. You're there every day. It's obvious you want to join. You like the Acroletes more than you like your major and lacrosse. Admit it."

I looked up at him. "What about you? Do you like your major?"

"If I didn't, I'd change it." Caz set the plate of brownies aside.

"You're taking a break from Betty?" I paused. "Shit's about to get real."

"Don't worry, baby," Caz said to the plate. "I'll be back once I set Hart straight." He leaned forward onto his knees and stared at me. "Why did you choose a Political Science major if you weren't interested in it?"

"You're talking to your food, and you expect me to take this conversation seriously?" I laughed and grabbed the utility knife off my desk, scraping the blade against the handle to remove the sticky residue left from the tape.

Caz leaned back with his arms out wide. "I got all day, Hart. Just answer the damn question."

I shrugged. "My dad wants me to be a senator."

Silence. And then a pillow pegged me in the head, hard.

"That's the dumbest fucking thing you've ever said. It's your life, dipshit. It's your future. Don't study something you hate just because your dad wants you to."

I threw the pillow back at him, and he easily deflected it with his hand.

"My dad pays the bills. If I change my major, he cuts me off."

"You actually believe that?"

I pushed the utility blade so hard against the handle, the metal screamed in protest. "Yeah."

Caz stared at me for a beat and then took another brownie off his plate. "So you get financial aid. Apply for scholarships. Get a job. You don't need him."

I thought for a moment. Maybe Caz was right. My lacrosse scholarship covered my tuition. I'd just have to find a way to cover my room and board. "What's your major?" I asked Caz.

"Biology. I'm Pre-med."

I laughed. "Funny."

Caz didn't laugh. "How is becoming a brain surgeon humorous to you?"

"You're serious?"

"As a tumor."

"That's...that's not...that's disturbing, dude." I frowned at him.

"Look. You have some time to figure this all out. It doesn't have to be today. It's too late to change your classes for this semester anyway, but get your shit figured out before spring. This is your life, not your dad's."

I nodded. "You're right." *Wait.* Did I just agree with Caz?

He stood up, brushing his hands together. "You wanna go blow off some steam?"

"What did you have in mind?" I sheathed the blade of the utility knife and tossed it on my desk.

The look on Caz's face was a risky promise. He picked up a brownie and tossed it at me. "Grab some fuel, buddy. I'm going to show you how to loosen up."

***

Caz shoved a key into the lock and then pushed open the door just enough that we could slip inside before locking it behind us.

"How'd you get a key?" I followed him into the trampoline room where he turned on the light, leaving the rest of the Acroletes gym in darkness.

"I can't give away all my secrets."

"Which means you stole it." I pulled myself up onto the nearest trampoline, launching my body into the middle of the bed.

Caz jumped up on the trampoline farthest from me with a Nerf football in his hand. "Heads up!" He drilled the ball across the room.

I jumped up, catching the ball with one arm and crashing down onto the webbing and bouncing wildly around. I was laughing when I finally managed to get to my feet. "Jesus. You throw worse than my grandma. No wonder you're a gymnast. Your spiral sucks."

"Fuck you. You don't need a good spiral for trampball. It's more fun when the toss sucks. Throw it back." Caz jumped high, and I threw the ball to him when he was at his highest point. "Yes!" he hollered when he caught it.

A knock came from the outside door we'd just locked, and I stopped bouncing. "Shit. Do you think it's campus police?"

"Nah, I invited some friends." Caz tossed the ball to me underhanded and hopped down to the floor. "What good is a trampoline without girls in spandex?" He jogged out of the room and returned less than a minute later with Amanda and Maureen.

"Hey, Alec." Amanda flashed me a brilliant smile and climbed up on the mat next to the first trampoline. "Thanks for inviting us."

"Are you finally going to give the tramp a chance?" Maureen asked, hopping up onto the second trampoline. She took a few small bounces to warm up.

I'd regularly been coming to Acroletes practice, but tonight was the first time I'd ever been in the trampoline room.

"Don't talk about Amanda that way, Maureen." Caz shook his head. "Just because she gives everyone a turn it doesn't mean she's a tramp."

Amanda rolled her eyes. "I didn't give you a turn, asshole." She pushed Caz off the trampoline that was next to me and claimed it for her own. She started jumping, and I wanted to kiss the man who invented trampolines. They paired so well with beautiful girls in tight clothes.

"What's Caz teaching you?" Maureen asked, mid-jump.

"Nothing. We're just here to play." I tossed the football in the air and then jumped up to catch it.

"Like hell you are." Caz threw a thick piece of canvas at me, hitting me in the chest. It had a buckle and metal rings on it. "That's a spotting belt. Put it on, candy ass. You're not leaving here until I teach you to flip."

"I thought we were playing trampball."

"Come on, Alec," Amanda begged. "Give it a try. It's fun."

My eyes followed her as she peeled off her T-shirt and threw it to the side before making her way back to her own trampoline. Well, if that was her way of convincing me, it wasn't a good argument. Given the choice, I'd rather sit and watch her and her tits bounce all night long.

"You gotta try it at least once," Maureen added.

Caz was a genius, inviting the girls. He knew male pride didn't know the meaning of the word "no" and it had no respect for the concept of "bad idea." I was either going to leave this room with a neck brace or a new addiction.

After putting on the belt, Caz hooked me into the spotting rig. He held onto a rope to keep me from falling on my head. In theory anyway.

"What now?" I asked.

Caz laughed. "Dude. Now you're going to fly."

Chapter 9

Taren

"Climb up." Doug's pointer finger poked through the opening in his tent bed and hooked in a come-hither motion. I chewed on my lip, unsure of what I should do. He stuck his head out, a cheesy grin plastered across his face. "C'mon, Denton. I won't bite. Much."

I was nervous, but also excited. Pickles seemed to be attracted to me, and I was totally up for a little romance. I climbed the ladder, pulling the sheet to the side before I crawled onto his bed. The inside was dark, and my eyes took a minute to adjust. Doug was sprawled on his back, fully dressed, *thank you Jesus*, with his hands folded behind his head.

"I thought you said you guys were having a party tonight?" I narrowed my eyes in mock suspicion. He smelled like alcohol, but he didn't appear to be drunk. Yet.

"Plans changed. The guys decided on poker night, but they wanted some cute girls to make the rushees happy. That's why I wanted you to bring your friends. You and I, on the other hand, are having a private *fiesta* right here."

"Are we?" I grinned and hoped he couldn't see my dopey smile in the dark tent.

"A party for two." He pulled me down next to him. "How was rush?"

"Okay, I guess. Weird. The synchronized dancing and chant singing freaked me out. It was like being trapped in *High School Musical*, but with a lot more floral furniture, and without any basketball players."

He laughed. "Wait until the serenading begins for Homecoming. That's some funny shit." He turned onto his side and inched closer to me. My heart thudded against the inside of my chest. "You went to every house today, right?" I nodded, and he played with a piece of my hair. "What did you think of Tri-Gam?"

I shrugged. "They were really nice. Pretty girls. Beautiful house." *Way out of my league.*

Doug laughed quietly and rumpled my hair. I frowned at him and smoothed it back down. I was not a freaking puppy. Besides, I had spent twenty minutes with the flat iron, getting it nice and silky smooth.

"Tri-Gam is the top house on campus, and you belong there, Denton."

Pickles thought I belonged in the best sorority on campus. A warmth spread through me, and I smiled up at him. Doug wasn't an expert in charm or romance, but he was interested in me, and that counted for a lot.

"Are you going to kiss me again?" I challenged him. "I seem to remember you promising me a private *fiesta*."

Doug smiled and then brought his mouth over mine, crushing his lips down forcefully. I felt like he was trying to suck the life right out of me. No, not forcefully, passionately. This was passionate, right? *Right?*

Doug rolled onto his back and pulled me on top of him. I struggled to keep up with the pace of his kissing. His lips and tongue were everywhere, licking me like an ice cream cone. I wasn't sure whether I was supposed to be grossed out or turned on. Was he going to lick my face right off? So much for all that makeup I put on earlier.

I shifted, trying to find a comfortable position, and Doug groaned as I accidentally ground my hips against his. I stopped moving and ended up nestled between his legs and felt...a third leg? *No, little chickadee, that is no leg.* Doug was definitely happy to see me, and his tongue was battling mine like they were a couple of gladiators fighting to the death.

Jesus, Denton. You're getting kissed. Why are you thinking about gladiators? Focus.

I turned my head to get a breath. Doug took the opportunity to suck on my neck as he slid his hands over my ass before slipping them up under the hem of my shirt. I stiffened. *Oh no.* What if he went for the bra strap? How many dates did I need to have before I gave guys access to the tatas? They should have given out handbooks at orientation for this sort of thing.

The sound of something ripping surprised me, and I yanked my head away from Doug's hoover lips.

"What was that?" I whispered.

"What?" He lifted his head to kiss me again, and I pushed him back down.

"That ripping sound. I heard something rip." I cocked my head to the side, listening again.

Then someone moaned.

Doug chuckled. "Oh. That was a condom wrapper. Watson must have a visitor."

"He's having *sex*?" I whispered those three letters like it was a curse word I wasn't allowed to say. "Right now? While we're in the same room?"

"Harder. Oh yes, harder!" The shout from behind bed tent number two could not be misunderstood. Watson and his visitor were indeed bumping uglies.

I buried my face in Doug's shirt. "Ohmygod."

He lifted my chin. "What's the big deal?"

"I...Fahrvergnugen." *Fahrvergnugen?* I word-vomited a German automobile advertising slogan? My mind was a strange, strange place.

Doug's mouth fell open, and he rubbed his eyebrow. "Hold up. Are you a *virgin*?" He said it like I was some sort of horrifying, mythical creature.

"It's not a disease, Doug. So what?" I challenged him, feeling angry with him for the first time. A wave of shame hit me next. I dipped my chin and looked away. So much for him thinking I belonged in Tri-Gam.

He rubbed the side of his neck, full of agitation. "Are you one of those girls who's waiting to get, like, a promise ring before you give up your V-card?"

I frowned. "No. But I'm certainly not having sex in a tent bed while someone else is in the room." My voice rose in indignation before I could stop myself.

"Don't knock it till you've tried it!" Watson moaned from tent bed number two.

***

At eight o'clock the next morning, Julie walked into our room like she owned the place. Alexis covered her head with her pillow, and I groaned and hid under my covers.

"Rise and shine, my pretties. We have business to attend to." Julie yanked the covers off of me and pulled the pillow away from Alexis. Placing both of our laptops next to us, she pushed Alexis over and got comfortable as she opened her own.

We had agreed to check house results together. I thought we'd do that at a reasonable time. However, Julie had a different plan. After entering our personal passcodes, we waited and whatever sleep still lingered in me, flew out the window. Anticipation buzzed through my body.

Julie screamed and bounced on the bed. "All three of my favorites are still here." She stood up and did a little dance. "I only got cut by two houses, but who cares? I think one was the place where I accidentally let it slip that their furniture reminded me of my Nana's. The other was definitely the one that smelled like burnt toast. I couldn't hack that smell twenty four/seven. Sometimes my brutal honesty hurts." Julie flopped back down on my bed.

"I got my favorites too," Alexis said, looking up from the screen. Her eyes danced with excitement. "It looks like I only got cut from one place. I'll have to choose the other three to cut now."

Julie leaned over to look at Alexis' screen. "But you still have Tri-Gam too, right?"

Alexis nodded and looked at me. "Taren?"

"I didn't get cut?" It came out like a question, and I pulled the laptop closer to me.

"You didn't get cut by Tri-Gam?" Julie held up both hands, fingers crossed for luck, and Alexis clapped her hands together.

"I still have Tri-Gam. I didn't get cut...by anyone. I guess they all liked me. How is that possible?"

Julie jumped up and down on Alexis' bed. "I told you Taren

Richards! You are hotter than Satan's nut sack!"

I threw my pillow at her. "Did you really just compare me to the devil's genitals?"

She laughed. "You gotta admit, that's pretty hot, though. Right?"

I didn't get cut by anyone. I sat back in my bed, staring at the computer screen. A sense of something new struck me. I was finally starting to believe I could be different. That it was my turn to belong.

Chapter 10

Alec

We were walking to Ratsies for calzones when I saw her again. The field in front of Memorial Chapel was filled with girls in sorority shirts, but my eyes were drawn to Taren like a heat-seeking missile. She was laughing and joking with a short, dark-haired girl, and I frowned. I'd forgotten how nice Taren's smile was.

She'd smiled plenty during the time we worked on our debate project. When it was just the two of us, we never had any problem getting along. Guilt clenched my chest when I thought about that night at the bonfire. All I wanted to do was ignore how I'd been the one to cause that smile to disappear for the rest of senior year.

Forget the smile, Hart. Forget the girl.

I tried to look away, but found it impossible. My gaze was pulled back to Taren against my will and damn if it didn't land on her skimpy skirt and the most perfect pair of legs I'd ever seen. The only way Taren's legs could look any better was if they were wrapped around my waist.

Wait. What?

I ran my hand across my forehead and then raked my fingers back through my hair. I sighed, closing my eyes for a second. I needed to get laid. If I was thinking about Taren Richards that way, it'd been way too long.

"Over here!" Caz yelled, demanding my attention. He was running down the sidewalk, looking over his shoulder at me with his hand outstretched. I pulled my arm back and threw the football to him. He caught it, and I grinned when he shook his hand to release the sting of the catch.

"Hey look," Caz said, stopping in the middle of the sidewalk and waiting for me to catch up. He pointed toward the crowd of girls. "It's your damsel in distress. You didn't tell me she was Greek."

I grabbed the football out of his hand. "Yeah, well I didn't know she was. In high school she was a geek." I tossed the ball in the air, catching it with my other hand.

Caz braced his hands behind his head and looked over at me. "A geek?" He laughed. "And you wonder why she hates you."

I didn't wonder why. I knew why. "The feeling's mutual."

"It didn't look mutual when you were groping her after her near death experience."

"I wasn't groping her." *Just...protecting her.*

"If you say so." Caz dropped his arms and shook his head, laughing. "So, tell me. How could you possibly hate a sweet little hottie like that?" His eyebrow was cocked in challenge.

I gripped the football between my palms, pressing my hands together until my muscles screamed in protest from the effort. "I thought we were going for calzones, not confessional."

Caz held his hands up in an unspoken demand for me to throw the ball. "I'm just curious. You saved the girl's life, and she was too pissed to even thank you. I want to know why."

My arm snapped forward and the ball sailed into Caz's outstretched hands. I shrugged. "Not much to tell. We were competing for the same scholarship at a debate competition. I needed it to get out from under my dad's iron fist." That scholarship had symbolized my freedom. "She won."

Caz stopped walking and frowned. "Let me get this straight. You humiliated her, and then she kicked your ass in a competition. I don't see how you could hate her for that." He chucked the ball at me, attempting to hit me in the chest, but I snatched it out of the air with one hand.

I took a deep breath and released it. "I was pissed about the scholarship because she won it with a project we had both worked on together. But that's not the reason I hate her."

Caz held his arms wide. "Enlighten me then."

I rubbed my chin in thought. "Imagine this. A group of seniors in a D.C. hotel at a debate competition for the entire weekend with only one chaperone."

Caz grinned liked he'd just accidentally wandered into the girls' locker room after gym class. Yeah. I had his attention now.

"So, one night my buddy and I decided to throw a party in our room. His brother even hooked us up with some beer. Brilliant right?"

"So did she puke on your bed or something?" Caz looked over at Taren, a small grin tugging the edge of his mouth. "She's pretty fucking hot, dude. I think I'd forgive her for just about anything."

"Guess who turned us in?" I asked him.

Caz's eyes widened in surprise. "She snitched on you?" He laughed and shook his head.

"Yeah, and it fucked up my senior year. No car. No parties. No dating. My father became my fucking shadow."

"For one mistake?"

"One mistake could ruin his perfect plan for me." I took a deep breath and looked away. "According to him, I couldn't be trusted after that."

Caz slapped me on the back. "Just proof that you should sign the Acroletes pledge. You and alcohol have a dark past."

I met his gaze and grinned, tossing the ball back to him. When he turned away from me to continue walking, my eyes were drawn back to Taren. She looked happy. The only other time I'd ever seen her happy was when she'd won the scholarship at the debate competition.

"You coming, man? I'm starving."

I tore my gaze away from her. "Yeah."

Caz slung his arm around my shoulder, turning me away from the field of chattering girls. "Don't even think about it."

"What?"

"About crossing the line. You say you hate her, but it's a thin line between love and hate. Besides, your high school nemesis is now a Greek. We're not their type."

"Speak for yourself. I'm everyone's type." My cocky grin slid into place.

Caz slammed the football against my chest, knocking the breath out of me. "Based on the Vulcan death glare she gave you the other day, I'd tend to disagree."

***

I stood up from my chair and stretched. Homework on a Friday night? Pathetic. I needed to go out and have some fun. I could probably bullshit my way into any one of the parties on Frat Row...

I grabbed my jacket just as my phone buzzed, and I picked it up to see that it was a text from Amanda.

Amanda: What are you doing?

Me: Studying. Caz went home. Bored out of my mind.

Amanda: Maureen did too. Mind if I come study with you? I'm bored, too.

Me: Sure.

We didn't have any classes together, and I had a feeling Amanda's version of studying would require naked skin. Charming her out of her shirt would be a lot more fun than trying to get into a Frat party.

Amanda: Cool. See you in 10.

I straightened up our room, tossing all of my workout gear into the closet. When Amanda arrived, I went downstairs to let her into the dorm.

"You look nice." I gave myself a mental high five for the tiny skirt she was wearing.

Her tongue peeked out to wet her lips. "Thanks." She held a bag from the convenience store. "I brought snacks. I know Caz doesn't have anything edible in his fridge." She handed me the bag of popcorn and bottles of water, and then followed me upstairs.

I stopped when we reached the common room. "Should we make popcorn right away?"

She nodded. "I missed dinner. I'm pretty hungry." Her eyes moved over my body like she was starved, but not for food.

I grinned to myself. I would definitely make sure she was satisfied. "Come on." Putting my hand on her lower back, I steered her into the mini-kitchen that was just inside the common room. I tossed the popcorn bag into the microwave and pressed start. Leaning back against the counter, I watched the bag turn around in circles. "Do you go home much?"

Amanda moved next to me. "No. My dad lives in Florida, and my mom works a lot on the weekends. There's no point."

"Don't you miss your friends from high school?" Her shirt was damn near see-through. All I could think about was continuing the kiss we had shared on the ropes course.

She turned, moving close without actually touching me. Her gaze travelled a slow path from my arms up to my face, and I clearly heard all the words she didn't say. She wasn't at my dorm to study or even for small talk. She was here for one reason only.

"Most of my friends are off at different colleges, and they don't come home much. I'd rather be here anyway." She shrugged and ran the tip of her nail along her lip.

The microwave chimed, and I pulled the steaming bag out, holding it up. "Want to watch a movie? Caz has a huge collection."

The smile that curved along her mouth made me wonder if she could read my mind. "Does he have any horror movies? They're my favorite."

Sure they were.

"Horror movies, huh?" I raised my eyebrows as I looked at her, and she pulled her bottom lip between her teeth. "I think we can find something for you."

Amanda grabbed my arm, curling her fingers around my bicep as I led her out of the kitchen and into the hallway. On the way down the hall, she leaned against me. I shook my head and smiled. Girls only liked horror movies for one reason, and I was totally on board with that reason.

When we entered my room, Amanda took it upon herself to create a makeshift couch on my bed with pillows while I browsed through Caz's immense Blu-ray collection.

"Do you want an oldie but goodie or a new release?" I asked.

Amanda came and leaned against me to peer over my shoulder. "Oooh. *The Shining*. I love that movie."

I raised my eyebrows in surprise as I tilted my head to look at her, but she'd moved away and was already crawling across the bed. She settled against the pillows, cradling the bag of popcorn in her lap. I smiled to myself and turned to put the movie into the player.

"Turn off the lights," she said when I stood up. She ran a piece of popcorn over her lower lip before eating it and licking the butter off her fingers.

I like the way you think.

The lights were out in seconds and I made my way over to the bed. I sat close to Amanda, spreading my arm across the pillow behind her. Five minutes into the movie, I could feel the weight of her gaze on me, and I reached into the bag of popcorn, which she had conveniently tucked between her knees. Her hand slipped into the bag at the same time, and she stroked my fingers with hers. As her fingers slid along mine, a thrill ran through me. All I could think about was her stroking me with that hand...

"Are you comfortable?" I asked. I sure as hell wasn't comfortable. My dick was already hard and I had zero interest in watching the movie.

Smiling, she curled herself into my side and rested her hand on my stomach. "I am now."

She tilted her face toward mine, and I leaned down to kiss her. She tasted like butter and salt, and when she slid her tongue into my mouth, I groaned, hungry for more. She buried her hands in my hair, making small noises in the back of her throat.

"You keep making noises like that," I murmured against her lips, "and I'm going to come up with all sorts of ideas that don't involve watching this movie." I tilted her head back so I could lick and kiss her neck. She moaned when my lips touched her skin, and my pulse picked up speed.

"That's what I was hoping." Her eyes closed and she held me close.

Reaching for her hip, I pulled her into my lap so that she was straddling me. My hands cupped her tight ass and she rolled her hips into me, pressing our bodies close. Jesus. I was hard as a rock. I kissed down her throat and looked down between us where her legs were spread around me. Her skirt was hiked up so that I could just barely see her panties.

I felt wild and I wanted her clothes off. I needed to be inside her.

Amanda rocked her hips into me, and I groaned against her skin, nipping the curve of her neck with my teeth. She jumped back and squealed like she'd seen a mouse.

My dick softened at the sound. *Fucking traitor.*

"Alec! I'm ticklish." Amanda slapped my arm, giggling. Then she pouted. "You need to lose this." She tugged on the neck of my shirt.

I reached behind my head and yanked it off, and then tossed it to the side. Her hands roamed over my chest as she leaned forward to kiss me again. She circled her hips, and the little moans she made sent an electric current straight up my spine. My eyes were focused on the tiny scrap of material between her legs, and my dick was back on his game again.

Amanda broke the kiss, panting. "I like you Alec." Her voice was needy, and she ran her hands over my chest and arms. "But I need you to understand that I don't do relationships."

Was this girl for real? "I guess it's a good thing I don't have time for one."

She grinned, still circling her hips against me. "Good. Now take my shirt off."

Amanda lifted her arms, and I pulled the fabric up over her head and tossed it to the floor. *Holy shit.* She wasn't wearing a bra. My dick twitched in appreciation. I slid my hands up her sides and then spread my fingers over her breasts, pressing their weight into my palms.

I bent down to draw a nipple into my mouth, and she arched into me. She whimpered and grabbed the back of my head, and I squeezed her other breast, rubbing my thumb across her nipple. Pressing her breasts together, I licked up the seam, imagining what it would be like to fuck them.

"You taste so good," I murmured against her skin. I moved my mouth back to her breast and nipped the tiny bud between my lips. She squealed again, pushing me away.

"I told you I was ticklish!" She giggled.

The chink in the armor—Amanda was hotter than hell, but her laugh was a literal cock block. I rested my forehead against her shoulder. Did she have any idea what that screeching did to the situation in my pants? Limp. Like I-just-saw-my-grandma-naked limp.

Fuck. Why was I thinking about that?

Concentrate, Hart. Amanda is half naked in your lap. You want to fuck her tits. She probably wants you to fuck her tits. Shit, she's probably going to let you fuck her tits if you can keep it together for more than ten seconds.

"Keep going," Amanda said, pushing my head back to her chest. "That felt so good."

Don't mind if I do. My tongue circled around her nipple, and I reached down between us, pushing her skirt up higher. I started kissing her again, keeping her mouth busy and my dick happy.

Amanda's fingers were at my waistband, fumbling with the button of my jeans.

Oh, hell yes.

She pulled her lips from mine to stare at me. "You want this, Alec?" she asked, rubbing her hand along the bulge in my pants.

"Like you wouldn't believe."

She slowly slid down the zipper, and I shifted so I was lying down on the bed with her still straddling me. "Tell me you want me," she whispered as she slid her fingers inside my jeans and stroked.

"I want you, Taren..." The sentence ended in a growl as I pushed my hips up into her hands.

Amanda's head snapped up. "What did you just say?"

"What?" I asked. *Why was she stopping?*

"Did you just say Taren? Is that a girlfriend or something?"

"What? No." *What the fuck?* Did I really just say Taren?

"Who's Taren?" Her hand was still in my pants, but now it felt like she was holding my dick hostage. The other hand was in the middle of my chest, pinning me to the bed, which was actually kind of hot except that she was glaring at me.

"Amanda," I said, "I don't have a girlfriend." I wrapped a long strand of her hair around my finger and pulled her face down to mine for a kiss. "No relationships, remember?" Her body relaxed, and then her hand started stroking me again.

My dick was straining against her grip and I pulled her closer, grinding my hips up into her. So fucking good. I just wanted to lose myself in her.

The door to my room swung open and crashed into the wall behind it.

"Honey, I'm home!" Caz called, flipping the light switch on.

Blinded by the sudden brightness, I put my hands up to shield my eyes, and Amanda made the strange squeaking sound again as she attempted to cover herself. I sat up quickly to try to shield her, and I accidentally knocked her off my lap and onto the floor.

"Aw, Christ," Caz swore. "Were you guys really sucking face to The Shining? That's some messed up shit."

I hurried off the bed, trying to hide Amanda from Caz's gaze, but he wasn't looking at her. He was staring at me.

"Dude. You have a boner. That's disturbing that you can get off while watching Jack Nicholson go fuckin' crazy on his wife and kid."

"What are you doing here? I thought you were visiting your family." I zipped up my pants, grimacing at the discomfort. Amanda had turned her back to us and struggled to get her shirt back on.

"I did. Now I'm back." He flopped down on his bed, unconcerned that he had interrupted my night. He picked up the remote and pointed it at his television. "Are you done watching this? I mean, it's not like you were anyway." He grinned, and I flipped him the bird.

Amanda grabbed her backpack off the floor and slung it over her shoulder. "I'll see you later, Alec," she said as she reached for the doorknob.

"Amanda..."

But she was already out the door and disappearing down the hallway.

"You could have warned me you were coming back tonight." I dropped down on my bed in frustration.

"I'll give you two very valuable pieces of advice." Caz grabbed the popcorn bag and shoved a handful in his mouth. "One, next time put a sock on the handle. And two, if you've got a girl in here, lock the door, dipshit."

Chapter 11

Taren

"Can I borrow a pair of earrings?" Alexis asked as she zipped up the back of my dress. We had another rush party tonight and were getting ready together.

I bent over and slipped on my heels. "Of course. Help yourself." I tipped my chin toward my dresser.

Alexis opened my jewelry box and rummaged around. "What's this?" She held up a long red ribbon.

My breathing faltered as I took it in my hand. This ribbon was a symbol to me of both pain and joy. I sat on my bed, running my fingers over the smooth satin. "I can't believe I still have this."

"Where did you get it?" Alexis sat next to me, securing a pair of silver hoops in her ears that Claire had given me for my last birthday.

My voice was low and flat. "You know how I was picked on in school?" Alexis nodded. "Sometimes it got pretty bad. This one guy liked to torture me. He was always doing things to my backpack. Dumping it in the toilet, kicking it down the hall—or my favorite—cutting the straps off so I had to carry it like a bag of groceries." I drew circles on the floor with my toes as I heard Alexis' sharp inhale.

"Oh, Taren. I'm so sorry." Alexis grabbed my hand and squeezed.

"It's over." I shook my head, dismissing her concern. "When I was working with Alec one day on our project, he noticed my backpack." I ran the ribbon through my fingers, the satin smooth and bright. "He used this red ribbon to fix the strap so I could carry my backpack again. It was part of the reason I thought his kindness was more than just friendship."

"It was a nice gesture."

"Yeah, well I'm a hopeless romantic. I wore this ridiculous ribbon in my hair when I went to the bonfire to ask him to the dance." I looked down at my hands, clasped tightly together. "Stupid." I rolled my eyes.

"Not stupid. Sweet. I love that you kept this." Alexis took the ribbon from my hands and placed it back in my jewelry box, shutting the lid. "Keeping this shows you never gave up. You were willing to take a risk, and you survived."

I swallowed around the lump in my throat and plastered a fake smile on my face. "Let's go. Jules will have a stroke if we're late." Alexis grabbed her sweater and opened the door. "And I think you just might be a hopeless romantic, yourself."

"I so am." She giggled as we walked down the hall together arm in arm.

***

I was in.

I was a Gamma Gamma Gamma.

They wanted me. They told me I *belonged* with them. And because sometimes, and only sometimes, things worked out the way they should, they also wanted Alexis and Julie.

"We're sisters! Real sisters! For life!" Julie cheered as we drank beers at our initiation party. Doug's fraternity hosted the party. They were considered our brother fraternity, which just meant we partied together all the time.

"I love your letters, Lex."

Alexis looked down and grinned. Her big sister, Tiffany, was our rush chair. As part of Tiffany's big sister role, she picked out Alexis' first sweatshirt with the letters of Gamma Gamma Gamma embroidered on the front. The navy sweatshirt with lime green chevron letters was adorable and very Alexis.

"Yours are so cute, too." Alexis pointed to my pink zebra letters. We learned that in the Greek system, letters were special. If you didn't go through the whole six week pledge period and get fully initiated into the sorority during a candle-lit, robed, oddly witch-like ceremony, you didn't get to wear the letters. All of the traditions still weirded me out a bit, but I wasn't going to complain.

Just as I was admiring the sweatshirts, lost in the emotion of belonging, a pitcher of ice-cold beer was dumped over my head. "Shit!" I screamed. I wiped the moisture from my eyes and wrung out my hair.

"Welcome to initiation, little sis!" My big sister, Kate, laughed and dumped a second cold pitcher of beer over my head. "Tradition dictates that we saturate your new letters in beer. Don't know why, but it sure is fun."

"Holy crap!" Julie screamed as her big sister threw one pitcher directly at her chest and another over her head.

I laughed, watching Alexis run from Tiffany, and then squeal as Asher Vance, President of Delta Epsilon, picked her up and held her. Tiffany poured beer on them both, but Asher didn't seem to mind a bit.

"Here, Denton." Doug handed me a towel, and I mopped my face dry.

"Thanks." I shrieked as Doug picked me up and twirled me around to face him, kissing me sloppily on the lips. I wished I could blame his clumsy kiss on his current state of drunkenness, but that was how he always kissed.

"Hey, Whistler." Julie slugged Doug in the arm before grabbing my towel.

"Not talking to you, Jules." Doug glared at her, and I raised my eyebrows at him.

"You just did, Whistler. Look, don't be mad at me about your boy, Lobo." Julie handed Doug the wet towel and looked across the yard. A pissed off Ricardo Lobo was perched against the back of the house with his arms crossed over his chest, glaring at her.

"I'll be back." Doug burped. "I need another beer." He staggered off toward the keg. He needed another beer like he needed that whistle around his neck again. I was going to have to find a way to lose that thing.

"I thought Ricardo was your Latin lover?" I whispered to Julie.

She rolled her eyes. "Chest hair."

"You're a mess."

"Me? What about our girl, Lex?" She nodded over toward Alexis who was lip-locked with Asher. "You never told me what happened after the boyfriend from back home showed up last week."

The corners of my mouth turned down at the thought of that shitty night. "He showed up, pissed as hell that she pledged a sorority. They started fighting, and I came to you." When that badass-looking guy cried, I knew it was my cue to get lost. "All she'll tell me is that they broke up."

Julie grinned and elbowed me hard in the ribs. Shit, she had pointy limbs.

"It appears Asher's lips are helping to make her feel better about her new single status." Julie cupped her hands around her mouth and hollered. "Hot damn, you two need to get a room."

Alexis pulled away from Asher, blushing as if she hadn't realized what she was doing.

Kate walked by and handed us more beers. One thing we did not need was any more beer.

"So, what happened with Ricardo?" I took a sip of the nasty, cheap drink.

"He's hot. I'll give him that, and he's a great dancer. Totally has that hot Latin guy thing down, but like I said, chest hair. Like a chia pet. Every time he took his shirt off, all I could think was cha-cha-cha-chia!" Julie shook her head and took a huge gulp of her drink.

I looked over at Julie and then at my beer. Julie always had some excuse when it came to guys. No matter how hot they were, within a few days she was picking them apart. *Must be nice to have the luxury of being choosy.*

"He's giving you the evil eye," I pointed out, refusing to RSVP to my world-class pity party.

"Well he can eye me all he wants as long as he leaves that shirt on."

I laughed. "You're such a bitch."

"You mean honest," Julie said as she eye-fucked her next victim.

I set my beer down and tried to wring out my sweatshirt. "I hate to be a buzzkill, but I need a hot shower and dry clothes."

Julie looked down at her clothes and shuddered. "Yeah, me too. I feel properly initiated. Let's go home."

"Bye." I hugged Kate and looked around for Pickles. He was nowhere to be seen.

"Say goodbye to lover boy." Julie pried Asher off Alexis' face, and we dragged her to the bus stop with us.

When the bus finally stopped at Denton, we stumbled out the door. A group of students was hanging out near the bus stop, but they didn't get on the shuttle.

"Blondie is hot!" Even in her drunken haze, Jules was ready to get her flirt on. She pointed to a taller guy in the group and licked her lips. She took a few steps toward him and then stopped. "Wait. What is he doing?"

Alexis and I craned our necks, looking to see what Julie had noticed. The guy she was talking about was tossing around things that looked like bowling pins. Oh dear god. He was juggling, like a friggin' circus clown. I rolled my eyes and laughed. What a weirdo.

"What are those guys doing?" Alexis hiccupped and pointed to the guys that were being cheered on by a crowd.

Two other guys seemed to be having a race along the sidewalk, but instead of running, they were walking on their hands. One of the guys' shirts had bunched up around his shoulders, exposing chiseled back muscles.

"Can a spine be sexy?" I grinned in appreciation. If so, his definitely qualified.

Alexis nodded with a grin. "Absolutely. Backs are hot when they look like that. Just think what the rest of him looks like."

The group rooting on the hand-walkers got even rowdier. Julie, Alexis, and I moved to the side, trying to pass. *Jesus.* These people were more embarrassing than the geeks that strutted around campus in their marching band outfits. If anyone knew embarrassment and geekiness, it was me.

When hot spine guy crossed the imaginary finish line, the strange group erupted into whistles and cheers. "Yeah, Alec!" a girl screamed out and hugged him.

I halted abruptly, causing Julie and Alexis to slam into me. "Alec?" I repeated.

At the sound of his name, the guy turned around and looked right at me. His mouth hung open and sweat dripped along his forehead and down his face. *Holy hell.* My stomach dropped to the floor. The sick feeling I had when he saved me from the speeding car came back like a punch to the gut. Alec Hart. I just couldn't get away from him.

"Taren? Is that you?" His eyes scanned me and stopped at my sweatshirt, taking in the sopping wet clothes. I was sure my hair and makeup were a total disaster, too. This was not the way I wanted Alec to see me. I fought the urge to cover up and revert back to high school Taren.

I narrowed my eyes and pursed my lips. Why did he sound friendly? He had humiliated me. He had accused me of busting up his party and getting him in trouble. Whatever hope I had of finishing high school under the radar had been squashed at that point. Did he think that saving my life the other day suddenly made us best friends? If he was arrogant enough to think my heart fluttered like a butterfly on crack when his arms were around me, he'd be wrong. Nope. Not at all. I also absolutely did not melt into a puddle of hormones when he asked if I was hurt. Nope. His deep throaty voice had zero effect on me. Not one bit. I was over my crush on Alec Hart. That ship sailed. Finito. It was over. Gone with the wind and every other cliché my mind could muster.

I crossed my arms over my chest and ignored the droplet of sweat that kissed the side of his face. "Yup. It's me, your old buddy Taren."

Alec smiled. "You look great!"

Asshole. Was that some kind of joke? I snorted and rolled my eyes. I kicked out my hip. "It's initiation night. I'm a Tri-Gam now." I pointed to my beer-soaked letters on my sweatshirt.

"That's great, Taren." His tone sounded unimpressed. *Arrogant asshole.*

I tipped my chin up. "Yeah it is." I cocked an eyebrow as I looked around at the motley crew. "Are these your friends?" I might have been a beer-soaked mess, but I was never going to let Alec look down on me again.

Alec's brow furrowed, and he crossed his arms over his chest. "Yeah, these are my friends."

Julie leaned close and whispered in my ear. "Juggler dude is back flipping on the lawn. Can we go? These people are freaking me the fuck out."

I muffled my giggle with my hand and watched Alec's jaw tighten.

Maybe it was the exhaustion, the cheap beer, or my own petty need to get even, but I wanted to hurt him like he had hurt me.

"I guess you were right, Alec." I stared down my nose at him, repeating the words he said to me only a year ago. "I guess we really aren't in the *same league*."

Chapter 12

Alec

As Taren walked away, irritation raked along my nerves. She acted like our last interaction had never happened, and it pissed me off. She'd almost ended up as some dude's hood ornament, for Christ's sake. A simple thank you wasn't too much to ask.

I fisted my hands at my sides. Taren had claws. She'd finally learned how to fight back, and I didn't like it one bit. The Taren who had just insulted me and my friends wasn't the Taren I knew. She'd never been outright cruel to anyone before. Even if she still hated me, I couldn't believe she would act that way.

Amanda came to stand next to me as I watched Taren and her friends enter Denton hall. "Who was that?"

I turned away, shrugging. "Just someone who went to my high school." Confessing her name would only make things worse. Amanda would make the connection. She wouldn't have forgotten what I moaned the other night.

Amanda didn't press the matter, and as our impromptu gathering broke up and people started leaving, I shoved away my thoughts about Taren.

"I'm gonna head out." Maureen stood up from the curb and brushed her pants off.

Amanda bent over to pick up her jacket before slipping her arms into the sleeves. "Since you're my ride, I guess I'm going, too."

"See you girls at practice," Caz called out to them, not breaking his rhythm as he and Jon tossed juggling clubs back and forth.

"Come on." I shoved my hands in my pockets. "I'll walk you to your car."

"That's so nice of you, Alec." Amanda pressed close to me, grabbing my hand and pulling my arm over her shoulder.

Maureen rolled her eyes at Amanda. "You really don't have to, Alec. It's not that far."

"Yes he does!" Caz hollered. "Hart has a hero complex. Let him protect your virtue, Maureen."

"What about mine?" Amanda yelled in mock anger.

Caz laughed, flicking the pin behind his back in a difficult move before tossing it to Jon. "That's just a lost cause, sweetheart."

"You're a prick, Caz."

"I love when you talk dirty, Amanda."

She stuck her tongue out at him, and they were still calling insults out to each other as we walked to the overflow parking lot.

"Your handstand is getting so much better." Amanda leaned her head on my shoulder and looked up at me. "I knew you'd win. You're a natural."

When we reached the car, she turned to face me. Her fingers traced along the muscles of my chest. "You want to come back to my place for a bit?"

I cleared my throat and reached up to scratch my chin. *I should say yes. Why didn't I want to say yes?*

"I can't. Coach called an early lacrosse practice tomorrow." I offered Amanda a small shrug and then reached behind her to open the passenger side door. She took the opportunity to lean in and press her lips against mine. She slipped a hand behind my neck and tried to deepen the kiss. I ran my tongue across the seam of her lips and kissed her back.

Nothing. Not even a twitch in my pants. What the hell was wrong with me? Amanda was hot. She was a sure thing, even she admitted that. I should be jumping at the chance to…jump that.

I pulled away, giving her an apologetic smile as I opened the car door wider. "Maureen's waiting."

Amanda pouted, but then slid into the seat. Her eyebrows pulled into confusion as she stared at me. I was confused, too. Lacrosse practice was a shit excuse, but it was better than giving her an even worse one—that I didn't want to go back with her.

"I'll see you guys at practice." I waved and then tucked my hands in my pockets, backing away as Maureen turned the car on and pulled out of the space.

Why did I turn Amanda down?

Jon and Caz were gone by the time I made it back to Denton. Fine by me. I was exhausted and bed sounded pretty damn good. Walking past the shuttle stop, I tripped over something on the ground. I bent over to see a small wallet attached to a lanyard.

That sucks. Whoever lost this wouldn't be able to do shit on campus without their ID. I opened up the wallet and groaned. *Fucking hell.* Why couldn't I catch a break? The smiling face on the card belonged to none other than Taren Richards.

***

I paused, my hand in a fist, before knocking on her dorm room door. If I hung the wallet on the doorknob, I could save myself the aggravation of having to talk to her. I looped the lanyard over the handle just as I realized her room key was attached.

Fuck. Leaving her ID and key outside her room was like a personal invitation to any drunk, horny, loser to waltz on in. She and her roommate would end up being a statistic on some university police report. I took a deep breath and then released it, shaking my head. Might as well do the right thing and face the shrew like a man. Besides, it was time to call a truce.

My fist rapped on the door twice, and the sound echoed down the hall.

"No, Jules. I already told you I don't want to watch that gross porn with you again. Once was enough." The door swung open, and Taren stood in front of me wearing nothing but a smile and a towel.

And just like that I had a fucking woody.

"Tell her I don't want her using her vibrator as a flashlight either!" A voice called out from behind Taren.

My gaze took all of two nanoseconds to scan every inch of Taren's wet, naked skin. She was wrapped in a small white towel that barely covered her ass and her hair was hanging down her back, wet and dripping. Motherfucking dripping down her body.

Iron. Clad. Wood.

"Uhhhh…" *Jesus.* My voice sounded like I was having sex with her. Which come to think of it...

"Alec!" Taren screamed and slammed the door in my face.

Christ. Get it together, fuckface. So what if she was naked and wet and…naked?

"What are you doing here?" Taren barked from behind the door.

I huffed out a breath and looked at the ceiling. Of course this wouldn't be easy. "Open the door, Taren."

"No. Why won't you just leave me alone?"

I fisted my hands. Why did she have to make this so difficult?

"I want to talk to you." My voice was low and demanding, which probably wasn't the best way to get her to cooperate.

"No. I have nothing to say to you, Alec. At least nothing that's nice. Go away."

I closed my eyes and rubbed the back of my neck. *Pain in my ass.* "You could say thank you since I found your wallet."

The door slowly opened, and Taren peered out from around the edge. She looked down and saw her wallet in my hand. "Oh."

As she reached for it, I pulled my hand behind my back. "Can we talk?"

She pursed her lips and narrowed her eyes. After a few seconds she held up her index finger, and I was glad she chose that digit instead of the one she probably wanted to use. She shut the door, and I heard muffled voices from behind it.

A moment later, a pretty blonde opened the door, glaring at me. "Come in." She motioned me in with her hand. She turned to Taren. "I'm gonna shower, but if you need anything, just scream." Her roommate gave me a pointed look and then grabbed a towel before leaving the room.

Taren stood next to her bed, hands clasped together. She'd gotten rid of the towel and was wearing shorts and a tank top. A very tiny, very thin tank top.

I swallowed loudly. "Look, I don't want to keep having these uncomfortable run-ins on campus." I watched her as she stared at the wall across the room.

Her eyes met mine. "Why can't we just pretend we don't know

each other?" She crossed her arms over her chest, and her breasts rose high under her tank.

Never. Ending. Woody.

"Pretending we don't know each other is awkward as shit." I crossed my arms and tried to avoid staring at her chest.

"Yeah, well so is getting humiliated in front of the entire school. Get used to it." Her hip was cocked to the side and her eyes blazed with confidence.

I held her gaze and neither one of us blinked as we glared at each other. "Look, I feel like an ass for what I did at the bonfire. But it's not like you're completely innocent either."

She tilted her head, and her forehead wrinkled. "I know you wanted to win the scholarship. So did I. We both worked hard on that project and deserved to win. You can't blame me for a decision someone else made." She stood up straighter, hands now planted on her hips, eyes flaring. With her chest jutted out in defiance, it was clear she wasn't wearing a bra.

Even my frustration couldn't subdue the way my dick twitched at the sight of her nipples poking through the thin fabric. Which only pissed me off more. Those tits belonged to a self-righteous harpy. My dick was a goddamn idiot.

I took a step toward Taren and narrowed my eyes. "I'm not talking about the scholarship." The hard edge of my voice made her flinch. "How about when you ratted out the hotel party? My father made my senior year a living hell for that."

"Are you serious?" She placed both her hands on my chest and pushed hard. I didn't move an inch, but a burn started to build inside me. Realizing she couldn't move me, she raised herself on her tiptoes and got in my face. "I never turned you in, Alec. The party was so loud the other hotel guests probably called security. I might have been a geek or a nerd or a goody-two-shoes, or whatever else you and your asshole friends called me, but I was never a snitch. I'm disgusted that you thought I was even capable of that."

She grabbed her wallet out of my hand and tossed it on the desk before stalking over to her bed. She yanked clothes from the laundry basket, folding them with vicious motions. "Thanks for bringing my wallet back. Hopefully we won't have any more awkward run-ins. If you see me, just turn the other way, and I'll do the same." She folded her shirt into something that resembled a wadded up napkin and slammed it down on the top of her bed.

I watched her attempt to fold a few more things. "You didn't turn me in?" My voice was rough. Regret was like a fucking boulder on my chest. All this time I hated her for a mistake I had made.

Her laugh was bitter as she turned around to glare at me. "Oh my god. Why are you still here?" When I didn't answer, she shook her head. "And why do I keep letting you hurt me?" she said under her breath.

"I never wanted to hurt you." I held my hands uselessly out to my sides.

"But you did." She looked like she was going to cry, and she crossed her arms again, her fingers gripping her biceps. "I thought we were friends."

"We were." My voice was firm and sincere.

Her laugh was full of scorn. "Yeah. As long as no one knew about it."

"I'm so fucking sorry." I walked toward her and placed both hands on her shoulders. I expected her to pull away and was grateful when she didn't. I bent my knees to meet her gaze, and I wondered if I sounded as guilty as I felt. "For everything."

She shuddered and took a deep ragged breath.

I gripped her shoulders tighter. "I wish I could take it all back."

Taren blinked quickly and then uncrossed her arms, her hands fidgeting together. "Me too."

"So what do I have to do to get off your shit list?" I grinned, forcing my hands to let go of her.

She sighed and then shrugged, a timid smile finding its way onto her lips. "Well, you *did* save my life."

"Twice," I reminded her, nodding toward the wallet she'd tossed on the desk. "One look at your picture and some douche would have been letting himself into your room later tonight."

Taren's eyes widened as the reality of the situation finally hit her.

"Oh...wow," she whispered, wringing her fingers together and looking between me and the wallet. "I didn't even think...Alexis could have been hurt." She stepped close to me and wrapped her tiny arms around my back, resting the side of her face against my chest. "Thank you for returning my wallet even though I was a total bitch outside." She squeezed tightly, pressing every part of her body against mine. My arms fell around her, accepting the impromptu hug.

Fuck. She'd know what she was doing to me in three, two...

"Oh." She gasped and pulled back.

I reached up and ran my hand through my hair. She was hot. Couldn't be helped. Besides, she started it.

Taren cleared her throat and extended her hand. "Friends?" She tucked some hair behind her ear, trying not to laugh.

I nodded and shook her hand. "Sounds good," came out of my mouth, but the words in my head were *for now*.

***

"Dude!" Caz yelled as I threw another perfect barani. "That was awesome. Now you have to do a full."

I laughed. "I just learned this. I'm not ready for a full twist."

"It's easy." Caz thought everything was easy. His judgment could rarely be trusted.

"The landing is blind," I said, stepping off the mat. "I don't like that."

"Come on," Caz said. "You're ready for the full. Do it." He grinned and I could see the wheels of mayhem turning in his head. "Or else."

"Or else what?" I sat down on the edge of the double mini tramp and leaned my elbows on my knees. Defiance only seemed to encourage him further.

"Or else I'll tell Amanda what you do in your bed at night." He collapsed on the mat and put his hands behind his head.

"I sleep in my bed, jackass."

"That's not what I'm going to tell her." He arched his eyebrows and then mimicked pleasuring himself. "Ah-manda. Oh Amanda, you feel so good," he moaned.

"You're a dick."

"Oh...Oh..." Caz continued to groan and mime-masturbate all over the mat. He opened his eyes. "Oh good. Here she is." He got to his feet and waved his hands like he was a hitchhiker flagging down a ride. "Amanda!"

"Fine." I stood up and pushed against his shoulder causing him to roll back onto the mat again. "Fine. I'll do it. You'll spot me, right?"

"Like a boss."

I walked back to the other side of the gym, swinging my arms in front of my chest like an Olympic swimmer to loosen my muscles. I'd never admit it to him, but I was glad Caz pushed me to challenge myself. If he didn't rag on me, I wouldn't be able to do half the things I'd learned in the Acroletes gym. We both knew it. He took my comfort zone and demolished it on a daily basis.

I stood at the end of the run, facing the double mini tramp, twisting my arms and chest as a last minute reminder to my body on how to rotate while flipping.

"Let's go, Maude. I'm waiting," Caz taunted. I stared at the double mini tramp a moment longer, and he started his ridiculous mime-masturbation again.

I took a deep breath and then started running. I leapt onto the first bed, rode the bounce high, and then came down on the second bed. As my body rose up out of the second bounce, I flipped, throwing my arms into the position Caz had shown me.

"Over-rotating!" Caz yelled, grabbing for my arm.

His direction was too late. I was too high, my rotation too far to stop, and the landing was blind. I came down hard on my ankle and heard an agonizing pop as I fell to the mat. Pain lanced up my leg and down my foot like knives splitting my bones. My body rolled awkwardly to the side, and I immediately curled up, pulling my leg close.

Fuck. I was going to throw up. I rocked back and forth, gritting my teeth.

"Shit!" Caz cursed, dropping down to the mat next to me.

"What happened?" Amanda yelled as she ran across the gym to us. "Alec, are you okay?"

"Get him some ice!" Caz grabbed my wrists, trying to pull them away from my leg. "Let me look at it."

I let him pry my hands away, and I hissed in pain. Leaning back on my elbows, I swore as I stretched out my leg for him to get a better look. The movement felt like someone was slamming a rock into an open wound.

"Dude. Shit." Caz jerked back away from me to sit back on his heels. "I'm so sorry." He was tearing his hands through his hair as he stared at my leg. His eyes were wide and full of panic.

"What?" I groaned and squeezed my eyes shut until light burst behind my eyelids. My leg hurt so fucking bad. "Is my ankle dislocated? Can you pop it back in?"

"I don't think so, dude. Shit." Caz muttered under his breath. "Alec...it's broken."

I opened my eyes. "It can't be." Shaking my head, I forced the words up and out of my chest.

"Ankles are definitely not supposed to look like that." For once, Caz sounded scared. His fear, more than the pain I was in, terrified me.

Gingerly I sat up and looked at my leg. I groaned, knowing with certainty that I'd fucked up royally this time.

I didn't have to be a doctor to know that recovery would take months. I didn't have to be a coach to know that I wouldn't be ready for the lacrosse season. At best, I'd be benched. I didn't even want to think about the worst—about what I might not be able to do if it didn't heal correctly.

I could hear Caz yelling for Amanda to get the coach and have him call an ambulance, but it sounded far away, as if it was happening to someone else. I stared at the unnatural shape of my ankle. My thoughts were a haze of dizziness. A dark cloud crept across my vision. I closed my eyes, and the noise around me faded into a dull drone.

One thought repeated with relentless certainty through my head: I'd just lost my scholarship. That thought was echoed by the absolute conviction that I'd also just guaranteed my father's wrath.

And then I really wanted to throw up. Not because of the pain, but because I risked it all. I'd gone all in on nothing but a high ace. I'd just gambled everything and lost.

A Year Later

SOPHOMORE YEAR

Chapter 13

Taren

"The devil came up from Hades with fire in his eyes. He said there's one thing wrong with Hell; there are no Tri-Gams. Oh, there are no Tri-Gams down in Hell. *Hell no!*" My sisters and I sang in unison, screaming at the top of our lungs when we got to the, *hell no*! "Oh, there are no Tri-Gams down in Hell. *Hell no*! Cause they're all up above, drinking beer and making love. Oh, there are no Tri-Gams down in Hell. *Hell no!*"

We stood outside of the Xi Upsilon fraternity house, serenading them to say that we had agreed to be their match for Homecoming.

"Ohmygod, I'm so happy the Xi U's asked us," Julie whispered in my ear as the members of Xi U sang back to us in response.

"Why do you care so much?" Alexis teased Julie. Julie's scowl made us both laugh.

"I'm seriously in love with their social chair, Damian Yoffee." She pointed one perfectly manicured finger to a preppy looking mass of muscle who was leaning against the banister of the porch. He saw Julie and raised his chin. "Did you see that?" she squealed.

"If that wasn't a declaration of love, I don't know what is." Alexis elbowed Julie and Julie nodded in agreement, missing the sarcasm that only one of her best friends could say with love.

***

"Are you planning on making your Friday morning history class, Jules?" I raised my eyebrow and pursed my lips in my best schoolmarm impression. Homecoming Week had arrived, and Julie had been dedicated in her role as Homecoming Chair for Tri-Gam. As such, she had attended everything…absolutely everything.

Except for her classes.

"Friday is the talent show." The light changed to red, and the pedestrian sign lit up, allowing us to cross Route One and head home. "I have to set up at six in the morning. Sorry babe, but history class is a distant second to that."

I rolled my eyes at her. Julie might not take her classes seriously, but I did. "You need to take classes you love. Once you get past core classes and take ones for your major, you'll feel differently." I loved every second of the required courses I was taking for my English Literature major.

"I can't start my design classes until I pass the stupid core fuckers." Julie threw her head back and groaned. "How the hell do you maintain such a good GPA and still have a social life?"

I threw my arm around her shoulders. "Easy. I study."

Julie wrinkled her nose at me as we walked up the pathway to our large white-bricked house. Moving into this beautiful old home still felt like a dream. Without my scholarship covering tuition and living expenses, I wouldn't have been able to do it. Several sisters sat on the front porch and waved when they saw us.

"Hey, Taren," Julie's big sister, Jen, called out. She knelt on the floor, painting a bolt and a nut onto poster board. "Are you sure you won't join the dance group for our talent show number? It's going to be so hot." Jen smiled, using her forearm to push her curly brown hair from her face since her fingers were covered in paint.

"Jen, I told you I have two left feet." I bent down to examine her poster. "Why are you painting tools on the sign?"

"T?" Jules yanked my arm, pulling me to a standing position. "You're my best friend, and I'm Homecoming Chair. How do you not know what our theme is?" She pointed to a large white sheet, stretched across four windows in front of the house. Painted on it were the letters of Gamma Gamma Gamma with a nut underneath. Next to that were the letters of Xi Upsilon and underneath their letters was a bolt. Written across the bottom of the sheet in bold black letters was, evidently, our slogan:

TRI-GAM AND XI U: TOGETHER WE SCREW!

Pornographic. And absurd. I didn't get it.

My eyebrows pinched together. "Oh shit, sorry Jules. I thought that was a joke. You know, like we're screwed. Meaning we lost." I rambled on, speaking rapidly and trying to explain my lack of attention. "The goal is to win Homecoming, so I figured you all were joking when you suggested that."

"We discussed your thoughts, T, and decided you were over-thinking things. We wanted to emphasize the fun, sexy element of the slogan. I think it's perfect." Julie smiled proudly. "By the way"—she pushed me through the front door— "why aren't you wearing your T-shirt?"

Looking around the formal living room of my sorority house, I could see sisters lying on sofas, reading magazines or playing on their phones. A group sat off to the left in the sunroom, working on a project for a class. Two of our new pledges shared a small side table by the fireplace, quizzing one another on Tri-Gam history. Every single one of them wore the same blue shirt with a nut and a bolt on the front.

"I...uh...forgot?" I grimaced, waiting for my best friend to unleash on me. She followed me as I walked into the dining room. Several girls were eating grilled cheese sandwiches and tomato soup from the table that was set up along the side of the wall. I took a plate and headed to the salad bar.

"Is this because of Whistler?"

My brows arched at her question, and I paused, tongs full of iceberg lettuce dangling in the air. "What do you mean?"

"Is Pickles making you feel bad about hanging out with the Xi U guys? He can be such a girl, sometimes." Julie crossed her arms over her chest and tapped her foot, waiting for my answer.

"No, it's not because of Doug. I seriously spaced out that we were supposed to wear the shirts today. I know you find this hard to believe, but I was focused on my classes."

"Lex is a terrible influence on you." Julie shook her head sadly. Once Alexis decided she wanted to go to medical school, she declared her major in Chemistry. The amount of work involved with that major forced her to buckle down. She and I were still roommates, now sharing bunk beds on the third floor of the house. Jules was right across the hall, but Alexis spent far more time studying than she did partying with us.

"I'm not letting anyone tell me what to do. Not Lex and not Doug." I tossed the lettuce onto my plate and then added strips of grilled chicken. "I'm just trying to balance my time between classes and Tri-Gam stuff." I poured dressing liberally over my salad, giving the bacon bits the stink eye and tossing on a few croutons instead. "Look, Doug isn't happy that we're partying with other guys, but he's partying with other girls. He'll deal."

Jules leaned in close to my ear. "Totally different. All of the Xi U guys are hot. Of course Pickles is going to be jealous." Julie clutched her plate to her chest.

"He has nothing to be jealous about. It's not like I'm trying to replace him."

Julie stepped back, frowning. "And why not? Have you two ever been on a date? Have you ever done anything other than hook up after a night at the bars or a Greek event? You're like fuck buddies...but with no fucking."

I tilted my head to the side in thought. "Nope, never been on a date." I straightened and sucked in a breath. "Look, Jules, I know my relationship with Doug is...odd. Doug's safe. He's dependable. Like my favorite pair of yoga pants. They might not be the most fashionable, but they're the comfortable, easy choice." What I thought, but didn't admit, was that with Doug, my heart was never at risk like it had been with Alec. I'd taken enough risks since I started college and wasn't ready for anything deeper than what I had with Doug.

Julie raised both eyebrows at me. "You do realize you just talked about your boyfriend like he was a pair of pants, right?"

Before I could come up with a good response, Julie screeched, and I jumped while attempting to steady my plate of salad perfection.

"What the fuck?" Julie's finger shook as she pointed to a sign hanging over the hot lunch portion of the table.

"Uh-oh. I think we're being punished. Who pissed Lisa off?" Our new chef, Lisa, was hired because the sisterhood had pitched a fit when the previous chef consistently made us carbohydrate-heavy, calorie-bloated meals like spaghetti, fried chicken, and mashed potatoes. Apparently, my sisters thought that high calorie meals in a sorority house was like an act of war against our waistlines. My stomach growled at the memory of chicken Alfredo. I missed that old chef.

"Somebody broke a rule." Jen stood next to me, wiping her paint-splattered hands on a paper towel. "Last night a bunch of girls came home wasted. A couple of them trashed the place with their carryout, but my little sis over here is probably the reason we're sanctioned right now."

Julie's mouth dropped open, and she glared at Jen. "What are you talking about?"

"Didn't you manage to pull a bunch of food from the padlocked fridge last night by squeezing your tiny arm through the opening?" Jen laughed at the wide-eyed look of shock on Julie's face.

"My dues pay for that food. Who does she think she's messing with?" Julie fumed and stomped her foot. "I'm starving, but I have to save my calories for tonight. I had a plan, and she's messing with it." She blew out a breath, and I bit the inside of my cheek to keep from laughing.

"Everything will be okay, Jules. Take a deep breath and let me get you some soup." I guided Julie to a seat and put my salad down next to her. Ladling her tomato soup into a bowl, I re-read the sign and chuckled. It was a sorority girl's nightmare. Hanging up in large letters on a yellow sheet of construction paper were the words:

No Fat Free Cheese For You

***

"Drink a beer. Drink a beer. If you can't drink a beer like a Tri-Gam can, then why do you have that beer in your hand? Drink a beer.

Drink a beer." My sisters and I chanted our serenade together.

"Welcome ladies!" Damian Yoffee's voice boomed out as we finished cheering.

We walked into the Xi U's house for another night of social bonding. When Julie explained what tonight's party was, Alexis burst out laughing and outright refused to attend. As I left our room to walk over to the party, she was curled up in bed happily studying.

"Your drinking buddy for this evening is wearing a name tag with your name on it," Damian informed us. "Brothers will be around to secure your handcuffs. Rest assured we do have keys. You and your drinking buddy will only be hooked together for the around-the-world portion of our party. You'll travel together from room to room, where a different themed shot will be served in each place. Everybody have fun!" Damian opened up a box of seriously legit looking handcuffs and beckoned us forward.

Was I really going to be handcuffed to a guy all night? Again, I thought Julie had been joking. I should know better by now. My palms began to sweat as I looked around the room. I should have stayed home like Alexis. Maybe the gods of partying would look down on me with favor, and I'd get a nice quiet guy as my partner.

"It's party time!" A tall guy with a curly mop of hair jumped on a coffee table and pulled his shirt off over his head. His physique wasn't awful...but I wouldn't call it mouthwatering either. I stood on my tiptoes to get a better look. Nope not even a single pack in that torso. Just a whole lotta beer belly that he wasn't shy about sharing with everyone.

"I hope I don't get him," I whispered to Julie, who nodded back with wide eyes.

"Jules! You ready to rock and roll? Let's head to the kamikaze room first." Damian walked up with Julie's name on his tag.

"Bring it on," Julie told him, flashing him one of her flirtiest smiles. Damian snapped a handcuff around her wrist and then on his own. He headed toward the first room, and Julie looked over her shoulder mouthing *Good luck* to me as she headed off.

"Ah, fuck! When I took off my shirt I lost my drinking buddy's name. I know it started with a T. Teri, Tara? No that wasn't it..." The tall guy on the table spoke loudly and looked around.

My stomach dropped, and I pressed my lips together. *No Bueno.*

"Was it Taren?" Jen asked with a giggle.

"Totally! Taren, baby! Where you be?" Beer Belly yelled.

Jen pointed at me, and I glared at her. "Sisters for life? I thought you had my back!" I spit out.

She shook her head and wagged a finger at me. "Maybe next time you'll join my dance group when I need you." Still chortling with laughter, Jen took off with her handcuff buddy.

I felt myself being lifted into a bear hug against a naked chest. "Taren! I'm Ed Tuckerman."

I extended my hand to shake his, but Ed only grinned bigger and snapped on my cuff, linking us together. He dragged me to the stairs, where we edged past a large group of people to hike to the third floor.

The room we entered first was lit by a black light, making strange things shine on each person. Teeth, eyeballs, even lint on clothing—everything white glowed. Music pulsed through the room, so loud it hurt my ears. Ed handed me a shooter, and I clinked my glass against his. I gulped it down, and the burning sensation in my throat caused me to cough. Ed slapped my back with enthusiasm.

Choking, I wiped my eyes. "What was that?" I screamed in Ed's ear to be heard over the music.

"Purple Jesus." Ed beamed. "That shit will make you have a come to Jesus moment. Or if over-served, a come to the white porcelain god moment."

Ed was funny. That would make tonight much easier. Laughing, I asked, "So Ed, what's your major?" *Wow. What an original and interesting question, Taren.* As I chastised myself, Ed groaned.

"Nobody calls me Ed, babe. I kind of go by my last name."

A fraternity guy who went by his last name? Real original. Seriously, what was wrong with first names?

Tuckerman guided me to our next stop, pointing to a room filled with red lights. "This one's Prairie Fire. Watch out, it'll put a little hair on your chest."

"What's in it?" I grimaced, my stomach still burning from the purple concoction.

"Tequila and tabasco sauce. Try it. I dare you." He winked.

As we entered the room, two of his brothers wearing cowboy hats raised their glasses in salute. "Fuckerman! You're here!"

Fuckerman? Figures.

Grinning down at me, he hollered, "Buckle up, baby. Fuckerman's going to take you for a ride."

Spending the night handcuffed to Fuckerman would be very interesting, to say the least. Aunt Claire would be proud.

***

Kira waved her hands in front of her as her voice became higher in pitch. "So then she gets out of bed, walks over to her desk, takes out the chair, pulls down her pants, sits down, and pees." Laughter echoed through the dining room, and Julie buried her face in her hands. "She even tried to flush the chair!" Kira, Julie's roommate, stood on a dining room chair, regaling all of us with stories about just how drunk Julie was last night.

"Are you feeling okay?" Alexis rubbed Julie's arm and then reached for a bagel. The unwritten rule in our house was that carbs were to be avoided at all costs. Except for Sunday mornings.

"I feel like death," Julie moaned, resting her head on her folded arms.

"Can I get everybody's attention?" Kate stood on her chair. "I posted the list in the hallway for assignments for Good Buddies." A few stifled groans filled the air, and Kate glared at the entire room. "We voted, girls. We picked this as our charity. I, for one, think it shows people that we're growing. Last year's pie eating contest to raise money for testicular cancer was weak. Asking the guys to eat pie, wearing only their boxers, was way too transparent. C'mon! Good Buddies is a great group. I think you'll all enjoy it." Kate jumped down and smiled when she met my eye.

"I'm looking forward to meeting my non-drinking, non-handcuffed buddy." I grinned at Alexis, pouring myself a large glass of juice.

Julie looked up and sighed, resting her chin on her hand. "I'm nervous. It's a year-long commitment. Plus, these are adults with disabilities. What will we even talk about?"

I shook my head, swallowing my orange juice. "Don't worry, Jules. Kate told me all about the program. The person we're partnered with usually doesn't get much social interaction. They work or attend programs on campus. They just need a friend."

"I'm excited to meet Stacy." Alexis took a bite of her bagel and chewed slowly. "I'm feeling like I need a wake-up call. You know, a reminder of life outside of college."

I pulled a garlic bagel apart and spread on veggie cream cheese. "I feel like I need to do something unselfish for a change."

Julie lifted her head and grinned slyly. "I'm sure Pickles feels everything you do for him is very *unselfish* of you." Rolling my eyes, I took a big bite and smiled at her, cream cheese still stuck to my lips. I then pursed my lips and blew her a kiss, making sure she got a good whiff of every bit of garlic.

"That smells so...disgusting...I'm gonna..." Julie slapped her hand over her mouth and took off for the bathroom.

Alexis met my eyes, and I pressed my lips together, holding my breath. She slapped her hand over her mouth, and we tried, for a whole two seconds, not to laugh.

Chapter 14

Alec

If I had any sense at all, I'd suck it up and study in my room. The only piece of furniture I had in there was a bed, but the discomfort of studying without a desk might be worth earning myself some peace and quiet to work.

I glanced over at Caz, who was sprawled out on the couch reading a comic book. He was distracted for now, but he wouldn't stay that way long. Studying in my room didn't mean he wouldn't come in anyway. Might as well go for comfort.

I collapsed into the chair at the table and then powered on my laptop—the one thing I'd managed to keep after my father kicked me to the curb. Recovering from a compound fracture took nearly nine months. Recovering from my father's rejection? I was still recuperating. Being disowned wasn't a speedy healing process.

"Don't you ever relax?" Caz asked me. His silence lasted thirty seconds longer than I'd expected it to.

"Don't you ever study?" I opened up the file that contained the notes from my Biology class and then dug through my backpack until I found my textbook.

"My grades are impeccable, and my question still stands. Don't you ever relax?"

I shrugged. "No time. I've only got three hours between the end of practice and the beginning of my shift. This is the only time I have to study." Frustration crawled up my spine, settling in my shoulders. None of my friends could understand the constant pressure I felt. Their tuition, room, board, books...hell even their fun was all paid for by their parents. I used to know what that was like, throwing around twenty dollar bets like it was chump change. Not anymore. Now I only bet when I knew I could win.

Caz sat up. "Why don't you ask your dad to help out?"

I grunted. "Not likely."

When I lost my scholarship, my father was furious. When I changed my major last spring, he damn near had a heart attack, and he still wasn't over it. He thought refusing to pay for tuition and my living expenses would bring me to my senses, but it only made me see things more clearly. For the first time in my life, I was doing what I wanted...and I was doing it on my own.

Caz closed his comic book and tossed it onto the coffee table. "It's been a year, dude. All you have to do is swallow your pride and ask."

"It's not that easy." I shifted in my chair, trying to get comfortable. "He blames Acroletes for taking away my future. Unless I quit the team and jump back on his Senator Hart campaign, he's not interested." I gave up worrying about what my father thought a long time ago. Now that I had a taste of freedom, it was unlikely he and I would ever find common ground again.

Caz got up from the couch and wandered into the kitchen. The fridge opened and closed. He then sat in one of the other chairs at the table, digging his spoon deep into a brand new can of icing. "Do you like working at Shell Shocked?"

I shrugged. "It's good money." I kept my attention on my textbook as I read the passage again for the third time. I was never going to get anything done if Caz hung around.

"Yeah, but aren't you afraid what Coach might say?" He tapped his spoon on the edge of the can until I looked up from my homework.

I sighed. "What do you mean?"

Caz glared at me. "You're a smart guy. Do you think he's going to be okay with you working at a bar? You signed a pledge to not drink."

"I don't drink, and I'm not a bartender. I work security." I leaned back and crossed my arms, frowning. "He can't be mad about that. I have to make money somehow, and Shell Shocked pays well."

Caz took another spoonful of icing and ate it in one bite. "You signed a drug-free pledge and you're a bouncer at a bar. You're playing with fire."

"I don't have a choice." I hated that Caz was voicing the arguments I'd already had with myself. Did he think I *wanted* to work at a bar?

"You always have a choice. You don't have to work there. That decision is all yours." Caz was uncharacteristically serious. "Be careful you're making the right one."

"I couldn't keep working three jobs and surviving on three hours of sleep a night. I need to make money. Something had to change."

"I understand." Caz snapped the lid back on his icing and stood so that he was looking down at me. "I just hope Coach does too when he finds out."

***

"Hart, you're going to be working the floor tonight while Jacobs works the door." Jimmy took a long drag from his cigarette and then flicked it with his thumb, scattering ash all over the floor.

Jimmy was the owner of Shell Shocked and he only ever called us by our last names. I was pretty sure it was because he had no clue what our first names were.

"We've got a local band playing tonight so the place is going to be packed," he warned me. "Let me know if you think you'll need an extra set of eyes on the floor with you."

"I will."

He slapped me on the back and then returned to his office where he'd probably stay for the rest of the night. Jimmy didn't show his face unless a fight broke out.

I leaned against the edge of the bar and watched the band set up. I'd only been working at The Shell, as most students called it, for a few weeks, but it was always the same routine. The place was dead until nine when the band started to play. Then all hell broke loose.

I was surprised Jimmy hired me, being that I was only nineteen, but he took one look at my size and offered me the job. When he told me how much money I could make, I accepted.

To kill time before the place got busy, I brought a few cases of liquor up from the basement and stacked them behind the bar.

"Thanks, hon." Jill winked at me before running her cloth along the bar to wipe it down.

"Let me know if you need anything else." I walked around to the other side of the bar and stood at the end, watching as people started trickling in.

The drummer tapped his sticks together, and the first riffs of music bounced off the walls drawing people away from the tables to dance. Soon the place was a wall-to-wall press of bodies, and the dance floor was a throbbing mass of groping hands, spilled beer, and clumsy dance moves.

Circling the darkened perimeter of the room, my eyes were drawn to every loud outburst. I lingered near a rowdy group of fraternity boys. They were regulars who were known for causing trouble.

A girl left the dance floor and headed to the bar, but was stopped when one of the fraternity guys stepped in her path.

"You've got a great set of legs. What time do they open, baby?" He held his arms wide, making her an offer.

I clenched my hands into fists, prepared to jump in if one of the guys took things too far.

Maybe Caz was right. Maybe I did have a hero complex.

She rolled her eyes and ducked under his arm. The laughter of the guy and his friends chased her away.

I was so engrossed in watching the asshole frat boys, that I was caught off guard when a girl stumbled into me, spilling her drink down my side. My entire body sighed in resignation. It wouldn't be a Friday night if I wasn't soaked with beer.

"Oh, sorry," the girl giggled. "I didn't see you there." When her eyes finally found my face, she smiled widely. "But I'm sure glad I found you." Her hand slid up my arm, and she leaned heavily on me. "Do you come here often?" Her words were already loose with alcohol.

"I work here." I tried prying her hands off so I could walk away and continue making my rounds, but she was still leaning against me.

"That's okay, sugar. I don't mind. My name's Julie. Wanna tell me your name so I know what to scream out later on?" Julie's hand was now on my chest, groping me.

I pulled her hand off, helped her get her balance, and gently guided her toward an empty table. "Thanks for the offer, but I'm on duty. You should be careful. Maybe you need to sit down and sober up a bit."

She recoiled and gave me a nasty look. "Be careful and sober up? What are you, my fucking daddy?" She turned away from me, but stumbled again.

I reached out to grab her to keep her from falling to the floor. *Christ.* That's all I needed was for this chick to pass out on the floor and give herself a fucking concussion.

"Jules, there you are. I've been looking all over for you." A girl with blonde hair came up beside Julie and grabbed her around the waist. "I got you a water," she shouted over the music.

"You should take her home. She can hardly stand." I glared at the backs of the girls as the blonde wrapped her arm around Julie to support her.

The blonde laughed without looking at me. "I've got her."

"Mind your own business." Julie waved me off as she turned to shout into her friend's ear. "I think I saw a hottie from one of my classes by the bar. Time to make my move." Julie turned to kiss the blonde's cheek, straightened her spine, and then proceeded to walk a fairly straight line toward the bar.

The blonde turned to face me, still shaking her head over Julie's behavior. "Sorry about that. She's a mess..." Her breath caught in her throat when she saw me, and her eyes widened in surprise. "Alec?" Her hand flew to her chest, covering the low cut shirt she was wearing.

"Taren?" I cleared my throat, tearing my eyes away from her hand and what the fabric underneath barely covered. "What are you doing here?" I hadn't talked to her in almost a year. Not since the night I found her wallet.

Her hand fell away from her chest and I could see how the top hugged every swell and perfect curve. "I'm here with my sorority sisters."

I thought nothing could beat seeing Taren in only a towel, but I was wrong. Dressed for a night at The Shell, she was sexy as hell. Her jeans were so tight I wanted to peel them off with my teeth. Her face was flushed from dancing, and the strap of her tight top had slipped down over her shoulder.

Knowing those jackasses in the corner were probably thinking the same indecent thoughts about Taren that I was, made me want to drag her out of the bar and send her home.

"Is she one of your sisters?" I nodded over toward her friend, Julie, who was now draped all over another guy.

Taren smiled and tucked a piece of hair behind her ear. "Yeah. Jules is a little crazy, I know, but she's got a good heart. She's one of my best friends."

"Well, keep an eye on her, okay? Some of the guys around here can be real assholes." I gestured over to the group of guys who had gotten my attention before Julie showed up.

Taren looked to where I motioned and frowned. "Those guys?" She lifted the strap of her shirt back in place and stood up straighter. "They're harmless."

I'd seen enough drunk guys in my short time at The Shell to know the difference between asshole and harmless. Taren was too trusting. She always had been.

"By the way." Taren leaned closer to talk over the music. "I heard you got hurt last year and lost your spot on the lacrosse team." She chewed on her bottom lip.

I rubbed the back of my neck. Of course she heard about it. We lived in a small town, and I'd been one of our high school's star players. "Yeah, well...unfortunately, I don't think there's a person from our hometown who didn't hear about that."

Taren looked down and shrugged. "My Aunt Claire is a bartender. Your dad kind of came in one night..." Her voice trailed off, and her eyes darted to my face as if she'd said something wrong. "Anyway, I'm sorry you lost your lacrosse scholarship. Claire said your dad was really upset about it." She looked down again.

"It's okay." I bumped her shoulder with my elbow so she'd look up. "Everything's good now."

"Really? You'd rather work in a bar than play lacrosse?" She slapped her hand over her mouth. "I'm sorry. I don't know why I said that. I didn't mean it that way."

I shrugged. "Don't worry about it. This isn't my dream job, but I'm happy."

Taren smiled, and it was a beautiful transformation. She was no longer the shy Taren she tried to hide behind in high school or the haughty one covered in beer that she pretended to be last year at the bus stop. I was seeing the Taren I'd only had a brief glimpse of in those few study sessions in the library and at the debate competition. This was the Taren that was confident and sure of herself.

"I'm glad," she said. "You look good, Alec."

"Is that so?" I grinned, crossing my arms over my chest.

Taren's gaze fell to my chest and biceps, and then her eyes darted back to my face, a blush spreading across her cheeks. "I just meant you look happy, that's all."

"Thanks." I had to bite back a laugh when Taren looked back to my arms. Her gaze was as hungry as mine was.

"Well, I should probably get back to my friends." She glanced over at Julie and then turned back to me. "It was nice talking to you again, Alec."

I liked the way my name on her lips ended in a smile. "Maybe we could get together some time," I suggested.

"Get together?" Taren looked nervous, and she reached up to rub her arm.

"Well, we're in the same Professional Writing class. Maybe we could study together sometime?"

"Oh." Her posture relaxed, and she smiled. "We are? I've never seen you."

"That's because you sit up front, and I'm usually late and sit in the last row."

Taren tucked her hair behind her ear again even though it hadn't moved. "Sure, that sounds great. Studying. We could study."

A guy appeared behind Taren and wrapped his arms around her middle. "Hey, baby." He was one of the fraternity guys I'd been watching earlier, and she jumped when he tucked his face into her shoulder, sucking on her neck like a goddamn leech. "You were supposed to bring me a beer."

I narrowed my eyes at him, and Taren peeked up at me, shame darkening her eyes. "Sorry, I ran into an old friend," she said to the guy as she nodded toward me.

Frat boy looked up as if just noticing me. I was sure the only reason he came over in the first place was to lay claim on her. I'd seen him in The Shell numerous times before with other girls, but never with Taren. She deserved better than a douche like him.

"Hey, bro." He lifted his chin in acknowledgment. "Name's Pickles."

I lifted my chin in response. "Pickles?" I glanced at her, and she shrugged, rolling her eyes.

"Come on, babe." Pickles grabbed the beer out of Taren's hand, took a swig, and then hooked his arm around her neck, pulling her away. "Let the hired help get back to work." He pretended to whisper it to her, but he said it loud enough to be sure I heard. He handed her the beer. She timidly took a drink and then glanced back at me once more before he led her away.

Fucking frat boy and his stupid nickname. What I wouldn't give for the chance to kick his ass.

I did another round of the perimeter of the bar, watching as drunk co-eds danced and sang while the band played. I passed the area where Taren was hanging out just in time to see Pickles grinding his hips into her backside and groping her chest. She pulled his hands away, laughing awkwardly as she scolded him, but I could tell she was embarrassed.

It occurred to me that ripping both his arms off could solve that problem.

Julie handed Taren a shot, and she pressed it to her lips before tossing it back in a swift, expert motion. Taren laughed as Pickles handed her another one.

When did she learn to drink like that? And why was she dating a guy like Pickles? She could do so much better.

I shook my head, annoyed with myself. I didn't have the luxury of worrying about Taren. She wasn't my responsibility. Besides, as I watched her hanging out with her friends, it became very clear to me that we were part of two very different worlds. We'd both made pledges for new lives, and I was positive those pledges could never co-exist.

Chapter 15

Taren

"C'mon baby." Doug moved on top of me, grinding his hips into my pelvis. I lay flat underneath him, my body rigid. The rhythmic motion was supposed to turn me on. Unfortunately, Doug's movements were jarring. Too many beers in one night had altered his coordination and his attractiveness. "We've been together for a year. I've been patient, baby. I promise I'll make you feel so good."

"Watson is playing video games on the couch. Cut it out." I pushed his shoulder, but he didn't budge. I wasn't ready to have sex. Doug shifted, dry humping my left thigh, and not my promised land. I almost asked him if he needed a map to find the right spot, but I didn't want to give him false hope.

Doug dragged his tongue up my neck, continuing up to my ear. He licked around the shell of my ear and then shoved his tongue deep inside. I scrunched my face and bit the inside of my lip to keep from groaning. He could mistake that groan for a moan, and he did not need any encouragement. Making out with Pickles was like getting greeted by an overly excited puppy—lots of enthusiastic licking that made me want to wipe my face off. I shuddered from the unpleasant intrusion of his tongue in my ear, and he grunted. *Shit. Did he think my response was from pleasure?* I pried open my eyes and looked up at his face, taking in his sloppy smile. I winced as he started in again on the leg humping. Yup. Definitely an overgrown puppy.

I cared for Doug. I really did, but I didn't delude myself. I wasn't in love with him.

"So? Tonight?" he asked hopefully, flicking a condom up between us so that I could see he was prepared.

"Pickles." I sighed, slightly annoyed that he was pressuring me, yet again. I understood that a year was a long time to wait for me to say yes. I always wondered if he might break up with me so he could have sex with someone else, but he never did. He just kept begging. "I'm not ready. I know that's not what you want to hear, but I'm not." I bit my lip and moved a piece of hair away from his eyes.

Doug's crooked grin vanished, and his eyebrows crinkled. "What do you need from me? What are you waiting for? A commitment? I'll give you one, if that's what you need." Doug moved off me and lay flat on his back. He dragged his fingers through his hair.

I turned onto my side to face him. My stomach was knotted with the guilt of what I was about to say. I didn't want to hurt his feelings.

"I like you, Doug. I really do, but I'm not in love with you, right now. Maybe we'll get there some day, but until then, the answer will be no."

"Virgins are hot. Way to make him work for it, T." Watson yelled out from below us.

Doug and I both groaned, and I buried my face in his chest. I stayed there for a few minutes, thinking about our relationship. Doug was goofy and a bit of a sloppy drunk, but he made me feel good about myself. The problem was, I wanted to feel passion and love. I didn't have that with Doug. I wasn't sure I ever would. I didn't want to have sex just because it felt like the time had come or because of some twisted sense of obligation to him. The last thing I wanted to do, though, was to hurt him. He was my friend, and he mattered to me.

"I'm sorry. I care about you, Pickles. You know I do. Give me some more time to figure myself out, okay?" I picked my head up, resting my hands on his chest and saw that my Whistler was sound asleep.

***

"I broke up with Damien." Julie sipped her Frappuccino and glanced at me out of the corner of her eye.

Slowing my pace, I blew on my own coffee before taking a drink. "You really liked him. What happened?"

"You wouldn't believe me if I told you." Julie grinned mischievously.

"Of course, we'll believe you. Spill it." Alexis leaned over me, narrowing her eyes to glare at Julie.

"He took a selfie."

Alexis stopped walking. "And? You take selfies every day."

Julie turned to face Alexis, and I crossed my arms over my chest, watching the show.

"He took a selfie at the *wrong* time." Julie raised her eyebrows, daring us to continue our questioning.

"People make mistakes, Jules. So he took a selfie at a bad time. If you really like him, I think you could get past that." Alexis worried about Julie all the time. She wanted to see her in a relationship with someone who cared about her, not serial dating anything that had a set of XY chromosomes and a nice head of hair.

"He took a selfie while we were having sex, Lex."

No one spoke. We faced forward and continued walking.

"You did the right thing. Sorry about that," Alexis mumbled.

Julie threw her arms up in the air. "Right? Thank you. What an ego-testicle prick!"

We laughed as we turned toward the Student Union where we would be meeting our assigned buddies for the first time. I couldn't stop smiling. The satisfaction from being a part of such an important program reminded me of how proud I was when Alec and I had prepared our anti-bullying bill for the debate competition. Doing something that could actually make a difference in someone else's life felt great.

We walked through the front doors of the conference building attached to the Union. Bright red and yellow balloons marked the doorway to the closest meeting room. A sign was perched on a tripod with the words, *Welcome to Good Buddies* in large, block lettering.

Leaving the topic of sex selfies behind, we moved into the room and found Kate standing near the doorway with a clipboard. "Ah, Taren. Great. Your buddy is waiting for you right now. He's seated at the last table on the left. Go on over and introduce yourself."

I headed in the direction of my buddy. Several of my sisters were already sitting with their respective buddies at small tables. Some shared cookies, pretzels, and sodas, while others looked at magazines together or sat chatting. At the last table on the left, a man was sitting alone. As I got closer, I noticed that unlike many of the other buddies, my partner didn't have Down syndrome. If I had to guess, I'd say he was older. Perhaps in his thirties? He appeared clean cut with closely cropped hair and a freshly shaved face. I waved and a wide, beaming smile filled his face.

"I'm Taren. It's nice to meet you." I extended my hand, and he shook it gently.

"My name is William. Good to meet you, too."

Pulling out a chair, I sat across from William, and he copied my movements, sitting back down.

"Thank you for being my buddy, Miss Taren." William smiled again, and my cheeks burned from my own never-ending grin.

"I'm excited to get to know you, William. Tell me something about yourself."

"Yup. Sure." William looked around the room for a few seconds before speaking. "I work every day. My dad got me a job at his office. I deliver mail. I like it. It is a good job."

"That's great you found a job you enjoy. I worry that I won't have the same luck when I graduate." That was an understatement. I loved to read and write, but I wasn't sure what career I wanted. I worried that I would graduate with a degree I couldn't actually use.

"What do you want to do?" William pushed a plate of cookies over my way and chose a small, broken chocolate chip one for himself.

Frowning, I selected the largest cookie on the platter, a thin sugar cookie, covered in sprinkles and handed it to him. His eyes lit up, and his cheeks flushed.

I played with the napkin in front of me. I had never told this to anyone. "I want to be a writer. I'd like to write a book someday, I think."

"Yup, yup, yup. I like books." William nodded and took a bite of his cookie, chewing thoughtfully. "I had a dream last night."

"You did?"

He nodded.

"What was it about?"

He swallowed and wiped his mouth with his napkin. "I met a girl who looked like sunshine, and she wanted to be my friend."

I smiled and broke off a piece of my own cookie. "Do you have many friends, William?"

"Yup. I sure do. Two, including you." His eyes shown with warmth, and a lump rose in my throat.

Something told me William would become my own form of sunshine.

***

"Taren!"

"Get down here!"

"Hurry!"

At the sounds of my sisters' frantic voices, I hopped off my bed and hurried down the stairs. Alexis slammed her book shut and followed behind. At the first floor landing, Julie and Kate waited, lips pressed together and eyes wide.

"What's going on?" I pulled my hoodie on and gathered my hair into a ponytail. Half of my sisterhood was crammed into the front of the living room, climbing over one another to look outside. The other half, it appeared, filled our front porch. The front door was open, but I couldn't see what was happening outside.

"Oh, you've got a big surprise out there." Kate giggled as she took me by the hand and led me outside to the porch.

Surprise couldn't accurately describe what I saw. The front yard of our house was full of piss-drunk members from Doug's fraternity. What beer they hadn't already consumed, they sprayed onto the lawn, aiming for a guy who was naked and hog-tied on the grass.

My eyes widened as I took in the scene. "God."

Julie leaned close to my ear. "Nope. Not God. Not even close. That's the Whistler, babe."

I couldn't move. I wasn't sure how I was supposed to react, so I just stared. The scene before me was like a gruesome car accident. I couldn't look away. Doug was lying on the front lawn of my sorority house, butt-ass naked, wearing nothing but his whistle. Duct tape bound his wrists and ankles, and he was covered in...everything. Ketchup, mustard, eggs, flour, pepper, beer, syrup. The entire contents of the Delta house refrigerator appeared to have been dumped on him. He was blindfolded, but yelling my name, all the while laughing and smiling the same sloppy grin that came after many, many alcoholic beverages.

"T, should I get him a sheet? To cover up?" Alexis whispered in my other ear. I nodded, wishing I could disappear and act like this had never happened. I brought my fist to my mouth, and Julie and Kate pushed me forward.

Asher moved away from the crowd, holding a gold necklace.

"Taren, our idiot brother has decided to place the highest honor we have on you. He has chosen to give you his letters. We, as the brothers of Delta Epsilon, do not take this lightly. For this reason, Pickles has been rightfully punished."

I looked away from Asher and into Kate's eyes. Doug was giving me his letters? My heart raced as panic filled my veins. Lavaliering was extremely rare in the Greek system. When a fraternity member allowed a girl to wear the letters he had worked so hard to earn, it was considered a sign of pre-engagement.

Pre-engagement? *Freaking balls.* What was he thinking? Didn't he understand a thing I said to him the other night?

Kate nudged me forward, and I took the necklace from Asher. "Congratulations," he said, grinning.

Alexis ran up with a sheet from my bed, and Doug's brothers rolled him over, removing his blindfold. Groans and exclamations of "ewww" filled my ears. Pickles was giving the crowd a full frontal, and it didn't appear to bother him one bit. He smiled when he saw me standing in front of him, holding his letters.

"Whaddya say, Denton? You wanted a commitment, right? I can't do much better than this." Doug's brothers hauled him to his feet, and I wrapped the sheet around his shoulders, holding my breath so I didn't have to smell him.

"Thank you." My voice was barely a whisper. I didn't know what to say. I never asked him for a commitment, and he'd totally put me on the spot in front of his friends and mine. This sort of declaration was supposed to make a girl happy, but I felt...embarrassed.

What was wrong with me? Doug wanted me. ME. His declaration was sweet and romantic...ish. Leaning forward he pressed his wet, sticky lips to mine, and I almost gagged when I tasted ketchup.

"I'm gonna go shower. We have poker tonight, but call me later, okay?"

I nodded and one of Doug's largest brothers picked him up and threw him over his shoulder. My sisters filed back inside, hugging and congratulating me along the way. My feet stayed planted right where they were. I was unable to move.

"Taren?" Alexis asked softly, turning me to face her. "Are you okay?"

I shrugged.

"Do you want this with Doug? This is a serious sign of commitment. If you accept his letters, you're basically pledging yourself to him."

I didn't answer right away. Instead, I stared at my feet as my mind raced and the ground tilted underneath me. What should I do? What did I want?

"Do you think you can trust him?" she asked.

My head snapped up as I looked at her. "What do you mean? Why wouldn't I trust him?"

Alexis shrugged. "Nothing. It's just that you guys have been together for a year and have never had sex."

"Yeah. So?"

"Well he goes out partying every night, but not always with you. And when he is with you, he's usually trying to get you naked."

She wasn't wrong, but what exactly was her point?

"Yeah. I trust him. He's nice to me." I didn't know what else to say. What I needed was some time to think. Everything had happened so fast. I wasn't expecting Doug to make a commitment to me, and now that it had happened, I didn't know how I felt about it.

"I'm just saying there is something he obviously wants from you, and after all this time, he still hasn't gotten it. Who's to say he isn't getting it somewhere else?"

I shook my head. "I don't think Doug would do that. If he was getting it somewhere else, why would he still be pressuring me for it?"

"Because you're a challenge," Julie interjected. "Bagging a virgin is like capturing the Golden Fleece."

"I...don't think so. If he just wanted to have sex, why lavalier me?"

Julie shrugged. "I didn't say it made sense. In fact, none of this makes sense."

She was right. None of it did.

Julie stepped forward and squeezed my hand. Her voice was quiet, and she swallowed hard. "I just want to say I'm scared for you, T."

I ran my index finger over my bottom lip. "I'm okay, Jules. I'm just a little freaked out."

"Me too. I think I'm going to need some serious counseling after tonight," she said. "I haven't had a flare up in over a year, but my microphobia is back with a vengeance. One look at that tiny pecker on Pickles, and I'm shaking from head to toe. Someone hold me." Her voice broke into peals of giggles, and we laughed until tears ran down our cheeks.

I wiped my tears away, and my stomach tightened. She was right. Unfortunately, Doug's tiny member really was the smallest of my worries right now.

***

Alec stood up and swung his backpack onto his shoulder. I zipped my shoulder bag and moved into the aisle. "Want to work on the job application letter this weekend?" I asked Alec, as we walked out of class.

"Absolutely." He grinned and opened the door for me.

We walked out into the sunshine, the fall wind whipping through the trees that lined the mall. I rubbed my arms, wishing I had thought to wear a jacket. "My place or yours?"

Alec cocked his head to the side and rubbed his chin. "Something tells me we'll be able to concentrate better at my apartment than we will at your sorority house."

Chuckling, I nodded. "Yeah, if my sisters get a good look at you, they'll be asking to join our study session. Guys with muscles are definite distractions."

Alec laughed. "Well, it's not like I plan to parade around shirtless or anything."

"What a shame," I mumbled to myself.

"What?"

I laughed nervously. "Nothing." I cupped my hands around my mouth and blew warm air onto my fingers, rubbing them together for friction.

"You cold?" Alec took off his zippered sweatshirt and handed it to me.

I hesitated, staring at him. He was wearing a tight dark blue T-shirt underneath. He didn't need to walk around shirtless. I could see the outline of his chest muscles through the thin material. His arm was extended as he held the sweatshirt out to me, and the veins in his forearm protruded out. I gulped in a breath. He was muscular everywhere, and I had the strangest urge to run my fingertips over the thick cords to see what it felt like. I was used to Doug's body. The only workout he'd done in the last year was lifting beer bottles to his mouth.

"I can't take your jacket. You'll freeze. You're only wearing a T-shirt." As the words came out of my mouth, another shiver ripped through me.

"I'll be all right," he said, motioning again for me to take the sweatshirt I so desperately wanted. "I'm always hot. I'm like my own personal heater."

At Alec's words, my brain was assaulted with thoughts of snuggling into his huge arms for warmth. My face immediately heated in shame. I was wearing Doug's letters, and I shouldn't be thinking about Alec that way. I could blame it on the crush I used to have on him—some habits were hard to break.

I took the offered sweatshirt and slid it over my arms. "Thanks. I'll get it back to you as soon as I can."

"Keep it 'til the weekend." Alec ran a hand through his hair. "You can give it back to me when you come to study."

"Taren!" I heard Doug's voice, and my palms began to sweat. *Damn.* I'd been ignoring his calls for the past two days.

I looked toward the sound of my name and saw Doug jogging my way. My fingers touched the fraternity letters that hung from my necklace. Ever since I put it around my neck, the letters felt heavy. I was weighted down with their meaning. I tucked the charm underneath my shirt. I still couldn't believe he'd decided to lavalier me. For what? So I'd have sex with him? I honestly didn't believe he was in love with me, so what other reason could he have?

What he'd done was a huge honor in the Greek system, and everyone expected me to say yes. Receiving his letters should have made me happy, but all I felt was shame. I had been the object of an action I didn't feel was deserved. I didn't know what this revelation meant for us as a couple, so I'd been ignoring him. I knew it was rude, but I was so confused.

Doug came up beside me and slung an arm over my shoulder. He kissed my cheek, and I glanced up at Alec. His face was tense, and the muscle in his jaw twitched as he watched Doug. My face flushed as my gaze darted between them. I felt embarrassed that my *boyfriend* had his arm around me in front of Alec. What was wrong with me?

"Alec, this is my...friend, Doug Pickles. You met him at The Shell the other night. Doug, this is Alec Hart. We went to the same high school and have a class together now."

Neither guy extended a hand to shake. They eyed one another up and down, and an uncomfortable silence surrounded us.

"Pickles is your last name?" Alec's eyebrows tilted up as he spoke to Doug. "That must suck, man. Thought that was a nickname."

Doug stared at Alec for a long moment without responding. Then he turned to me, and he dipped his chin down, pouting. "Friend, Taren? Really? I mean, c'mon." He pulled out the necklace from where it was tucked underneath my shirt.

Looking up, Alec watched me in confusion. His eyebrows pinched together as he stared at the necklace. Doug placed it on my chest and ran his finger over it before moving behind me. I stiffened as he wrapped his arms around my shoulders, and a queasy feeling turned in my stomach. Doug Pickles was staking claim on me. He might as well have lifted his leg and pissed all over me like a territorial dog.

"You know what this is?" Doug asked, pointing to the necklace. Alec gave him a death stare and didn't respond. "My letters. That means she's my girl. We just made it official. Right baby?" Doug kissed my cheek again, and queasiness crawled up my throat.

Alec stood as still as a statue, not budging or saying anything.

"Come on, babe." Doug released his grip on my shoulders and grabbed my hand. "I'll walk you to your next class."

"Um. Yeah, thanks." My eyes darted up to Alec's face to find his mouth pressed into a tight line as if he wanted to say something. "I'll see you on Saturday?" I smiled and hoped he could see the apology in my eyes.

He hitched his backpack higher on his shoulder. "See you then."

When Doug placed another kiss on my temple, Alec turned and walked the other way.

"You're seeing him on Saturday?" Doug snapped once Alec was out of earshot.

"We're in the same class, and we're getting together to study." I wrapped my arms around my stomach as Doug turned, guiding me up the sidewalk. He hadn't commented on the oversized sweatshirt I was wearing. I wondered if he had noticed it wasn't mine. I let out a slow sigh and my shoulders slumped. I felt like shit for not telling him who it belonged to.

"You haven't returned any of my messages, baby." Doug's arm fell away from my shoulder and slid around my waist. His fingers stroked under the edge of my shirt to find skin.

I shivered, and subtly cringed away from his touch. "I'm sorry, I've just been busy studying," I lied.

His hand slid down over the swell of my ass and slipped into my back pocket. "Come to The Shell tonight and hang out with me." He leaned in to kiss my neck.

My eyes darted around, wondering if people were watching the way he was touching me. "I don't know—"

"Can't you put aside the books for one night? I want to party with my girl." Doug stopped and turned to me. He used his fingers to tilt my face toward his and gave me his best puppy dog gaze—the one that had made me feel special so often over the past year.

My lips were parched, and my throat tightened as I blinked, trying to find the words to respond. "I...It's just...I have a test tomorrow." I couldn't even commit to seeing him tonight, and a fresh wave of guilt washed over me. I had to look away from him. He was my boyfriend. He'd been patient with me for the most part, and was the first guy to notice me. That had to count for something. What the hell was wrong with me?

He released a frustrated sigh and looked over my shoulder. His mouth pulled into a tight line. "Fine. Maybe you'll be able to pencil me into your schedule tomorrow." He leaned in and gave me a quick kiss on the lips, and then he walked away without another word.

As I watched him disappear into a group of students, the necklace, hanging around my neck, was heavy with the weight of my regret. I was the worst girlfriend ever.

***

I slammed the book shut and looked at the clock. The band at The Shell would have just started playing. If I left now, I would have plenty of time. Doug's words had been echoing through my head all day, and the shame over the way I'd been treating him was too loud to ignore. I was his girlfriend. He had made a commitment to me and wanted to spend time with me. Why was I in my room studying instead of hanging out with him?

Alexis looked up from her bed and watched as I stood up and went over to the closet and rummaged through the clothes. "You're heading over to The Shell, aren't you?"

I let out a deep breath and shrugged. "We're dating. I should start acting like it." I pulled a pair of skinny jeans out and my favorite top.

Alexis closed her book and hopped off her bed. "I could use a study break." She smiled as she picked out her own outfit.

"Lex, you don't have to go." I tossed my pajama shorts on my bed and shimmied into my jeans.

"Of course I do. Julie is out on a date, and I'm not letting you walk there alone. Besides, I could use a drink. It's been a long week."

"Fine." I leaned over and kissed her cheek as I buttoned my jeans. "As long as it's not because you feel the need to babysit me."

She laughed. "I haven't been out drinking in a while. If anyone needs babysitting, it'll be me."

We finished getting dressed and made the walk over to The Shell. The walk may have been short, but in heels, it always felt ten times longer than it really was. We flashed our fake IDs to the bouncer and he opened the door for us with a wink and a smile. The band was already playing, and the dance floor was packed by the time we made it inside.

"You sure he's here?" Alexis leaned over to shout into my ear. The place was filled with people and so dark, we had a hard time seeing anything but flashing lights and bobbing shadows.

I looked toward the corner where Doug usually hung out with his frat brothers, but he wasn't there. I lifted my hand and swirled my finger to indicate I was going to walk around. "Watson and a bunch of the other guys are over there. He's got to be here somewhere. I'm just going to go look for him."

Alexis squeezed my other hand. "I'll go get us a couple of beers." She pointed to the bar, and I gave her a thumbs up.

I walked around the edge of the dance floor. My hand crept up to my neck as my fingers found Doug's letters. I smiled and could already feel the guilt fading away. This was where I should have been hours ago. Doug was my boyfriend. Avoiding him, especially after he put himself out there in front of all of our friends, was just wrong.

I walked over to Watson, and when he saw me, his eyes flew open wide in surprise.

"Hey, Watson." I smiled.

"Hey, Taren." He took a long gulp of his beer as his eyes darted past me. "Does Pickles know you're here?"

"No. I came here to surprise him. Do you know where he is?" I turned around to search the immediate area, but still didn't see him. Odd. He usually stayed close to his brothers.

Watson put his arm on my shoulder. "Hang out here with the boys. I'll go look for him."

"You don't have to do that. I can find him." I brushed off his hand and waved. "I'm here with Alexis anyway." I headed toward the edge of the dance floor where she stood with two beers. She stood frozen, staring at the people dancing. She really did need to get out a little more often.

"Hey. Thanks, babe," I said with a smile, snagging one of the beers out of her hand. I pressed it against my lips and tilted my head back, letting the liquid slide down my throat. Yum. I should bring Alexis more often. She bought the good stuff.

Her head swung to look at me. Her eyes were full of concern.

"Oh, sorry. Is this yours?" I tried to hand it back to her.

"No. Taren, it's..." Her eyes flashed back to the dance floor, and that was when I saw why she looked so worried.

My Whistler.

Shock slammed into my chest.

His tongue was down another girl's throat, and my hand immediately covered my mouth. His hands gripped her ass while his hips ground into her like he was going to fuck her into tomorrow.

I teetered on my heels as if someone had knocked them out from under me. "What the hell?"

Alexis reached out to steady me. "Taren. Are you okay?" She gripped my arm, trying to get my attention, but I couldn't look at her.

I couldn't see anything except for the blurry form of my boyfriend humping another girl. In public. The tears were hot and angry as they crowded past my eyelids. I wiped them away with the back of my hand and handed my beer back to Alexis. "Hold this for me." What I really wanted was to break it over Pickles' head.

I stomped onto the dance floor, and Watson intercepted me, placing his hands on my shoulders. "Taren, it's not what it looks like."

I turned an angry glare on him. "Back off, Watson before I knee you in the balls." I shrugged off his grip, and he backed away, hands up in defense.

I shoved my way through the crowd, and although I was small, my fury parted the crowd like the Red Sea. Every memory I'd had with him–the good and the gross–as well as my misplaced regret, fueled my rage. When I reached Pickles, I tapped him on the shoulder and put my hands on my hips.

He pulled his lips from the girl. "What the fuck do you want?" he asked, swinging his drunk gaze in my direction. When his two functioning brain cells made the connection, he stepped away from the girl as if burned. "Taren?" He looked between me and his dance partner. He extended his arms toward me. "It's not what you think, Taren."

I shifted away from his reach. "Really?" I crossed my arms over my chest. "Because I think you were hooking up with another girl." I reached up and wrapped my fist around his letters. I glared at him in disgust and yanked on the chain so hard it broke. My neck burned from where the chain cut into my skin.

"No." He tried to grab for me, and I stepped out of his grasp.

"You were hooking up with another girl less than a week after you lavaliered me? Seriously, Pickles?" I was revolted.

"No. Come on, babe. You know that's not true. It was just a dance." He reached out to touch my arm, and I recoiled. I couldn't believe he had the balls to try to lie to me with the lip gloss smeared evidence still standing next to him, watching us argue.

"I'm not stupid, Pickles." I grabbed his arm and turned it so his palm was up. I dropped the necklace into his hand, feeling a thousand times lighter than I had since he had given it to me. "You obviously don't know the meaning of the word commitment."

I turned to walk away when he grabbed my arm, spinning me back around. "You can't just throw away a year." Doug growled, digging his fingers into my arm.

I pulled my arm out of his grasp. "I didn't throw it away. You did." I spun around and walked back to Alexis as fast as I could and with as much dignity as I could muster. Which to be honest, wasn't much. I was so stupid. Watson knew. All of Pickle's fraternity brothers knew. I felt like I was back in high school, staring at Alec Hart, embarrassment coursing through me. Once again, I thought a guy liked me and I was wrong. I was nothing but a joke.

Tears filled my eyes as Alexis took my hand without a word. The truth was, deep down, I never fully trusted Doug. My chest ached at the thought, and I wrapped my arms around myself. He had never *needed* to be with me. Hanging out with me was an afterthought for him. I was the warm set of lips and free grope that he could count on when he was in the mood. Of course, he didn't need to have sex with me. He was probably getting it from other places. My friends had been right. I was a challenge. That's why Doug stayed with me even though I refused to have sex with him. My chin trembled. Realizing my insignificance hurt.

Doug ran in front of us, trying to keep us from leaving. "Don't, Taren. Don't do this."

A tear slid down my cheek, and I brushed it away. "You just made me feel worthless." I took a deep breath and choked down my emotion, refusing to cry in front of him. "And I promised myself that those days were over."

"Taren, wait!" Doug shouted as I led Alexis around him and walked away. "You're making a big mistake."

I shook my head and headed for the door. Before we left, I looked back and saw Doug staring at the letters in his hand.

Was he feeling hurt? Confused? Pissed? *Welcome to the club.*

***

"What is new, Miss Taren?"

I joined William at his table, and he passed me a cup of lemonade. "Oh, too much, William. My head is swimming." I took a sip of lemonade and sat back in my chair. "Yum. Thank you."

William grinned. "Reminded me of sunshine, like you."

William was so kind and gentle. He made me feel comfortable and at peace in my own skin.

"What is hurting you?" He sipped his drink and waited patiently.

How did he always know when something was wrong? Even though I was there to talk to him, I couldn't keep myself from opening up to him about my life when he asked. I took a deep breath. "I've had a boyfriend for the last year. The only boyfriend I've ever had. But..." I sighed and looked away. "He's wasn't always the best boyfriend, and we broke up."

William nodded. "Did you love him?"

"No." I answered before realizing the word had flown out of my mouth. "I didn't, but when I was with him, I wasn't alone. Before I met him, I was alone a lot. Does that make any sense?" I stared into my glass of lemonade, feeling the weight of my admission.

"I'm alone a lot. I do not mind it." William took another drink. "I think it is better to be alone and listen to yourself than to be with someone you do not love, listening to them."

My smile was tentative but grew bigger as his words hit me. *Holy cow.* He had a point. I had been wasting my time with Pickles. For an entire year. Why? Because he made me feel like I belonged. That wasn't enough of a reason anymore. I wanted to feel a connection to someone. I wanted to feel a spark. Passion. Love. I belonged with my sisters and my friends. They were always there for me. I didn't need that from Doug. I nodded at William, a fluttery feeling developing in my stomach and flowing through my body as I listened to his parting words.

"No more hurting, Miss Taren. Listen to your heart. Yup, yup."

Chapter 16

Alec

"Dude, what are you doing?" Caz was sprawled across the couch, watching TV.

I rushed around the living room, picking things up and tossing them into the hall closet. I'd figure out where everything went later. "Taren's going to be here soon. I don't want the place to look like a dump."

"Taren? I don't recall giving my blessing to anyone named Taren."

"I don't need your blessing for shit. But you've actually seen her before." I grabbed the sneaker and T-shirt that were slung over the arm of the couch and flung them into the closet before shutting the door. "Remember that girl I went to high school with?"

"Wait...no way, is she the sorority girl eye candy?" Caz sat up straight.

"We have a class together. We're studying." I went into the kitchen and started putting the dirty dishes in the dishwasher.

Caz burst out laughing. "I thought you hated her. So do you like her now or are you just trying to make amends?"

The plates knocked against each other as I shoved them into the lower rack. "She's coming here to study. That's all." The silverware clattered as I dropped them all into the side basket and then slammed the door shut.

"Then why are you trying to impress her like you're planning to get her naked?" Caz yelled back.

"I'm showing you what decent manners look like in case you ever man up and bring a girl home." I wiped my hands with the dish towel and then walked into the living room, flinging it at Caz's head. "Besides. Taren has a boyfriend. Some fraternity douche named Pickles."

He tossed the towel back at me, and I caught it in my fist. "I told you those girls belonged to the guys on frat row."

I walked over to the closet and tossed the towel in with everything else. "And I told you that we were just studying." Turning to face Caz, I leaned against the closet door. "I thought you guys were going out."

"We're leaving now." Jon walked into the living room, fresh from a shower. He looked around the apartment. "Nice. You cleaned up."

"No he didn't." Caz tossed his comic book on the coffee table. "He threw all our shit in the hall closet. So if you're looking for your tighty whities later on, you know where to find them."

"Those are yours." Jon grabbed his jacket off the back of the chair and put it on. "You're the only one in this apartment who wears them."

"You mean I'm the only one hung well enough to need them." Caz swiveled his hips like a low rent Elvis impersonator. "My junk likes to be secure when I'm throwing triples in the gym. It's too massive to be swinging free with that kind of rotation."

Caz was always bragging about his size. One thing I knew for certain from living with him was that you should always sanitize the ruler before using it. Chances were, he had used it last to measure his dick.

A loud buzz echoed through the apartment, and Caz beat me to the intercom.

"Speak," Caz ordered.

I pushed him out of the way. "She's not a dog, dickhead." I pushed the button again to speak into the intercom. "Taren?"

"Alec?"

I pressed the button to buzz her in. "Come on in. I'll meet you down in the lobby." I grabbed my keys and headed for the front door.

"Hey." Caz came jogging after me. "Don't forget the rules buddy."

I frowned. "What rules?"

"Don't forget to put a sock on the door this time and lock it just in case."

I shook my head. "I told you this isn't a date. We're just studying."

Caz opened the hall closet and grabbed a dirty sock from the pile I'd tossed in there, and then he flung it at me. "Don't say I didn't warn you."

***

"Where did your roommates go?" Taren took off her jacket and laid it across the arm of the couch.

"They went rock climbing." I couldn't afford to go to the climbing gym with the guys. Usually it bothered me, but one look at Taren in her skin-tight jeans and low cut top and the only thing I could think about climbing was her body. With my mouth. Although I knew it couldn't happen, I'd take this pleasurable torture any day.

"You didn't want to go?" She set her backpack on the floor.

"I have too much work to do. Besides, they won't be back before I have to go to work." I picked up her jacket to hang in the closet, but then stopped before I opened the door as I remembered all the shit I'd hidden in there. Instead, I draped it over the back of one of the chairs at the table.

"Oh." A small frown pulled the corner of Taren's mouth down. "You have to work tonight?"

"Every Thursday, Friday, and Saturday night. Sometimes other nights when I can pick up extra hours, but those are my regular shifts. Want a drink?" When she nodded, I went to the kitchen and grabbed two bottles of water. I came back into the living room and handed her one. "Will you be there tonight?"

"No." Taren played with a piece of her hair. She looked away from me as she settled into the corner of the couch, kicking off her shoes, and tucking her legs underneath of her. "Doug will probably be there, so I don't really want to go."

"Why not?" I sat on the arm of one of the chairs and opened my water, taking a long drink.

Taren glanced up and her hands fell into her lap as she twisted a ring on her thumb. "I gave him back his letters. I haven't talked to him since I found out he was hooking up with other girls."

"Shit." I set the bottle on the coffee table and wiped my hands on my jeans. I'd seen him with other girls at The Shell before, but I didn't know how new their relationship was or how open. "I'm sorry."

Her laugh was bitter, and she shook her head. "Don't apologize. It's not your fault. I just can't believe it took me a year to figure it out."

Fuck. A year? "I know it's not my place to say, but you deserve better than him, Taren." I leaned my elbows on my knees and tried to look her in the eye.

I thought I saw her roll her eyes as she leaned over to pull her laptop out of her bag. "Yes, well I won't hold my breath."

"What do you mean?" Why was she even dating Pickles in the first place? She was too smart to be with a loser like that. Especially for a year.

She traced the design on the top of the laptop with her finger. "Doug was my first kiss." She immediately ducked her head, burying her face in her hands. "That sounds so sad, I know," she mumbled under her breath. After a few moments, she peeked through her fingers at me. "Doug was my first kiss, but I can't say it was exactly by choice. There weren't a bunch of guys to choose from or anything."

Taren had been awkward and unpopular in high school, but there was nothing awkward about her now. "I have a feeling the issue wasn't a lack of interest, but your lack of availability."

"Maybe." She shrugged as if she didn't want to continue talking about it.

"So, you want to work here?" I asked, pointing to the couch.

"We can work at the table if you want." She started to get up.

"No, no. This is fine." I stood up and reached out to stop her. Taren sat back down and powered on her laptop. Grabbing my own laptop off the table, I sat down on the other end of the couch.

Taren looked back at me, and the sweet pink of her lips curved into a shy smile. "Do you already know what you're writing for your application letter?"

I leaned back against the arm of the couch so I could face her. "Yeah. You?"

Taren nodded and then licked her lips. "After we're done writing, we can read each other's letters and critique. Does that work?"

"Sure." I stared at her mouth. Her lips were still wet from where she had licked them, and I wanted to lean forward, kiss her, and capture every word that came out of her mouth.

We both started up our laptops and ten minutes later, I was still staring at my screen, imagining just how sweet Taren's lips would taste.

Fuck. If I was being completely honest with myself, I was thinking about how sweet every inch of her body would be.

"You're not typing." Taren's face was tilted down toward her screen, but she was peeking over the edge of it at me. She bit her bottom lip and fought back a smile.

"You're not either." I rubbed my chin with my hand and smiled back. "Does the brilliant Taren Richards have writer's block?"

A breathy laugh escaped her, and she scrunched up her nose in an adorable way. "I already wrote it?" Her admission came out like a question.

"The whole thing?" I lifted my chin in question.

She released a defeated sigh. "I'm sorry. I don't want you to think I'm wasting your time. I was just so afraid if I came here, and I was alone with you all" —she gestured to me with her hands and shook her head— "with you all gorgeous and muscular and...hot...that I wouldn't be able to concentrate," she rambled. "Oh shit. And now I sound like a complete idiot." She dropped her head into her hands again.

"Gorgeous, muscular, and hot?" A small laugh rumbled in my chest. "Do you sweet talk all your study partners this way?"

"Forget I said that." She groaned. "Please?"

"No way." I reached across the couch between us and pulled her hand away from her face. "I like a compliment as much as the next guy." I lifted her chin up so she would look at me. "Besides, I already wrote mine for the very same reasons."

"Oh?" She frowned in confusion for a few seconds before my meaning hit her. "Oh." Her mouth curved into a smile. "Okay. Well should we just trade then?"

She reached up to smooth down her hair, and I was happy that she was at least as affected by me as much as I was by her. We switched laptops, and I read her application, every word valuable insight into the new Taren.

"You're going into Physical Therapy?" She tilted her head to the side, still reading my letter. "I thought you were studying Political Science." Her index finger tapped on her bottom lip as she thought out loud.

"My father wanted me to go into politics." My jaw clenched as I remembered his reaction to my accident. "I never wanted to be a politician. When I lost my spot on the lacrosse team, I decided to change my major to something I was interested in."

"What did your dad say?" The skin around her eyes was creased with concern.

I shrugged. "He cut off financial support."

"Is that why you work so much?" Taren chewed on her bottom lip, waiting for my answer.

I shrugged. "Apparently following your dreams is an expensive proposition." I smiled to make the truth less harsh.

She was quiet for a moment, but her eyes never left mine. "That's really brave of you, Alec. I respect that you followed your heart and that you're making it happen on your own. I'm sure it can't be easy."

"It's a lot easier than doing something I'd hate for the rest of my life." I ran my hand through my hair. Taren was looking at me with something close to admiration, and it felt damn good. After everything I put her through, earning her respect wasn't something I took lightly.

"Look at you, Alec Hart. You've changed. For the better." She leaned back into the couch, crossing her arms as she scanned my face.

I looked her up and down. "You've changed too, Richards."

She smiled. "Change is good, right?"

"It is."

"So," she said, fiddling with a bracelet she was wearing. "Do you talk to your dad much?" She looked up at me.

I took a deep breath, trying to decide what to say. The last thing I wanted to talk about was my broken family.

"Not really. I see him when I go home for the holidays. My mom asks me to come home more often, but being around him is just too hard. If he starts drinking when I'm around, things get ugly."

"Oh." Taren swallowed in discomfort, and I wanted to kick myself for adding that last part. "That's horrible, Alec. I'm so sorry."

"Forget about it. My family is dysfunctional. Shit happens. No big deal." I shrugged. "Not everyone gets the perfect dad."

She laughed, but it was flat. "I know what you mean. My dad left my mom when I was little. I've never even met him."

I was an ass. Here I was complaining about a father who was too involved in my life and Taren had a father who was completely absent. "So it's just you and your mom?"

"For a little while it was. My mom died when I was in elementary school. My aunt raised me."

Shit. Guilt hung heavy in my chest. Not only did Taren spend most of her time in school getting picked on, but she suffered through it without the love and support of her parents. Knowing what she'd gone through just reinforced to me how strong and resilient she was. "Jesus. I had no idea, Taren. I'm sorry."

She shrugged as if it was no big deal. "I barely remember my mom, but Claire is great. A little unconventional, but I'm lucky. I know she loves me as if I were her own." She opened her mouth as if to say more, and then changed her mind. After a few seconds she asked, "You don't have any brothers or sisters, right?"

I shook my head. I always wished I'd had siblings. Bearing the load of my father's expectations would've been so much easier if I had someone to share it with. "Nope. I do have some cousins, though. I'm really close to one. He's great. Probably the best thing to shake out of my family tree."

"That's awesome you have someone in your family you're close to." Taren smiled for the first time since I'd started dumping my family troubles on her.

"Yeah." I pressed my lips together. "He's the closest thing I've ever had to a brother."

"Oh god." Taren's eyes widened, and she clutched her chest. "Can you imagine?"

"What?" I rested my elbow on the back of the couch and leaned my head against my hand.

"Two Alec Harts? The world wouldn't be able handle that much good looks and charm." She shook her head and stuck out her bottom lip.

"You think I'm charming?" The corners of my lips turned up.

Taren's leg stretched out, and she pushed against my thigh with her foot. A playful grin tugged at her lips. "Don't act like you don't know."

I reached down and ran my finger up the bottom of her foot, tickling her. She squealed and pulled her leg back. Our eyes locked, and my voice dropped low. "I just like hearing you say it."

Her smile was shy as she broke eye contact. "Well, good looks and charm can only get you so far. Let's finish studying." She straightened the laptop and started reading again.

Oh, I was studying all right, but it certainly wasn't my classwork. I could only focus on the one girl I was stupid enough to chase away... fucking charming. I'd show her just how charming I could be.

***

My handle rattled noisily, and then someone began beating on my door.

"Go away, asshole." I turned over and covered my head with a pillow.

I heard a shuffling noise and then the sound of metal scratching on metal. "Aha!" Caz's voice was triumphant. The door slammed against the wall behind it as it was pushed open, and I lifted the pillow to see Caz standing in my doorway with a key.

I needed a deadbolt.

He walked over to my bed and yanked the pillow off my head. "Since you're staying in bed, do you mind if I hang out with the pretty girl in our living room?"

"What?" I groaned and rubbed my forehead.

He slammed the pillow back down on my head. "It's ten in the morning, dickflap. Apparently you had a study date with Taren. She showed up with coffee and a box of donuts."

"Shit!" I bolted upright, wrestling my way out of my blankets and grabbed my phone. *Why didn't my alarm go off?* "Tell her I'll be out in a minute."

"Take your time." Caz walked toward the door and then turned to toss the key to me. "I'll just be out here eating all the donuts and testing out some new pickup lines. How about this..." His voice dropped low. "Taren, your lips look lonely. Would they like to meet mine?"

I threw the pillow at him, and he ducked. "Just tell her I'll be there in a minute. And don't say that shit to her."

He held up his hands in surrender and backed out of the door with a wicked smile on his face.

I stumbled around looking for something to wear. Finding a pair of track pants that were in my basket of clean laundry, I pulled them on. *Shit.* I passed out as soon as I got home from work last night, and I probably still smelled like a bar. I wished I had time for a shower.

I couldn't risk leaving Caz alone with Taren for long, though. He was probably already halfway through her box of donuts or trying to convince her to rappel off the balcony of our apartment. I settled for a quick tooth brush and some fresh deodorant.

"Hey Taren." I could hear Caz all the way down the hallway. "Is your dad a baker? Because you have a nice set of buns."

Jesus Christ he was a jackass. A frustrated growl vibrated in my throat and I tossed the blankets back over the mattress and hurried out of my room and down the hallway. Taren sat at the table with Caz, who had a donut in each hand.

"Sorry, I overslept." I ran my hand back through my hair, trying to make myself look presentable.

Taren looked up at the sound of my voice, and she dropped the donut she was holding. She stared at me with her mouth hanging wide open. She didn't say anything.

"What did you do to her?" I strutted toward Caz, fisting my hands at my sides.

He turned to answer me with a mouth full of chocolate and sprinkles. He looked between Taren and me a few times and then slapped the table with his hand, barking out in laughter.

"Shit, dude. Put on a shirt. It's too early for me to see your nipples." Caz shook his head and gestured toward Taren. "I think your girl's in shock." He waved his hand in front of her face, and she finally looked away from me and at him. "They don't make them like that on Frat Row, do they, sweetheart?"

"Uh..." Her eyes darted back to my chest before her gaze slid up and over my shoulders and down my arms. The look in her eyes was heated, and my muscles flinched under her careful inspection.

I wanted to feel her fingers touching me the way her eyes did. I wanted to take her back to my room and peel her shirt off. Hell, I wanted to peel it all off. I wanted her lying naked underneath me, staring up with the same look of desire she had on her face now.

"Ignore him, Taren. He's an ass." I rubbed my palm across my eyes, trying to get visions of a naked Taren out of my mind. She was here to study. I needed to get that through my thick skull.

"Be nice or I won't let you have any donuts." Caz pulled the box toward his chest and wrapped his arms around it.

"Don't you have plans today?" I glared at him, hoping he'd take the hint and get lost.

"Nope." He gestured toward the window. "Was going to go mountain biking today but the weather sucks."

Jon wandered out of his room and down the hall, wearing only his boxers. He yawned and scratched the top of his head. "Did I hear someone say donuts?"

Taren's gaze found his bare chest, and then as if embarrassed to be caught looking, she glanced at me. Her eyes were drawn to my naked torso almost against her will. With a small gasp, she looked away, her eyes settling on her donut, the only non-nipple place to look, apparently.

Caz reached across and patted her hand before rooting around in the box. "Disgusting, isn't it? They always walk around half-dressed."

"Don't you guys have something to do today?" I repeated. They were never around during the day on the weekend.

Jon yawned again. "Nope. Staying in and playing Xbox all day." He reached across the table to help himself to a donut.

"Guess you and Taren will just have to study in your room, buddy." Caz took a huge bite and motioned toward my room with his head. "You don't mind, do you Taren?"

She glanced at me, almost nervous. "No, that's fine."

***

"Sorry about them." I led Taren into my room. "I had no idea they were going to be here today." I picked up my laundry basket and shoved it into the closet as she hovered just inside the doorway.

"No, it's okay. They're nice." She stared at the bed, and I was sure she was realizing, just as I was, that the only place to sit down in my room was my half-made bed.

"We could always go to the library." I braced my hands on the back of the only chair in the room. "I know this isn't ideal for studying." I nodded toward my bed. I didn't want to go to the library. I liked the idea of having Taren to myself in my room. Just the thought of her sitting on my bed made my blood pulse hotter under my skin.

She tucked her hair behind her ear. "This will be fine. As long as..."

"I won't try anything, I promise." I stood up, crossing my heart with my finger and giving her my most trustworthy half-grin.

She laughed. "I was going to say as long as you put on a shirt. I won't be able think straight if you don't."

I chuckled and pointed at my chest. "You find this distracting?"

"You have no idea." She stretched the words out in a slow confession. Her smile vanished. Her expression was shy as her gaze darted away from me, and she bent down to dig through her backpack.

"Well we can't have distractions, can we?" I found a T-shirt and put it on while she rummaged through her bag and pulled out books. When she looked up and saw I was fully clothed, she breathed a sigh of relief.

Grabbing the textbooks I needed, I sat on one end of the bed and reclined against the wall. Taren was still standing in the middle of the room, looking unsure with her books cradled against her chest.

"You coming, Richards?" I grabbed my pillow and then leaned over to set it against the wall at the other end of the bed for her. I patted the mattress. "These are five star accommodations." The corners of my mouth curved into a grin.

Heading for the other end of the bed, she shook her head as if clearing it, and a smile fought its way across her lips. She sat on the edge and then scooted backward until she was leaning against my pillow. She curled her legs underneath her body and set a book in her lap. "Thanks for letting me hang out to study. It's so much quieter here without the sorority house interruptions."

"I don't know." I glared in the direction of the living room even though the door was closed and locked. "Caz is king of interruptions."

Her laugh was quiet, and she turned to look at me. "He can't compete with the house; it's crazy. I love my sisters, but someone is always barging into my room to borrow clothes, gossip, or just hang out." She reached up to her face to tuck her hair behind her ear. "My roommate is studious, but Julie can be a menace if she's bored. It's hard to get anything done there."

"Sounds like life with Caz." I pulled my laptop out of my bag and powered it on. She opened her book and then relaxed into my pillow as she started to read. I opened the file for the essay I was working on.

An hour later, Taren lifted her arms overhead to stretch. My fingers stilled on the keyboard as my eyes were drawn to the sensual curve of her body. She closed her eyes, pulling her body into a graceful arch. Her hair tumbled around her shoulders as her head fell to the side. My body thrummed with the need to lean over and devour the smooth curve of her neck.

Taren hummed with contentment, and the sound went straight to my cock.

She straightened her body and opened her eyes. "What are you working on?" She reached out and grabbed a book off the top of my stack.

I swallowed down the need that was burning hot in my chest and cleared my throat. "An essay about myths and legends in different cultures. Mine is about the red string of fate. We're supposed to discuss how the subject matter of the myth might be related to similar stories in other cultures."

"I've never heard of the red string of fate." She opened the book and flipped through some of the pages, stopping to look at illustrations.

"It's an East Asian belief that a red string connects two people who are destined to be together." I grabbed the book she was holding and flipped through the pages to find an old drawing, and then pointed to the illustration. "The Chinese version believes they're tied by the ankles. The Japanese version says the pinky fingers. Both believe the couple will continually cross paths and even though the string might get tangled or messed up, it will never break. Their connection means that they're destined to always be together or help one another."

"Wow. What a cool story. Is that for a core class?" She didn't look up from the book as she studied the illustrations. The thoughtful way she examined the page reminded me of our days working on the debate project. She was so full of passion that it was hard not to get sucked into her excitement about things.

I cleared my throat, trying to quell the desire to keep staring at her. "It's a diversity class. I needed something to fulfill some of my core requirements, and it fit into my schedule."

"It definitely sounds more interesting than my core class." She sighed and turned the page, inspecting another illustration.

"What are you taking?"

She finally looked up, and a thrill burst through my chest to have her intensity focused on me. "Introduction to Art Theory. I thought it would be fun looking at art. I had no idea we were going to have to analyze it. Way over my head." She waved her hand over her head and rolled her eyes before reclining against the wall to read her book again.

Silence fell between us, and I found myself stealing glances at Taren. She was running her tongue along her bottom lip as she concentrated. I imagined that her lip tasted like powdered sugar from the donut she'd been eating earlier. I had the urge to lean over and take a taste to see if I was right.

Taren cleared her throat, and for a moment, I thought she'd caught me looking. "You know, maybe we're connected by a red string."

"Yeah?" I raised my eyebrows in question.

She shifted on the bed to get comfortable, setting her book to the side. "Yeah. Our paths seem to keep crossing. First in high school, then last year, at The Shell, and now in our class. Even though things were a mess in high school, we're friends again now, right? It's crazy. What were the chances we'd meet at college? I mean, we're so different, but we work well together." She chanced a look up at me.

"So you're saying we're meant to help each other?" I crossed my arms, giving her a teasing smile.

"Well, maybe you've done most of the helping so far." Her smile was shy, and her laugh was nervous. "You saved me from getting hit by a car, you found my wallet, you loaned me your sweatshirt." She ticked each item off on a finger. "And you fixed my backpack."

"You remember that?" I figured the memory of her backpack repair had probably been wiped out soon after I embarrassed her in front of everyone.

Taren shrugged. "I always remember when people are nice to me, especially since those days were pretty rare back in high school." She shook her head before turning to look at me again. "Anyway, maybe someday I'll get to return the favor and help you. I mean, since we're destined to keep running into each other and all." She smiled and pushed my knee playfully.

I grinned. "You're right. It must be fate." Was it fate? I wasn't sure, but I was fucking thrilled our paths had crossed again.

She continued to watch me, her mouth slightly open as if she was going to say something. No matter what I promised earlier, I couldn't stand another minute on this bed trying to ignore the fact that I was attracted to her. Being study partners wasn't going to be enough for me anymore. I needed to see if she tasted as sweet as I imagined she would. I wanted Taren, and I didn't intend to screw it up this time.

Chapter 17

Taren

Alec bent closer to me, his gaze fixed on my mouth. A swarm of butterflies danced in my stomach, and my heart caught in my throat. "I promised I wouldn't try anything. I want you to trust me, but I want to kiss you so fucking bad. Is that wrong?"

I sighed, closing my eyes for a split second to relish the moment. I looked up at him and leaned forward, just enough. "I've been wanting to lick your chest since you walked out of your room this morning. Is that wrong?" I stilled and squeezed my eyes shut. *Oh shit, oh shit, oh shit.* I opened them, one at a time, and twisted my lips. "I said that out loud, didn't I? I'm such a—"

He cut me off by pressing his mouth against mine. My heart pounded against the inside of my chest like a caged animal. Gripping my waist, he pulled me closer, and my arms wrapped around his neck. His lips were warm, and when they parted, his tongue lightly swept against mine.

A moan slipped out before I could stop it, and his kiss became more demanding. His fingertips pressed into my hip. With every sweep of his tongue, my blood pounded through my veins like liquid fire. He tasted amazing, mint and…all man. I loved the way his lips kissed the corners of my mouth, my chin, my neck, my shoulder, before they raced back to my mouth with greedy desperation. Our tongues tangled with one another, and our lips only parted so they could come back together again, hot and slippery. Another moan escaped me, and his fingers clenched me tighter.

He pulled back and cupped my jaw with his hand. "Taren." My name came out strangled, like a long, low groan before his mouth descended on me again. I threaded my fingers into his hair and tugged the short strands. I was on fire. I had to be. He was burning me from the inside out, and every press of his lips made me feel more alive. Releasing his hair, I dragged my fingers down his back, fisting his T-shirt.

When his hands slid up my sides and to my shoulders, tiny fireworks exploded under my skin and in my chest. This was it. This was the feeling I'd been waiting for. Something in me had always known Alec Hart would kiss like this. Nothing about it was sloppy or messy. His lips were absolute perfection, as if they were made just for me.

His fingers slipped into my hair, cradling my head. My tongue met his in teasing licks as my breathing picked up. I moved onto my knees and tentatively touched my fingers along the bottom of his shirt, inching inside.

When my fingertips finally skimmed the hot, hard skin of his stomach, his muscles jumped in response. I pulled back to look at him. His jaw was clenched, and a vein in his neck throbbed as he gritted his teeth.

"Sorry," I whispered, withdrawing my hands. My already flushed face burned with embarrassment. I was moving too fast…doing this all wrong. He was probably used to girls with so much more experience. I tried to swallow past the lump in my throat as I sat back on my heels, twisting my fingers together. The thought of this ending—of not kissing him anymore—was torment.

He reached over his head to pull off his shirt in one swift motion. Even that was ridiculously sexy. "You can touch me, Taren." He placed my hand where it had been just moments before. "I want you to." His eyes met mine, and the intensity stole my breath. "Please."

I thought I might burst into flames having my hands on him again. So many times I had thought about this when I was in high school, and now he was begging me to. I bit the inside of my lip, trying not to smile in triumph, as my fingers skimmed along the ridges of his stomach. My palms pressed against him, exploring the tight, hard muscles.

Alec's gaze held me captive, and desire smoldered deep inside as he watched me touch him. When I licked my bottom lip and pulled it between my teeth, he groaned. That sound, rumbling deep in his throat, went straight to my core. His muscles twitched under my fingers, and a feeling of power overtook me. My breaths were shallow, and my fingers trembled with excitement.

In an entire year with Doug, I had never felt one second of what I felt right now. He never set my body on fire. He never made me feel desperate. I'd never known what it was like to really crave something until now. I craved Alec. I would never get enough of his lips or the way his eyes held mine when he said my name.

Feeling bold, I placed my palms flat against Alec's chest and pushed him back against the mattress. His eyes flared, and then he shot me a sexy smirk. I pressed my lips together, and moving on my hands and knees, I straddled him.

Holy shit. I was straddling Alec Hart. Instead of ruining the moment and doing a victory dance, I let my eyes roam over his chest and face.

"You're so beautiful," I told him. The urge to lick him was relentless. My body vibrated with energy and lust when I leaned forward and lightly licked his collarbone before placing a soft kiss on his chest.

His body went rigid. He exhaled in a groan, and closed his eyes. When he opened them again, he searched my face where my lips were poised over his chest.

"Taren." His voice was low and rough, and his face strained. "Do you have any idea how gorgeous you are?"

My racing heart tripped. Skipped a beat. I looked back down to his chest before he could see the vulnerability in my eyes. I'd come a long way in a year, and I knew I was pretty, but I never expected to be called gorgeous. By him. Was this even real?

I bent to place kisses on his chest, ribs, biceps, and shoulders. With each touch of my lips to his skin, I wanted to leave a small piece of me. I wanted to mark him.

Alec pulled me up to his mouth for another kiss, and my body lay flush against his. I moaned when our hips made contact, and Alec continued kissing me as he sat up so that I was straddling his lap. I moved my hips forward in gentle rocks, and I could feel him growing hard underneath me.

Alec cupped my face with both hands and looked into my eyes, breathing hard. "Fuck, you feel so good."

My hips slid backward and forward, grinding against his lap. Instead of answering, my lips met his, urgent and fierce. He groaned again, and I wanted to capture every sound that echoed through his chest.

It was too much and not enough. I wanted more. I had to have all of him. My hands ran over his arms and chest leaving trails on his skin. I felt frantic and out of control. I wanted him to touch me. I wasn't ready to go all the way, but dear god if I didn't feel his hands on my skin, I was going to shatter.

"Touch me, Alec," I whispered. "Please."

He ran his hands down the sides of my neck, but he was in no hurry. His pace was slow and agonizing. When his fingertips brushed my shoulders, I shivered, and he kissed me harder, trading needy sounds between our lips. His hands continued across my shoulder blades and over the swell of my chest, cupping me gently while his thumbs feathered over the center of my breasts.

"Yes." I closed my eyes, my words a whimper, as I tilted my head back.

He leaned forward to kiss my neck, gently rubbing his thumbs across my pebbled nipples. His palms caressed the underside of my breasts through the fabric of my shirt. Tiny moans slipped out of my mouth and into his as I rocked into him.

Alec pulled his lips from mine, and I wanted to cry out from the loss. Then he pressed them to my neck and sucked lightly. "Are you close, Taren?" His mouth moved against my skin as he said the words.

What was he talking about? I couldn't get closer to him than I was now. All I knew was that a force of nature wouldn't be able to get me to stop moving against him like this. His erection rubbed against me, and everything deep inside tensed in anticipation.

The doorknob rattled and then there was a loud knock. My eyes opened, and I slowed my movements as I looked toward the sound.

"Well, at least you locked the door this time. Can I eat the rest of the donuts?" Caz's voice was loud and unwelcome from the other side of the door.

Was he coming in here?

Alec turned my chin back toward him. "Eyes on me." I felt his words right between my legs and loved how his simple demand was possessive and full of the same need I felt.

"I'm going to take your silence as a yes." Caz called before we heard him stomp off down the hall.

Alec's large hands were on my waist, coaxing my hips back into their rhythm. "Are you close, Taren?"

I studied his face. His expression was tight and his chest heaved as he drew in air. He was the sexiest damn thing I had ever seen.

"Close to what?" I managed to say.

"This." He captured my mouth with his. His hands slipped around to my ass, and he pulled me down to him as he pressed up against me. His erection was rubbing me in just the right way, and I moaned in response. His body mirrored mine with every dip and roll, our hips moving together in a rhythm that made my heart race to keep up.

I took a few stuttering breaths before I stopped kissing him and buried my face against his neck. My words, a quiet, breathless, chant filled the space between us. "Oh god, oh god, oh god." My body jerked, and my voice shook as his hips kept thrusting. Wave after wave of sensation flooded through me as sparks of bliss exploded through my body. I gripped his shoulders and held my breath, clinging to the pleasure until it faded. Finally, I collapsed against his hard chest.

Alec held me tightly, and I was draped against him, loving the way our breaths came in deep, messy pulls.

"Oh my. That was...amazing." I scattered small lazy kisses along his shoulder blade.

He lifted my chin to look at me, tucking a chunk of hair behind my ear. "Yeah, you are."

"That was a first for me." I buried my face against his chest and wrapped my arms around his back. I wanted him to know. I just didn't want to admit it while he was looking at me.

Alec's hands wrapped around my upper arms, and he pushed me back to put space between us so he could look at me. "Are you serious?" His forehead was wrinkled in confusion.

I shrugged.

He smirked and pulled me to him, kissing my forehead. "Well I'm glad I was your first."

Me too.

The wait had been worth it. Alec Hart had given me my first orgasm. He...he...I froze as realization slammed into me. He hadn't had one. *Oh, crap.*

I peeked down and stared at his lap, at a very hard, very bulging, very large, and I was sure, very unsatisfied, erection. My face reddened. "Can I…" I blew out a breath. "I mean, would you like me to…" I wrung my hands together. "Or should I say how can I…?"

Alec rested his hand on my clasped ones and rubbed his thumb along my skin. "I don't want to rush you."

I quirked an eyebrow at him.

"I'm fine." He shifted uncomfortably, but he smiled. Then, he winked as if he knew an inside joke that I wasn't privy to. "For now."

I cocked my head as the corners of my lips turned up. "For now?"

He was right. We should take it slow. I glanced up at him and licked my lower lip. But not too slow.

I smiled, a confident, albeit devilish, smile. "Want to study again tomorrow?"

***

"So…I want details. Lay it on me." Julie sat on the floor of my bedroom, carefully polishing her tiny toenails a bright, cherry red.

"He's quite possibly the sexiest guy on the planet." Laying on my stomach, I rested my head on my crossed arms. I let every warm, delicious memory of the day before invade my thoughts.

"So you hooked up?" Julie paused from her methodical stroking of the brush and looked up at me.

"Yes, and it was amazing. Earth shattering. Life changing. I didn't know it was supposed to be like that." I shook my head and grinned.

Julie paused, her brush suspended in the air. "What? Hooking up?"

"Yeah." I buried my face and muffled my words. "And orgasms." A flush of embarrassment heated my cheeks.

"The hell? What do you mean you never knew? Did Pickle the Dickle not know how to ring your lady bell?" Julie's voice rose in volume.

Lifting my head, I laughed. "Ring my lady bell?"

"Orgasm. Pickle never got you there?"

I shook my head. "Nope. My bell was never rung. Now I think I'm addicted."

"It's about time. It's like getting a hug from the good Lord above. Not that I've hugged the Lord, but I imagine it would feel pretty darn great. And a good orgasm feels fucking fantastic, so I'm just saying."

I stared at her in silence. She was so…weird.

"So what's the problem? What aren't you telling me? My best friend radar is shooting glitter bomb warnings at me." Blowing on her toes, she screwed the cap back onto her polish and then straightened her legs in front of her. "I'm not leaving. I need proper drying time before my top coat. You can't get rid of me so keep talking." Her grin was both impish and prim. She was winning this one.

"Okay, okay. He's gorgeous. His body did things to me that I will never forget, and he's sweet. He's also paying his own way through college, so totally responsible and hard working."

"Sounds kind of perfect, T. What's the problem then? Does he make a terrible O face? I dated a guy who did that, and I dumped him in a New York minute. The look on his face scarred me for life." Julie's expression was so serious that I couldn't keep from laughing.

"No." I giggled and sat up on my bed. "My only hesitation is that he totally humiliated me in high school. Talk about scarred for life." My laughter faded, and I hugged my pillow to my chest.

Julie pressed her lips together and nodded for me to continue.

"After he embarrassed me, the rest of my senior year was miserable. The bullying got worse, if that was possible. Almost every day someone would tease me about that night and remind me what a loser I was."

"Pecker heads. Seriously, T, what I wouldn't give to go tell them all to go fuck a duck." I would have paid anything to see her tell my worst attackers to go fuck a duck.

"Thanks, Jules. I love you, too." I smiled. "But seriously. What if he changes his mind and rejects me again? I really like him and that would destroy me. I feel more for him after two days than I felt with Pickles in a whole year."

"T, sometimes you've got to take the leap. You're awesome, and if he can't see that, he doesn't deserve you. If he is stupid enough to break your heart again, so help me God, I will ruin him." She got up off the floor and sat next to me.

"Your nails, Jules. Be careful." Julie took her beautifying rituals seriously. She'd be in a funk for hours if she smudged her perfect piggies.

"Yeah, well…you're worth it." Julie wrapped her arms around my shoulders and hugged me tightly. "I mean it. You're worth it."

***

"Wait up, Denton." Doug jogged after me. I zipped up Alec's sweatshirt, the one I had conveniently forgotten to return to him a few days ago, and turned to face my ex.

"I can't talk. I've got a class in ten minutes." I bounced on the balls of my feet, desperate to avoid a conversation with Doug.

"Really? We dated for a year, and you can't give me five fucking minutes?" Doug scowled. I wanted to remind him that after finding him sucking face with another girl I didn't owe him jack shit. Instead, I shrugged, hoping that listening would get this over more quickly.

"What is it?" I kept my hands in the pockets of the sweatshirt so I wouldn't be tempted to punch him in his cheating face.

"Are you really breaking up with me just because of one dance?" He paced back and forth in front of me and ran his hands through his hair.

"First off, I don't think it was just that one dance. And by the way, it wasn't just a dance. You were humping her on the dance floor and shoving your tongue down her throat." I glared at him. "My sisters have been telling me for months that they've seen you flirting with girls. I'm not surprised you took it to the next level. You've never had the best judgment…especially when you're drinking." I raised an eyebrow at him, and he rolled his eyes.

"Taren, trust me. It was just a dance. I gave you a year and my letters. That's a big commitment. I can't believe you're just over us, like it was nothing." Doug stopped pacing and stood in front of me.

"What you and I had wasn't nothing, but it also wasn't love. You wouldn't have cheated on me if it was."

Doug frowned at me. "Taren…"

I held up both of my hands, palms facing him as I cut him off. "What you and I always were was friends. Let's stay that way.

Friends?"

He hesitated and then sighed. "Okay, Denton. We'll try this your way, but I know you're gonna miss me. You'll be asking me to take you home by the end of the month." He winked.

Clearly his cocky attitude hadn't been affected by our breakup. I opened my mouth to argue, but stopped. I'd give him the last word. His pride was damaged, and I knew what that felt like.

There was only one guy I wanted and he wasn't named after a vegetable. His nickname might even be god, based on the number of times I called it out when we were together.

Chapter 18

Alec

I propped my head up on my hand so that I could look at Taren. She was lying next to me on my bed—her shirt tossed on the floor, her long blonde hair a beautiful mess of tangles, and her lips still marked with the touch of mine.

"I love kissing you. I could kiss you forever." Taren reached up to run her fingers lightly down my arm. I noticed that she touched me a lot, like I was a piece of art her body had to memorize.

"We've got a pretty good start on forever. I don't think we've been out of this bed in hours." I nipped at her shoulder, and she giggled.

As soon as my bedroom door had been shut and locked, our study session had turned into a frantic kiss-fest. Our books lay forgotten on the floor, our need to study falling victim to our need for one another. Later on, when I was up all night doing the work I had neglected, life would suck. Right now, I didn't care.

I leaned down to kiss Taren again, and her mouth immediately parted. Her tongue twisted with mine as if we'd been kissing each other our entire lives. The slick warmth of her mouth was like fucking heaven.

When I moved my lips from hers, she let out an adorable growl of frustration until they touched her neck and she realized my kisses were heading to where my hands were tracing the edges of her bra. She arched up into me, and her head pressed into my pillow as she closed her eyes.

The way she placed her trust in me made me wild with the urge to protect her, to keep her innocence all to myself. That need to keep her safe was in constant battle with my darker side—the side that needed to claim her. I wanted to own every sexy sound that ever came out of her mouth.

I reached around her back until my fingers found the clasp of her bra, and when her eyes opened, I thought that she'd tell me to stop. Instead, her lips lifted into a shy smile. The clasp snapped open under my fingertips, and her eyes closed again. She reached up to the back of my head to pull my face into her skin.

My nose ran along the lacy edge of her bra where I could smell her perfume and Taren sighed. My thumbs slowly eased the fabric up until it was draped across her collarbone. Nothing but my heavy breaths were between my lips and the smooth skin of her breasts. Hunger gnawed at me. She was so beautiful I wanted to savor every inch of her skin with my tongue. I wanted to devour her.

I leaned down and kissed the curves of Taren's perfect chest, stealing a glance up at her face to see her reaction. I wondered if she'd stop me. I hoped not. I wanted her to trust me.

We were taking things slow, but I was going to make sure that when we were apart, she'd still feel the echoes of where my mouth and hands had been. I wanted her to ache for me.

"Don't stop." She threaded her fingers into my hair and pulled me into her until my lips touched her again.

"You're so damn sweet. I can't get enough of you." My voice was rough against her skin, and my body was rigid as I held myself over her. I licked her nipple with a flick of my tongue before drawing it fully into my mouth. She pressed up into me as if she couldn't bear for any part of her body to not touch me.

"God, yes…" She let out a thankful groan when I settled my weight between her legs, rolling my hips into hers. "I need you." She pleaded, trying to press our bodies closer together.

She didn't need to beg. The taste of her kisses, the smell of her skin, every soft and exquisite curve—I could never get enough of her. I would give her whatever she needed.

***

Taren sat down on the opposite side of my bed, her eager gaze reeling me in like I'd swallowed not only the bait but the entire hook. I crawled across the mattress toward her, and she held up her hand.

"Hold it. Before we get started, I want to know how late you stayed up last night to get your work done."

I smiled. "I like it when you're bossy. It's pretty damn hot." As I started to make my way over to her again, she pulled her backpack into her lap like it was a shield.

"Tell the truth, Alec. How late?"

"Three in the morning." I shrugged like it was no big deal.

Her forehead wrinkled with worry. "Don't you get up at six to work a few hours in the physical therapy office before class?"

"I'm used to it. I used to work three jobs. Now I only have two. Three hours of sleep is an improvement." I'd give up sleeping entirely if it meant more time with Taren.

Her face became serious, and I was reminded of the straight-laced Taren I knew from high school. "That's not healthy, Alec. I don't want to be the reason you're exhausted."

"You're worth it." Leaning forward, I inched toward her again. My hands and lips itched to get a taste of her.

Her eyes flashed, and I could see my eagerness reflected in them. Her lips parted and I could tell that she wanted me to kiss her. Instead, she shook her head slightly as if she were clearing her head. "I'll make you a deal." She held up her finger and looked at me in determination. "For every item you accomplish off your study list, I'll reward you."

I stopped my slow crawl toward her. The smile that crept across my mouth held back all the wicked things I wanted to say. "Reward me?"

She narrowed her eyes. "If you're a good boy and do your work, I can make it worth your while." When I didn't answer, she lifted her eyebrows and jutted her chin out in defiance. "Do you doubt me?"

Remembering our last few nights together, doubt was the furthest thing from my mind. Her lips however..."You're serious? Not even a kiss?"

She pulled a book out of her bag and opened it up, without looking at me. "The sooner you get started, Alec, the sooner you get rewarded."

Shit. Talk about knowing how to motivate a man. Maybe Coach could take some pointers from Taren. None of his pre-show speeches had ever done what her promise of a reward could. I hurried to get my books and heard her giggle. When I looked up to say something, her face was a picture of calm.

Three hours later I'd checked everything off my list, and I watched as Taren stood to remove another piece of clothing. She was putting on the slowest goddamn striptease known to man. I hated it as much as I loved it. So far she'd lost the jacket, shoes, T-shirt, and tank top. She still hadn't let me touch her at all. I was in agony with want. I wanted my hands on her. I needed to feel the slick warmth of her mouth on mine. My body was strung so tight, one fucking touch from her would probably snap me in two like a damn wishbone.

She unbuttoned her jeans and then hooked her thumbs into the waistband as she wriggled the tight material down her body. My eyes hungrily feasted on every inch of skin as it appeared.

In nothing but her cute little boy shorts and lacy bra, she looked almost shy as she stared at me. She started to speak but then hesitated for a moment. "I'm still a virgin."

"That's okay." A deep rumble of caveman satisfaction reverberated through my chest and I wanted to howl in triumph. Relief coursed through me knowing that douche Pickles had never claimed that part of her. Another first that could be mine. *Fuck yes.*

"I'm not ready tonight." She crossed her arms over her chest, rubbing her hands up and down her arms.

My eyebrows drew together in confusion. "Did I make you feel like you should be?" The last thing I would ever do was pressure her for sex.

"No, no!" Her hands snapped up to ward off the question. "Not at all. It's just that I've been doing this slow striptease..."

"Which I appreciate immensely." I leaned back on one arm and made a show of running my gaze up and down her body.

She rolled her eyes. "I just thought I should make things clear before I come over there." Her hand fluttered in front of her, motioning toward me. "I'm not trying to be a cock tease. I was just trying to make studying fun."

"Did sweet Taren Richards just say the word, cock?" I feigned shock.

Her skin flushed from head to toe in embarrassment.

"Come here." My words were softer, and I sat up, holding my arm out to her. "I'm just teasing. You tell me what you want, and that's all we'll do. We won't do anything you're not ready to. I promise."

She regained her confident posture as her smile lifted back into place. She crossed the room and sat down next to me on the bed.

"So what do you want, Taren?" I reached up to run the backs of my fingers down her cheek.

She bit her bottom lip as her eyes roamed over me. "I want you to take off your clothes." Her words were quiet, but determined.

I lifted my eyebrows at her request. Not what I was expecting, but I was only too happy to oblige. I reached back and grabbed the neck of my shirt, pulling it over my head in one quick motion. "More?" I threw my shirt to the side.

She nodded, and her eyes flared in excitement as she bit back a smile.

I stood and undid the button on my jeans before pushing them down and then kicking them away. I arched an eyebrow. "More?"

Taren was quiet for a moment, and her eyes shifted to my boxers as if considering how dangerous saying 'yes' to that question might be. Finally, she shook her head 'no.'

"We're even now." Her gaze raked over me, shameless and ravenous.

"I don't know about that. I just spent the last three hours in torture, wanting to kiss that beautiful mouth of yours while you sat half-naked and untouchable on my bed. I think you deserve to suffer a bit."

Taren crossed her arms. The haughty movement hid her breasts which had only been covered by a tiny lace bra. She glared at me. *Bad move, Hart. She's covering up...that's a step backward.*

"Well if this is such torture." She got up and walked toward her pile of clothing. "I could always put everything back on." Her eyebrows lifted in challenge.

Just as she bent to reach for her shirt, I couldn't take it any longer. "Fine. You win, Richards. We're even." The words came out like a growl.

She tilted her head and lifted her eyebrows in question. She motioned with her fingers, coaxing more out of me as she slowly slid her arms into the fabric of her shirt.

"I owe you a...reward?" I'd give her anything she wanted as long as that fucking shirt didn't go back on.

"Now we're talking." She dropped the tiny piece of clothing and crossed the room, quickly finding her way into my arms, just as easily as she'd been finding her way into my heart the last few days.

I pulled her down on the bed with me, running my fingers up and down her side with light pressure. The delicate touches made her eyes flutter shut, and her body pressed into me.

The feel of her skin against mine was heaven. Like an addict, I wanted to have everything at once. Instead, I let my fingers and lips savor her. I kissed her, deep and slow, making sure she felt it all the way to the tips of her toes.

Taren's hands worshipped my body. Her lips followed the path of her fingers to brand every part she touched. The heat spreading through me was a slow burn; the kind that snuck up on you. The kind where you didn't know you were in trouble until it was too late and you were lost in a blazing inferno.

If I wasn't careful, Taren would consume me.

Maybe I wanted her to.

I groaned when she pressed her hips into me, melding her body into mine. My heart hammered in my chest. The only things between us were a few pieces of thin fabric and a promise. No matter how hard it was, I would keep that promise until she was ready for more.

"These study sessions are going to be the death of me." My blood was thundering through my veins with urgency. My chest was tight with need. I wanted to own her. Make her mine.

"Yeah, but it would be a good way to go," Taren said between kisses.

Hell yes, it would be a damn good way to go.

Chapter 19

Taren

Julie was in my room, rummaging through my closet, looking for something to wear. Tonight was Wednesday, better known as Ladies Night at The Shell.

"You'd have more luck looking in your own closet." I closed my laptop and stretched my arms over my head. "You have a much better selection."

"Yeah, but I'm trying to get that bass player's attention. I want to wear something I've never worn before." She pulled a hanger off the rack and inspected the small piece of fabric hanging from it. "Speaking of getting someone's attention," she said without looking at me. "What are you going to wear for Alec?"

"He doesn't work on Wednesdays." After spending the past week together, I'd learned his schedule. I hadn't had the chance to check in with him yet today and I wondered if he'd be relieved that I had plans to go out with my friends. At least he'd have time to do all the studying that I'd prevented him from getting done.

Julie spun around holding the tight, shiny top she'd picked out for me a few months ago. "Perfect. Invite him. He'll be more fun to play with if he's not working." The smile she gave me was wicked.

"I hadn't even thought of asking Alec to meet us there." I picked up my phone to look for any missed calls. "I never really had to invite Pickles out to party with me. He was always just there." I had to admit, the idea of spending the night dancing with Alec was one of the best ideas Julie had ever had. That was saying something, considering the girl was full of brilliantly fun plans.

I looked at the display on my phone, and the screen read three o'clock. Alec was still in class. I'd have to send him a text and hope he saw it when he got done.

"You're inviting him?" Julie grinned as I starting typing.

"Yep," I answered with my own smile.

"Nice. Tell him to bring one of his studly friends. That guy with the spiky blond hair wasn't bad to look at."

I paused in my typing to look up at her. "I thought you were trying to impress the bass player?"

Julie gave me a perplexed look. "Yeah, but how am I going to show off my best moves without a dance partner?"

I laughed as I texted Alec.

Me: Are you working tonight?

Julie tucked my shirt over her arm and headed for the door. "Be ready by eight o'clock, sweetcheeks. I don't want to miss any of Bass Boy's set tonight."

"Yes, ma'am." I gave her a mock salute, and she gave me a finger wave as she left.

"T?" Alexis raised up on her elbows and looked down at me from her place on the top bunk. "Are you sure about this?"

"About what?"

"Alec hurt you in high school. Are you sure you can trust him?"

Alexis' forehead wrinkled as she bit her thumb.

I turned my phone over in my hand, running my fingers over the edges. "I'm not going to lie. There's a part of me that worries one day he'll look at me and see the same loser I was in high school. But I'm different now and so is he. We've both made mistakes, and as much as I needed a fresh start, I want to give him one, too."

Alexis smiled. "I like seeing how happy he makes you."

He did make me happy. So freaking happy. I hoped with all my heart that he felt the same way.

An hour later I got a response from Alec.

Alec: No. I'm not working tonight. Why?

Me: I was hoping you'd meet me at The Shell.

A few moments passed before his short text came through.

Alec: I can't hang out at The Shell.

Me: Because you work there?

Alec: No. Because I took a pledge not to drink.

Me: But you work there.

Alec: Working there is one thing. Hanging out would be wrong.

I honestly couldn't see the difference between the two, but I wasn't going to argue about it.

Me: I kind of promised Jules I'd go to ladies night with her. Are you sure you can't come? We could dance and have fun. You don't have to drink.

I was hoping Alec would change his mind, but his text back was short and terse.

Alec: I have practice tonight until 10.

Me: Come after.

Alec: Sorry. I can't.

My stomach sank. The disappointment was more crushing than I could have anticipated. Tonight was just one invite, one small rejection. I stood up and paced the length of my room. *Why does this bother me so much? Why does it feel like he's blowing me off?*

Alexis popped her head up from the book she was reading. "Is he meeting you at The Shell?"

"No, he has practice." I chewed on my lip and continued my pacing. We hadn't been on an actual date in public. We only studied together and hooked up. Not that I was complaining, but the thought plagued me that Alec could be embarrassed to be out in public with me. We got along fine in high school, too...as long as it was in private.

"Umm, you're wearing a hole in our carpet because....?" Alexis tapped her pencil against her book and waited.

"Do you think maybe he doesn't want his Acroletes friends to know he's dating a sorority girl?" I stopped and hung my head. "Are we too different for this to work out?"

Alexis slammed her book shut and sat up. "There is nothing wrong with being in a sorority. He chose a different path than you, but neither one is wrong. If you're going to make this work, you have to put the past and your insecurities behind you. You have to believe in the person you've become."

I heard her words, but my heart was still working on believing them.

***

Today was my weekly Good Buddy visit. I was supposed to meet William at the Student Union. Instead I found him sitting on a bench outside the meeting room, typing on his phone.

"Hey, William. How are you today?" I sat next to him on the bench. He looked up, tucking his phone into his jacket pocket. He flashed me that genuine smile that I had grown to love and need. Everything about William was real.

"Call me 'Will' now." He straightened his shoulders, looking proud of his nickname.

"Will." I tapped my lip in thought and pretended to try it on for size. "I like it." William grinned, and my heart swelled. Being with him was easy. I couldn't even call it charity work because time with him was precious, grounding, and most importantly, uplifting. He'd become a good friend.

"Would you like to go for a walk?" I pointed to the glass doors that allowed sunshine to stream inside. "The weather's nice today. I thought it would be fun to go over to the McKeldin Mall." I'd caught him people-watching several times before, and no place was better for that than the mall.

"Yup, yup." William put on his coat, and we made the short walk to the grassy area that was home to the reflecting pool in the middle of campus. He didn't speak, but his eyes were full of joy. William watched the students hurrying into buildings or sitting in groups, talking and laughing. I'd discovered that it didn't take much to satisfy him. Seeing others happy was something he particularly seemed to enjoy.

"So, how are you this week?" I walked over to a bench by the reflecting pool and sat down. He moved closer to the edge, bending over to examine the water before sitting next to me.

"I am happy today, Miss Taren. How are you?"

How was I? That was a good question. I wasn't sure how to answer it. The time I spent with Alec had been fantastic, but I still wasn't sure about my future with him. Especially after his rejection last night.

Alec had matured a lot since high school. He was the same smart, confident guy he'd been back then, but now he was also humble, and funny, and protective. The problem was, we'd yet to actually interact in a social situation, and that was starting to bug me.

Was there any part of his life I fit into aside from studying? Better yet, was there a part of my life he fit into?

Hooking up with him was great—better than great—but did I want to get involved with someone who didn't have anything in common with my circle of friends? Should I lust after someone who couldn't find time for me in his life?

I blinked and tore my gaze off the reflecting pool. I wasn't unloading all of that emotional baggage onto my buddy, William.

"My weekend was good." I gave him a half-smile and then blew out a breath.

"But?"

I tilted my head at his question. "But what?"

William shrugged. "It was good, but..."

I smiled. Leave it to him to pick up on my unsaid words. I sighed. "Have you ever liked someone and weren't sure if you should, Will?"

He nodded, his face solemn. "I liked a girl named Sarah. We went to school together, and she had long red hair. So pretty."

I turned to face him. "What happened? Did you ever tell her you liked her?"

"I did. She liked me, too. We even kissed a few times." He grinned, ducking his head down and studying the ground.

"So..." I nudged him with my elbow.

"Her dad found out. Said we could not date. He said it was not right. That I was not right. You know...in the head." William pointed to his head, his eyebrows scrunched together.

I scooted closer to him and rubbed his back. My heart hurt to hear his words. I was pissed off that someone could think awful things like that about a guy as sweet and kind as William. Just because he was different, didn't mean he was less. That was so far from the truth the idea made me sick.

I still didn't know what William's official disability "label" was, and it didn't matter because nothing could change the wonderful person he was. Labels didn't mean anything. They couldn't even begin to scratch the surface of the complexity of the people they were attached to. I should know. I had my share of labels in high school, and none of them were really me. The real shame was that some people were too closed-minded to see William for the beautiful soul he was.

"I'm sorry, Will. That had to be hard for you. Did you ever talk to her again?"

He nodded and looked at the pool of water. "Yup. I did not give up. I told her, we might be slow, but we still feel love. I kissed her again, but her dad saw. He told me if I touched her again he would call the police."

He shook his head, and I reached out to hold his hand.

"I would never hurt Sarah. I would never hurt anyone." William looked at me, tears glistening in his eyes. I had to swallow the lump in my own throat to keep from crying.

"I know that, Will. Some people aren't open to new ideas or to things that are different from what they're used to." The words came out of my mouth, and my stomach dropped. What a hypocrite I was. I could judge Sarah's father, but I was doing the same thing he'd done. I was hesitant to consider a possible future with Alec because he had a different lifestyle. Would it really be that hard to have a real relationship with him?

"Tell me about your fellow." William squeezed my hand gently in his. I was amazed how he knew what I was thinking about.

I waved my other hand dismissively. "You don't want to hear about it."

"Sure I do. We are friends. Friends listen to one another."

He was right. He'd confided in me. "You sure?" I asked.

William nodded.

"His name is Alec. We actually went to high school together. I liked him a lot back then, but he didn't like me. He hurt my feelings."

William frowned. "I am sorry. I know how that feels."

I smiled sadly in return. "Now it turns out we're here at the same university. When I first saw him here I was cruel. We both hurt each other, but we've grown up now. This semester we're in the same class and started hanging out together." No way was I going to elaborate further.

"Then what is wrong?" William cocked his head to the side, waiting for my response.

"We lead very different kinds of lives and have no friends in common. My friends are very important to me since we do things together all the time. He wouldn't be a part of that. He wouldn't understand my life with them. Alec and I are complete opposites."

Was that true, though? Alexis didn't always come out and party with us, but Julie and I were still good friends with her.

Then I remembered that Alec chose not to hang out with me even after his practice was over. "Besides, I'm not sure he likes me as much as I like him."

"Miss Taren, does he make you feel happy?"

I hesitated to really think about what William was asking. Just being near Alec made me feel a lot of things. Mostly toe-curling things I couldn't discuss with William, but was it happiness? I thought back to our study sessions and the easy banter and friendship we shared.

"Yes." I sighed, picturing Alec's face...his hands...his lips.

"That is it, then. What else is there? Just happiness. Yup, yup." William looked at his watch and stood up. "Time to go."

"Already?"

"No worries, Miss Taren. I will see you again next week."

I smiled to myself. The way he said it, I felt like he was donating his time to hang out with me, not the other way around. I guess that was how real friendship worked. I rose to my feet and walked back toward the Union with my good buddy William, thinking about what he had said.

What else is there? Just happiness. Was it really that beautifully simple?

***

Alec: Come to the bball game? I'm in the halftime show. I want you to see the Acroletes perform.

I bit my lip in nervous excitement. I hadn't talked to Alec in person since his rejection two nights ago. He'd worked last night so I didn't text him to ask him to study because I knew he couldn't. He'd texted benign little comments throughout the day, but I held back, protecting my heart. I had to admit I took great satisfaction in the idea that he was reaching out, that he wanted to see me.

Me: Sounds good. Julie, Alexis, and I were planning on going anyway. We'll go early to get seats up close.

Alec: Cool. See you then.

A Friday night and Alec wanted to see me? Hope surged through me.

***

"We have a special halftime show for you today, Terp fans." The words bellowed over the speaker system. "The University of Maryland Acroletes are here to perform their death-defying halftime show. Watch them spin, twist, and flip as they barely avoid mid-air collisions. Please give a huge Terp welcome to the Acroletes vaulting team!"

The entire building filled with cheers as the Acroletes ran to the middle of the court, waving to the crowd. They were dressed in black and red uniforms that made them look like professional gymnasts despite the fact that they were part of a university club.

"Oh. My. God. The guys wear spandex? You can see everything!" Julie shrieked and then cupped her hands to her mouth to yell out her approval.

"Is that Alec?" Alexis pointed to the most muscular guy on the court, who was busy searching the crowd for something. He smiled when he saw me sitting with my friends.

"Yeah, that's him." I made eye contact with Alec and waved. He raised his hand in acknowledgment and then lined up with the rest of his teammates. Two lines of gymnasts faced a vaulting box and two sets of small trampolines. They looked like they were prepared to run perpendicular to one another.

"He's hot, T. And built like a fucking Greek god. Holy cow. No wonder you have a crush on him." Julie fanned herself with her hand.

"Yeah," I breathed out on a sigh. Every muscle in Alec's lean body was cut and defined. My crush on him was about way more than his body, though. Alec had always drawn me in with a force that surprised me.

A pounding techno beat blared loudly throughout the Xfinity Center. I could feel my seat vibrating. People around us clapped in time to the music while I held my breath as the two lines of gymnasts ran toward the vaulting box. They hit the trampolines in alternating precision as they flipped and twisted over the box, crisscrossing and barely missing one another.

Avoiding mid-air collisions indeed. I was almost too afraid to watch. The only problem was, I couldn't take my eyes off of him. He was one of the last people in line each time, along with Jon and Caz. Their timing was so perfect that it looked like one wrong move would send the three of them crashing into a pile of broken bones and torn muscles.

"I really like the idea of spandex," Julie shouted, leaning closer to be heard over the deafening noise of the crowd. "It's a little disturbing to look at since it leaves very little to the imagination, but at least you know what you're getting. Not a micro-penis in the bunch, T. And that Alec. Whew, girl. He's no Pickles, that's for sure. That boy looks well-hung. I give my approval."

I took another look at Alec as he ran across the wood floor, hitting the trampoline with power, forcing it to vault him into the air in a series of somersaults. My face flushed as I vividly remembered our last study session. Alec was definitely in no danger of Pickles' tiny affliction.

A few more runs took place, where people were piled on top of the vaulting box to create a giant wall of bodies as the Acroletes flipped over them. My stomach was in knots, expecting a wreck with every gymnast that went over the pile. When the stack of people reached six high, I couldn't bear to watch. I was reminded of watching a horror movie. One where the guy with the chainsaw was about to lay waste to the naive blonde girl who tried to run away in high heels.

"You can look now," Alexis peeled my fingers away from my eyes. "He made it. They're taking a bow."

I emerged from behind my hands and clapped while everyone around us chanted, *"Fire Hoop. Fire Hoop. Fire Hoop."* People pumped their fists in the air along with their chant. The Acroletes rushed back into a single line as a metal hoop was lifted over the vaulting box.

Oh god. I thought it was over. More potentially life threatening danger was about to take place?

One of the coaches reached up with his hand and when the lighter he was holding touched the hoop, the entire thing burst into a circle of hungry flames. The building exploded with roars of approval. The crowd screamed as the Acroletes threw themselves on the trampoline and flipped thought the ring of fire.

I breathed a sigh of relief when Alec and his roommates made it through the flames unharmed. *Holy mother of God.* I was going to have a freaking heart attack watching this performance. I had no idea the university allowed Alec and his friends to risk their lives like that. Their act was dangerous. When the Acroletes lined up for their final bow, I clapped madly along with everyone else, glad it was over so my heart rate could go back to normal.

The music changed into a powerful, sexy ballad and the athletes and coaches folded up the mats and cleared the floor of the vaulting equipment. Alec walked to the middle of the court with a brunette who was rocking a plain black leotard. Only a person with zero percent body fat could look amazing in an ensemble like that. Not a jiggle or a dimple was in sight. I shifted in my seat and sucked in my stomach. *Hello insecurity, nice to see you again.*

The girl slowly walked around Alec like a jungle cat stalking its next meal. Alec reached out his hand, and the girl took it. She stood right next to him as they stared into each other's eyes. My stomach rolled. They were so close–intimately close. I didn't like anything about what I was seeing.

He lunged slightly with his left leg bent, never taking his eyes off her, and she tucked her foot onto his thigh. One swift pop of his body, and she was in a handstand on top of his hands.

"Wow. That's so cool." Alexis scooted to the edge of her seat, leaning forward so she could see better.

Alec pressed his hands up, straightening his arms so that the tiny girl was balanced high above his head. She spread her legs wide until they were parallel to the ground. I could almost feel the rise of thousands of instant boners from every guy in the stadium.

"She's really...flexible," Alexis pointed out, looking at me warily.

Alec dropped his hands, and gasps filled the stadium as the girl plummeted toward the ground, only to be caught by Alec tightly against his chest. They ended up in some sort of acrobatic sixty-nine position, or maybe that was just my jealousy noticing.

"Dude. Your boy's face is right in that chick's hoo-ha." Julie snorted. "She's got a good view, too, though."

Nope. Not just me noticing.

Alexis grabbed my forearm and squeezed.

Alec flipped the brunette to the side in a cartwheel move, and they continued to maneuver from pose to pose. Their movements were completely in sync, as if they shared a body. My stomach felt like it was filled with lead, and my hands were clammy with sweat. *Gymnastics my ass.* They were all over each other. No way in hell they were only friends. One couldn't touch and move like that without full knowledge of the other person's body.

Julie squirmed in her chair and then leaned in close to me. I looked over, and she wasn't watching the show anymore. She was watching me.

I wanted to run down there and rip the skinny, Acro-bitch's hands off Alec. My breaths came faster and more ragged as I dug my nails into my palms. I clenched my teeth together so hard, I thought I'd break a tooth. I didn't want to, but I forced myself to look. I watched Alec and his partner perform one amazing, erotic pose after another, and each movement chipped another piece off my ridiculous heart.

As I focused on them, realization hit me, and I felt sick. He didn't hang out with me on Wednesday because he was at the Acroletes gym. With her. He'd made his choice that night, and it clearly hadn't been me.

Why did he want me to come watch this? I'd been an idiot to think that a few kisses meant that he wanted something serious with me. I'd just been the body on hand to satisfy his needs at the time. Alec was no different than Pickles.

Jealousy clawed at my heart as Alec held the girl's hand and spun her into his body, dipping her backward while gazing at her. People whistled and catcalled, which only made me feel worse. I had to swallow past the gigantic rock in my throat as his palm slid down her arm until he reached her hand to twine their fingers together. Their faces were so close they were almost kissing.

I hated how amazing they looked together, like they were made for one another. My chest tightened with humiliation; something I hadn't felt since the night of the bonfire. I was stupid to stick around and watch the rest of the show. Alec wasn't just hurting me this time, he was crushing me. Catching Pickles cheating on me was painful and embarrassing, but my heart was never invested in Pickles. Breaking up with him had almost been a relief. Watching Alec with another girl, however, was a thousand times worse. I hadn't even realized how hard I'd already started to fall until that moment.

My chin trembled as I spoke. "Can we go? I'm not really in the mood for basketball. Besides, I need a drink. Like yesterday." I cleared my throat and looked at Julie and then over at Alexis. They stared at one another, faces pinched, before they nodded. I kept my head down as we made our way up the aisle toward the exit.

"That's my girl." Julie slung an arm around my shoulder. "Don't worry about that ridonkulously good-looking human specimen. Guys like that don't date sorority chicks anyway. I heard the Acroletes are drug-free or something. They don't drink anything other than protein shakes. No fun."

I blinked my eyes to fight back the tears. She was wrong. Alec had been more than fun, but that didn't mean we were right for one another. The problem was, I'd gotten him, for just a minute, and that loss now cut me deep. A tear rolled down my cheek, and I brushed it away with my fingertip.

"You okay?" Alexis looped her arm in mine as we made our way across campus toward Route One. Her eyes were soft, and her smile was strained.

I had worked hard to become stronger. I didn't need the girls worrying about me, but I loved that they did. "Yeah. I thought he actually liked me. Stupid." I swallowed hard and wiped away another stray tear. "I hadn't realized that I wasn't the only girl in his life. I don't want to be one of many. I want to be the one. You know?" My voice cracked, and I bit my lip. "I guess it's better I realized that now before I got too attached." I glanced away, each of those words feeling like a stab in my chest as I spoke them out loud.

"Just because they perform together, doesn't mean they're hooking up." Alexis wrapped an arm around my shoulder.

"Oh, they're total fuck buddies." Julie chortled. "Did you see the way his hand was all over her ass in that third pose?"

"Jules!" Alexis glared at Julie and squeezed me harder.

My breath caught in my throat. Julie's honesty was brutal, but that was also one of the things I loved about her. Besides, she wasn't saying anything that I wasn't already thinking.

"What?" Julie stopped in front of us. "It's the truth, and so what if he's hooking up with that chick? Taren doesn't need him. She's sexy and fun. She can go out tonight and have her pick of guys." Julie hooked her arm in mine. "Just like I do."

Her last words were softer. Julie thought she was fooling everyone, but not Alexis or me. We knew she wanted the same thing we both wanted, to be the one to the right person. Julie just weeded through guys much faster.

I chewed on the inside of my cheek to keep from letting my shame get the best of me. Alec and his partner looked and acted like a real couple, while he and I…did not. We hadn't even been on a real date yet.

I looked at Julie and sighed, my throat too thick to speak. Her face fell, and she reached for my hand, but I pulled away, waving my hand in front of my face. I was not going to lose it. I was not. What I was going to do was to move on and forget about high school crushes. The best way to do that was to party.

"I'm sorry I can't go with you guys. I have a huge Chemistry test tomorrow." Alexis changed the subject, and I was so happy I wanted to kiss her.

"How can you go through college not partying? Studying is so not worth that." Julie shook her head, and Alexis rolled her eyes.

I smiled sadly at Jules, glad I had friends to help me forget my heartache. "She wants to be a doctor and save lives. That's a hell of a lot more noble than drinking with us, Jules."

Julie wrinkled her nose at me. "Don't tell me you agree with her. I can't afford to lose my dancing partner." She shoved her tiny elbow into my side, and I forced out a laugh.

"Not a chance, sister. I'm totally ready to get hammered and dance tonight." I needed to release the bad feelings lodged in my chest, and a night with Jules was my answer.

"Good, because you don't have a choice." Julie looped her arm through mine.

As we exited campus, Alexis hugged us and crossed the street to our house, while Julie and I waved and turned to walk to The Shell. We pushed open the door to the bar. The bouncer inside was a nice guy. Julie always flirted with him, and he pretended not to notice our fake IDs.

"Hello, ladies." He glanced down at our offered IDs and then opened the inner door to the bar. "Have fun."

Julie hugged him, and we walked inside. The pulsating music surrounded me and filled my confused brain with nothing but blessed noise. No room existed in this bar for any sadness, jealousy, or self-pity. The time had come to have some fun.

"I'm getting us a drink!" Julie shouted in my ear, and I nodded, moving to the music. I licked my lips and took a deep breath. Game face on.

"I'd say it's a liquor kind of night, right?" Julie asked when she returned from her trip to the bar. She handed me a pink drink, and I swallowed it in one gulp. Cranberry and vodka. The combination went down easy and did the job well. I could feel my cares slipping away. Perfect.

***

My shoulders swayed to the music, and I tossed back another drink. I'd lost count of how many Julie had already brought to me. I was buzzed and feeling loose. The house band was on stage, and Julie squealed in delight. "That bass player is so unbelievably gorgeous."

She pulled me onto the dance floor, and I studied her newest fixation. Wow. Absolutely hot, just not at all her type. The guy's arms were almost fully sleeved with tattoos, and his short dark hair was messy and spiked. She waved, coyly, but he completely ignored her.

"Let's show him what he's missing." Julie grabbed my hips, and I shimmied closer to her. I ran my hands up through my hair, and she rolled her shoulders, jutting her chest toward me. We held hands and laughed at the show we were putting on for her clueless obsession.

As we continued to dance, her gaze was drawn over and over again to the stage. "What an asshole. He's not even looking." Julie's attention was fixed on the bass player, but he only had eyes for the instrument in his hands and the way his fingers mastered their way across the strings. She frowned in confusion as he continued to ignore her, despite the fact that she was pulling out all her best dance moves.

"Drinks!" she shouted in irritation, pulling me off the dance floor.

The bar blurred in front of my eyes, and the people standing around it were foggy. Having another drink was probably a bad idea, but I was feeling so much better than I had before. I didn't want to let the happy haze disappear. My insecurities would come crashing back in on me too easily. I could feel them lingering, waiting for the moment I sobered up. I shook my head, clearing away the fuzzy lines of the bar and smiled up at the handsome bartender.

"Two tequila shots, please." Julie leaned over the counter and shouted her order. "And two beers."

The glasses slid across the worn wood of the bar top. I reached for one, and the liquid sloshed wildly against the edges with my clumsiness.

"To forgetting." I clinked my shot glass against Julie's before slamming back the nasty liquor. I coughed and then laughed when Julie handed me my beer.

"Chaser," we said in unison. We clinked bottles, and I drank quickly.

"I'm so going to regret this in the morning, but at the moment, I don't care." I yelled in Julie's ear, and she swallowed her beer in large gulps.

"And that's why we party, chica. The booze makes it all better." She gave me a wet kiss on the cheek, and I threw my head back in laughter.

"Taren." A large hand gripped my shoulder, and I turned to see who called my name. The room tilted and spun. I closed my eyes to gain my bearings but stumbled off balance. *Oh. Bad move.* I opened them to find Alec glaring at me. He had changed out of his Acroletes costume and was wearing his Shell Shocked bouncer uniform.

"What's up?" My voice was clipped and defensive as I turned to face him. I waved to Julie as she took off with a group of our sisters onto the dance floor. They began, what looked like, a good old-fashioned twerk-off.

His large arms were crossed over his chest, and he scowled down at me. "Did you leave early? I looked for you after halftime ended. Your seats were empty."

"Yeah, I got bored." *Hello bitchy Taren, where did you come from?* No one in that entire arena thought any part of the Acroletes show was boring.

The flash of hurt in Alec's eyes was brief, but clear. "You got bored?" His jaw clenched, and his eyes narrowed.

"Well, not bored with the show exactly. I got bored watching you basically dry hump that girl in front of eighteen thousand people." I crossed my arms and narrowed my eyes right back at him. The room spun around, and I did everything in my power to hold my stance. "Why didn't you tell me you had a girlfriend? I know what it's like to be cheated on. I don't want to be that chick. I don't want to hook up with another girl's guy."

The anger wiped clean off his face, and his gaze softened as he laughed. "You're mad about Amanda? Holy shit. She's not my girlfriend. We're just balancing partners."

I huffed, and my eyebrows pinched together. "Right. I'm not that naïve, Alec. At least have enough respect for me to tell me the truth. It's obvious you're hooking up with her." I could hear myself slurring the words. I should stop drinking before I ended up passed out in a corner somewhere choking on my tongue.

"No." Alec stopped smiling and bent his knees, making sure to look right into my eyes. His hands gripped my shoulders, and he squeezed gently. "I'm with you."

My heart raced, and I had to look away. "Have you ever been with Amanda?"

Alec shifted, looking to the side as he dropped his hands. "We messed around freshman year a few times. Nothing serious."

My laugh was bitter. "Right. You haven't hooked up since last year. Sure, Alec."

"Taren—" Alec's scolding was cut off when Doug picked me up and twirled me toward him.

"You're slowing down, Denton. Shots! Let's go." He handed me a glass filled with liquor.

Alec grabbed my hand. His nostrils flared, and lips curled as he pulled me close. Some of the liquid in the shot spilled over the rim and down my arm. "I thought you broke up with him." Alec snarled, nodding toward Doug.

"Oh." I shook my head and plastered a large, fake smile on my face. "He's not my boyfriend. He's my *drinking partner*," I shot back. "Look, you've got a beautiful balancing partner, and I've got an eager drinking partner. I'm here to party."

My voice fell at the end. I looked away before lifting the glass Doug had given me. I threw it back, not caring what it was. Whatever had been in the glass burned like a mother going down. I swayed and Doug grabbed my elbow to steady me. A wobbly smile formed on my face, and I gave Alec a smartass wave as Doug led me away.

"You don't really like that meathead bouncer do you? I saw him at the halftime show. He's a freak." Doug glared at Alec over my shoulder, and I stared at Doug's chest, trying to find my balance. The soft round bulge of his belly was outlined in his old, faded Greek Week T-shirt. If I closed my eyes halfway and let them blur the image before me, I could picture the contours and ridges of Alec's chest that I remembered all too vividly. My head was spinning, but I wasn't sure if it was from the memory or my intoxication.

I looked over at Alec. His furious eyes were focused on me, and my heart hammered in my chest. "I don't know. I like him, or I used to. We're tied by a string of fate." My words jumbled together as I leaned back against a nearby table. The more I drank the easier it became to lie.

"You're tied with a string of tape? That's weird—even for you." Doug reached up and tucked my hair behind my ear. "Let me take you home and tuck you in. You need to sleep this off." He pulled me against his body, and I could feel the clumsy press of his lips against my neck. "Come on, Denton. Let me take care of you. You know I know how."

Sleep. Getting tucked in. Sounded good.

Wait. No. I pushed back against Doug's chest. "I'm not going home with you, Pickles. You cheated on me!"

Before I could continue my rant, Alec's hand wrapped around my elbow, and he pulled me away from Doug. "I need to talk to you, Taren."

"She's staying right here, bouncer boy." Doug stood taller, and he protruded his beer gut out in a way that I think was supposed to be menacing. I giggled. Was he trying to intimidate Alec with his cushy softness? The more I thought about it, the more I laughed. I couldn't stop.

Doug grabbed my arm and tried to pull me toward him. Alec pulled back, and I felt like frayed rope in a game of tug of war. My arms were stretched between the two, and my hair hung in my face. As they pulled, my stomach churned, and I prayed I wouldn't get sick in the middle of the bar.

"Both of you let go." I twisted my body to yank my arms free. They ignored me.

"She broke up with you. She's way too drunk to go anywhere with you." The muscles in Alec's neck stood out as he stepped toward Doug. "If you touch her again, I'll toss you out myself, and I'll make sure you're banned from here for good." Alec reached for my arm again, and I shrugged him off.

Doug clenched and unclenched his fist, bringing it up to point at Alec. "You can't ban me."

"You sure about that?" Alec's voice was raw.

"Why do they even let you work here?" Doug snarled. "I bet your boss doesn't know you're in that drug-free club. You're bad for business."

Doug snatched my hand again and yanked hard to pull me toward him. I started to fall, but Alec reached out to steady me. He leaned forward, his large body looming over Doug.

I was tired of this stupid pissing contest. Neither of them cared about me. All they cared about was treating me like a possession. I wanted to get away before the argument turned into a full blown fist fight.

"You guys are idiots." I tried to pull my arm free but neither would let go.

"Walk away now while you still can." Alec pushed his face even closer to Doug and pointed toward the exit with his other hand, long muscled arm outstretched. Even in my inebriated, jilted state, I wanted to lick that arm.

Doug glared at both of us, but then he pushed my elbow away, and I stumbled into Alec.

"You're going to be sorry about this." Doug growled before walking away. I wasn't sure if he was talking to me or Alec. Honestly, I didn't care.

Turning around, I faced Alec. "I'm leaving, too." I lifted my chin in challenge as I glared at him. I didn't know where things between us stood, and my insecurity over what I'd seen at the halftime show was still too fresh to spend the rest of the night near Alec. I needed some time alone to think.

"Call Alexis." Alec grabbed my shoulder to keep me from walking away. "There's no way I'm letting you leave here alone, and I can't walk you. I'm working." He held me close to speak into my ear, and I shivered from his hot breath.

"I'll be fine." I pulled away, stumbling a little as a wave of dizziness hit me. "And stop manhandling me."

His face turned red. He leaned closer and spoke through gritted teeth. "Do not leave here alone, Taren. I'm not asking you. I'm telling you."

"Fuck you, Alec," I bit out before jabbing my finger in his chest. I turned back toward the dance floor, but moved too quickly and bumped into a table, knocking over several beer bottles. I straightened and stumbled once again as the room tilted before my eyes. Shit. I could feel the room going dark. I leaned over the table, pressing my face to the slick wood. I closed my eyes. I'd just rest for a minute until the room stopped spinning.

"That's it," Alec growled.

I forced my eyes back open as he scooped me into his arms and headed toward the door.

"You're coming with me." He tightened his hands around me, holding me close. My head rolled uselessly onto his chest. I didn't even have the strength to hold it up on my own anymore. The last thing I saw before I passed out cold was the frigid glare coming from Doug Pickles.

Chapter 20

Alec

I readjusted the pillow underneath my head again, but it did no good. My floor was so fucking uncomfortable. Being noble was highly overrated. I hadn't slept at all, and the sun was already battling its way through the blinds.

I took a deep breath, but couldn't relax. All I could do was listen to Taren's breathing, getting more frustrated with her by the second. She'd been so drunk the night before that she could hardly walk. I hated how reckless she'd been with her safety and our relationship. Every time I tried to close my eyes, I was tormented with images of just how vulnerable she'd been. She'd almost left with Pickles for fuck's sake. What if I hadn't been there?

I turned my head. She was curled up on my bed, facing me. With her hand tucked under her cheek she looked so peaceful. I had a hard time believing that I'd spent most of the night holding her hair back while she puked her guts out.

She made a tiny moan like she was in pain, and then she curled tighter into a fetal position. I ran my hand back through my hair in irritation. No matter how pissed at her I was, the thought of her being hurt made my chest tighten with worry.

I sighed and then pushed up from the floor. Her eyebrows were pinched together in discomfort, and her body shifted under the blanket, but she didn't wake up. I stood up and then sat on the edge of the bed. I lightly ran my fingers over her knotty hair and then down her back. Her makeup was smeared, but the sight of her in my bed clenched my heart. As angry as I was with her, I still wanted to comfort her, which only pissed me off more. She might not have earned my sympathy, but I continued to skim my fingers over her until her face and body relaxed.

Taren had become my biggest weakness.

Stepping away from the bed, I dragged my hands down my face and released a harsh breath. I had no idea what I was going to say to her when she finally woke up. Was she trying to punish me by partying with her ex? Did she want to hurt me that badly?

Pacing back and forth, I ran my hands through my hair and pulled at it until it stood on end. I didn't have time for her insecurities. I couldn't tolerate the possibility that whenever she wanted to hurt me, she'd do it by putting herself in danger.

I wanted to wake her up and yell at her, but I also wanted to crawl in bed and wrap my arms around her and keep her safe from her own stupidity.

The screen on my phone lit up, and I bent over to see that it was a call from my boss, Jimmy. I snagged the phone off the floor and walked into the hallway, shutting the door behind me.

"Hey, Jimmy." I made my way into the living room so I wouldn't wake up my roommates.

"Hart! What the hell happened to you last night?" he shouted into the phone.

"Sorry. I had to leave." I rubbed my forehead with my palm and collapsed onto the couch.

"You had to leave?" His laugh had zero trace of humor in it. "Shit. A fight broke out on the dance floor. Jacobs had to leave the front door to break it up because we couldn't find you. Breaking up fights is what I hired you to do. You're the muscle. I pay you to keep the peace."

"I'm sorry. It was an emergency. I didn't have time to find you, and I've been too preoccupied to call."

"I don't give a shit about *your* problems, Hart. I pay you to take care of *mine*."

"It won't happen again." My shoulders slumped. He was right. I had a job and I'd abandoned it. That wasn't like me.

"Fuck right it won't! If it does, you're fired."

"It was a one-time thing, Jimmy." My voice was firm. I couldn't afford to lose this job. I also wasn't going to sit back while he tore me a new one. Like he said, he hired me to be the muscle, not a fucking doormat. I hadn't gotten out from under my father's boot just to crawl under Jimmy's.

He laughed. "Just so we're straight, you're working Wednesday night. Unpaid."

I flinched. That would mean missing Wednesday night practice and not even making money for it. "Jesus Christ, Jimmy. I made a mistake, but I'm not going to work for free."

"Then don't bother coming in tonight." When I didn't answer he asked, "What's it gonna be kid?"

I needed my job. Jimmy paid well, and he knew it. I leaned forward, closed my eyes, and pinched the bridge of my nose. "I'll see you tonight."

He chuckled. "That's what I thought. Don't be late, Hart. In fact—" He paused, and I braced myself for his next words. "Why don't you come in an hour early? You can help the band set up."

An hour early on a Saturday night. Fucking hell. Saturday nights at The Shell were longer, busier, and shittier than any other night.

"See you at seven." I slumped back into the couch before ending the call. I leaned my head back and closed my eyes. I had no idea how I was going to make it through work tonight.

After a few seconds, I sat up and reached for the textbook I'd left on the coffee table. Since sleep wasn't an option, I might as well get some work done. I'd barely had a chance to crack open the book before I heard footsteps coming down the hallway.

"You're up early." Caz sat in the chair across from me.

"It's not early." I turned the page and forced my eyes to focus on the next paragraph.

"It's way too fucking early to study." He grabbed my book and pulled it to him, scanning the page. "Econ? On a Saturday morning? That's the way to ruin a weekend."

"Fuck off." I snatched the book out of his hand.

"Dude, you're moody when you don't get sleep." Caz leaned back in his chair with his hands behind his head. His eyes were narrowed as if he could read my mind if he stared hard enough.

I ignored him, hoping he'd go away. Five minutes later he was still sitting there. Caz wouldn't leave until his curiosity was satisfied. I was surprised he'd managed to stay quiet that long. He had to have set a personal record.

I looked up from my book, slamming it shut. "Jimmy called this morning and threatened to fire me." I crossed my arms and pressed my mouth into a tight line.

"Fire you?" His face screwed up in confusion. "Why?"

"I left work early last night without telling anyone." I shrugged.

"He didn't take it well."

He chuckled. "Your boss is an ass stain. You'd be lucky if he fired you. I keep telling you that job isn't worth it."

I clenched my jaw and rubbed along my chin. "I need the money." I hated the desperation in my voice.

"Not that bad, dude. Trust me." Caz got up from his chair and stretched. "Guess I better go shower. Maureen is coming over to pick us up to go to the climbing gym." He turned to face me. "You should just quit. Get a better job."

I looked back down at my book and shook my head in annoyance. I couldn't just quit. Rent had to be paid.

Just as Caz started to walk away, the screen on my phone lit up with another call, and he paused to look at it. "Why is Coach calling you on a Saturday morning?"

I looked at the screen in confusion. "I have no idea."

"Well shit, dude. Answer it."

"Are you hanging around to eavesdrop?" I glared at him.

Caz huffed. "Do you even have to ask?" He plopped down in the seat across from me again and kicked his feet up onto the table.

I answered the phone. "Hey, Coach."

"Alec." Coach's voice was somber. "I hope I didn't wake you."

I took a deep breath. "No sir, I've been up for a couple of hours."

"Good. I have a serious problem I need to discuss with you." Even over the phone I could tell he was scowling.

"Yes sir." My heart thudded in my chest, and I shifted in my seat.

Coach sighed heavily. "I've been told through an anonymous source that you work at Shell Shocked."

My chest was empty and hollowed out as all the air rushed out of me. *An anonymous source?* Who the hell would tell? I looked at Caz, but immediately tossed that thought out the window. He might not agree with my job, but he was a loyal friend. He'd never get me in trouble. Who else would tell though?

I swallowed slowly. My head hung low, and I ran my hand up the back of my neck as I leaned my elbow on my knee. "Yes sir, I work there."

"So it's true. You work at a bar?"

I could hear the disappointment in his voice, and for the first time since taking the job, I was ashamed of it. Coach was a good man, and I craved his approval. Gaining and keeping his respect had been one of my greatest accomplishments.

"I'm a bouncer there, sir." I stood up and began to pace back and forth. "I haven't broken the pledge in any way."

Coach sighed. "I trust you, son. You know I do. The problem is appearances. You know that our group is mostly supported by the generosity of the College of Health and Human Performance, right?"

"Yes, I know that." I stopped behind my chair and gripped the edge of it until my knuckles turned white.

"Well, that financial support is given in exchange for the Acroletes promoting a healthy lifestyle, mainly a drug-free and alcohol-free lifestyle. If the college were to find out that members were not adhering to that pledge, we could lose our financial support."

"But I haven't broken the pledge, sir. I promise." I looked up to see Caz leaning back in his chair with his arms crossed. He had an "I-told-you-so" look smeared across his face.

"I believe you, Alec. I do. The problem is that after the halftime show, you're a bit more recognizable. When students see you promoting a drug-free lifestyle in our show and then later you're working in a bar, they get mixed messages. This puts me in a very difficult position."

His words were like a punch to the gut. "I understand."

"Do you still want to be part of the Acroletes?"

"What?" I couldn't believe he was asking me that. "Yes, of course. You know how much it means to me."

Coach released a long breath before answering. "Well, in that case, I'm going to have to ask you to find a new job. Until you do, you'll be on probation."

"Probation?" The word left my lungs in a long exhale of disbelief. I couldn't survive without Acroletes. I needed it.

"You won't be able to perform or come to practice until you cut ties with that place. I'm sorry, son. I know you're paying for all of your own bills. A well-paying job is a means to an end, but I hope you can understand why it needs to be this way. I can't risk the rest of the team because of your situation."

"Yes, sir."

"If it helps, I know of a couple of positions available on campus. I could give you a recommendation."

"Thank you, I might take you up on that." Shit. I'd probably have to take five of those jobs to make the same pay I was getting at the bar.

"Keep me updated on your decision."

"I will."

Coach said goodbye, and after he hung up, I tossed my phone on the table, dropping my head into my hands.

"Dude, that sucks," Caz said.

I looked up. "You heard everything?"

Caz nodded. "What are you going to do?"

Why did he even have to ask that question? "Get another fucking job, what do you think? I'm not quitting the team."

A satisfied smile spread across Caz's mouth. "Good. Just making sure you were going to do the right thing. I didn't really feel like convincing you otherwise. I haven't had enough sugar this morning for a battle like that."

I grunted in response.

"Hey, buck up, little camper. Don't worry. Everything will work out." He stood up and came around the back of his chair to punch me in the arm.

"Get the fuck off, asshole." I pushed him away. He had a way of making me laugh even when I didn't want to, and I felt like being in a shitty mood.

Caz reached up and tried to ruffle my hair like I was four years old. I grabbed his arm, and we were locked in a mini-wrestling match as we knocked into the back of the sofa.

A sudden clearing of a throat forced us to stop. We both turned to see Taren standing just inside the room, staring at us. I was holding Caz in a headlock.

"Alec?" She looked confused, embarrassed, and sick to her stomach.

"Holy shit." Caz pushed my arm off his neck and stood up, gesturing toward Taren. "I didn't know Donuts spent the night. What the hell are you doing out here studying when you had her in your room?"

I glared at him. "None of your business."

"Hey, did you bring donuts again?" Caz tilted his chin at Taren, and his eyebrows rose in question.

Taren's face paled at the mention of food, and she shook her head.

"She doesn't look like a woman who has been pleasured properly," Caz said to me. "I think you did something wrong last night."

A pink flush crept over Taren's cheeks, and she looked at the floor. She wrapped her arms around her middle as if she'd been violated. I wondered if she remembered last night at all. Even though I was still mad at her, I didn't want her to think I'd take advantage of her.

"It wasn't like that, dickwad. Why don't you go take a shower before Maureen gets here?"

"If it wasn't like that, what was it like?" Caz had his hands on his hips, challenging me.

Taren's eyes flicked up to my face with the same question.

"Taren had a little too much to drink and passed out." I was speaking to Caz, but holding Taren's gaze. "I brought her here so she could sober up." Her eyes flew wide and flashed with shame. "I slept on the floor." My voice was firm, needing her to know I never would have hurt her.

"Ah." Caz nodded his head as a knowing smile tugged at his mouth. "So drunk donut girl was the reason you left work early. No wonder Jimmy was pissed."

Taren's eyes found Caz. "Who's Jimmy?"

"Alec's boss. Seems he got in a little bit of trouble for rescuing the damsel in distress. That's you." He pointed to her.

"I'm sorry." Her voice was quiet and shy as her eyes met mine. "I don't remember much about last night. What did I do?"

I took a deep breath and crossed my arms. "You accused me of dating Amanda, and then you got so drunk you almost let that ass Pickles take you home."

She blanched at my harsh words and rubbed her arms. Her face flushed pink in embarrassment. "So that girl wasn't your girlfriend?"

I huffed out a breath and shook my head, curling my lip in disgust as I spoke. "How big of an asshole do you think I am? Do you honestly think I'd hook up with you and then invite you to the performance to show off a girlfriend?"

Caz laughed. "Well, in donut girl's defense, some of those moves you and Amanda do are pretty questionable."

"Shut up!" I shouted at him. "Shouldn't you be showering?"

"And miss all this drama? No way. I'm about to make a bucket of popcorn. This is better than *Judge Judy*."

"Did I really almost go home with Pickles?" Taren's arms were now tightly across her chest as she held onto her shoulders, and her face pinched with worry.

"Who's Pickles?" Jon yawned as he came out of his room.

"None of your business," I said.

At the same time Caz responded, "I think it's donut girl's ex-boyfriend."

"Can I talk to you in private?" I grabbed Taren's elbow and led her to my bedroom.

"Come on!" Caz threw his hands in the air. "Don't deprive me of my entertainment. You know I'm just going to listen at the door anyway."

Once we were in my room, I slammed the door behind me and locked it to keep Caz out. A few seconds later the knob rattled, and he swore.

Taren turned to look at me. "I'm sorry I don't remember much about last night. I'm so embarrassed. Did I really almost go home with Doug?" She was wringing her hands together.

"Yeah. And he wasn't too happy that I kept that from happening."

"Thank you for taking care of me." When Taren looked at me, I could see the apology in her expression, but then she dropped her gaze to the floor. She wound the hem of her shirt over her finger nervously. "I was really out of it last night, wasn't I?"

I took a deep breath and released it in a frustrated rush. "Why would you do that to yourself? You were piss drunk, and then you just drank the shot that Pickles gave you without a thought. For all you know, he could have drugged it."

Her eyes found mine again, and her eyebrows furrowed in disbelief. "He wouldn't do that."

"You should know better than to take a drink that you didn't see get poured. Especially from a guy as shady as Pickles."

"I know he's sort of a jerk, but he—"

I took a step toward her and held my hand up to silence her. "Look, I didn't stay up all night watching you puke your guts out just to argue about your asshole ex." I was pissed and jealous that her first reaction was to defend him.

She bit her bottom lip like she was trying not to cry. "I'm sorry. I don't remember." She rubbed her forehead as if that would make everything clear.

Disgust crawled up my spine and I felt my shoulders stiffen in anger. She had no idea how much danger she'd been in, or how much I'd risked by doing the right thing. I paced back and forth, unable to look at her. When I tripped over a sneaker, I bent over to pick it up and then threw it into my open closet. It ricocheted against the back wall and knocked things off their hangers.

Taren flinched. "Alec—"

"You need to leave." I turned from her and flung the covers back over the bed before grabbing a pillow and tossing it roughly over top. I couldn't look at her. I refused to let her wounded expression affect me. I was done.

"You want me to leave? Now?" Her voice was quiet, tugging at me, begging me to give her whatever she wanted. From the corner of my eye, I saw her reach for me, but I moved away before she could make contact. Her touch had the power to undo me, and I wasn't going to let that happen. Not now.

"Yeah. I have some job hunting to do before I go into work." I crossed the room, and kicked a pile of clothes into my closet before slamming the door shut.

"You're leaving The Shell? Why?" She stepped to my side, and I turned to look at her.

"I'm on probation with Acroletes until I get a different job." Shit. Until I said it out loud, it hadn't really felt real. I thought being Taren's hero would feel so much better than when I was the villain. I just hadn't realized how high the price would be to do the right thing. I hadn't known I'd have to make such a huge sacrifice.

I walked over to my desk where I'd left her jacket and shoes. I thrust them into her hands and didn't even feel guilty when I saw the look of hurt on her face. "You can let yourself out."

She swallowed, and her bottom lip quivered. "Alec, I'm so sorry. Can we just talk about what happened last night?"

"I don't have the time. I've got a lot of shit to do today." She flinched, and I walked over to my bathroom before turning back to face her. "Do me a favor."

She was staring at her clothes, but she looked up reluctantly, almost like she didn't want to meet my eyes.

"Don't ever drink like that again. I might not be there next time to make sure you're safe."

She was still staring at me as I slammed the door. I turned the shower on to drown out the sound of her leaving my room.

***

I sat in the small lobby, waiting for my turn to be interviewed. Pictures of university sporting events lined the walls which were painted in red, black, and yellow stripes. I really needed this opportunity. The stadium security office at the University didn't usually hire students, but the director was friends with Coach and offered to give me a chance at an interview. I hadn't been able to find a job to replace The Shell, and I'd already missed a week and a half of practice. In addition, Jimmy had been asking me to come in an hour early almost every shift—an hour he wasn't paying me for. He'd sniffed out my desperation like a fucking bloodhound.

I noticed a stray thread hanging off my polo sleeve. Reaching up, I wrapped the thin, red string around my finger and then yanked, pulling it free. The stitches along the seam were loose and weak.

I was always amazed at how quickly everything could unravel. Just when things were going my way, I made an impulsive decision and fucked my life up beyond all recognition. The time had come to get my focus back. I needed to nail down a job and ace my classes. I needed to get back to the Acroletes gym. I needed to remove the distractions that were getting in the way of my goals. I couldn't afford to risk what I'd worked so hard to gain.

I stared at the red thread that was wound tightly around my finger.

Right now, Taren was a risk. My first instinct was always to jump in and save her, but if she self-destructed, she could take me down with her. She didn't trust me and expecting the worst of me had been too easy for her. I'd spent most of my life living with a father who always expected the worst of me. I sure as hell didn't need it from my girlfriend. Perhaps having her in my life right now wasn't what was best for me—for either of us.

Unraveling the thread, I rolled it into a ball between my fingers.

"Mr. Hart," the secretary said. "Ms. Miller is ready to see you now."

I took a deep breath and stood before following the woman down the hall. It was time to get my future back on track.

As I walked by the secretary's desk, I tossed the ball of thread into the trash can.

Chapter 21

Taren

Wind whipped my hair around, and I pulled my jacket closer. A light, cold drizzle fell and the gray day matched my mood. I walked slowly toward the Student Union, keeping my head down to block the wind and the rain from my face. As much as I loved seeing William, I was dreading today. I had missed our last meeting. I just didn't show up. Not that I had planned to ditch him, but I was too hungover from that disastrous night after the halftime show. I was devastated over how things ended with Alec so I went home, climbed into bed, and slept. Right through my time with William. And the kicker was, being with him was one of the things I most looked forward to these days.

As soon as I had remembered, I called him. His voice had sounded so small over the phone. He was hurt and confused.

All because I was insecure.

I opened the door to the Union and a blast of warm air hit me. William sat on a bench in the hallway, watching the people bustling all around him.

"Hi, Will." My voice was quiet. I pressed my lips together; worry filled my gut like a heavy weight. I felt queasy from the thought that he might be mad at me.

"Hi, Miss Taren." William stood up and opened his arms for a hug. A big, bright smile stretched across his face, and I let out the breath I'd been holding. I gave him a small grin and felt the weight leave my stomach. At least this part of my life would be okay.

I moved into his embrace, wrapping my arms around his waist and pressing the side of my face into his chest. William was tall, at least three or four inches taller than me. He hugged me back tightly before pulling away.

"I'm sorry, Will." My face pinched, and tears stung my eyes. I wasn't sure why I was so emotional, but it was probably embarrassment. I was humiliated. I had hurt the people I cared about most.

"I changed my mind." William's expression became serious, and I stiffened. The heavy feeling returned to my stomach, and my heart beat faster.

I looked down at the ground and twisted the ring on my thumb. *Changed his mind? About me? Did he not want to be my buddy any longer?* I couldn't take more rejection right now. I looked up at William; his face was an unreadable blank slate.

"About what?" I whispered. My eyebrows furrowed and my mouth dried.

His eyes focused on mine. With a strong and confident voice, he said, "Call me Billy."

Laughter burst out of my throat before I could contain it. I buried my face in my hands and peeked out at him. The relief coursing through me felt fantastic. He still wanted to be my friend. At least my stupidity hadn't ruined everything.

I couldn't wipe the grin off my face. "Of course. What made you change your name?"

William cocked his head to the side and squinted as if in thought. "Will seemed kind of boring, don't you think?" He nodded his head as if answering his own question. "Yup, yup, Will is boring. I think Billy is more fun."

This time I nodded as well. He had a good point. "Well then Billy, can I buy you a cup of coffee?"

"Yes, I like coffee, but I am buying." William led the way to the nearby coffee stand, and we placed our orders. With coffee in hand, I found a small table nestled into a semi-private nook in the noisy area.

"Thank you. The next cup is on me." I pulled the lid off of my Styrofoam cup and poured in some creamer, stirring it slowly.

William opened sugar packets two at a time and dumped them into his cup. He winked and took a sip of his overly sweet drink. I smiled and blew on my own coffee before taking my first sip. Warmth filled me, and I relished the simple act of sharing time with a friend.

"I really am sorry I missed our last meeting. I overslept. I wasn't feeling well." Chewing on my lip, I wiped away the drops of moisture that ran down the sides of my cup. "That's not an excuse, I know that, but still...I'm sorry."

William studied his coffee cup, avoiding my gaze. "I forgive you, Miss Taren. I was just scared. I thought something happened to you. That you got hurt."

I reached out and placed my hand on his wrist. He looked up. His big brown eyes met mine, and I sucked in a quick breath. "You were worried about me?"

"Of course." He smiled shyly. "You are my friend."

I shook my head, smiling back at him. Just like the Grinch, I felt my heart grow three sizes larger. Like a slap in the face, realization hit me that my stupid, selfish actions had hurt two of the people I cared most about. I squeezed William's hand in mine. Both he and Alec worried about me, and I had let my jealousy and insecurities make me act like an idiot. I needed to grow the fuck up because this was not the person I wanted to be.

"I have something I want to give you." I reached into my purse and pulled out the red ribbon. William looked at the piece of satin and a wrinkle formed on his forehead.

I closed my eyes, allowing myself a moment to remember. "This was given to me by my friend, Alec. He's the one I told you about before." I tilted my head to the side and William nodded. I stretched the ribbon straight out across the table, and then folded my hands in my lap. "Back in high school, he used it to fix my broken backpack so I could carry my books home." My throat tightened at the memory.

William grinned and moved his fingertips along the smooth, glossy fabric.

I cleared my throat. "A couple of weeks ago, Alec and I were studying together, and we talked about how we were connected by a red string of fate." My heart beat faster and my stomach filled with butterflies. I *loved* being with Alec. Whether we were studying, talking, kissing, or touching, I was happy. Anytime I was around him, I felt centered and alive. I was ashamed at how easily I'd given in to doubt and jealousy. I wondered if Alec would ever be able to forgive me.

Almost two weeks had passed since the night of the halftime show. He no longer sat next to me in class. He hadn't invited me to study with him. He hadn't answered any of my texts. I had completely gotten our string snarled into a knot I might never be able to untangle.

"What does a red string of fate mean?" William spoke each word slowly as his eyes narrowed in confusion.

I picked up one end of the ribbon and handed it to him. I took the other in my hand. "It's an old folktale. To be connected to someone by the red string of fate, means that you are tied together. Your lives are connected. No matter what happens, you will always be close and will find your way back to one another."

I gestured between us with my end of the ribbon. "You and me. We're connected by a red string of fate, too. You're not just my buddy. You're my friend. No matter what happens, we're tied together. If I mess up again, which I'll try really hard not to do, don't give up on me. We're friends. We'll always be connected."

"Friends." His smile lit up his face.

"Keep this to remember." William's eyes creased in happiness as I placed the ribbon in his hand. I wouldn't need a physical reminder. The impact of my bad decisions weighed heavy on my heart.

I had one more person I had to make amends to before I could begin to forgive myself. Alec might think our string was broken, but I would do everything in my power to convince him otherwise.

***

"Come in!" Alexis hollered from the top bunk where she was busy studying.

Julie walked in with a pile of her own books and settled on our floor.

"What's up?" Alexis asked her, smiling at the look of frustration on our laid back friend's face.

"Hard dicks and helicopters." Julie smirked, and Alexis groaned loudly.

"Nice, Jules." I laughed as I sat at my desk, pulling on a pair of knee-high riding boots that perfectly matched Alexis' brown sweater dress I was borrowing.

"I have a shit-ton of French homework." Julie sat cross-legged on the floor, staring at her open textbook. "French. Who even speaks French anymore? *Parlez-vous* jack hole?"

Alexis climbed down the ladder, laughing, and turned to stand in front of me with her arms crossed over her chest. "You look nice, T. Where are you going?"

I wrapped my finger in the chain of my necklace and bounced my knee. "I'm going to talk to Alec. I'm hoping he'll forgive me for being an idiot. I need him to give us a chance." I rubbed at my chest. I felt like I was having heart palpitations for goodness sake.

"Good for you." Alexis shot Julie a hard look before turning back to me, her hands clasped tightly together. "I'm sorry again. I should've texted you when you didn't come home that night. I feel horrible."

"I've apologized to each of you like a gazillion times already." Julie huffed and looked up to the ceiling. "When Alec carried her out of there, I assumed she was going to his place to hook up. I had no idea she was passed out. I thought he was just being romantic. It looked hot." Julie stood up and grabbed my hand, squeezing it. "I really am sorry."

I grabbed my jacket, shaking my head at both of them as I slipped it on. "My stupidity is not your fault, Julie. Both of you need to stop apologizing. I learned my lesson. I'm only sorry that the person who suffered the most in the whole thing was Alec." I sighed heavily as I pictured the look of disappointment and anger on his face. The pressure of my regret was crushing. I steeled myself and stood up straight. I had to make things right with him.

"You know I found out that it was that knuckle dragger, Pickles, who turned Alec in for working at The Shell." Julie was looking at her nails and picking at the polish. "Jen overheard him telling some of his brothers the other night. He was also bragging that he had cheated on you all along." She dropped her hands and rolled her eyes. "He's such a prick stain."

I swallowed away the bitter taste I got whenever I thought about Doug, and grabbed my purse. "Pickles is old news. We're no longer friends. We're no longer anything. I just hope Alec will still give me a chance."

"Girl, you look smoking hot in that dress." Julie whistled as she looked me up and down. "Alec can say no to booze all he wants, but he's gonna want a tall drink of you. No guy in his right mind would turn you down looking like that."

"Thanks. Wish me luck." They waved, and I took a fortifying breath as I stepped out of the room. I closed the door behind me and headed for the stairs. I wanted Alec to say yes to me, not because I looked good, but because he felt the way I did. We had an unbreakable connection, right? I had to trust that the mess I made could be untangled.

***

"Speak!" Caz yelled into the intercom outside his apartment.

"Hi Caz, it's Taren. Can I come up?"

"Do you have food?"

I laughed and could hear scuffling in the background. Then Jon told me to come up. As I walked up the stairs to their door, every single worry I'd been obsessing about ricocheted around in my head. I wiped my hands on my dress and blew out a breath. I prayed that my heart would stop hammering like it was going to tear out of my ribcage. Two more steps and I regretted that I didn't have something in my hands to keep them from trembling. I should have brought donuts.

What if Alec said no? What if he turned me down? Again. The possibility was strong that I could have a repeat of bonfire night, but I had to try. I had to know for sure if I had any chance with him.

The door swung open just as I lifted my fist to knock. Half a second more and I would have knocked on Caz's chest. I jumped back, but he laughed, dragging me into the living room.

"It's cold as a witch's tit out there tonight, Donuts. Get in here where it's warm."

"Is he here?" I looked around the living room, and my stomach flipped. I was just as nervous and excited as the first time I rode a rollercoaster. I felt like I had just ascended to the top of the steep hill, and I was dangling over the first plunge.

"He's in his room doing God knows what. I'll warn you…he's grumpy as shit. Enter at your own risk." Caz pulled the coat off the back of my shoulders and then froze. I turned to see his eyes bulging out as he did a double take. Jon walked out of the kitchen eating an apple, and he stopped, midstride, mouth wide open.

Oh no. What was wrong? I looked down, tugging on the hem of the tight dress, making sure everything was covered and nothing was hanging out. That would be just my luck to have the back tucked into my panties or something. I crinkled my nose and arched my neck back to check behind me. Nope. Everything seemed to be in place.

"Wow. Taren, you look…" Jon's words were hesitant, and then he swallowed loudly.

"Holy shitballs. I've been a good boy this year. Why, Santa? Why can't I be on the nice list like Alec?" Caz fell to his knees, hands clasped in prayer. "And boots. Boots! Love me some hot girls with boots. Those boots can walk all over me anytime." Caz spread out on the floor on his stomach. "Come on, Donuts. Have at it."

"Stop drooling, ass nugget." Jon threw a pillow from the couch at him before ushering me down the hallway toward Alec's door.

After Jon returned to the living room, I could hear him and Caz bickering. I knocked on Alec's door and waited, my stomach freefalling. The roller coaster was plummeting down the hill and approaching the first bend in the tracks. Alec would have the ability to totally derail me if he told me to go away.

"What?" Alec's voice was loud and flat.

I paused before I went in, holding onto the knob, desperately hoping that I could fix the mess I made. I walked into the room, shutting the door behind me. Alec sat on his bed wearing headphones and reading from a textbook.

"Hi." My voice quivered, and the smile on my face felt forced. I tucked a lock of hair behind my ear, unsure of what to say now that I was in front of Alec.

He looked up at the sound of my voice and yanked off his headphones. "Taren." The look on his face was anxious. "What are you...?" He stopped mid-sentence as his eyes moved from my face and slowly trailed down. I felt the heat of his gaze as it devoured me. His eyes slid over every curve and dip of my body that was visible through my dress. I could feel myself responding as if he'd already touched me. My skin tingled, and I wished it were his hands and not his gaze, caressing me so intently.

I stood in front of him, waiting for him to finish his question. I wanted to go to him—but I needed him to make the first move. His eyes widened when he got a look at my boots. My legs were shaking in anticipation, ready to close the distance between us, ready to be wrapped around his waist.

Alec took a breath, and his lips parted. His eyes darkened.

"Lock it!" Jon yelled from the other side of the door. "I can only hold him back for so long."

The sounds of a struggle were louder on the other side of the door. Caz yelled out, "Don't worry about being quiet. Be as loud as you want, you naughty kids."

Reaching behind me, I felt for the lock, securing it without taking my eyes off Alec's.

"What are you doing here?" Alec tossed his book to the side, and he moved off the bed, approaching me. His worn jeans and long sleeved T-shirt did nothing to hide his beautiful body. I laced my fingers together so that I wouldn't reach for him before I could tell him all the things I needed to say.

"I wish I could go back and change the way I acted after the halftime show. I feel horrible that I made assumptions and accused you. I'm embarrassed that I let my jealousy come between us." I squeezed my fingers together. "Most of all, I hate that I hurt you." My voice cracked, and I cleared my throat. "I'm so sorry, Alec. Please forgive me." I took a step toward him, and he mirrored me, moving forward, until we were almost touching.

"Why are you sorry?" His voice was raspy, and my tears welled. I missed him so much that my heart hurt, just hearing him speak. Being this close to him reminded me of how much I'd lost.

"For drinking too much. For doubting you. For being selfish. For costing you your job. For hurting your place on the team. For not telling you how much I want you—"

His lips cut my apology off with a kiss as his hand cupped my cheek, and I opened my mouth, frantic to taste him. I fisted his shirt in my hands. Alec's tongue moved into my mouth, and I moaned, rising on my tiptoes to give me better leverage to kiss him back. Alec grabbed my ass, lifting me up so I could wrap my legs around his waist. *Yes.* He groaned, and I felt how hard he was against me. My tongue delved into his mouth, and I pressed myself as tightly as I could against his chest, not able to get enough of him. *God.* Only two weeks had passed, but it felt like forever without him.

I gently bit his lower lip and then moved my mouth to his ear. I whispered, "Does this mean you forgive me?"

Alec's breaths came quick as he pulled back to look at my face, walking us over to his bed like I weighed nothing. I stayed wrapped around him. My hands rested behind his neck while my fingers played with the ends of his hair.

"We've both made mistakes, Taren. There are probably a million reasons why this thing between us might never work, but we only need one reason why it will. We can't stay away from each other." He stroked my back and kissed the corners of my mouth.

"I want you, Alec. I've always wanted you. I know that we don't seem to be compatible, but opposites attract, right? Do you really want me to stay away?" I asked again.

His steely blue gaze scanned every inch of my face as if memorizing it. "No," he finally answered. "If you hadn't come over tonight, I would have come looking for you. I can't stop thinking about you." He kissed my lips. "I need you."

I closed my eyes for a second, letting those words echo through me. *I need you.* I needed him, too. I wanted nothing more than to belong to Alec. Smiling, I pulled him back in for a kiss, but his finger came between our lips.

"No more games. No more flirting with Doug. I'm fucking serious. If we're going to do this, I want to know that he's completely out of your life. I want us both to be all in. You and me. A real relationship. Not just study buddies who make out. All in." Alec looked at me, and my eyes burned with tears of relief. He didn't just want me, he wanted *more* with me.

"That's what I want too. I want to be all in with you." I pressed my lips to his, feeling relief unfurl through my body, curling into fingers of desire.

"Taren?" Alec asked between kisses. "Can I touch you?" His hands were still under my thighs supporting my weight. Even though I was groping him with desperate need, he hadn't tried to touch me anywhere else. I loved the way he asked permission, as if access to me was a gift, not an assumption. The power he gave me to decide, made me want to give him everything.

"Please." My voice was breathy, and I gripped his shoulders tighter. My pulse raced with anticipation.

He set my feet back on the floor so he could reach up to my face. He ran his thumbs over my cheeks like I was precious. Cherished. He'd become my protector in so many ways. He made me feel as if my heart and body were safe with him. How had I ever doubted that?

I reached down between us to grab his shirt and lifted it over his head, eager to have access to more of him. Leaning forward, I kissed him again. Our tongues tangled together and we both moaned. Alec grabbed the hem of my dress. He inched the fabric up before smoothing it back down over my legs, almost as if he was doing it against his will. After he repeated this several more times, I smiled against his lips as we continued to kiss. My heart was slamming against my chest, begging him to just take my dress off, but he was waiting for my permission. I ran my hands up his chest, wishing I could convey my feelings to him through touch alone. His hesitation and his respect was like an aphrodisiac to me. I wanted him, desperately.

"It's a little unfair I'm so over-dressed," I whispered against his lips. My voice wavered, and my hands shook. I had no experience in seduction, and here I was, trying to tempt the hottest guy I'd ever met in my life. I licked my lips and swallowed hard. My eyes lifted up to meet his, and the lust-filled look I got in return caused me to shudder with apprehension. *Get it together, Donuts,* I scolded myself. *He's not going to believe it if you don't.*

"Do you know what you do to me when you look at me like that?" He squeezed his eyes shut and pressed his lips against my shoulder. "Fuck. You're driving me crazy." Alec's voice was rough, and his words made me ache.

I could do this. I could be sexy. I looked up at him and smirked. Then, I reached down to the bottom of my dress and with a slow wiggle, I gradually slid the tight material up my body. Alec leaned back to watch as my naked skin made an appearance inch by inch. His fingers twitched like he wanted to help me, but his arms hung by his sides as his gaze followed the progress of my hands.

When the dress finally made its way over my head, I was left in nothing but my carefully chosen lingerie and boots. I wasn't ready to go all the way with Alec tonight, but I was ready to move to the next level. Tonight was about baring myself to him both physically and emotionally. I was ready because he was worth the risk.

Excitement and nerves vibrated under my skin, and I ran my hands up his arms, wrapping them around his neck. "Well?" I was proud that my voice was confident.

Looking down, Alec gave me a crooked smile. "You can leave the boots on."

His hands rested on my waist, and I giggled as he spun us around so that the backs of my knees hit the edge of the bed. He lifted his chin toward the mattress and his was voice soft. "Is this okay?" He brushed my hair back from my face, his fingers tracing the edge of my jaw with reverent gentleness.

I nodded and he lowered me to the mattress.

"I dreamt about this." Alec dragged his fingertips down my neck and to my hair that lay splayed across his pillow. He leaned over me, and his weight rested on his forearms. "I pictured you just like this. Laying in my bed, your hair spread out on my pillow, your scent on my skin." He swallowed, his Adam's apple bobbing in his throat. "Your lips begging to be kissed." Alec slipped his tongue along my lower lip. "I missed your taste. I missed…you, Taren." He dipped his tongue inside my mouth, pulling me in for a deep, slow kiss.

The words coming from his lips were too much. I moaned into his mouth as emotion stung the corners of my eyes. He was hard as he pressed against me, and my eyelids fluttered shut as I lifted my hips into him. My hands ran all over his arms, and my fingers molded themselves to the muscles of his shoulders and back. I would never have enough time to feel him. Never.

Alec's kisses were eager, his lips pressing against mine with such intensity I hardly had time to catch my breath. He moved down, trailing his lips along my neck until he reached my chest. Every place he left a kiss felt hot, and I felt flushed.

"I missed the way you tuck your hair behind your ear when you're nervous." His lips branded my right shoulder. "I missed the way you smile when you know you're out-debating me." His mouth traced the words into my skin before leaving a scorching touch on my rib cage. "I missed the way you can get lost in a book and fall into its pages." His kiss settled between the swell of my breasts, and his breath feathered across my skin.

A tear rolled down my face as emotion overwhelmed me. I wasn't just another body. He saw me. The real me.

He looked up and propped himself up on his elbow. He reached up and wiped the tear away with his thumb. He left his hand on my face and gazed down me. "What's wrong?" His fingers stroked my cheek.

I closed my eyes, taking a deep, shaky breath. "I'm so happy we get a second chance." Another tear escaped me, and his face pinched as he reached up to wipe that one away, too.

"Second chances don't change the past. They just prove we can learn from our mistakes." He pressed his face into my neck, his mouth just below my ear. "I'm not the same guy I was in high school. I'm going to prove that to you." He kissed the curve of my neck.

"Please, keep going. I don't want you to stop. I need this." My voice was strong, and I threaded my fingers into his hair.

He raised his head, watching as his fingers skimmed across my shoulders and down over the swell of my breasts, tracing the edge of my bra. He unhooked the clasp on the front and then pulled back the lace. He inhaled sharply when the tips of his fingers caressed me.

"I can't get you out of my mind. You're...amazing." His gaze followed the path of his fingers. The reverence in his voice sent my heart soaring in a thousand different ways at once before it slammed back in my chest. Alec's hand cupped the weight of my breast before his thumb lightly circled the center. I pressed my lips together to hide my moan, but his triumphant smile was proof that he heard me. He brought his mouth to my other breast while his thumb continued to massage my nipple. His gaze never left mine.

As soon as I felt his warm, wet tongue, I closed my eyes. The feeling was so sweet that light burst behind my eyelids. My breaths came quickly as he sucked and nibbled. I squirmed and writhed beneath him, his touch both gentle and demanding. All of my questions were gone.

I had no doubts, no worries, only trust. Alec's embrace was the one place I belonged.

He moved down my body, kissing my belly until he got to my panties. He lifted his head in question.

I licked my dry lips and gulped in a breath. "Not all the way. But—" I swallowed hard. I needed to tell him exactly what I wanted, but I was embarrassed to say the words aloud.

"My hand?" He pushed up to press another kiss to my lips, coaxing away my apprehension. His tongue stroked mine, and I relaxed. Pulling away, I nodded.

His grin was wicked as he inched his way back down my body and then slid my panties down my legs. He reached down between us to stroke me, sending pulses of heat racing through me with every touch.

My hands were buried in his hair, gripping the strands in desperation. Alec's fingers moved along the warmth between my legs, dragging with sweet tenderness, before circling along my center.

I gasped, clutching him tighter to me and arching up into his hand. He'd never touched me like this. If I felt like I'd been on a rollercoaster before, I was wrong. Pleasure surged through my body, and I held on tight as he took me to the edge before kissing me gently.

Alec stilled his fingers and looked up, his eyes searching my face. "You still okay?"

This man. I loved that he didn't want to push me too far, but right now I needed him to keep going.

"Please," I groaned, and he smiled, relief filling his face. He slid two fingers into me, watching my face as he moved them in and out. Each stroke of his fingers sent delicious tremors through me. I tensed, squeezing my eyes shut. "Yes," I dragged out the word and just when I thought I would crack and fall over the edge, he changed the rhythm...the angle...the pressure. Dear god I hoped he'd never stop.

"Alec..." My eyes locked onto his as my body thrummed with pleasure. Tears filled my eyes again. Tears? This couldn't be sexy. I kept crying, but everything about me was out of control right now. My body, my heart, my mind, raced to keep up with him. All I could do was hang on.

"Taren. You feel...Jesus you look so beautiful." Alec's voice cracked, and his lips trailed up my neck, as he sucked and groaned against my skin.

"Alec." I began to shake as his name shuddered out of me with every breath.

Finally, my body became lax, and Alec lay next to me on the bed, pulling me in close. I pressed my nose against his neck, nuzzling against him, and smelled the scent of his hot skin. He kissed my temple, and I tangled my legs with his jeans-clad ones.

Hold the phone.

I was butt-ass naked, and he was still wearing his jeans? This was wrong on so many levels. Easing out of his grip, I moved down his body, licking along my favorite ridges and contours. He grinned and settled back on his pillow. His head rested on his bent elbow as he watched me. His eyebrow cocked as if wondering how far little miss goody-two-shoes was willing to go.

I'd show him I wasn't the same girl he knew in high school. More than anything, I wanted to bring him the same pleasure he had just brought me. I knelt next to him and paused, biting my lower lip. I might not have been experienced compared to other girls in college, maybe even other girls he'd been with, but I was a quick learner. My pulse quickened, and I sucked in a breath.

I slid the button at his waistband through the hole and unzipped his pants, my hand trembling. Alec sat up and covered my hand with his.

"You don't need to do this tonight." He smiled and kissed me softly.

"I want to do this." I took a deep breath. "I want to make you feel as good as you made me feel. I'm just not sure I'll do it right."

"Taren." The scorching intensity in his eyes almost knocked me over. "Anything you do will be perfect."

I loved the confidence I felt from the fact that he trusted me. Slipping my hand inside, I rubbed along his hard length and my own body lit up in response when he grunted.

Threading my fingers into his belt loops, I pulled his jeans down his legs, and he helped by lifting his hips. My gaze was trapped for a few wonderful moments as it found the bulge in his boxers. When I looked up, he grinned as he caught me checking him out. My face flashed hot, and I shrugged. I didn't care. I was like Julie with an Internet connection and a no-limit credit card. I was going to enjoy every moment of this free-for-all.

I ran my hands up his thighs and his body tensed. I slid his boxers off and took a minute to appreciate the view. Straddling his knees, I traced my fingers up and around his hip bones. Once I found the tight cluster of muscles on his stomach I ran my fingers over them, too. Alec Hart was big and gorgeous all over.

My fingers followed the path of his abs down. I wrapped my fingers around him tentatively and he groaned.

"Fuck. Taren, yes." Alec propped himself up on his elbows, watching me. Heat coiled through my body, knowing he liked what I was doing.

I moved my hand up and down his length in a slow rhythm. *Holy shit.* He felt amazing. Hard, hot, pulsing. As many times as I had imagined touching Alec like this, reality was so much better.

"Is this good?" My words were quiet, but excitement shot through me.

"Fuck yeah. Just a little harder. A little…faster." Alec's lips parted, and he closed his eyes.

I squeezed him harder, and his body tensed even more underneath me. I moved my hand faster, and his breathing increased.

An ache pulsed deep inside me, and I wished I could squeeze my legs together. I was more turned on doing this and watching him than I had ever been before. I wanted to push him to the brink, just like he had taken me. I needed him out of control, just like I had been.

I tightened my fingers around him even more.

"Yes." His voice took on an edge. When I picked up the speed of my hand, Alec groaned and thrust his hips up. His breaths came deep and harsh.

Oh, hell yes. He liked it. Donut girl for the win.

The thought spurred me on, and I leaned over to kiss him. I let the naked skin of my breasts slide against his sweat soaked chest as I moved my hand faster between us.

When Alec's stomach muscles bunched together, he reached up to grab my face with both hands. He kissed me hard as he moaned into my mouth. I swallowed his sounds but kept moving my hand.

He tore his lips from mine, his voice husky. "Babe, I'm gonna come. Shit, you'd better move."

I bit my lip and kept going, fascinated by the way his face and body tensed. Finally he sighed, long and low, his mouth hanging open and chest heaving as his release spilled through my fingers and between us.

He stared at me for a moment. His hands cradled my face before he eased me down onto the mattress next to him. He kissed my eyes, nose, and lips while he used a towel to clean us up.

After he was done, Alec pulled me close and brought his lips to my ear. "You and me, Taren. You and me," he whispered. "We're all in."

I smiled, pressing my face against his neck, and curled up next to him.

Me and him.

Chapter 22

Alec

The time had come for me to get my girl out of her comfort zone.

I handed Taren the pair of shoes I'd borrowed from Maureen as I led her to the fifty-five foot freestanding climbing wall on campus. She stopped and stared up at the students making their progress up the wall.

"You can't be serious, Alec. *This* is our date?" The terror in her eyes was clear.

"Come on." I put my arm around her waist and led her forward. I leaned over to whisper in a deep voice to her. "It'll be fun."

"You know what would be fun? Going back to your apartment and peeling me out of these clothes." She smirked and batted her eyelashes at me.

Visions of a naked Taren flashed through my mind, and I reached up to run my hand back through my hair. "You could tempt a fucking saint you know that?" I glared at her, and she continued to smile. I wasn't going to give in. "Don't worry. We'll get to that later. But first we're going to have a little fun." I put my hands on her shoulders and turned her toward the sign-in desk.

"I didn't think you'd actually be able to convince her." Maureen sat behind the counter and handed me two harnesses.

"I'm *not* convinced." Taren pouted at Maureen and then cast another worried glance at the wall. "In fact, I haven't even agreed. I don't have muscles like you, Maureen. I'll never make it up that thing. My idea of exercise is running for the campus shuttle."

Maureen laughed. "Don't worry. Alec will belay for you. He's not going to let you fall."

Taren's eyebrows pinched together as she looked at me. "What does belay mean?"

I put my arm around her. "It means I'll be holding the spotting belt, babe. Don't worry. I work here, remember?" Maureen had gotten me the job so I could pick up some extra hours on the weekends. I didn't think I could trust Taren's safety with anyone else. I knew I'd never let her fall, and she knew it, too.

I took Taren's elbow and steered her over to the beginner section. She rubbed her arms and gazed helplessly up at the towering wall and the people dangling from it.

I slipped my finger under her chin and turned her to face me. "Do you trust me?"

She looked at my lips and then her gaze found my eyes again. I could see fear, but that faded as her faith in me took over. "You know I do."

"Then you know I'm not going to let you fall." She swallowed and then nodded. I leaned in to kiss her, my lips lingering longer than I meant to because I didn't want to break the contact. "Ready?"

She nodded, and I stepped back to slip on my harness. Taren watched with fascination as I tightened all the straps. I held her harness out so she could step into it. When she hesitated, I leaned forward and kissed her again.

"If you're a good girl and give this a try, I promise to make it worth your while." Her eyes narrowed, and she fought to hold back a grin. She'd said the same thing the night she forced me to study. "Do you doubt me?"

She tapped her foot and cast another terrified glance up at the wall before meeting my gaze. "It better be worth it."

My eyes traveled down her body, and she shifted under the heat of my gaze. "It will be so worth it that your toes will curl."

She blushed and then moved toward me, holding my shoulders for balance as she stepped into the harness. I might have taken a little longer than necessary to tighten the straps along her inner thighs, and I caught her smiling when she noticed.

"Don't start something here you can't finish." Her words were a threat, but her tone was playful.

I ran my fingers along the edge of the harness from her hip to the top of her thigh, and she shivered. "You can do this," I told her.

While we waited for her turn, I explained to her how the belay system worked. "Whatever happens, don't panic. Use the commands to tell me what's going on and trust me to keep you safe. When you're ready to come down, whether you're at the top or halfway there, just call 'Take,' so I know you're ready. I'll lock the rope so you can let go of the wall, and then I'll yell up, 'Got you.' Then you can call, 'On rappel,' hold onto the rope, and enjoy the ride down. Okay?"

"What if I forget the signals?"

"You won't, but if you do, I'll help you."

She nodded and took a deep breath, sending another wary glance upward as the person on the wall rappelled down. When it was her turn, I tied the knots and loaded the rope into the belay device. Taren watched my hands with a strange look on her face and then smiled.

"What?"

"The rope is red." She pointed out with a shrug. "Our red string of fate."

I was surprised I didn't notice it first. I grinned down at her. "See? I told you everything would be okay."

With renewed confidence, she allowed me to finish the prep work and then stood in front of the wall.

"On belay?" she asked, just like I had instructed.

"Belay is on," I responded to let her know I was ready.

"Climbing."

"Climb is on," I told her.

Taren reached out to the wall and tucked her foot into the first crevice and pulled up. She wobbled a bit, and I pulled the rope a little tighter to let her know she was safe. She straightened herself out and reached for the next grip. As she made her way up the wall, her confidence grew. I wished she could see just how amazing she was tackling the wall despite her fears.

I watched closely as she made slow progress up the wall, clinging to it with every ounce of strength she had. She stopped a few times to catch her breath, but she never gave up. She was about three quarters of the way up when she called out, "Take!"

I pulled the rope with two long strokes to take out the slack before calling, "Got you." Gingerly, she let go of her handholds and then gripped the rope.

"On rappel," she said.

I lifted the locking mechanism just enough to let her slowly descend the wall. She kept her feet out like I had instructed, gently pushing off the wall to control her rappel. I couldn't keep the grin off my face when her feet touched the ground and she turned around with a look of pure delight.

"Oh my god, Alec. That was...amazing. I can't believe I almost made it to the top."

"I knew you could."

Taren threw herself into my arms, and we were a tangle of red rope, carabiners, and kisses.

Behind me I heard a throat clearing. "You forgot to say 'Belay off.'"

Taren and I turned to see a guy glaring at us. He was wearing a Go Climb a Rock shirt and an arrogant expression. I quickly untied the knots in our ropes to release us.

"Now, belay off," I told him as I handed him the rope. The guy flipped me the bird, but I didn't give a shit. Taren trusted me and had conquered her fears. That was the only thing that mattered.

She grabbed my hand. "Let's get the belay out of here." She kept her face straight for all of two seconds before dissolving into giggles.

***

Taren was becoming my new addiction. I couldn't get enough of her. And seeing her tackle my world by taking on that climbing wall? My girl was a winning hand...a fucking royal flush.

I rushed through the front door of my apartment, kicking it closed behind me, before I jogged down the hall to my room.

"What's the rush, princess?" Caz yelled as I passed the kitchen. He stood at the counter, eating brownies right out of the pan with a fork.

"Taren's on her way over," I said as I jogged down the hallway. She'd be here in ten minutes, and I still hadn't taken a shower. Spending the afternoon with my cousin had seemed like a great idea a few days ago, but I had forgotten how easy it was to lose track of time when I was with him.

I shut my door behind me and stripped out of my clothes on the way to the bathroom. Just as I was about to get in the shower, I heard the intercom buzz and when I heard Caz answering it, I jumped into the shower before it was completely warm. Shit. Time to pull off the fastest shower of all time.

I stood under the spray and quickly lathered up as the hot water kicked in and filled the small room with steam. I was washing the last of the soap off my body when I heard my bathroom door open.

"Need a hand?" Taren's voice was as hot and sultry as the air in the room.

I grinned to myself as I imagined her hands sliding over my wet body as she licked the water off me. Even though my promise to her was still intact, her modesty had been shattered months ago. My hands and mouth had memorized her body so perfectly that I knew it as well as I knew my own. Not having sex was surprisingly satisfying. I was still looking forward to the day Taren was ready, but until then, I was happy to explore the alternatives.

"Don't tempt me. We'd never leave if I let your hands help." I shut off the water.

The shower curtain ripped open, and Taren stood on the other side of the tub with my towel in her hand. My eyes took in every inch of her, from her head to her... Shit. She was wearing my favorite boots, and her jeans were tight and hugged her body like a second skin.

"You really don't have a choice in the matter." She leaned against the sink, allowing her eyes to travel across my naked skin. She sucked on her lower lip as she eyed me below the waist before bringing her gaze back to mine. "I'm early for a reason."

She handed me the towel, and I ran it over my body before wrapping it around my waist.

"I love when you talk in riddles." I hooked the neckline of her shirt with my finger and gently pulled her into me for a kiss. When her lips touched mine, I folded my arms around her, pressing her against me. I kissed her like I hadn't seen her in days.

Her hand went to the back of my neck deepening the kiss. When I pulled back and saw the way her shirt clung to her chest, almost transparent from my damp hug, I smiled.

"You're trying to make me lose control." I gave her a quick kiss on her cheek and then grabbed her hand to lead her back into my room. I spun her around to look again at the damage my freshly showered body had done to her outfit. "I got you all wet. What a shame." I cupped her breast in my hand and her nipple hardened under my palm.

"You're an expert at getting me wet." She put her hands on her hips and looked down to watch me fondle her.

"Good point." I leaned in for another kiss, intending it to be innocent.

Before I could pull away, Taren's hands were at the edge of my towel, pulling it away from my waist.

I groaned against her mouth. "You gonna help me get dressed, babe?"

"I told you I was early for a reason." Her fingers and voice were confident. "You always take care of me." She let the backs of her fingers brush against my abs as she leaned in to kiss a water droplet off my shoulder. "Always putting my needs above yours. Everything you do makes me feel safe, or happy, or desired." She looked up at me from where her lips hovered just above my chest. "Now it's my turn."

She let the towel fall to the ground and then dropped to her knees. Our eyes were locked on to one another and she licked her lips. Her hands reached out for my thighs. "I've been wanting to do this for so long." The longing in her confession was like an electrical current straight to my spine.

Holy. Fuck. I took a deep breath. "You don't have to do this, Taren. There's no rush."

Her hands were on my hips, and her thumbs pressed into my skin with gentle circles. "I want to do this. I trust you with my body and my heart."

My chest swelled with emotion, and I had the desperate urge to pull her up into my arms and kiss her to make sure she was real. Even after everything she'd been through in high school because of me, she had faith in me to protect her. That kind of trust wasn't something I took lightly. "I care about you, too."

She grinned and her hands moved across my thighs in an excruciating slow pace. "Just tell me what to do, to make it good for you."

My throat was dry, and I swallowed. "I promise you that whatever you do will be fucking brilliant." My voice was low and laced with so much need I could barely get the words out.

She smiled and her palms slid up my thighs. Her fingers spread wide as she pressed her hands up my sides, across my abs, and then down. Taren was always beautiful and brilliant, but seeing her exposed and vulnerable in front of me was almost enough to undo me.

She wrapped her hand around me, licking her lips once more before her mouth drew me in. Hot. Wet. Tight. Perfect. I gripped the back of the chair behind me, holding on so tight the plastic dug into my palm. My hips wanted to thrust forward so I could plunge deeper inside her mouth, but I stayed still. I ran my fingertips underneath her jaw and slid my thumb across her cheek in adoration.

Fuck. Taren's mouth was heaven on earth. Her eyes cut up to me briefly as if asking for direction. I moved my hips in and out a bit. "If it's tight and wet, babe, it'll feel good." I ran the back of my fingers down her hairline.

She pulled back, dragging her hand and lips along me in a slick, sucking motion as she kept her eyes on me the entire time. I inhaled sharply, my breath hissing through my teeth in its rush to reach my chest. The movement of my hips urged her on, and she soon found a rhythm. Taking lead from the way my moans tumbled out of me, she sucked and stroked just the way I liked it.

"So good." I groaned. I couldn't stop staring between us, where I disappeared into her fist and mouth over and over again. Reality was so much better than anything I'd imagined. The fact that she wanted to do this lit me like a fuse, and my body was on edge, ready to detonate.

I moved my hands to the back of her head, and she closed her eyes, moaning when my fingertips slipped into her hair. Her tiny sounds vibrated along my bones, and sparks of lust and need shot through my body. *Christ.* Did she realize how much she was testing my willpower? I threaded my fingers into her hair, gripping it because I had to hold on to something so I wouldn't lose control.

Taren's hands were on my hips again, sliding around to my ass. She pulled my hips in to meet the plunge of her lips, and my willpower crumbled as my hunger took over. I thrust into her mouth with as much restraint as I could muster. She groaned and when her eyelashes fluttered open and she looked at me, I was gone.

Her fingers dug into my skin, holding on as our movements sped up. When I felt the wave of my release rushing up my spine, I pulled out and my hand replaced her mouth. "Fuck. Taren." Her name left my throat in a groan. She watched, greedily, her lips still wet, as my body shuddered and jerked as I came in my hand. After a moment, I dropped down to my knees in front of her. She grabbed my discarded towel and gently cleaned me off while I pressed light kisses all over her face.

She was smiling at me, and after she tossed the towel aside, I pulled her in for a deeper kiss.

"Good?" she asked between kisses.

"No. Not good. Fucking brilliant."

Her face brightened with mischief. "Maybe I should thank Julie for making me watch all those videos." Her eyebrows arched up in question. "She was right. Research was a good idea."

I slid my hand around the back of her neck and pulled her forward until our mouths were almost touching. "Are you telling me that sweet Taren Richards studied porn so she could give her boyfriend a kickass blowjob?" Her lips pulled back in a sassy smile, and I kissed her. "I feel like I should be jealous. You were looking at another dude's dick, but I'm still too turned on to care."

She laughed and ran her hands up my chest. "If it helps, I can tell you I never want to see those videos again." She looked down between us and licked her lips. "I want to do that again soon, though."

My head dropped back, and I groaned. "You're killing me, woman. What did I do to deserve this torture?"

Taren giggled and pressed a kiss to my chest. "You make me so happy. Just like I always knew you would."

I lifted her chin and kissed her mouth, slow and sweet. Taren was my new addiction. We might be a long shot, but she was worth the gamble.

***

Three days. That's how long it had been since I'd seen Taren. I had so many part-time jobs I couldn't remember where I was going half the time. The thought crossed my mind that I should probably head home and catch up on sleep or studying, but my need to see Taren was an itch that couldn't be denied. I pulled out my phone to text her.

Me: I don't have to work tonight. Want to hang out? We could get dinner.

I stood outside the Student Union and leaned on a bike rack, waiting for her to respond. My phone pinged with a message a few seconds later.

Taren: :(I wish I could. I have to study tonight. I have a huge exam tomorrow.

Frustration and need clawed through my chest. I had class with her in the morning, but I didn't want to wait that long. I wanted to see her tonight.

Me: Come to my place. You can study there.

Taren: Ha! We both know the only thing I'd be studying at your place is your naked ass.

I smiled and chuckled to myself.

Me: Perfect. I accept.

The typing icon blinked and a few seconds later the screen was filled with sad emoticons.

Taren: You don't play fair. I really need to study. This exam is worth half my grade. I'll make it up to you tomorrow, I promise.

The typing icon blinked again.

Taren: I miss you.

I pushed off the bike rack and snatched my backpack off the ground, slinging it over my shoulder in frustration before typing my response.

Me: Ditto.

I started down Campus Drive toward my apartment and a Taren-free night. I shook my head in disappointment. Three nights had been too long. I understood that she needed to study and I respected how hard she worked for her grades. But three nights?

Screw it. I made a sudden right hand turn to cross the street. She was too busy to come to me, but she never said I couldn't come see her. I was a fucking genius. Problem solved. I'd pick up a pizza and bring her dinner. Pizza and a back massage while she studied, how could she say no to that?

***

Jesus Christ. I'd never been to Taren's sorority house before and I didn't expect it to be so nice. Standing on her front porch, ringing the doorbell, I felt like a ratty ass pizza delivery guy. With huge columns and a classy brick front, her house looked like a mansion. I was still in my workout clothes, holding a greasy carryout box.

The door opened, and I half expected to see a butler. Instead, a girl wearing a Tri-Gam shirt stood in the doorway. She was staring at the pizza box and had a horrified expression on her face.

"Can I help you?" Her voice was hesitant like I was lost and needed directions. When she managed to stop staring at the pizza like it was going to bite her, she looked up at me. Her eyes widened in surprise. She did a quick scan of my body and then smiled, running her finger along the neckline of the low cut shirt she was wearing. "We didn't order a pizza."

"I'm actually here to see Taren." I looked through the open doorway and could see shiny hardwood floors and elegant furniture. The place looked like a five-star hotel.

"Oh." The girl pouted and sighed. "Let me get her for you. We're just having a chapter meeting." She opened the door wider and let me into the foyer. "I'll be right back."

Chapter meeting? I thought Taren was studying. The girl walked around the corner into the next room where I could hear girls chattering.

"Taren, you have a visitor." The sound of voices died down.

"Who is it?" Taren sounded confused.

Why would she be confused? Who else would be visiting her? I clenched my jaw in annoyance.

"Shoot. I forgot to ask his name. I think it's a pizza delivery guy." The girl's answer came out like a question.

"Pizza?" One of the other girls said the word like it was a curse. "Taren, that's like contraband. You can't bring that in here! I don't care how stressful studying is."

Taren laughed. "I didn't order a pizza, Jules. Let me go see what's up. I'll be right back. Go on without me, I'll catch up later."

Footsteps echoed across the floor, and when Taren rounded the corner, the sight of her took my breath away. She was wearing a pink tank and shorts, and her hair was in a loose braid. She didn't look like the girl you took out bar hopping; she looked like the girl you wrapped yourself around on a lazy Sunday morning.

"Alec?" She stopped, and her hand reached for her neck, rubbing it nervously. "What are you doing here?" Her eyebrows pulled together, and she looked from the pizza box to my face. "And why do you have pizza?"

"Since you couldn't go out to dinner, I thought I'd bring it to you." My eyes made a quick scan of my surroundings before settling back on Taren. The girls in this house probably ate gourmet meals. What was I thinking bringing a fucking pizza?

Taren rubbed her arm, and her face twisted with apology as she slowly walked toward me. "We already ate. The chef serves dinner at six."

A fucking chef? Of course they had a fucking chef. This place was like the Ritz Carlton. I took a deep breath and rubbed the back of my neck, forcing out a laugh. "Yeah. I guess pizza was a bad idea." I cleared my throat, hating that she looked so uncomfortable. My driving thought had been to see her, but now that I was there and she wasn't jumping into my arms with happiness to see me, I didn't know what to do. I felt so...out of place.

As if coming to her senses, Taren grabbed my free hand and twisted her fingers between mine as she plastered a smile on her face. "No. It was really sweet."

"So, a chapter meeting?" I nodded toward the room.

She looked over her shoulder, and her hand flew up to tuck her hair back. "Yeah. We have them once a week to go over house stuff. They're really boring." She squeezed my hand. "Hopefully it doesn't last much longer because I really do need to study, and I'm starting to freak out a little."

"Is that your way of kindly telling me to get lost?" I grinned at her and pulled her hand up between us so I could kiss the backs of her fingers.

Her eyes opened wide. "No! You know I'd really rather spend time with you." Her thumb ran across the back of my hand, and her bottom lip pouted out. I wanted to suck on that lip. I wanted to push her up against the fancy ass wallpaper and kiss her until she forgot all about her meeting and studying.

"Time with me, huh?" I slid the back of her hands across my lips, and her eyes drifted shut. "Then I guess it's a good thing I took off work Friday night so I can take my girl on an actual date. Jon told me about this great restaurant in National Harbor."

Taren's eyes flew open. "Friday night?" The words were almost panicked.

I nipped her thumb between my teeth. "You can wait that long can't you?"

Her expression fell, and she bit the corner of her lip. "I can't on Friday. I'm so sorry." She shifted and took a deep breath, and her eyes couldn't meet mine. "I already committed to going to a happy hour that night with my sisters." She looked over her shoulder toward the room she'd come from.

My arm dropped, and our hands hung between us as our fingers barely linked together. I felt like she'd punched me in the chest. She turned back to face me and I stared at the wall behind her.

"Oh." My voice caught in my throat, and my lungs burned with the need to take another breath. My response hung in the air between us, icy and distant. I knew that she attended social events with her sisters when I was working. Did I expect her to change her plans just because I didn't have any?

Yes. That's exactly what I expected, and that irritated me.

She tightened her grip on my fingers. "Can you get off another night? I'd love to go to the National Harbor with you. Having Alec Hart all to myself for a romantic date would be just the way to celebrate acing my test." Her eyes begged me to forgive her, and my chest loosened.

I forced myself to smile. "Sure. I'll see you tomorrow at class, and we'll pick another night."

I leaned in to give her a light kiss, and her hand wrapped around my neck. The heat of her mouth and the sweep of her tongue teased me. I almost threw her over my shoulder so I could go find the first empty room.

Instead, I pulled back and ran my thumb over her bottom lip. "I better let you go so you can finish your meeting and get back to studying." She pouted, and I gave her one more kiss. "Good luck on your test, babe."

Her smile was sad, and I turned to leave her house with the pizza box still in hand. "Alec." The desperation in Taren's voice forced me to turn. She was standing in the doorway with her arms hanging at her side like she wanted to reach out and beg me to stay. All she had to do was say so and I would. "Thank you for coming to surprise me. I..." She paused as if she wanted to say something but couldn't. "I'll see you tomorrow in class."

I nodded and flashed her a smile. I descended the steps and then as I made my way up the sidewalk, I heard the door close. I huffed out a breath and opened the box to pull out a slice of pizza.

What a shitty way to end the night. On the bright side, though, I had an entire pizza to myself. That is, if I could finish it before I got back to my place and Caz found it. I followed the sidewalk away from the Graham Cracker, where Taren's house was located, and made my way past Frat Row.

I hadn't gone far when a familiar voice yelled to me. "Yo! Bouncer boy. Where you heading?"

Hell, this night just got better and better. I looked up to see Pickles and a few of his friends heading toward me, likely on their way to a party. I ignored him and moved to the side to walk around him.

"I haven't seen you at The Shell," he taunted. "Are you a delivery boy now? Talk about a downgrade." He laughed, and his friends joined in.

"Fuck you, Pickles." I said the words with indifference, but I wanted a fight.

"No thanks. I'll leave that to Taren."

Every muscle in my body tensed and the edge of the pizza box flattened where I crushed it in my fist. I turned around slowly to glare at him. "Shut up, asshole." I took a step toward him. "Don't talk to her. Don't think about her. Don't even look at her. She's off limits to you." My heart pounded against my ribs, begging my fists to shut him up permanently.

Pickles chuckled and tucked his hands into his pockets. "Off limits? Pretty hard to do that when we'll be partying together Friday. It's always a happy hour when Taren's around."

My head tilted against my will, and I knew the moment when he realized he'd gotten to me. She was going to happy hour with this bag of dicks instead of going out with me? I didn't care if she made a promise to her sisters. I wasn't okay with the idea of her hanging out with Pickles.

"Aw. Didn't she tell you?" His forehead creased in mock sadness. "I guess she didn't want you to know. I'm her dirty little secret." My eyes squinted, and his face lit up when he noticed. "Don't worry, buddy." He reached out and clapped me on the shoulder, and I fisted my hand to keep from reaching out and ripping his fucking arm out of its socket. "I'll keep my eye on her for you." He winked and then turned around to walk away with his friends.

When he looked back over his shoulder at me, the grin he gave me said, "I win, fucker." My body was so rigid with fury I was afraid that if I moved, I would go on a rampage and destroy everything I touched.

I watched him until he disappeared, and then I threw the entire pizza into the nearest trash can. Jogging across the road, I headed for the stadium steps where I knew I could get some release.

I needed to chase my demons away before I did something I'd regret.

Chapter 23

Taren

I slid into the seat next to Alec's. "Hey, you." I kissed him on the cheek and his jaw tensed under my lips. *What the hell?* We looked forward to Tuesday morning seminar all week. This was our only class together this semester, and probably the last one we would share. For our final two years of college, every other course we took would be required for our majors.

"What's wrong?" I looked around the room. The teaching assistant was passing out papers, and neighboring students were focused on their phones or completing the daily crossword in the campus newspaper. What could possibly have pissed him off?

Alec turned to face me with a stony expression. My stomach fell to my feet. Had I done something wrong? He seemed fine when he left last night.

"You never mentioned spending happy hour with Pickles." A muscle twitched in his jaw as he clenched his teeth.

Crap. Until he mentioned Pickles' name, I'd forgotten that he'd be at the happy hour with my sisters. I bounced my knee, nervous energy coursing through me. "I'm sorry. I knew we had a happy hour with

Delta Epsilon, but I didn't even think about Pickles. I avoid him like the plague." I reached over and rubbed Alec's forearm.

He scowled and squeezed his hand into a fist. "Why would you want to go anywhere Pickles will be? He cheated on you. He's a dick. I don't want you anywhere near him."

I placed my hand on his fist and pulled his fingers apart so that I could slide mine in between his. "He is a dick. That's why I hadn't given him a second thought. I promised my sisters I would go to happy hour, and I don't want to ditch them. I'll just have a few drinks and talk with the girls. There'll be no interaction with Pickles at all." His shoulders relaxed, but he looked up at the ceiling. "Alec, look at me. Please."

His eyes met mine, and his mouth twisted to the side.

"You don't have to worry about him. He never crosses my mind. You're the only guy on my mind. You're the only one I want to kiss or touch." I took a deep breath. "Or taste." My body tingled from the memories my words conjured. Alec's pupils enlarged, and his lips parted. "Now that I have you"—I shook my head and grinned—"There's no room for anyone else in my head or my heart. Believe me."

Alec stared at me for a long minute and then leaned forward to press his lips to mine. His tongue darted out, sweeping into my mouth for a brief second. I groaned and felt him smile in return. He pressed his forehead to mine and whispered, "I believe you, babe. It just makes me crazy to have to share any part of you with him. I can't get enough of you."

Just like that the two hour seminar that had been one of my favorites became a very painful exercise in restraint.

***

"What do you mean you're only going for an hour?" Julie stomped her foot. Her clunky heel made a surprisingly loud sound on the hardwood floor of our room.

Alexis rolled her eyes. "I have to study. I always have to study. I sound like a damn broken record." She leaned closer to the mirror and dabbed on a light pink lip gloss. "Organic Chemistry is meant to weed out all the lazy asses who won't hack it in med school." She smacked her lips together and stood up straight. "I refuse to be weeded out."

I winked at her and then sobered my face for Julie. "I might not stay the whole time either. Alec has off tonight. I think I might leave early to spend some time with him."

Alexis sat on the chair and fixed the strap on her sandal. "Is Alec okay with you going to a party with Pickles?"

No. No he's not. "Well…"

"Don't even tell me you are going to be one of *those* girls. Everything is fine and dandy until you meet some guy and then you ditch us to hang out with him all the time." Julie shook her head and pressed her lips into a tight line.

I rubbed lotion on my hands and arms. "I'm not ditching you. I'm going to happy hour, just like I promised, but Alec is important to me, too. I can understand why he doesn't like the idea of me hanging out or drinking where Pickles is going to be."

"Taren, you're in a sorority. You're going to be drinking with guys. This is what I'm talking about. Alec doesn't understand Greek life." Julie placed her hands on her hips. Alexis stood up, looking between the two of us with a frown.

Irritation crawled under my skin, but I tried to remember that Julie had always been on my side. "No, he doesn't understand why Tri-Gam is so important to me, but the Acroletes are a mystery to me, too. The important thing is that we're trying to understand one another and learn to live with our differences."

"Your lives are completely opposite. Don't you think that lack of understanding is a pretty big deal?"

"We understand each other in the ways that matter. He's so good to me, Jules." I slung my arm around her shoulder and squeezed. "Maybe you just need a little time to get to know him better."

Julie looked at Alexis who nodded encouragingly. Julie rolled her eyes. "Okay, fine. But only if you promise there will be no juggling."

I burst out laughing and hugged her. "No juggling, but I do have to warn you about his friend, Caz."

***

"Hit me!" Pickles bellowed and slammed his glass on the bar. The group of rowdy fraternity brothers surrounding him cheered, egging him on.

Alexis sighed and glanced at her watch. "I'm sorry, Taren. I'm going to head out. I have a lot to do, and I've had about as much of *that* as I can take." She hooked her thumb behind her to where I could hear Pickles harassing the bartender to hurry.

I looked toward Pickles to find he was already staring at me with a sloppy smile on his face. He'd reached the level of drunk where he would think it was appropriate to paw at me. Time to go. I stood up from my barstool. "I'm out, too."

She frowned. "Jules is going to be pissed we're leaving at the same time."

"Nah, she's lip-deep in a new flirtationship. Her happy hour is getting happier by the minute." Alexis giggled, and I grabbed her hand. We wove our way through the crowd to hug our friend goodbye.

We left the bar, and Alexis was shaking her head as the door swung closed behind us. "I wonder how long that one will last?"

I snorted. "If he lasts longer than two weeks it'll be a record." I hooked my arm through Alexis'. "What about you? Are you and Asher serious?"

She looked up at me with a sad smile. "The only thing I'm serious about is school. I don't have time for a love life."

We walked along the sidewalk, but I stopped when Alexis turned to go toward our house. "I'm going to see Alec. I'll be back later." I couldn't keep the grin off my face, and I felt bad because Alexis deserved to have the kind of happiness I had with Alec.

Alexis pinched her eyebrows together. "How do you know he doesn't already have plans?"

"He said he was studying. He always studies at his place." I waved and headed for the apartment complex where Alec lived. The walk was short, and I got lucky enough to be able to follow a group of people into the lobby so I didn't have to buzz in. I rode the elevator up to his floor, and excitement grew in my chest as I imagined the look on his face when he answered the door.

The television was loud coming from inside the apartment, and I had to knock a few times before the door finally swung open. When Caz saw me, the goofy smile he was wearing fell, and he frowned at me.

"Donuts?" He opened the door wider and looked around me to find only empty hallway. "What are you doing here? I thought you and Alec were going to the National Harbor."

My head tilted in confusion. "No. I had a happy hour with my sorority tonight." The words came out slow and unsure. Why would Alec tell Caz we had a date? "I left the party early. Alec told me he'd be studying so I came to see him."

Jon appeared behind Caz. "He's studying at the library."

Caz whirled around to glare at Jon. "I thought he took the night off to take Donuts on a date?" Then he turned his glare on me. "You stood him up for happy hour?"

Guilt gnawed at my stomach, even though I hadn't done anything wrong. "No. It wasn't like that. I already had plans when he asked me out." Why was I explaining this to Caz? My relationship with Alec was none of his business. "Which library did he go to?" I asked Jon.

"McKeldin. But he won't be there much longer. He just texted to see if we wanted to meet up with him for racquetball." Jon held up his phone.

Caz's face brightened, and he backed away from the door. "Fuck'n A. He deserves an ass kicking. Where the hell did I leave my racquet?"

My excitement at seeing my boyfriend sputtered and died as Caz disappeared into the apartment. Even though Alexis had mentioned it, I hadn't expected Alec to have plans. My shoulders sagged as I backed away from the door. "Okay. Thanks, Jon. I guess I'll call him later." I turned to walk down the hallway.

"Taren?" I looked over my shoulder to see Jon leaning against the doorjamb with a serious expression on his face.

I turned and wrapped my arms across my chest, wondering if he was going to give me some sort of lecture on my choice to spend time with my sisters. "Yeah?

He sighed and shook his head. "Do you know where the racquetball courts are?"

"The lower level of the building where you practice, right?" Hope bloomed in my chest.

Jon nodded. "He took the night off to be with you." He gave me a suggestive arch of his eyebrow and then pushed off the wall and went inside his apartment, closing the door behind him.

I nearly ran down the hallway to the elevator.

***

The gym was almost empty as I made my way to the racquetball courts. Small doors that led to each court lined both sides of the hall. Only one of the rooms had any sounds coming from it, and I peeked through the tiny window to see Alec punishing a tiny blue ball as he slammed it against the wall. He'd taken his shirt off, and his muscles flexed and strained as he chased the ball down, crushing it with each swing of his racquet. He was so delicious to watch that for a moment, I'd forgotten the reason I'd come.

After drooling for a few minutes, I pushed the door open and ducked as I stepped into the room. "What did that ball ever do to you?"

Alec spun around, the ball forgotten as it continued to bounce around the room. The surprise on his face morphed into appreciation as he took in my outfit. He stalked across the room, and when he stopped in front of me, he was so close I could have licked his chest. God, I wanted to.

He placed his racquet behind my waist and used it to pull me against him. His skin was hot, and I thought I might melt into a puddle at his feet. "You're here." He grinned. "This is so much better than racquetball." He dipped his head down to my shoulder and nuzzled his lips against my neck.

My head tilted back as a pleased sigh echoed in my throat. "I couldn't bear the thought of not seeing you tonight."

"Ditto," he mumbled against my skin.

"Want to get out of here? I want to show you something." I gasped as he nibbled the soft skin of my neck. "And I got dinner." The last few words were breathless as I jiggled the bag of food I'd bought.

"I'm only hungry for you." He kissed me on the lips, and then he smiled when his stomach growled. "But whatever you got smells fucking delicious. I guess I'll just have to have you for dessert."

I laughed and pushed him away when he tried to dive back in for a kiss. "Come on. No dessert unless you eat your dinner like a good boy."

Alec groaned but went to the corner of the court and grabbed his shirt. He put it on and then grabbed my hand, sliding his fingers between mine.

We found a nearby bench and I laid out a spread of subs and sodas. As we ate, I looked up at the sky. Noise from nearby traffic reminded me that Route One was close, but here, in this moment with Alec, I felt secluded. I felt a peace I'd never known.

"So where are you taking me?" he asked as he ate the last bite of his sub. We tossed our trash into a nearby can and his fingers found mine again.

"I don't want to ruin the surprise." I rubbed the inside of his palm with my thumb, loving it when he squeezed my hand tighter in response.

"You couldn't surprise me anymore than you did when you walked through that door. You have no idea how much I needed to see you tonight." He pulled me to him and placed a lingering kiss on my lips, stealing my breath with the demanding heat of his mouth and tongue.

"I have some idea." I exhaled a pleased moan.

He laughed and released me so we could keep walking. "Did you have fun hanging out with...your sisters?" His jaw tensed, and he looked straight ahead. I could hear the unspoken words. He was worried about Pickles.

"I did, but I'm glad I'm here with you now." I squeezed his hand, and we walked in comfortable silence across campus. The darkness made it feel as if we were in our own little world.

"Here we are." I led him off the sidewalk and down the hill to the small dark tunnel that went under Regents Road near the chapel. The edges of the tunnel were overgrown with weeds and ivy so that it was almost hidden. Once we stood in the opening of the tunnel, I turned to face him, and his arm circled my waist, pulling me close.

He reached up with the other hand and tucked my hair behind my ear before leaning down for a kiss. "Where are we?" Each word was punctuated with the gentle press of his lips.

"This is the kissing tunnel." I tilted my head up so I could see his expression. He gazed down at me with such adoration that my knees almost buckled. I couldn't believe I almost missed out on this tonight. "It's supposed to be one of the most romantic spots on campus."

"The kissing tunnel?" His smile was dangerous as he slid both hands into my hair and lowered his mouth until it hovered just above mine. "I love that you came to find me tonight." His lips descended, smoldering against mine. "I love that you brought me here." His mouth branded a trail along my jaw to my ear. "And I'm going to love kissing every part of your body until you beg me to never stop."

He pulled me close, and as he kissed me in the moonlight, my soul felt like it was lodged in my throat. My heart beat erratically because with every part of me, I was sure.

I know it. I love him. I love Alec Hart.

Chapter 24

Alec

I wrapped the grips around my hands and Caz shoved his hands into the chalk bucket next to me.

"How's Donuts?" Caz's tone was serious, and my eyebrows pulled together as I looked down at him.

"Good." The word was short and clipped because I had the sense I wasn't going to like his train of thought.

He rubbed his hands together, spreading the chalk over his palms. "Do you think she's going to choose you?" He met my eyes, and his jaw tensed.

"What the hell is that supposed to mean?" Anger laced my words.

He slapped his hands together in a cloud of chalk dust. "You planned a date night, and she ditched you for happy hour."

"You don't know what you're talking about."

"Really? At some point she's going to have to choose between her party life and her drug-free boyfriend. Do you think she's going to choose you?" He walked between the parallel bars and reached up to grip one as he stared at me.

"I'm not asking her to choose. She doesn't have to." I glared at him.

"I hope you're right." He turned away from me.

I bit back the words that I wanted to say, that on Friday she did choose me and that was enough. Caz had no idea what he was talking about. I looked over at him, ready to tell him so when I remembered the truth: Taren came to see me after she'd already been to happy hour.

Had she really chosen me or had she just made room for me in her busy party schedule?

Fuck. Caz's comments were like poison, worming their way into my brain and planting doubt I didn't need.

***

We grabbed a quick dinner at Marathon Deli, and then I took Taren on the second part of our date, which was back on the other side of campus. When we arrived at the building where the Acroletes' practice was held, she looked at me strangely.

"I thought we were going back to your apartment. Don't tell me you want to play racquetball instead?" She pouted, and I leaned over to suck her bottom lip between mine in a gentle kiss.

I pulled back and grinned. "Just a quick stop in here. It'll be fun."

She tucked herself under my arm and let me lead her inside the building. I pulled Caz's duplicate key out of my pocket and unlocked the side door to the gym.

"They let you have a key?" Taren's eyes widened in surprise. "I can't believe they give everyone a key."

"This is Caz's actually. And he doesn't know I have it." I winked at her and led her into the gym.

"Huh. Well that actually makes less sense. Out of anyone, I can't believe they gave Caz a key." She frowned in disbelief.

"He never told me how he got it, but I seriously doubt anyone gave it to him. Follow me."

I led Taren into the gym, and I saw her glance around at all the equipment. I remembered the first time I came to the gym, having no idea what the Acroletes were all about. She gasped when we entered the trampoline room.

"Want to?" I asked her, gesturing to the first one.

She flashed me a giddy smile and then hurried up the steps and onto a bed.

"Don't jump too high at first." I followed her up the steps. "These are a lot more powerful than the backyard variety."

Taren jumped, and I sat down on the mat to watch her. She took small bounces, jumping in the air, giddy and breathless. I was content to watch her, happy that she was in my world and enjoying it.

"This is so much fun!" she exclaimed. "Come jump with me."

I was a smart man. No way could I resist her. When I walked onto the webbed bed, I pulled Taren into my arms and kissed her. We were wrapped around each other. The sweet touch of her lips transformed into kisses that were insistent, demanding, and urgent.

"I want you." She was breathless as she bounced and kissed me feverishly.

My body ignited as my mind raced with dangerous thoughts. I wanted her here in this room. A goddamn fantasy come to life.

"I want you, too. I always want you." I pulled us down to lay on the trampoline and pushed her knees apart, settling between her legs. I buried my face in her neck, kissing and licking along her shoulder until goose bumps rose on her arms. She arched, pressing her body into me. When my hips followed hers back down, the trampoline dipped, rocking our bodies into a delicious friction. I felt like a fuse about to blow. Hooking up on the trampoline was suddenly my new favorite sport.

"I need you, Alec." Her voice was pleading as she pulled her hands out of my grasp and ran them inside my shirt and across my skin.

I rose up on my knees, my heart hammering with the sight of her spread beneath me, and begging for my touch. The trampoline still rocked gently beneath us. I held her gaze as my hands slid under her shirt, pushing it up past her ribs. When my fingers reached the lace of her bra, her eyes flared with lust before fluttering shut.

"Every inch of you is so fucking soft it makes me crazy." I growled as I pushed her shirt up and over her head and then bent to kiss the sweet skin between her breasts.

I kissed my way down her stomach, loving the way her breath caught in her throat with every touch of my tongue on her skin. When I got to her jeans, I took the edge of the waistband in my teeth and pulled until she opened her eyes and pushed up on her elbows to look at me.

I hooked my finger in the waistband. "I'm going to take these off, and then I'm going to see how sweet you really taste." I said it like a command, and her mouth fell open with a surprised intake of breath. When I raised my eyebrows in question, she nodded, and I held her gaze for a moment as her cheeks flushed.

She watched as I unbuttoned her jeans and slowly pulled them down her legs. I kissed my way from her thighs to her ankles, and the tremors my lips caused on her skin sent fire racing through my limbs. Every part of my body was filled with need for her. To touch. To taste. To have.

When I pulled her panties off, she pressed her legs together, and I could almost see the blush creeping along her entire body. I placed my hands on her knees and pushed them open with gentle pressure.

"Trust me, babe. I want to see all of you." My hands slid down her thighs, and when I bent down so that my breath fanned across her, she shuddered. That little movement made me so hard, I had to take a deep breath to calm the fuck down.

She moaned quietly when I swept my fingers across her slick skin. The minute my tongue touched her, her body bowed off the trampoline as she called my name. In that moment, I felt like a starving man. I'd never get enough of the taste of her or the way she responded to me.

I licked her with slow teasing strokes of my tongue, forcing moans out of her. I pushed two fingers into her as I sucked and licked the skin just above where my fingers were. Her hands gripped my hair as if she needed to hold on to keep from flying away.

My tongue flickered over her as my fingers moved in and out. Her hips rocked up into me as if unable to control the bucking of her body and the springs squeaked with her frenzied movements.

"I'm so close. I'm so close, Alec." The words were a chant that I didn't think I'd ever get out of my head.

When I groaned against her, her hips shot off the webbed bed, pressing against my lips. She cried out as she came, and then her body fell limp against the trampoline.

I collapsed next to her, pulling her into my arms and hooking my legs around hers.

Our hands ran over each other in soothing caresses as we lay together. We kissed unhurriedly, our bodies continuing to feed the small rock of the trampoline. I pulled back to look at her, and she smiled at me, causing my heart to trip over itself.

"These are mine." I ran my thumb over her lips, and her smile was lazy as she closed her eyes. "These are mine." My hand cupped one breast and then the other as I skimmed her nipples with my thumb and she giggled. "This is mine." My hand rested at the top of her thighs, and my finger slipped along the wet seam between her legs. She sighed and laid her head against my chest. "And this...this is mine." My hand flattened over her heart, and she lifted her head to meet my gaze.

"Yes." She barely whispered the word, but I heard it.

Taren Richards was mine. She was the fucking love of my life.

Chapter 25

Taren

"A hot dog-eating contest?" William grinned and then took a long drink of his juice. We headed out of the sandwich shop and waited to cross Route One.

I nodded and smiled. "Yes, sir." The light turned red and we walked back onto campus. Spring was my favorite time of year at College Park. Spring break was just around the corner, and flowers bloomed all around us. On days like today when the weather was on the warm side, students were laying all over the grass on the mall, sunbathing and most likely skipping classes.

"I think I would like that." He took another sip of the juice he had bought for his trip home.

"Well, I lost miserably. I barely ate one and none of the girls could eat even half as much as the guys." I never quite understood the allure of eating contests. Watching people shove food down their throat made me feel ill. Luckily, William was up for a much-needed, calorie-burning, walk outside today.

"And why were you doing this, Miss Taren?" William stopped to pick a dandelion, and then he handed it to me, his eyes sparkling.

"Make a wish."

I closed my eyes and thought. My only wish was to slow time. Everything was as it should be right now. My life was a perfect balance. I still went out with my sorority sisters a few times a week, and I looked forward to every moment I got to spend with Alec. He was amazing and owned every piece of my heart. We hadn't said any declarations of love yet, but with every smile, word, and touch, he showed me how important I was to him. I couldn't forget about William. My time with him was just as important.

Taking a deep breath, I opened my eyes and blew the fragments of the dandelion into the air.

William nudged my arm with his elbow. "Bet you didn't wish for a hot dog!" He threw his head back and laughed, murmuring to himself, "Good one, Willy, good one. Yup, yup."

I placed my hand on his arm. My eyes widened and eyebrows lifted. "Willy? I thought you were going by Billy now? Are you changing your name on me again?"

"Billy is fun; that is true, but Willy is more...friendly. I would want to be friends with Willy." He nodded as he spoke, and I bit my lip to hold back my grin.

"I'd be your friend no matter what your name was." We walked again, heading toward the Student Union.

"Tell me again about the hot dogs. Why did your friends eat so many?"

I hooked my arm in his and sighed. "It was a stupid contest that's part of Greek Week, Willy. Every spring the Greeks get together and play games, kind of like the Olympics. You've seen the Olympics before, right?"

He nodded.

"Well, fraternities and sororities pair up in teams and compete against each other." This year's theme for Greek Week was based on the television show Survivor. The goal was to outwit, outlast, and out-Greek. Corny, but at least this theme was better than the one chosen for Homecoming.

"I see. Do you win money?"

I shook my head and pressed my lips together to suppress my giggle.

"A prize?" he asked, cocking his head to the side.

"Nope, no money or prizes. I think there might be a trophy, though." William stopped walking, and I turned to face him.

"You do these things for a trophy?" William's brows were smashed together.

"Well, people really try to win so they can say they won. That they're the best." I pointed toward the semi-circle of grass in front of the U-shaped gathering of fraternity houses. An obstacle course was being set up for tomorrow's games and a slip and slide was being hosed down. The smell of highly processed meat still lingered in the air. "That's where we'll be doing an obstacle course tomorrow."

"That looks like it might be fun." William shrugged.

"Have you ever competed in something just for fun?" I asked, running my finger along my lip.

He put his hands in the front pockets of his pants as he studied the ground. "No. I have never been part of a team or anything. But my mom always said you can be a winner by doing something for someone else. She said I am a winner because I help people." William looked into my eyes, uncertainty etched across his face.

"You know what, Willy? Your mom is right. You're definitely a winner, and I won the day I got you for a buddy, that's for sure." When he smiled, happiness filled my chest, and I couldn't keep from grinning back at him.

"How is your fellow? Are you still happy?"

I was happy. Truly and fully happy. "More than I've ever been, Willy." I slipped my hand into his big gruff one, and we turned back toward the Union.

"Then I think we both won, Miss Taren."

***

The door to Alec's bathroom opened, and he came out, his half-naked body illuminated by the light behind him. He flipped the switch, depriving me of the one view I'd never get tired of seeing.

"Wait, can you turn the light on for a minute?" I leaned up on my elbow. "I can't find my—"

The light switched back on, and I grinned as I stared at my favorite view again. "There you are."

Alec laughed as my eyes feasted on every bare spot of his muscular chest and arms. "I love when you're naughty."

My heart skipped a beat when he said love. I loved him. I loved everything about him. I just wasn't brave enough to admit it to him yet. He flipped the light off again, and the bed dipped as he pounced on the mattress. He was propped up above me. His arms and legs, on either side of my body, caged me in. I could barely see him in the darkness, but I couldn't miss the hunger in his eyes.

Reaching up I played with the strands of hair that hung on his forehead. "When can I see you perform again?"

"You gonna stay the whole time?" He cocked an eyebrow at me.

I looked toward the wall. "I'm sorr…"

He cut me off with a chaste kiss. "I was teasing. No more apologies. The school visits stopped last week. Our last performance for the season is Friday night at the Xfinity center." He placed small kisses down my neck, and my pulse quickened. "I was hoping you'd come."

"I do love to come." I giggled.

He hung his head and groaned. "You make being good so hard."

I frowned. "Is it hard?" I moved my hand to cup him, and he made a pleased sound in the back of his throat. He was indeed, hard. "Seriously, though, I wouldn't miss seeing you perform. Of course, I'll be there." I continued to stroke him over top of his boxers, and his eyelids became heavy.

He growled. "I don't want you to stop doing that…ever… but I should get a few hours of sleep before work tomorrow."

My chest tightened. I was so selfish when it came to our time together. No one worked harder than Alec, and then I demanded even more of his time.

I stuck my lower lip out in a pout. "I know. I just couldn't resist one last touch." I squeezed him gently, and he pushed his hips into my hand. "Okay, I'm done now." I flipped over, turning my back to him and curling up with a pillow, on my side.

"Like hell you are." He climbed over me and kissed me so that I could feel the smile he was wearing. He hooked his hand under my knee and wrapped my leg around his waist. Then he pushed his hips against me to prove that he was wide awake.

Lucky me.

Alec's hands framed my face. His thumbs traced over my lips from the center to the edges. "I never knew I could be this happy." His thumbs stopped at the edges of my mouth, and he kissed me again. My heart raced, and my skin burned hot. I wanted him. I wanted it all with him.

"Alec—" I gulped in a breath, my mouth now dry. "I'm ready.

Now. Tonight." I placed my hand over his heart and felt the rapid beating beneath my fingertips.

Alec's eyes blazed, and he stilled, holding his breath and searching my face. "Are you sure you're ready?" His voice was gravelly, and the sound made me want to wrap my legs around him.

I'd been thinking about this for weeks. Nothing had ever felt more right than Alec being my first, and if I was really lucky, my only. "I've never been more sure about anything. You know I trust you completely."

Alec closed his eyes, and the veins in his neck stood out, corded and tight. Opening his eyes, he kissed my lips. "I'm going to take care of you, babe. I promise."

My stomach fluttered, my face burned, and most embarrassingly of all, I couldn't stop smiling. I loved him, and he was going to be my first. I was nervous, excited...and ready.

I tucked my hands into the waistband of Alec's boxers, pushing them down past his hips. He pulled them all the way off and then tossed them to the side. I reached up to run my hands down his chest, over his stomach, and around to his back. He was hard and so male, and I wanted him all over me. My heart felt like it was going to crash through my ribs, and I could feel the echoes of it pulsing through my entire body.

Alec traced the outline of my chest over my T-shirt. When he slipped his hands underneath the fabric to pull it off and saw that I wasn't wearing any panties, he groaned.

"Christ, Taren. I want to devour you." His lips sucked along the tender center of my breast causing me to purr in response as I pushed up into him. His tongue swirled around before his lips sucked and pulled on my nipple again.

"Kiss me." I gripped his hair, and he lifted his head from my skin for only a second before he moved his body higher, and his lips crashed against mine. Neither of us seemed to be able to tame or quench the need we had for one another.

His knees spread mine apart, and he broke off the kiss to capture me with his gaze. Alec trailed his fingers from my collarbone, between my breasts, and over my stomach, leaving goosebumps in his wake. When his hand slipped between my legs, he stroked me with gentle pressure. His fingers dipped inside me, and my hips lifted to meet him.

"Holy shit. You're so wet." His voice was raw, and he looked between us to watch his hand move on me.

Muscles deep inside tightened, and I was filled with a rush of desire. I wanted him inside me so badly I could hardly think straight. I reached between us, sliding my hand up and down his hard length.

His forehead dropped to my chest, and he groaned, pushing his hips into the stroke of my hand over and over again.

"What happened to my good girl?" Alec was breathing hard as he pushed up onto his hands to look down at me. I continued to move my hand on him, and he leaned over to reach into his nightstand drawer, pulling out a condom. I watched as he ripped open the package and rolled it on.

He studied my face. "I'll go slowly so it doesn't hurt too much. You can tell me to stop."

"I trust you." I leaned up to kiss him, and his lips melded against mine.

He paused, hovering over me. "Don't look away." He shifted his body, and the tip of him pressed against me. Watching my face the whole time, he pushed in just a bit. I gasped a sharp intake of air when the pain hit as he slowly moved into me. The feeling passed quickly, and then Alec was filling me with heat and want and…him. I circled my hips, moving slowly, feeling pleasure spark through my body.

"Taren." He groaned. "I've never felt anything so perfect." His hips moved in time with mine, small thrusts and rocks that forced tiny whimpers out of me.

"Alec." My voice shook with emotion, moved by his complete and total possession of me. He had the ability to surrender his heart to me with just a few words, a touch, and a look.

"You're so tight." He squeezed his eyes shut, slowing his movements, making them long and deliberate. He blew out a breath, tucking his face against my neck, kissing and murmuring words I couldn't understand.

I slid my arms around his back, gripping his shoulders as I lifted my hips, urging him on. I couldn't get close enough to him. I didn't want him to ever stop.

"I love—" My tongue tripped over the last word before I spoke it aloud. I worried that what I felt for him was so much stronger than what he felt with me. We'd only been together a few months. As much as I wished I could forget it, the memory of his first rejection was still with me. I didn't want him to misinterpret me and think I was putting pressure on him. If I said "I love you" and he didn't feel the same way…I didn't think I would recover.

His eyes opened, and he moved in and out. His pace was slow, forcing me to feel every inch of him. "Yes?" he asked, plunging deeper inside of me. I moved to meet him halfway with each strong, sure thrust.

"I love…being with you, Alec." My voice was thick in my throat. "I never knew I could be this happy either."

He released a breath with a heavy exhale. His forehead dipped into the space between my shoulder and the pillow as his lips found my neck. Then, his hands reached around underneath me to hold me to him.

"I love—" He paused. In my head I imagined he said, you, even though he never did. I wanted to hear those words so badly, and yet I was too afraid to say them myself.

Alec groaned as our bodies fell into a rhythm. Our hips rolled more quickly against each other. My hands were in his hair, guiding his mouth to mine, begging for more of him as his thrusts became more frantic. His hands were still under me, pulling my body against his.

"More." I writhed beneath him, begging, and something in Alec's eyes flashed.

He let himself go, thrusting into me. "Oh, god. Yes." I pressed my head against the pillow as my orgasm rushed through me, an avalanche of sensation.

Alec pressed his mouth to my neck, saying my name as he came. Finally, he collapsed on top of me, breathing hard. He kissed the spot underneath my ear. "I love...being with you, too," he mumbled against my skin.

The love I felt from his touch and from hearing that he wanted to be with me, too, was enough.

For now.

***

"Five minutes until the obstacle course, people!" Asher stood on the porch and yelled down to us. "Find your assigned partner!"

We were enjoying a Greek Week happy hour at the Delta Epsilon house. Even though we were paired with Doug's fraternity for Greek Week, I'd managed to avoid him at all of the events.

Next to me, Julie sipped her beer and looked around the front yard of the fraternity house. The area was roped off with caution tape, keeping "underage" drinkers out. Underage was really just code for those poor saps without a fake ID.

"What time did you roll in last night?" Alexis asked, drinking the rare beer she allowed herself to indulge in.

"To be clear, I rolled in this morning. Alec walked me home on his way to work." I hid my grin behind my bottle of beer.

Julie raised an eyebrow. "Please tell me he finally popped your cherry."

I choked on my sip, coughing and wiping my mouth with my hand.

"For the love of God!" Alexis scowled at Julie, who wore a shit-eating grin on her face.

"I'd hoped to talk to you guys somewhere more private, and not use the term cherry or pop, but I guess that's not happening…" I grinned and both girls squealed.

"How was it, Taren?" Alexis held her breath and pressed her lips together.

"I waited for the right guy, and it was the perfect time. He was gentle, and passionate, and it was…" I sighed. "Perfection."

"Blah, blah, blah. Did you have an orgasm?" Julie tapped her foot, waiting for my answer.

My eyebrows squeezed together, and I leaned back. "Um, yes. Doesn't that always happen?"

"No! That does not always happen. Marry him, or tie him to his bed. You can't let a guy who knows his way around a g-spot get away. Mark my words. He's a keeper." Julie took a long sip of beer and turned to Alexis. "Ah, our lone virgin. Want me to get Asher wasted tonight? You can have your way with him and not be the oldest virgin ever living."

Frowning at Julie, I wrapped my arm around Alexis and hugged her to me, but Alexis moved out of my grasp, her face pink.

"That's not necessary. I'm not…a…that. All set here, thanks." Alexis stammered, and Julie looked at me, jaw dropped and eyes bulging.

"Who? Asher?" Julie braced her hands on her knees and heaved in a breath. "When? I need details. I feel so lost and confused."

Alexis shook her head. "Not now. That's a story for later. Right now we celebrate Taren."

We clinked beers as Asher headed our way. He gave Alexis a quick peck on the lips. "You and I are partners." Alexis blushed and slipped her hand into his.

"I'm actually running this event, so I'll see you all down there." Julie wished us luck before running onto the grassy field in front of the house.

"DENTON!" Pickles' voice boomed behind me, and I jumped. "Partners! As it should be."

No fucking way. My body felt like it was freefalling off a cliff. My vision blurred, and I walked back a step.

"Sorry, Taren." Asher frowned at me. "Pickles picked you as his partner and threatened to go ape-shit crazy if anyone else tried to pair up with you."

"That's because Denton and I have the best chance of winning this thing, dillhole," Doug hollered as he wrapped his arm around my neck, trying to pull me into a hug.

Alexis leaned close to me. "You don't have to do this, Taren."

I pushed Pickles' arm off and looked at all the other match-ups, noticing no one would look me in the eye. Heat crept up my neck, and

I couldn't seem to close my gaping mouth.

"Watson?" I asked, begging him to switch with me.

"Sorry, Denton. Bros before hoes."

I rolled my eyes. "Is it any wonder you don't have a girlfriend?"

"Denton? You trying to get rid of me?" Doug asked.

"Been trying for months now," I mumbled under my breath.

"Competitors! Time to get tied up. Take your asses to the starting line!" Jules called over the speakers.

"You don't have to do this." Alexis placed her hand on my arm, her jaw set.

Shit. I promised Alec I wouldn't drink or party with Pickles. Would he understand being partners in a game? Or would he be pissed? My chest hurt at the thought of breaking my promise. I rubbed at my chest and, my brain whirled around as I tried to decide what to do. I had to tell everyone I was out. But if I forfeited, our match up would lose Greek Week. This was an obstacle course. We weren't drinking together or dancing. There was no intimacy here.

I sighed, looking around at all the other pairs. I remembered some of the crazier things I'd done in the name of Greek life, like being handcuffed to Ed "Fuckerman" during the Around-the-World drinking party. I survived that; I could survive this. I squared my shoulders. Alec would understand that this was innocent fun.

"It's just a game, right?" I looked over at Doug. He swayed on his feet as he tilted another beer back against his lips. He was well on his way to drunk. We'd be lucky to make it past the first obstacle. Actually, we'd be lucky if we didn't. Then I could get out of this nightmare early.

"C'mon, Denton. Let's tear this bitch up." Doug grabbed my hand, and I yanked it away from him. He reached over and held on with a tight grip. "We gotta go get tied up, babe." His eyebrows wiggled suggestively, and I fisted my hands to keep from slapping him in the face.

"Don't call me babe." I gritted my teeth and pushed him away with my elbow.

My stomach was queasy, and my palms began to sweat as organizers bound our wrists and ankles together with rope. *This will be over soon. This will be over soon.* I chanted in my head over and over again.

Doug kept trying to hold my hand, and I kept shaking him off. "Cut it out, Pickles. The rope is just to make sure we work together."

"Lighten up, Denton. Just trying to make sure we work as a team. We gotta stay close or it's not going to work."

"Well, we don't need to hold hands to do that. Okay?"

"Whatever you say." His grin was sloppy and confident—just like every other time I'd been around him. *Damn.* I couldn't believe I used to date him.

Once all of the couples were lined up at the starting line, Julie picked up the mic. "On your marks, get set...go!" she yelled as she fired the starter gun.

Following the crowd of tethered Greeks, Doug and I trotted over to the tunnels. I got down on my hands and knees and crawled through the plastic tube. Doug followed close behind me. When his hand landed on my ass pushing me forward, I looked over my shoulder and hissed at him.

"Hands to yourself, Pickles!"

He chuckled. "Relax. Just helping you out, Denton."

After we got through the tunnel, and I stood up, Doug slapped me on the ass with a little squeeze. "Nice job, Denton. You have no idea how much I enjoyed that view."

"Argh," I grumbled out an unintelligible sound. This was mortifying and degrading, and yet my stupid ass had agreed to do it. I groaned again. "You're such a—"

I didn't get to tell him what he was before he was running toward the next obstacle and dragging me behind him.

The walls were next. Doug lifted himself onto the top of the first wall, and when he noticed me dangling below, he reached down to grab my arm and pull me over with him. He grunted, lifting me over the wall, and tears pricked at my eyes. *Why was I doing this?* I had promised Alec I would stay away from Pickles. We toppled to the ground on the other side, Doug landing first with me sprawled on top of him. Shame burned in my veins and a light sheen of sweat covered my skin. I didn't have to imagine how funny we looked, Julie was commentating the entire ordeal.

"Taren Richards is using Doug Pickles to soften her fall like he's some kind of mattress. Come on guys, we don't need a play by play of what you used to do in that tent bed." Julie screeched with laughter over the speaker system.

Holy hell. I was going to kill her after this. I didn't know who had thought it would be a good idea to let her commentate after she'd been drinking. She was inappropriate enough when she was sober. My chest, face, and ears burned red hot. I had the strongest desire to flee. I looked around, trying to decide if I could make a run for it. *You are tethered to Pickles, dumbass.*

Right.

As soon as we crossed the finish line for the obstacle part of the race, one of the coordinators waved us on to the next station.

"The last station is the passing station," Julie announced. "Competitors have to pass objects to one another without using their hands. Anything goes!" Someone handed Julie a beer, and I watched her take a large gulp before clapping her hands together in excitement.

"Oh shit. How do we do this?" I peered down at the objects on the table in front of me.

Doug jumped around in excitement. "Whatever it takes. We're in second place. C'mon, c'mon. Let's go, Denton."

I stared at the first object, a peach, and tried to figure out if I was coordinated enough to use my elbows without squashing it to a pulp. I bent over at the waist, attempting to use my arms as chopsticks, only to realize I was not as flexible as I thought I was.

"Just use your mouth!" Doug shouted. "We can win. C'mon, Denton!"

My mouth? Shit. "Fine," I snapped. I bit down on the peach and stood up. Sticky juice dripped down my chin as I turned toward him. Doug leaned forward, mouth opened wide, and bit on the other side, pulling it from my teeth before spinning around and dropping it into his basket.

I looked down to see that next up was a cucumber. *Oh, fuckity fuck fuck.* Of course it was something shaped like a dick. A juicy peach and a dick-shaped vegetable. Why was I not surprised? The Greeks and their love of all things sexual. What if Alec were to see this? How bad would it look? *Bad.* The answer was *way fucking bad*. The problem was, I wasn't sure how to stop this runaway train. I bent over and bit down on the end of the cucumber, desperate to just get the stupid game over with.

"Look at the tubular vegetable skills, people. The way Taren Richards has her lips wrapped around it to keep it secure...it looks like she's done this before, folks," Julie yelled through the mic. "And here's Pickles on the receiving end. Will he? Can he? Yes! Yes! Doug Pickles, instead of grabbing it with his neck like all the other pansy ass guys, has taken the other end in his mouth like a pro! It doesn't look like any of the other guys were willing to take one for the team like our man. It's almost unfair how good Taren and Pickles are at this."

I glared at Julie as Doug dropped the cucumber into our basket. I knew she couldn't see me, but I would get her back for that comment.

"Hurry, final race to the finish line! Go, go, go!" Julie screamed.

Doug whooped, taking off at a sprint and dragging me behind him. I tripped, unable to keep up. Doug reached down and threw my one free leg and arm over his shoulder. I was hanging upside-down while still partially tethered to him.

"Put me down!" I yelled, smacking him on the back as he ran full speed across the finish line.

"We won! We won!" Doug jumped up and down while I struggled to get him to release me. "Keep doing that, Denton. You're rubbing me in all the right ways."

"Pickles!" Julie yelled as she ran up behind us. "You're disqualified, moron. She had to run on her own. She couldn't be carried." Julie was red-faced and pissed. Doug had probably cost our match-up the Greek Week trophy. That meant I had done all of this…for nothing. I stared at the ground, not sure if I should laugh, cry, or scream.

"Fuck. I need a brewski." Pickles roughly set me down and cut our bindings. I rubbed my raw wrist, glaring at him and trying to decide what I wanted to shout at him first.

"Sorry, Denton. Hope I didn't hurt you, but I had fun with you today. Just like old times." Before I even realized what was happening, Pickles grabbed my shoulders and placed a wet, sweaty, beer and peach-flavored kiss on my lips.

Oh, hell no. I shoved him off and then wiped my mouth with the back of my hand, which caused him to laugh. I turned away, dragging large mouthfuls of clean Pickles-free air into my lungs.

His laughter turned into a grunt of pain, and I spun around, everything around me moving in slow motion. Someone dressed in a bright yellow campus security jacket shoved him down, wrenching his arms behind his back. From the terrified look on Doug's face as it was pressed into the muddy ground, it wasn't one of his friends fooling around. I tore my gaze away from Pickles just as the guy on his back looked up at me.

Nope. Not a friend at all. The guy with his knee in Pickles' back was one hell of a furious boyfriend.

Alec.

Chapter 26

Alec

I pulled Pickles' arm back a little higher, pleased when it caused him to bark out in discomfort. "Don't ever touch her again." The words were almost a growl as I pushed them through my clenched teeth. My body vibrated with rage, and I wanted nothing more than to introduce my fist to his face. This prick needed to learn a lesson.

I leaned forward, and my knee dug further into his back. He grunted and satisfaction curled through my limbs, urging me to make him hurt so he'd never forget.

"Alec! No! Don't do this." Taren grabbed at my arm, but I shrugged her off.

She should have stopped this from the start. She knew how I felt about him, and she'd made a promise. I was almost as angry with her as I was with him. My hands were shaking with the need to break something.

"You will never touch my girl again. Do you understand me, asshole?" I wanted to rip him to shreds.

Doug turned his head as his face contorted into a sneer. "I'm only giving her what you can't."

I pulled his arm up higher, and he squirmed against the pain. "I asked if you understood." I could barely control the words as they came out of me in a snarl.

His face turned red, but he didn't answer.

"So help me God, if you ever touch her again…I. Will. End. You." My voice shook as I said each word. Then, I pushed off his back and stood up. He rolled over, glaring up at me as he lay sprawled on his back, rubbing his wrist.

I lifted my eyes to find that we were surrounded by people who gave us wary looks. I scanned the crowd, ready for his Delta Epsilon brothers to pounce on me, but they didn't. Pickles pushed up from the ground, and when he got to his feet, he narrowed his eyes at me.

I took a step forward, towering over him. "Walk away now while you still can."

He leaned in and spoke low so only I could hear him. "Next time we meet, you won't have the safety of that security jacket to hide behind." His lip curled in disgust, and he turned to walk away, pushing through the circle of people around us. I watched his retreat until he disappeared into the crowd. A long moment passed before I noticed that Taren was talking to me.

"Alec?" Her voice was panicked, her eyes wide with worry.

She reached for me, and I looked down to see that her hand was on my arm. The same hand that had just been tied to her ex. I pulled away enough that she flinched from my rejection.

"I'm sorry about that…" Her words were full of regret, and she glanced over her shoulder toward the race course. "We had to be partners."

"Right. Had to be." I scowled at her and crossed my arms. "You had no choice in the matter." I shook my head. "That fucking asshole cheated on you, and yet here you are, partying with him like you're best friends. You let him touch you. You broke your promise to me." The words tasted dirty as I said them, and I both loved and hated the look of hurt that flashed across her face.

"That's not fair, Alec." Her voice cracked, and she pursed her lips to keep from crying. "You knew I was here for the Greek Week games. I explained this to you last night. You knew what I'd be doing." She reached out to touch me and I uncrossed my arms, so that her hand fell away from me.

"I didn't know you'd be doing your ex." I glared down at her and my arms tensed at my sides like I was ready to go into battle. I blamed Pickles, but Taren had let it happen. I wanted my words to slice deep, to punish her. "You failed to mention that you'd be tying yourself to your ex so he could treat you like you were his fucking whore." That last word ripped out of my throat, taking a piece of my heart with it.

"Excuse me?" Her voice rose in indignation and she stepped back. She put her hands on her hips and her eyes blazed with fury. Her regret and remorse evaporated before my eyes, leaving nothing but disgust.

"Did you like it when he kissed you and grabbed your ass, Taren?" I ground my teeth together, remembering what Caz had said last year. That I wasn't her type. That she belonged to the guys on Frat Row. "Do you like being treated like you're just another one of his hookups that he can yank around and grope at will?"

Taren's lips pressed together and she took a deep breath. "Stop it. Don't say anything you can't take back, Alec." The anger in her eyes flared. "This wasn't about me and you. I did that race for my friends. If I had refused to participate, we would have forfeited and lost."

I threw my hands up in the air. "It's nice to know a race is more important than your promise to me." I wasn't buying her bullshit, and she knew it.

"You're making a much bigger deal out of this than it really is. It was just for fun. It didn't mean anything. I needed a partner. He picked me and I got stuck with him."

A harsh laugh escaped me. "Right." I huffed and looked around before I fixed my eyes on her. I leaned in and unleashed the bitterness that was clawing at me. "Wasn't that the same excuse you used for dating him?" I wanted her to feel the betrayal I felt when I saw Pickles with his hands and mouth all over her.

Taren's expression was a mixture of heartache and outrage. She pressed her mouth into a tight line, and I looked away. I couldn't stand the sight of her lips. Lips I'd kissed earlier in the day. Lips which had just been on the receiving end of a kiss from Pickles.

"I thought we were all in," she whispered as she choked back a sob. "Don't you trust me?"

"Trust? Really?" My words were sharp and clipped. "How can I trust you when you keep making bad decisions involving that asshole?" I refused to look at her, to give her the power to make me feel guilty. She was wrong here. She was the one who totally fucked up and now she was turning it on me, trying to make me feel guilty. Yeah, not happening.

"You did not just go there. You want to talk about trust? I trust you when you put your face in your partner's hoo-ha during routines. On a daily basis, might I add." She pushed against my chest and I still wouldn't look at her. I couldn't, I was too pissed.

"You tell me it's just for fun, and that you're only partners." Her voice shook, and she took a deep breath. "Well, this was for fun. We were only partners. Trust is a two way street." The strength in her words caused me to look at her. "I trust you—now you need to trust me."

I crossed my arms and shook my head. "There's a difference. Pickles wants in your pants." I leaned close so our faces were only inches apart. "You promised you'd stay away from him, and instead, you're leading him on." I needed her to feel the same misery I felt.

Taren stepped back like I'd physically slapped her. "Leading him on? Is that what you really think?" She was breathing hard, and her eyes watered. "I know you're upset. I am too, but Pickles is my past. You're my now. You know that."

I looked away.

She turned my face toward her. "Look at me. You know that right?"

I didn't have an answer for her. All I knew was that my girlfriend had let her ex manhandle her in front of hundreds of people. When she had to make a choice, it hadn't been me.

Julie came up behind Taren and threw her hands into the air. "I can't believe that idiot totally fucked up the end of that race." She stomped her foot and made a noise in the back of her throat, balling her fists at her sides. "Now we have to win the talent show to even have a chance at getting the trophy." Julie looped her arm through Taren's. "C'mon, T. Let's go get something to drink."

"Alec?" Taren resisted Julie as she locked eyes with me. She looked drained. "Please."

At the sound of Taren's plea, Julie looked between us. "What's wrong? Did I interrupt something?"

"I'll talk to you later, Taren." My eyes flicked over to Julie. "When we don't have an audience. I need to get back to work."

Taren reached out to grab my arm as I was turning away. "Alec, please. I don't want to leave things like this."

I shrugged her off and stepped back. "I gotta go, Taren, and so do you." We both needed some space to cool off.

She grabbed my jacket, refusing to let me walk away. "We're going to be okay, right?" Her eyes searched my face for the unspoken answers I couldn't give her. "I'll see you later tonight?"

I gave her a terse nod. I was on empty and that's all I had left to give.

She leaned in as if she were going to kiss me, but I tilted my head away. "I'm working, Taren." Her mouth opened, and she sucked in a quick breath. My rejection seemed to crush something inside her, and yet I still couldn't bring myself to tell her everything was okay. "Do us both a favor. Stay away from Pickles."

Julie rolled her eyes. "Calm down, cowboy. Your girl is safe with me." She gave another tug on Taren's arm. Taren resisted for a moment. Her eyes pleaded with me to say something. Tell her everything was okay. Forgive her.

I took a step back, and she finally allowed Julie to pull her away in the opposite direction. I kept waiting for her to stop and come back, to choose me over her Greek life. If I was her "now," she needed to fucking prove it this time.

She disappeared into the crowd, and my chest ached.

Trust was such a fragile thing, easily bent and broken, impossible to put back the same way it had been. I'd done it again. I'd gone all in. I gambled my heart this time. As I took in the scene around me, a world so different from my own, I was beginning to think that more than my trust would end up broken.

Chapter 27

Taren

We won Greek Week.

My sisters and the brothers of Delta Epsilon screamed and jumped around, hugging each other in celebration. I stood off to the side, watching them. A bittersweet sadness came over me. These things used to matter to me, too—the games, the parties, the traditions—they used to be important to me. I sighed and held my Solo cup to my chest. Falling in love with Alec had changed me. I had just been too afraid to admit it.

Today was a cluster fuck. I didn't want to upset Julie or Kate or Jen. I was afraid to rock the boat.

I had become the opposite of unique.

I had lost who I was. I lost my focus…my center. My need to feel like I belonged had consumed me and I continued to make horrible choices. From dating Pickles, to getting stupid-drunk, to agreeing to partner with someone who had been cruel to me and rude to my boyfriend…what price was I willing to pay to fit in? Was I willing to sacrifice my own happiness or that of the man I loved?

No more. Time to fight those fears.

"You okay, T?" I turned around at the sound of Julie's voice. She stood next to me with her arms crossed over her chest and a frown on her face. We were on the edge of the chaos, watching our friends celebrate the big win.

I shook my head. "Not really, but I will be. I need to talk to you." I motioned to the front steps of the Delta Epsilon house, and we both sat down.

I rubbed my clammy hands on my jeans. I didn't want to hurt Julie, but I had to be honest with her and myself. "I love being your sister." I looked over at her and smiled, all our memories playing before me. I blew out a deep breath. This was much harder than I had thought. "I can't keep participating in these fraternity parties anymore." I blurted out the words.

"What? Why?" Julie sputtered.

"Partying with random guys who are looking for a hook up isn't right for me anymore. Before I met Alec it was one thing, but I can't keep doing that."

"You're not leaving Tri-Gam are you?" Julie's chin wobbled, and tears filled her eyes. Her reaction was so unexpected that my eyes watered. Julie loved me in her own way. I just never thought she'd be so sad if I left.

"Of course not! I love all my sisters so much, especially you and Alexis. You both helped me find myself. I'm confident and strong because I always knew I had friends like you behind me." The tears slid over my cheeks, matching the ones on Julie's face.

"But why do you have to stop coming to parties?"

I took a deep breath before letting it out slowly. "I hurt Alec today, Jules. I did something I wasn't comfortable with because I didn't want to let you all down. Agreeing to do the obstacle course with Pickles was a huge mistake. He'll never respect me or my relationship with Alec. Alec saw the way Pickles touched me, and he heard the commentary you made. That gutted him, and he didn't deserve to feel that way. I love him."

"He was hurt? I didn't mean anything by what I said; I was just having fun. Wait a minute. Did you say you love him?"

The corners of my lips lifted. I should be beaming at the thought of loving Alec Hart, but I was worried I might have blown my chances with him after today. "I love him so much, and I fucked up. I really hurt him. I should have withdrawn from the race as soon as I realized Pickles was my partner. I should've known better."

"I'm sorry you felt pressured to do something you didn't want to. I might get on your ass about things, but you know we're friends no matter how many parties you go to or how many events you do. We're sisters. Always."

I smiled. "Yes we are."

"And I love you because you accept me for who I am, flaws and all. You never, for one second, make me feel less than." She wrapped her bony arms around me in a tight hug. Every time I tried to pull away, she squeezed me tighter, causing both of us to laugh.

"I have to go. Alec is expecting me to be at his show."

"Fine." She pulled away, planting a kiss on my cheek before releasing me. "Apologize to him for me?"

"I will." I stood up, checking my watch and groaning. "Shit, I'm late. I'm going to have to run like hell to get there."

"Go." Julie stood up and placed her hand on my back, pushing me forward. I waved as I ran down the steps of Delta Epsilon.

Knowing I had the support of my sisters to be who I wanted to be was empowering, but the time had come to listen to my heart. I needed

Alec to understand just how much I loved him.

Chapter 28

Alec

The arena was full of excited voices and last minute sound and light checks. We only had an hour until show time. I should have been excited. I should have been warming up. I should have been thinking about my acts and all the new skills I'd added in the last few weeks. Instead, all I could think about was Pickles and Taren. Images of Pickles touching her ass, picking her up, and joking with her like they were still a couple tormented me. Thoughts of Pickles kissing what was mine drove me insane.

I couldn't focus.

"Hey." Caz patted me on the shoulder. "Help me carry this mat over to the beam. The girls need to warm up."

I followed him over to high bar and picked up the other end of the heavy mat. My muscles strained as we lugged the mat across the floor, but we didn't speak. My thoughts were on a continual loop.

I didn't know you'd be doing your ex.

Christ. If there was an award for asshole boyfriend of the year, I'd won it with that comment. Taren had promised to come to our show tonight, but I hadn't talked to her since I finished my security shift at

Greek Week two hours ago.

Was she upset over our argument? Was she drinking? Was she with Pickles?

We set the mat down next to the beam, unfolded it, and pushed it underneath.

"Thanks," Amanda said.

I gave her a terse nod and turned away.

Amanda grabbed my elbow. "What's wrong? You look upset."

I looked down at where her hand rested on my arm. Where Taren had touched me. "I'm fine."

"Hey." Amanda's voice softened. "You can tell me what's wrong. We're friends."

The sound that came out of me was meant to be a laugh, but it was bitter and tired. "It's not anything I want to talk about."

Amanda sighed. "Is this about Taren? You can talk to me. I'll understand. Don't let this come between us."

"Nothing is coming between us, Amanda. We're partners. That's it. There's nothing to come between."

"Is she coming tonight?"

"Of course Donuts is coming." Caz shoved between us as he walked away from the beam. "We saved her a seat right up front. Even got some for those hotties she's always hanging with." Caz indicated the four seats in the front row that we put reserved signs on—one for my cousin and the other three for Taren and her friends.

"I'm sure she'll be here." Amanda rubbed my arm like she was trying to comfort me.

Amanda couldn't possibly understand. Taren and I were being pulled in two different directions. If today was any indication, we might never be heading the same way. Her obligations to her Greek life had taken priority over our relationship.

My phone rang, and I pulled it out of my back pocket. When I saw the name on the screen, my chest clenched with disappointment. Instead of Taren's name, it was my cousin's.

"Hey, Lee." I walked away from the beam and stared at the four empty seats I had reserved. "You still coming to my show?"

"You forgot to give me my ticket. I am waiting outside."

"Ah. Sorry, bro." I'd been so distracted I forgot to put his ticket at will call. "I'll be up in a minute to let you in."

I slid my phone in my back pocket and jogged up the stadium steps to find Lee. He was outside by the ticket booth, examining the Testudo statue near the stadium entrance.

"This is just like the one on the McKeldin Mall." He touched the nose of the turtle, and the spot under his hand was a bright, polished, golden color from being touched so often.

"Yeah, there are a couple on campus. It's apparently good luck if you rub the nose," I told him. I reached up to run my hand across the statue. Superstition or not, it was a habit all UMD students followed.

"You don't need luck." Lee's smile was brilliant, as usual—a permanent fixture on his face.

"Everyone needs luck."

Lee shook his head. "Nope. You just need to make the right choices."

***

The overhead lights flickered, announcing to the audience that the show was about to start. I pulled out my phone to text Lee.

Me: Is Taren here yet?

Lee: Not yet.

Was she really going to be a fucking no-show? We hadn't parted on good terms, but she said she'd see me tonight. I assumed that meant she was still coming to the show.

Me: Can you text me when she gets here?
Lee: Okay.

Tossing my phone onto my bag of costumes, I paced back and forth. I ran my hand through my hair, rubbing the back of my neck.

What if she got caught up in the fun at the talent show and afterparty and drank too much? I wouldn't be there to take care of her.

But Pickles would.

I found myself over by the curtain, pulling it back to check the front row myself. Lee was playing with his phone, next to three empty seats.

"Dude. You've got to stop obsessing about this." Jon put his hand on my shoulder and pulled me away from the curtain. "If you don't get your head in the game, you're gonna mess up big time. You can't afford to be thinking about anything but the show. It's dangerous."

"I know."

"Your warm-up sucked major donkey balls," Caz added. "Vaulting is first up and we're depending on you. You're middle man." He referred to the fact that I flipped between him and Jon during the alternating runs in the flipping passes.

Caz and Jon's words were a reminder that my actions not only affected me, but everyone else in the performance. We depended on each other's timing, strength, and skill to stay safe. They were right. I needed to get my head in the game.

"Have you called her to see where she is?" Jon asked.

"Yeah. No answer." I could only think of two reasons why she wasn't answering. Either she couldn't, or she wouldn't. Either way, my chest felt like it was in a fucking vice grip, and I wasn't sure whether I should be worried or pissed.

"She probably just lost track of time. She'll be here." Jon smacked me on the back as he walked away. Caz followed him, but not before I saw the look on his face. Pity.

I picked up my phone and checked it again.

No new messages. I tossed the phone back on my bag.

If she meant what she said about trust and me being her now, then why the fuck couldn't she take the time to call me? Why wasn't she here yet?

When the lights finally went out, the darkness that blanketed the arena went soul deep. I heard Coach begin his introductions over the speaker system, and I went to join the rest of the Acroletes. I stood in line, watching the glow of my phone from afar until it blinked out.

***

The music was loud. I could feel the beat of it coursing through my body. The noise usually fed my adrenaline, forcing me to run harder, jump higher, twist faster. Tonight everything was muddled by my thoughts as if I was wading through tar. My body remembered the tempo and speed, but I didn't feel the exhilaration that I normally got from performing. I felt thin and empty. Splintered.

The lights along the front of the stage were bright. But somehow I knew those seats just beyond the edge of the darkness were still empty. I couldn't shake the worry that maybe Taren *couldn't* come, that I hadn't been there when she needed me.

I felt a smack on the back of my head. "Head in the game," Caz said as he peeled away, running for the other side of the stage.

We were in two lines, ready to alternate our flipping passes. I looked across to the line Jon and Caz were in, waiting for my turn. Jon nodded at me and then started running toward the vault box and his mini trampoline. I waited a second and then ran after him, heading for my own mini trampoline. Out of the corner of my eye, I could see Caz following behind him. I had a split second of perfect timing to squeeze between them. We'd been doing this all year. It was almost second nature.

As I leapt for the trampoline, I knew something was wrong. Jon was already landing on the mat. I was too late. Caz was hitting his trampoline at the same time as me. I'd been running too slowly. Panic slammed me back into reality, and the haziness was gone as my heart hammered with perfect clarity.

We both shot into the air at the same time. Bailing was no longer an option. My only choice was to go through with it like a NASCAR driver and hope we could avoid crashing in mid-air. I threw my flip, aware that Coach was yelling my name. I could sense Caz rocketing toward me.

We slammed into each other, two cannonballs of flesh and bone. The force of Caz's rotation was like getting hit with a wrecking ball. I was rocked off course, my arms and legs leaving my tight tuck as I reached out for safety. Spotters lunged for me, grabbing for my shirt or leg or anything they could hold onto as I soared over their heads.

I saw Caz tumble to the mat in the grasp of two spotters, and in that split second, I was relieved. I careened away from the safety of my own mat toward the floor. I tried to get my feet under me, but only one foot touched down before it buckled with a loud pop. Pain lanced along my leg as I crashed onto the hardwood and my body crumpled like a crushed can. I couldn't stop my momentum, and my head snapped back, slamming against the floor. Light burst across my eyes in a blinding flash of agony before my vision went dark.

Chapter 29

Taren

Crap, fuck, hell, shit, dammit. My heart beat wild in my chest. I was so screwed. Pausing, I checked my phone to text Alec that I was running late. The stupid battery was dead. I ran my hands through my hair, pulling at the ends. I had to haul ass. I pumped my legs, pushing myself to run faster. My life was quickly becoming a shit storm of epic proportions.

I panted, gasping for air. Sweat trickled down my back and my side ached. Damn, I was out of shape. Marathons were definitely not in my future.

With the Xfinity Center in sight, I slowed my sprint to a walk and tried to catch my breath. The sound of sirens echoed nearby. Flashing lights and emergency vehicles were in front of the building.

Shit, shit, shit. My lungs tightened like they were being squeezed. Something bad had to have occurred at the show. Panic slid through my veins, turning my blood ice cold. Ignoring the pain in my chest, I sprinted toward the entrance.

"Taren!" Jon called my name and waved me toward him.

Why was Jon outside? I whipped my head around. A crowd of people were standing outside in Acroletes uniforms. Shouldn't they be in the middle of their performance? Where was Alec?

A paramedic slammed the back doors to the ambulance shut, and it sped away. I stood frozen, watching the flashing lights against the dark sky. A chill ran through my body and my heart sank.

"What happened? Who got hurt?" I gasped for air. "Where's Alec?" I looked around and recognized a few faces, but not the one I wanted to see.

Amanda was standing next to Jon. Her lips curled and her face twisted. "Alec and Caz got hurt." She spoke through gritted teeth.

No. My stomach rolled, and a wave of nausea hit me. "Oh my God." I turned toward Jon as my hand flew toward my mouth. "How bad are they hurt? Is Alec okay?"

"He and Caz collided during vaulting. Caz is shaken up and has a twisted ankle, but he'll be fine. I don't know about Alec, but it looked bad." Jon's face was pale. "They just took him away in the ambulance."

No, please God, no. My legs shook so badly I had to lean against one of the bike racks along the sidewalk.

"This is your fault you know." Amanda's voice rose in fury as she stepped closer, jabbing a finger into my collarbone.

"My fault?" My voice faltered as my hand pressed against the skin on my throat. I couldn't catch my breath. Air wasn't filling my lungs.

"Not now, Amanda." Jon tried to grab her elbow and turn her away, but she yanked free of him.

"You heard me. This is all your fault. You were supposed to be here, and you didn't show. Alec was worried sick about you, so he got distracted. That's why he had the accident. Because of you."

He was worried about me? I stepped back, shaking my head no. Guilt crashed over me in waves until I felt like I was drowning in it. I never meant to make him worry. We had an argument, but I trusted he had faith in us. I looked at Jon, hoping he'd tell her she was wrong, but he stared at the ground, rubbing his chin.

"Is that true, Jon?" My stomach churned viciously, and I covered my mouth with my hand, afraid I might vomit.

Jon slowly drew his gaze back to me and frowned. "We don't know what caused the accident. Alec was upset about something before the performance. He seemed distracted. He kept looking at the seats he saved for you." His voice trailed off.

I looked away and took a deep, pained breath. "I was running late."

"And you can't pick up your phone and let him know?" Amanda sneered at me. "He called and texted you like twenty times." She put her hands on her head and paced back and forth. "You couldn't be bothered to pick up your fucking phone and wish him luck."

I tried to swallow past the regret that was lodged in my throat. "My phone died," I said meekly, knowing that it was a lame excuse. "I...I was on my way. I was running late. I'm sorry..." Tears filled my eyes. All I wanted...no, all I needed, right now was to see Alec and know he was okay. That we were okay.

"Well, you were too late. Way to make your *boyfriend* a priority." Amanda gave me another nasty look as her gaze traveled over me from head to toe. "You don't deserve him." She spun angrily, her ponytail whipping across my face as if she'd slapped me before she stomped away.

Amanda was right. I *didn't* deserve him, but I wanted to. I would do anything I could to make things better and keep Alec in my life.

"I think you're Alec's kryptonite." Jon focused on the road the ambulance had taken. "But I don't think that's going to keep you away, is it?"

Tears spilled down my cheeks, and I shook my head. "Jon, I need to see him. I love him."

Jon turned to me. "Okay." He nodded slowly. "I was just about to head out to the hospital. You can ride with me if you want."

Full body tremors coursed through me as I followed him. *I let Alec down.* I wiped away the tears from my cheeks and took in a shaky breath. He'd forgiven me the last time I hurt him, but I wasn't sure if he'd be able to do that again.

"Let's go." Jon headed toward the nearest student parking lot. Neither of us spoke the rest of the way to the hospital. No words were needed. I had fucked up.

Again.

And once again, Alec had paid the price.

***

I shifted in my chair. The small, hot waiting room smelled of burnt coffee. Jon and I, as well as almost every other member of the Acroletes team, had been here for hours. I'd picked off all of my finger nail polish, and Jon had worn a path in the linoleum flooring. We weren't allowed to see Alec, and we had no idea what was going on with him.

The doors swung open, and my eyes flew up. Alec's dad walked in, tall and in command. Alec's mother clung to his arm. Her face was streaked with tears. They walked straight to the front desk, and Alec's mom leaned in, speaking to a nurse. Mr. Hart turned to face the waiting room.

We took up every chair and bit of floor space available. Every other person in the room wore a red and black warm-up suit. When Mr. Hart's eyes landed on me, they widened. He bristled and, his mouth formed a tight line. My face flushed, and I squeezed my hands together. He knew who I was. He blamed me for his son's suspension.

The Acroletes' coach approached Mr. Hart and introduced himself, drawing the man's intimidating glare away from me. Coach held out his hand to shake with Alec's father, but the big man crossed his arms over his chest, refusing to extend a hand. I watched as Coach's face reddened, and his posture stiffened. The two men spoke, each getting louder with every word. Mr. Hart shook his head, poking his finger into Coach's chest. The tension in the room was thick, and I held my breath, waiting to see what would happen.

Mr. Hart shouted something at Coach, and Alec's mother turned from the nurse. She put her hand on her husband's arm and then spoke in low tones to both men. After a moment, a nurse ushered the Harts through the swinging doors, and they disappeared without another word.

Coach approached us and cleared his throat. "I know everyone is worried about Alec." His gaze traveled over the entire group before resting on me and Jon. "His parents have assured me that he is stable. He broke his ankle and is currently in surgery to have it repaired. He also broke a few ribs and has a concussion."

Worried whispers and questions ricocheted through the room, and the Coach put his hands out in a calming motion. "He's going to be okay. Once he's released, he'll be going home with his parents." He rubbed the back of his neck. "At least, next week will be spring break, and he won't miss his classes." Coach took a deep breath and nodded. His eyes darted around the room before they settled on us. A forced smile spread across on his face. "They asked that everyone go home. They'll be in touch."

Right. From the way that Alec's father had interacted with Coach, a voluntary exchange of information didn't seem likely.

"Let's all go get some rest," Coach said. "We need to be up early tomorrow to get the equipment out of Xfinity. Bad news is the show was cancelled. We won't be able to reschedule because of spring break, but Alec's going to be fine and that's really all that matters."

People got up to leave and headed for the doors. I stayed right where I was. Mr. Hart could try to keep me away if he wanted, but I wasn't leaving. I'd let my friends lead me away from Alec in the middle of our fight. I'd be damned if I made the same mistake twice. I was here for the long haul.

Amanda stopped in front of me. "You don't think you're actually going to get to go back there and see him do you?"

"What I think is none of your business," I snapped back. Even if she was right and I was the reason Alec got hurt, I wasn't leaving without seeing him first. I was his girlfriend.

She snarled at me. "Alec is more my business than—"

"Just go home, Amanda," Jon interrupted. He placed his hands on Amanda's shoulders. "We're all tired and worried, but you heard what Coach said."

Amanda gave an annoyed huff, but after another glare in my direction, she turned and left.

Jon stood up and grabbed his jacket and keys. "I'll take you home. Caz is probably ringing a silver bell, expecting me to wait on him hand and foot."

I sat in my chair and crossed my legs. "Actually, I'm staying."

Jon's eyes softened. "I know you want to see him, but his dad hates the Acroletes. He especially hates me and Caz. I don't know what kind of history you and Alec have, but from the look his father gave you, it doesn't look like you have any better chance than the rest of us of getting to see him. Best you can do is go home and wait for Alec to call you."

"I can't leave without trying to see him. I can't let him think that I wasn't planning on coming tonight. You don't understand. We argued earlier. I have to talk to him." My voice started out steady and strong, but cracked at the end.

Jon pinched the bridge of his nose. "You can't stay here alone. You have no way to get home."

"I'll call one of my sisters to come hang out with me." I lifted my chin high. He wasn't going to change my mind.

"I thought your phone was dead." Jon cocked his head to the side.

I sighed. "Oh. Right." How could I have forgotten that?

"Here." He dug his phone out of his jacket. "Call your friend. I'll hang out with you until she gets here."

"Thanks." I took the phone from him and dialed Alexis' number. All of my other friends were probably still out partying and celebrating our win. If I could count on anyone right now, it'd be Alexis. My eyes were full of unshed tears. Tears of worry. Tears of regret. Tears of guilt.

Jon put his hand on my shoulder. "He's going to be okay."

"I know." My lip quivered as the events of today hit me full force. "I'm just not sure if *we're* okay."

***

"Ms. Richards."

My name was almost a bark, easily rousing me out of sleep. I opened my eyes to see Alec's father towering over me. I sat up, rubbing sleep out of my eyes. Alexis was nowhere to be seen. I didn't remember falling asleep, but I remembered that she'd come to stay with me before Jon left.

"I sent your friend to get some coffee for the drive home."

My heart began to pound. "Drive home?"

"You need to leave, Ms. Richards." Alec's father stared at me, and my stomach twisted.

I sat up straighter, attempting to look more presentable. "I want to see Alec first. Please," I begged.

"That's not possible. He doesn't want to see anyone. His mother and I agree that what he needs right now is some rest."

A lump formed in my throat. "But if you tell him I'm out here—"

"He knows, and the answer is the same. Let him get some rest. He had a traumatic accident tonight, not to mention the surgery he had to endure. If he wants to contact you when he's feeling better, he will."

Tears stung my eyes. "But—" I stood up, arms outstretched. I had to see him. I had to apologize.

"I've had about enough of this stupidity. Losing his scholarship. Risking his life doing unsafe sports. Involvement with worthless distractions." A look of disgust crossed his face. I looked down at my Greek Week T-shirt, still dirty from the obstacle course I'd run with Pickles. "As for now, there will be no visitors. It's time for you to go home, Ms. Richards." With that, Mr. Hart was gone, leaving me with nothing but crushed hope and a heart full of worry.

***

Four days had passed since the accident.

I called and emailed Alec hourly.

He never answered any of them.

I was broken.

And so was my heart.

Chapter 30

Alec

My father loved his lake house in Deep Creek. I hated the place. Probably because he loved it so much. Right now I hated him, so by default I hated Deep Creek and everything in it.

"Dinner time, honey," my mother said as she came out on the back porch where I'd been lounging all day long. My foot was propped up on a pillow that she insisted on fluffing every half hour.

I felt trapped, which was probably why my father brought us out to Deep Creek in the first place. He said it was so I could recover, but I knew it was so he could keep me under his thumb. The seclusion gave him more opportunity to feed me all the bullshit I'd managed to escape since last year.

"Did you hear me, Alec?" my mother asked, setting her hand on my shoulder.

"Yeah. Sorry, Mom. Just bored out of my mind." I leaned my head back to look at her.

She ran her fingers through my hair. "Sorry, but the doctor said until your dizziness fades, you shouldn't do anything that strains your eyes. That means no TV or laptop. You just need to take it easy and relax."

I laughed to myself. Even if I found a laptop, there was no Wi-Fi connection at the lake house. I was living in the fucking dark ages. Not to mention the fact that my phone was lost. My duffle bag had been recovered from the Xfinity Center and returned to my parents at the hospital, but my phone hadn't been inside. Which meant that I was stuck in the middle of nowhere, with nothing but a massive headache, a bum ankle, and three broken ribs. I was at the mercy of my parents.

"Come inside and have some dinner." My mother tugged on my shirt sleeve, and I closed my eyes.

"Is Dad home yet?" The one good thing about the lake house was that my father spent a lot of time fishing or at the local bar.

My mother sighed. "I know your father isn't easy on you, but he means well. He just wants what's best for you."

"No." I shifted my position. When the jostling sent pain shooting through my leg, I drew a breath in through my clenched teeth. "He wants what *he thinks* is best for me."

She sighed again and grabbed my crutches, holding them out for me. "Dinner is getting cold."

"Can I borrow your phone?" I asked instead of taking the crutches. I didn't care about dinner. I needed to talk to my friends. I wanted to know that Caz was okay. Even more than that, I wanted to know what happened to Taren the night of the show. I'd had nothing but time to rehash our argument and the events leading up to it. She didn't come to the show or answer my messages. Did that mean she'd made her choice?

"You can on Friday." she reminded me. "No technology this week. Remember?"

How could I forget? Without distractions, all I had to keep me company was regret and uncertainty. Was Taren okay? Was she worried about me? Or was she spending her spring break partying with her friends, determined to forget me?

***

"I think this happened for a reason," my father said, piercing me with a glare. Years ago, that glare would have made me grovel to do his bidding.

I looked at him across the table. My mother was seated between us, almost like a referee. Not much had changed since high school. Well, not much except for me.

"Yeah. My timing was off, and I had an accident." I shoveled food in my mouth so I wouldn't have to talk to him.

"Alec, it's obvious that this hobby of yours is way too dangerous. You need to take your future seriously. Once you quit your little gymnastics group, you'll have more time for your studies." He took a sip of his drink, watching me over the rim of the glass. "You can switch back to Political Science. I'll pay for your tuition, of course, with the expectation that you get an acceptable internship next year. I have some good contacts—"

"I'm not switching majors." The words were sharp and confident as I stared across the table at him.

My father's face contorted in anger. "Sir."

"No need to call me Sir," I said with a smirk. "Just Alec."

"What?" he bellowed. He stood and slammed his palms on the table. His hands clenched into tight fists and the muscles in his forearms twitched like he wanted to take a swing at me.

"Calm down, Alexander," my mother said, looking between us warily. "Why don't you go into the den? I'll bring you something to drink."

My father cast me a look of disgust and tossed his napkin onto his plate. He pushed back from the table, rattling the plates, and stormed away in fury while yelling over his shoulder, "We're not finished here!"

I leaned back into my chair, feeling a sense of victory. He could yell at me until his voice gave out, but I wasn't changing my major. I felt a sense of satisfaction in knowing the only power he held over me was the power I gave him. I had no plans of letting him control any part of my life again.

"Why do you provoke him?" My mother started gathering the plates and taking them to the kitchen sink.

"Why does he think he can manipulate me? I've worked hard for what I have. He can't take that away from me. As soon as spring break is over, I'm going back to my life. The one I chose."

My mother set the plates gently in the sink and then rested her hands on the edge as she looked out the window. "I know," she whispered.

***

I shifted in the seat, trying to get more comfortable.

"Are you sure you aren't dizzy anymore?" My mother gave me a worried glance before returning her eyes to the road. She'd agreed to bring me straight to school after leaving Deep Creek, but only because my father and I both had agreed I couldn't go home with them. Besides, I'd missed hanging out with Lee. He'd left multiple messages on my mom's phone asking me to come see him as soon as I was back in College Park.

"I'm fine, Mom." I stared out the car window, and my fingers tapped a nervous beat on my thigh. I was actually as far from fine as I could get. Frustration crawled up my spine, settling in my shoulders, and I tilted my neck to the side to release some tension. I hadn't talked to any of my friends since the accident. I'd missed work with all three of my jobs, which could mean I had no jobs to come back to. Even if I did still have my jobs, how could I possibly do my security work? I had no idea how I was going to make ends meet if I lost that job. I ignored the small voice whispering in the back of my mind that told me things could be so much easier if I would accept my father's help.

No. That would mean giving up my dream. No matter how hard things got, I'd never give that up.

The worst part was that I still didn't know where I stood with Taren. I asked my parents if she'd come to the hospital. My mother couldn't remember, and my father told me that the only people he saw in the waiting room were my Coach and a few other members of the Acroletes team.

That was like a knee to the groin.

If Taren had been hurt, I would have done anything to be at her side no matter how angry I was with her.

Maybe she didn't know I got hurt, or maybe she didn't care. Maybe she decided she couldn't give up partying with her frat-loving ex-boyfriend. Why else hadn't she come to the show?

My mom pulled up alongside the curb. "Are you sure Lee is going to meet you here?"

"That's what he said." I shrugged. "He said it was important."

"How are you going to get back to your apartment?" Her forehead creased with worry.

"Don't worry Mom; they have buses." I gestured to a bus that was passing us on the other side of the road. "I'll be fine. Besides, I live just off campus. I can always make it back there on my crutches if I have to."

"I know." She reached over to squeeze my arm in a soothing gesture. "I just worry about you."

"I'll be fine." I met her eyes with a smile, and she let out a deep sigh. "I promise."

She leaned over to kiss me on the cheek. "I don't say it enough, Alec. I'm proud of you, and I love you so much."

Her words caught me off guard. I wasn't used to praise from my parents. "Love you, too Mom." I opened the door and swung my leg out.

She put the car in park and went to open her door. "Here, let me help you."

"Nah, I got it." I waved her off. I swung my leg out, and then reached behind my seat to grab my duffle bag.

"Wait." My mother grabbed my arm and stuffed an envelope in my hand.

"What's this?" I opened it up to see that it was full of money.

She shrugged. "I wasn't sure if you'd be able to make it to work with your—" She swallowed as she looked at the leg hanging out the door. "With your injuries." She ran her fingers along her hairline tucking her short hair behind her ear. "I wanted to make sure you'd be able to pay your bills. The doctor said it might take up to three months for you to be able get around well without the crutches." She blinked, her eyes shining with tears.

"Mom, you shouldn't have done this." I stared at the money, and my breath lodged in my throat as relief coursed through me. I looked up to meet her gaze. "Dad's going to be pissed."

She gave me a stern look. "You might think your father makes all of the decisions, but that's not true. You're just as much my son as you are his. I can take care of you if I want. I'm proud of you, Alec. As long as you're happy and living the life you want, I'm happy for you."

"Mom—" My voice was thick with emotion. I leaned over and pulled her into a hug, and her arms wrapped around my back.

She sniffled against my chest. "Don't get all mushy on me now, Alec."

I laughed, grateful for her lightening up the mood. "Thanks, Mom."

"Don't thank me." She leaned back in her seat and wiped under her eyes with her finger. "It's the least I could do considering we kept your phone from you all week."

My head snapped up as my eyebrows furrowed. "What?"

She lifted her chin and straightened her shoulders. "We both agreed that you needed rest. Since the doctor said you shouldn't be straining your eyes by looking at screens, we kept your phone hidden. I put it back in your bag," she said, nodding to my duffle.

Christ. Did she have any idea how much less stressful it would have been if I'd been able to make calls this week?

"It was for the best. Go." She nudged me out the door. "Lee is waiting for you."

I decided that it wasn't worth it to argue about the phone. I was healing; I was home, and I was ready to get my life back on track.

I got out of the car and then turned, leaning down to peer back inside. "Thanks for the ride, Mom." I held the envelope up and shook it. "And for the money."

"You're welcome. I love you, honey. And Alec?"

"Yeah?"

"Prove him wrong."

I stood on the sidewalk and waved as my mother left, feeling for the first time in a week that I could breathe. As soon as she was gone, I dug around in my bag looking for my phone. I found it and pressed the button on the front.

Figures. Of course it was dead. I shoved it back inside and slung my bag across my shoulder as I settled my hands on the grips of the crutches.

Now. Where the hell was Lee?

Chapter 31

Taren

I sat on a bench near the reflecting pool, waiting for my weekly meeting with William. He had texted and asked that we meet here today. Tilting my head back, I looked up at the clear blue sky filled with white fluffy clouds. I stretched my legs out in front of me. The bright sun warmed my skin, but the cool breeze kept the weather mild. A day like this made me want to smile, but instead, I blinked away tears.

I picked up my phone and texted Jon again.

Me: Have you heard from him?

I kept calling and texting Alec, but he never responded. I was terrified that he was hurt so badly, he was unable to respond to any of us. I just needed to know that he was okay.

Jon: Nope. Calls keep going to voicemail. Texts not answered. Did you go to his house?

I had told Jon that since it was spring break, I thought Alec would be at his parent's house.

Me: Yes. I drove to his house and knocked on the door. No answer.

The thought that he either refused to talk to any of us, or physically couldn't, made me sick to my stomach. I closed my eyes as I leaned back on my hands. This week had been hell, but seeing William would make it better. He always made everything better.

I could hear the conversations of people walking by. Two girls spoke in high pitched squealing tones about a cute boy in their art class, and I wanted to punch them. My mind was finally numb, and I wanted to keep it that way. The sound of metal scraping against the sidewalk in a halting rhythm made me cringe. I didn't want to open my eyes to see what it was. Reality was a big old bitch these days. I wanted to stay in my own little world of darkness for a bit longer.

"Taren?" Alec's voice was raw and gravelly.

My eyes flew open at the sound. I gasped and my jaw dropped. Alec stood in front of me, leaning on a set of crutches. *Thank God.* He was here. He was okay.

"What are you doing here?" His eyes tightened, and his jaw set. He stared at me as if my presence alone caused him pain.

"I'm here to meet a friend..." I shook my head. "What are you doing here?" I wanted him to say he was looking for me, but the glare on his face said otherwise. He had a duffle bag slung across his chest, and a cast on his left leg.

I was torn. I wanted to run up, throw my arms around him, and kiss him senseless. The look he was giving me, however, told me to run the other way.

He looked away. "I'm meeting my cousin here." His voice sounded flat and empty.

"Oh." The taste of disappointment was sour. "Where have you been? I've been trying to call you."

His eyebrows furrowed. "You have?" Doubt dripped from his

words.

Hurt coiled in my belly, sick and vicious. "I've called, texted, and emailed you non-stop for the last week. Why didn't you answer? I was worried about you."

The look in his eyes hardened. "Why didn't you return my calls the night of the show? Why didn't you come? You promised you'd be there."

He wasn't holding back any punches. "I tried to text you to tell you I was going to be late, but my phone was dead. I came to the show, but I was late because of—"

"Fucking sorority stuff." He cut me off. His words were harsh, but his scowl was worse. "I know. Believe me, I know."

"You don't understand, Alec. Can't I explain?"

"You don't need to explain anything, Taren. I'm not your priority. We're too different, and maybe it's a good thing we've figured that out now before things got too serious."

Too serious? How much more serious could it be than giving someone your virginity? Than trusting them with your heart? I loved him. Nothing had ever been more serious in my life.

"How can you say that?" I asked, my voice breaking.

"You've made it pretty clear how important parties are to you. My life is all about hard work and discipline. We're pretty different." Alec's voice was sharp, like he was tearing pieces of my heart out with every word.

"Don't say that! I was late because I was explaining to Julie that I wasn't going to be attending parties anymore. You're more important to me than that stuff. I was coming to see you because I chose you."

"Only you didn't see me, did you?"

"I was on my way," I argued, tears threatening to fall. My lungs felt constricted with panic and I couldn't take a deep breath.

"Did you even know I was hurt before today? I mean, you looked surprised to see me, but you didn't look surprised that I was injured. If you knew I was hurt, why didn't you come see me in the hospital?"

"What?" I felt the color drain from my face. "I did come see you in the hospital. I was terrified for you."

"Those must have been some pretty strong painkillers because I certainly don't remember you visiting."

I clenched my teeth. "I was there. So was Jon, Coach, and all your friends. Your father wouldn't let us into your room to see you. But you would know that if you checked your damn phone or email," I spat out. "I called you at least a dozen times a day since you've been gone! Were you ignoring me to hurt me? If so, it worked."

"My phone was dead, too," he retaliated.

We glowered at each other. We were both hurting. The knowledge that our trust was broken made my heart ache.

Alec closed his eyes. "I think I should go."

"You're just going to leave? Things get hard, so you're just going to give up?"

He looked down at the ground and shook his head. "Isn't that what you did at the obstacle course? Things got tough, and you left me. I don't know if I can trust myself right now." He looked up and took a shaky breath. "I haven't seen you for a week. All I know is that what I saw between you and Pickles on Frat Row broke me." He looked past me, his jaw clenched as he spoke. "You didn't come to the show. You didn't send me a message to let me know you were okay. I was so worried about you that I couldn't focus. My distraction hurt someone else and ruined an entire show." He directed his gaze back on me and swallowed loudly. "I know it's not fair to want you to give up something you love for me, but I hate that frat parties and guys like Pickles matter so much to you. Can't you see how destructive we are to one another?"

That shattering? That was my heart. No words had ever hurt as much as the ones Alec had just said. Some of what he'd said was true. I did mess up. I did let him down. What I needed him to understand was that nothing in my whole life mattered more than him.

"Miss Taren?" William's kind voice almost made me sob out loud.

I jerked my head away from Alec, and I wiped away my angry tears before either of them could see.

"Hey, Willy. You're early." The words shook as they left my mouth. I pressed my lips together and took in a deep breath. My stomach was filled with lead, and my chest hurt. For the first time, I worried that my relationship with Alec was irreparable. Even if I thought we were worth the effort, it wouldn't matter if he didn't think we were, too.

Alec stared at William, and I was glad to see it wasn't with pity or discomfort. I didn't think my heart could handle it if Alec mistreated my friend. "How do you know Lee?" he asked, hooking his thumb toward William.

I looked at Alec in confusion. "This is my friend, Willy."

"His name isn't Willy." Alec looked angry and frustrated.

William chuckled and approached me to give me a hug. "Hi, Miss Taren. Good to see you." I accepted William's hug and pulled him tightly to me. It was nice to see a friendly face.

"Lee? Taren? My head's fucking killing me. Can one of you tell me what's going on?" Alec rubbed his forehead and then grimaced, clutching his ribs. His breath hissed through his teeth, and he clenched his eyes shut. As upset as I was with him, I felt awful that my anger had made me forget how badly he was hurt just a week ago.

"I'm not sure who Lee is." I arched an eyebrow at William in question. "But Willy started out as my assigned buddy through the Good Buddies program here at the university. Now he's my friend."

Alec's eyes widened in surprise before he carefully gestured toward William. "Lee's my cousin. I told you about him. He's pretty much the best part of my family. Remember?"

I laughed. "Willy is your cousin? Wow." I squeezed William's arm and smiled up at him before facing Alec. "As different as we are, at least we have one good thing in common."

Alec tipped his head as if considering my words, and then looked away again.

"Willy, can we meet another day? It looks like you guys have some catching up to do. I'll talk to you soon, okay?" I went to pat William's hand, but he gently clasped mine in his own.

"Wait, Miss Taren. Please." William smiled, and my heart warmed. I couldn't say no to him. Not when he had always been so good and understanding with me.

"Sure, Willy."

He pulled me closer to him and grabbed Alec's hand too.

"Guess I have some explaining to do, huh? Yup, yup." He laughed to himself, and I couldn't help but grin. Looking over at Alec, he had a small smile on his face as well. "See, when I heard that Miss Taren was my buddy, I remembered right away that she was the girl that stole my cousin's scholarship."

My jaw dropped, and I looked over at Alec. He was stunned.

"Alec and I talk a lot." William grinned at his cousin. "I also remembered he had hurt you in high school when you asked him to go to the dance, Miss Taren. He was not nice to you." William's face sobered, and he frowned at his cousin. "He felt bad about that. He was a jerk. Did he tell you?"

I shook my head.

"Then he got in trouble for that party, and he thought it was your fault. So he was not super happy to go to the same college as you, you know that?" William dipped his chin down, watching my reaction.

I nodded, catching my bottom lip between my teeth. I knew that much was true.

"Oh, but then he told me he saw you around campus. He said you changed. You were not so...how did you say that, Alec? She did not have anything up her rear end anymore?"

Alec groaned and closed his eyes as I huffed out an angry laugh. "Nice, Alec." I let go of William's hand and crossed my arms over my chest.

"Now do not get upset, Miss Taren. He liked you. He used to watch you, and it made him feel good that you were having fun in college. Even if...what did you say Alec? A lot of the time it sucked for you?"

William and I looked at Alec, but he turned away, studying the fountain.

"This year, when we became buddies, he was talking about you again because you had a class together. He even used to stare at the back of your head during class. How funny is that?" William snorted, and I bit my lip to keep from smiling.

"Geez, Lee. I thought you knew how to keep a secret. Why not tell her all my embarrassing stories from when we were kids?"

William ignored Alec. He was clearly on a mission.

"I knew you and Alec did not get along in school, but when I met you, you were like sunshine. I knew my cousin needed that kind of a bright light girl in his life." William leaned over to whisper loudly in my ear, "His daddy is not very nice, you know."

My eyes welled up again with tears, and I hurried to brush them away.

"You talked to me during our visits about a boy you liked and when you called him Alec, I thought my heart would explode. You both liked each other! How funny is that? You both just needed a little help."

"Wait a minute, Lee," Alec addressed his cousin. "This whole year when I talked to you about Taren, you knew she was your buddy and you never said anything?"

William nodded, a big-ass smile all over his face.

"Why did you lie? I thought we told each other everything."

William frowned. "I did not lie. I just listened. Listening is the most important." He reached into his backpack and pulled out the red ribbon I had given him weeks ago.

I held my breath. This was so embarrassing. Alec would probably recognize it and know I had kept it all these years. *Way to look like a weirdo, Taren.*

Alec looked at the ribbon, and then his eyes met mine. He obviously remembered. He remembered everything.

William took one end of the ribbon and tied it onto my wrist. "Miss Taren gave me this. She told me the story of how you fixed her backpack with this ribbon, and she wore it in her hair when she asked you to the dance. She saved it and when she hurt my feelings one time, she gave it to me. She told me the story about the red string of fate and that she and I were connected."

William took the other end of the ribbon and tied it to Alec's wrist.

"Now I am part of your string of fate. I listen and I help. You two were always connected, you just need a good buddy to make sure you stayed that way. Yup, yup."

"Jesus." Alec swore quietly as he stared at the ribbon that connected us. I couldn't tell what that one word meant.

"Willy, you're very sweet, but just because you want us to be together, doesn't mean we can be. We're so different from each other. We hurt each other too much."

William ignored me and turned to Alec. "Do you love her?"

Alec was silent as he raised his gaze to mine. My heart ached. I loved him, but I still hurt him without meaning to, and he had done the same to me.

Alec took a deep breath and then blew it out. "Yes. Of course I do. You know I do, Lee. I already told you that."

My breath caught in my throat and I pressed the palm of my hand to my mouth. My heart raced as my brain processed the words I had been dreaming of hearing. Did Alec just admit he *loved* me?

He reached for my hand and took it in his. His thumb rubbed over the back of my hand. "I think I've loved you for a long time, Taren."

"And what about you, Miss Taren? Do you love him?" William searched my face for my answer, but I couldn't stop staring at Alec.

"So much I can barely breathe," I admitted softly.

"Well," William dropped the ribbon from his hands and stepped away from us. "Well, okay then. Happiness and love. You are tied by fate. Always have been. Yup, yup."

William turned and walked away.

"Wait! Willy!" I was about to chase after him before I remembered I was tethered to Alec. A subtle one, that William was.

"Yes, Miss Taren?" Only William's head turned back toward me.

So many questions swirled around in my brain. Some were for William, some were for Alec, and some were for myself. Only one came to mind at that moment. "If your name is Lee, why do you go by William, and Will, and Billy, and Willy?"

"My name is William, but my family always called me Lee since the day I was born. Never liked it. After I met you, I thought I would try a few others on for size. See how they fit, but I know for sure what my name is now."

He walked away again, and I called out, "What did you decide?"

William turned fully around and laughed. "William. Yup, yup."

We both watched as William walked away. He didn't look back. He kept his head up high as if he knew we didn't need his help anymore.

Alec laughed softly and linked our fingers together. "What the hell just happened? I know I got hit in the head pretty hard, but I'm pretty sure we just got completely played by my cousin."

"Someone needed to talk some sense into us. Remind us that we're all in. Right?" I leaned in and kissed him lightly, still a little unsure.

When I tried to pull away, Alec reached up and slid his fingers around the back of my head bringing my lips back to his. I opened up for him and let him kiss me more deeply, and he groaned.

"You really love me?" he asked.

I held his gaze. "Completely." I leaned in to kiss him again.

"I missed you," he whispered against my lips. "You have no idea."

"I missed you, too. It was killing me that I couldn't find you. I even drove out to your parents' house and knocked on their door."

Alec pulled back so he could look at me. "You did? I didn't think..."

"I was so worried about you. I wanted to fix things."

Alec kissed each corner of my mouth. "My dad took me to Deep Creek. They thought it would be good for me to recover there at our cabin. No phone. No computer. No you." He kissed me square on the lips. "No fun."

"I thought you were avoiding me because you were mad. Your dad said you didn't want to see me." The relief I felt at knowing he didn't purposely ignore my messages made me feel lighter than I had in a long time.

"My fucking father… Look, I was hurt. But I would have talked to you if I could. I thought about you the entire time." He pressed his lips against mine again, and I loved the way his kisses wrapped possessively around my mouth. I wanted him to remind us both just how much we belonged to one another.

"I think William's right. We're tied by fate. We'll always find our way back to one another."

Alec grinned. "So, you're sticking with me?"

I held up our joined hands with our wrists tied by the ribbon that had changed, and continued to change, my life. "You don't have a choice. We're bound for good. I love you, Alec."

He lifted up our hands and kissed the inside of my wrist where the ribbon was tied. "I love you, Taren."

Chapter 32

Alec

I pulled the car into the parking lot, and although she didn't say anything, Taren looked at me like I'd lost my mind. Tonight was supposed to be a special date—our last weekend of freedom before we started classes at UMD as juniors. I was sure she was wondering why I'd brought her to our old high school at night. Our car was the only one in the parking lot.

Perfect. That's what I'd been hoping.

"Ready?" I asked her.

An easy smile swept across her mouth. "Sure."

I retrieved my duffle bag out of the back seat and met her in front of the car, taking her hand in mine. Taren was wearing a sundress that made me want to toss her back in the car. I wanted to christen the back seat with her in a mass of sweaty limbs and sweet kisses. Those cowboy boots weren't helping matters any. I could almost imagine them wrapped around my waist while...

Focus, Hart.

I tugged on her hand, and she smiled as I pulled her toward the football field.

"What's that?" she asked, pointing to the glow we could see in the distance.

I lifted our hands to kiss the backs of her fingers. "You'll see."

We walked hand in hand until we reached the area of scorched earth that was filled with at least a hundred lit candles. I finally looked over at Taren to see that her eyes were bright with happy curiosity. I set down my bag and pulled out a blanket and spread it open across the grass just outside of the circle.

"What is this? Are we having a night picnic?" Taren asked, staring at the circle of candles which looked like a sea of flame. "God. How beautiful."

"Yes, you are." I reached up and tucked a piece of hair behind her ear. In the flickering candlelight, she looked like an angel. I would have to remember to thank Taren's aunt Claire for helping get this ready in time.

"So what's going on?"

"I'm re-writing history," I told her.

"Oh really?"

I took both of her hands in mine and pulled her close to me. "Ask me to go to Homecoming, Taren."

She tilted her head in confusion. "What?"

"I wish I had said yes when you asked me to go to Homecoming. I wish I had known myself enough then to make the choice that I wanted to make—and not the choice that everyone else expected. I didn't know myself back then, but I do now. So, we have our own bonfire." I gestured to the candles. "Will you ask me to go to Homecoming? I really want to say yes."

She looked over at the candles, and I saw the moment when it registered with her that this was where I'd broken her heart and trust that awful night. She shook her head as if I was being ridiculous, but when she turned to me, her smile was brilliant. Taren bit her bottom lip before looking up at me through her lashes. "Will you go to Homecoming with me, Alec Hart?"

I was surprised at how strong my relief was and how much I needed a do over on that night.

"I thought you'd never ask." I wrapped my arms around her back while still holding her hands. Her body arched into mine, and I bent over to claim her mouth with a kiss. "Yes. Anything you ever want. Yes," I whispered between kisses.

She laughed. "I just want you."

"I just want the chance to finally dance with you." I let go of her fingers, and she reached up to wrap her hands lightly around the back of my neck. My hands found her waist. With her body pressed up against mine, we danced in the flickering light of hundreds of candles on a night of second chances.

Taren brought her hand to my cheek, and her thumb caressed my skin. "You know, as hurt as I was when you said no, now I'm glad it happened that way."

"Why would you be glad that I hurt you?" We swayed, and I kissed her shoulder. My lips traced a path up her neck until I reached the tender skin under her ear. Taren leaned her head back and sighed. My mouth moved down the front of her throat to the neckline of her sundress.

"We weren't ready for each other then. Now I'm stronger and so are you. I know we'll make it through anything because we love each other." The words were breathy, pleading for me to show her just how much I felt the same way. How much I'd changed from the boy I was in high school.

I reached into my pocket and pulled out the old red piece of silk that had been through so much with us. I twined my fingers with Taren's and then brought our hands up between us. She watched as I weaved the ribbon in and around our hands and wrists. I tangled us together so tightly that no matter what we faced in the future, we'd never fall apart from each other again.

"We've both made pledges that are important to us and the things we believe in, but this time, my pledge is to you. I don't ever want you to doubt the way I feel about you."

"I don't doubt you." She leaned up on her tiptoes to kiss me.

"I know, but I'm making this official. I should have said yes all those years ago. I want you to know that you will always be my yes. I promise that no matter how life might try to tear us apart, no matter how tangled things get, I will always come back to you. I promise to believe in my trust for you and not my own insecurities. I promise to always be *all in* with you. I promise to love you with every piece of my heart. Tonight, I pledge myself to you."

Taren searched my eyes, before her gaze fell hungrily to my lips. "Pledge yourself to us."

"To us," I said, lifting our hands to kiss her wrist.

My lips had barely left her skin before her mouth crashed into mine. I wrapped my free arm around her, and she pushed me backward until I was sitting on the blanket. She straddled me and then kissed me so desperately I could barely catch my breath.

She finally leaned back to look at me. Her free hand roamed under my shirt until her fingers rested over my heart. "This moment is so perfect. After everything we've been through, this means so much."

She brought our bound hands between us looking at the red ribbon twisted and tied around our wrists, fingers, and hands. "I love you, Alec

Hart."

"I love you more, Taren Richards."

A wicked smile curved along her lips, and she bent over our tied hands to take one of my fingers into her mouth. She wrapped her tongue around it, sucking as she pulled back.

Holy. Shit.

"Naughty little Taren." My words came out in a groan.

"I pledge to us, too. Always." She kissed my fingertips and curled her body into my lap.

Taren Richards owned me, body and soul. I couldn't think of anything else in the world I wanted more than to belong to her.

Chapter 33

William

Love was strange. Alec and Miss Taren loved each other for a long time, but they were afraid of it. I was afraid of lots of things.

But not love.

Love was the only thing that helped people make the right choices. I listened to people all the time. I learned a lot by sitting still.

People could be mean. They were cruel to one another. Sometimes they were cruel to me. Life would be better if they knew what was really important. Happiness and love. That was all that mattered.

I was not in love. Not yet, anyway. I loved my parents. I loved Alec. I loved Miss Taren like a friend. The love like I saw with Alec and Miss Taren? I did not have that. I wanted it, though.

I thought I might be able to love Sarah. Her Dad said no. That we were too slow.

He was wrong. Nobody was too slow to love. Everyone could love. They just needed to find the right person.

That was the hard part I think. It was like shopping for shoes. Me, I liked a black gym shoe with Velcro straps. Easy to put on and comfortable when I walked to the bus stop. I had to try on a lot of shoes before I found the ones that fit best. Some people, like Alec and Miss Taren, found their match when they were young. But sometimes when you are too young, you are not ready for that match.

I was older than those two love birds. I was ready. And waiting.

I sat on the bench and checked my digital watch. I had fifteen minutes before my bus came to take me to my apartment. I was proud that I moved out of my parent's house. I had a roommate who did not talk much, but that was okay. I listened when he did. I wished I had more friends, though. Right now my only friends were Alec and Miss Taren.

Today was a really good day. I spent time with Miss Taren. She was happy, so that made me feel really good inside.

Sunlight shone off something on the ground and made a rainbow in the air. I smiled, as I always did when the sun was shining and especially when I saw a rainbow.

"What is that?" a girl asked. She was standing next to me, pointing at the ground.

I looked up to see happy brown eyes.

"I don't know, but it makes a rainbow." I stood up and stuck out my hand. "My name is William."

The happy brown eyes creased in the corners when the woman smiled. "I am Stacy." She shook my hand. She had a nice handshake, not sloppy. "I like rainbows, too." She pointed to a clip in her brown hair. I smiled back.

"Very pretty." I sat back down on the bench and patted next to me. "Would you like to sit?"

"Yes, I would." She sat next to me, hugging her purple purse to her chest. She looked over at me. She had a small grin on her face. "Are you in Good Buddies like me?"

"Yup, yup." I nodded and angled my body to face her. "My buddy is Miss Taren. She is the sweetest."

"Nah, my buddy is the sweetest. Her name is Alexis." Stacy's face lit up when she said her friend's name. Ah, she had the sunshine in her, too. "Hey, can you find what was making that rainbow? I would like it for my collection."

"Yup, yup." I bent down. I studied the ground and found a small crystal. It looked like it was a charm on a necklace once. As I picked it up, light shined off it on to Stacy's shoes.

I looked over and laughed.

"What is so funny, William?" Stacy sounded upset.

"I was looking at your shoes."

"What about, 'em?" She frowned, looking down at her own purple gym shoes.

"I like them. Especially the laces."

She looked over at me and smiled again. "Thank you. I thought they were special."

"They are. Do you have time for me to tell you a story?"

Stacy tilted her head to the side and then looked over her shoulder. "No bus. I have time."

"Great." I looked down once more at the bright red laces on each of her shoes. "Have you ever heard about the red string of fate?"

Don't miss the next story in the College Bound series!

The Color of Us

by Laura Ward & Christine Manzari

*The following excerpt is subject to change.

The Color of Us

Chapter 1

Those inspirational posters were nothing but lies. Rain didn't always bring a rainbow. There wasn't always calm after the storm. And not every ending meant a new beginning.

I only needed one violent night for those dreams to be shattered. The truth was, when things ended, there was no promise for a bright, new, shiny beginning. The only guarantee was that things would change.

I hated that things had changed.

I hated that the rain stole my rainbow. I hated that the storm tore my family apart and left nothing but broken bits inside each of us. I hated that when my sister's life ended, so did my rosy view of the future.

Unusual silences. Empty places. Unfinished conversations. The pain came in waves, and sometimes I thought I might drown under the weight of losing her.

I always thought the worst part of grief was the moment when tragedy struck, but that's not true.

The worst part came after the last casserole was finished and everyone went home. The worst part came a few weeks later, after the consoling phone calls had long gone silent and the last flower petal had withered away. The worst part was seeing the empty chair at the dinner table every single night. The worst part was the silence in the mornings...silence that used to be filled with my sister's teasing voice and beautiful singing. The worst part was hearing people laugh or seeing them smile, never knowing if I'd be capable of either of those things again. The worst part was the finality of it all. Samantha really was gone and everyone just kept on living and breathing and moving as if my heart wasn't some crushed, mangled mess inside my chest.

The worst part was that I missed my sister, and it was so fucking unfair that I had to live a life without her.

***

"Time to get up, Alexis." My mother's order was quickly followed by a blinding brightness as she threw open the curtains in my bedroom.

"Mom!" The sunlight pierced through my eyelids and I cringed, hiding my face under the blanket. "I'm sleeping," I groaned.

Her footsteps echoed across my floor and then my comforter was torn away. "You've spent the first few weeks of summer in bed. You've got to get out sometime." Her voice softened and my closed eyes stung with unshed tears. "Your father and I want you to try and enjoy what's left of your break."

I rolled over and wrapped my head in the pillow. Yeah right. Enjoy my summer. As if that was even possible. The only thing I enjoyed was losing myself in movies and books. That's the only time I could stop thinking long enough to find peace.

"Today is your first day of driving school. You don't want to be late." Her voice wavered just enough that I peeled the pillow away from my face to brave the light streaming in through my windows.

My eyes narrowed sleepily as I stared at her. I tried to swallow but my throat felt like it was clamped shut. Driving school? Was this some kind of sick joke? "What?"

"Come on. You've been looking forward to this." She met my eyes with her patented calmness, but the way she clutched my comforter in her fist betrayed her. She held onto it like it was a lifeline to keep her from drowning.

"Mom." I shook my head. "That was before...I don't...I don't want to learn how to drive. Not after..."

She sat down on the edge of my bed. Her hand lifted as if to comfort me and then she cleared her throat and her hand fell to the mattress. "We're all devastated by what happened, Alexis, but you can't keep avoiding life. Sam wouldn't want that."

Avoiding life? I wasn't avoiding life. I wanted life. Sam was life and more than anything, I wanted her back. She pushed boundaries and lived on the edge. She was passionate and brave. She was charismatic and adventurous. The limelight craved Sam. Without her, everything just felt...less. Pointless. Lifeless. Colorless.

"I don't want to." I rolled over, facing the wall. If there was one thing I knew, it was that mom wouldn't force me to go to driving school. No way. Not after...

"Alexis Marie White!" The pillow was snatched away from me and my head crashed into the mattress. "Do not turn your back on me. I know you're hurting and so am I, but I'm still your mother. I know what's best for you." I felt the mattress rise as my mom stood up. "So you're going to get out of this bed. You're going to get dressed. And you're going to driving school." The door clicked closed behind her.

Damn. She took my pillow.

***

I walked into the small, dark classroom of EZ Driving School and searched for an empty desk. I spotted one in the back row and went to claim it before I was forced to talk to someone. The desk had just enough room for a notebook and pen, and the top was covered in so much graffiti the wood was barely visible. I dropped into the seat and looked down at the scarred surface.

Right in the middle, someone had written, "Speed is a tempestuous lover." Next to that, the words "Jesus Rocks" were carved near fancy script that said, "No Regerts." I rolled my eyes and tried to ignore the urge to fix the mistake. At least it wasn't a tattoo. That would have been truly regrettable.

My eyes roamed the rest of the artwork, which was mostly just a series of names and pointless phrases. I finally noticed that on the edge, someone had scribbled a crude drawing of a dick. Nice. At least it was anatomically correct. I shook my head and covered it with my notebook. Out of sight, out of mind.

I took a deep breath and ventured a look around the classroom. Everything was dingy and the air reeked of stale cigarettes and mildew.

If my mom thought this form of hell was better than my usual method of coping, she was sadly mistaken. I don't know why she felt the need to drop me off at the curb of this god forsaken building. She left me with nothing but a happy wave and a wish to have a good time. Seriously? If she wanted me to heal and move on with my life, this was the last place I should be. I wasn't capable of being normal or happy right now. Especially not if a car was involved.

I crossed my legs under my desk and opened my notebook, my hand shaking as I tried to forget where I was and why it bothered me so much.

"This seat taken?" A gravelly voice pulled me out of my dark thoughts and I looked up to see…trouble. There was no other way to describe him. He was dressed all in black. Black tight t-shirt, black jeans, black belt, and black boots. Even the leather-studded cuff on his wrist was black. He wore his light brown hair in a messy, spiked jumble on his head. I couldn't tell if he worked to make it look that good or if he just rolled out of bed and left his house without looking in the mirror.

He stared at me and I finally managed to say, "No." I watched as he folded his lean, tall body into the seat next to me.

"Name's Liam." He acknowledged me with a gruff nod of his head and I smiled politely in return.

There were plenty of guys like Liam at my school. They were usually off sneaking a smoke, cutting class, or causing general mayhem. I didn't associate with them.

"Don't have a name?" His head was tilted toward me and he stared with an intensity that made me feel as if he could read all of my deepest, darkest secrets. His green eyes flashed with mischief and I felt a twinge of guilt for not answering him.

"Sorry. I'm Alexis," I said quickly. Why did I feel like I was out of breath? "I wasn't trying to be rude."

He nodded and bounced his leg restlessly underneath his seat. "Didn't think you were." His gaze travelled from my face and down my body in a quick scan. "You look a little old for this class."

"Yeah, I'm eighteen. Just getting around to it." I watched my finger as it traced the metal spine of my notebook before I looked up at Liam again. "You look a little old yourself."

"I'm eighteen too. I already have my license, but I got myself into a little traffic situation." He grinned and ran his hand through his hair, which only made it look more wild. "Asshat lawyer convinced the dipshit judge that repeating this lame class would put me on the straight and narrow." He gave me an arrogant wink and sat back in his seat, stretching his legs in front of him. "Too bad for them I don't do straight and narrow."

I blinked a few times, staring at his cavalier expression. Wow. He was trouble with a capital "T." My mom would choke on her pearls if she knew I was talking to someone with a criminal record.

Good thing I had no intention of telling her.

"All right people. Quiet down now." A balding man wearing a short-sleeved button-down shirt and a tie entered the room. Conversations died out as students settled into their seats. "Good morning, I'm Mr. Weinberg and I'll be your driver's education teacher. Let's get started."

I turned in my seat to face forward, preparing to take notes. Beside me, Liam chuckled and when I looked at him, I noticed he was staring at me with a smirk on his face. His hands were resting lazily on his desk and he didn't have anything with him to take notes. "You're taking this seriously, aren't you?" His eyes were practically laughing at me as ne nodded toward my pen and notebook.

My mouth opened to argue with him, but there was no point. Guilty as charged...I took everything seriously. I turned toward the instructor again and took down a few notes as Mr. Weinberg spoke.

"Hey, Lex?" The words were a husky whisper and against my will, I turned toward Liam again. I wanted to tell him that no one ever called me Lex, but then he licked his lips and I almost stopped breathing. I decided then and there he could call me whatever the hell he wanted to as long as it came from that mouth.

"Yes?" I managed to say.

"You ever driven a car before?"

I swallowed and shook my head.

"If you want to learn to drive stick, I'm the guy for the job." His gaze dropped to my desktop. When I saw where he was looking, I blushed ten thousand shades of red. *Christ on a cracker.* The dick drawing was peeking out from under my arm and he was staring at it.

Liam started chuckling and I slid my notebook over to hide the drawing. He wasn't just trouble, he was temptation personified.

What really scared me was how much I liked it.

I turned my eyes toward the front of the room, my lips pressed together as I held back a smile. I desperately tried to ignore the guy in black who strangely made things feel a little less dark.

The rest of the class passed by as I took notes and avoided looking at Liam. We dismissed two hours later and I quickly grabbed my things, knowing my mom would be expecting me to come out on time. I walked out of the building, searching the parking lot for her car.

"Need a ride?" Liam stood next to me, lighting up a cigarette and inhaling deeply.

"No, thanks." I hugged my notebook to my chest and peered sideways at him. Smoking usually disgusted me, but Liam looked so effortlessly cool when he lifted the cigarette to his mouth. All I could do was stare. I shook my head as I realized what he'd asked me. "Wait, you're still allowed to drive?"

He blew out smoke and flicked the end of the cigarette with his thumb. "I got my license suspended in June. So, technically no. But fuck that, I gotta drive. I'm only here so I can get my license back before school starts."

"Oh." His parents let him drive without a license? What kind of parents would do that? Not mine. I cleared my throat. "Where are you going to school in the fall?"

"Community College." He ran his tongue along the front of his teeth like he was getting rid of the taste of the words in his mouth. "You?"

"College Park."

"Ah, your last few weeks of freedom before you head off to the university. Sweet." Liam grinned and then took another long drag from his cigarette.

Mom's minivan approached. "That's my ride. See you tomorrow." I smiled politely and gave him a small wave as I headed to the car.

"I'll save you a seat tomorrow, Lex," Liam said as I walked away.

My heart stuttered to hear him call me Lex. My family always called me Alexis. I was the good girl. I was predictable. I did what was expected of me. But Lex sounded like someone who knew how to have fun. Lex sounded like she tested boundaries. Lex sounded like someone Sam would have hung out with. I wouldn't mind being a different person. I wouldn't mind being Lex.

When I got in my seat and buckled in, I chanced a look out the window to find Liam was staring at me with a wicked grin. My heart beat faster under his gaze and I had to look away.

"Who were you talking to?" Mom pulled out of the parking lot and headed toward our local grocery store.

"Uh...no one. Just a guy from class. He sat next to me."

She looked in the rearview mirror. "He looks like trouble." She said the last word like it was a communicable disease.

I smiled to myself. Liam didn't just look like trouble, he was trouble. For once, that didn't sound like such a bad thing, no matter how my mom said it. Liam was nothing like me, and I was drawn to his darkness and inappropriate charm. My life had been nothing but endless rules that I followed without question. Maybe my mom was right. Maybe I did need to try and enjoy my summer.

Maybe a little trouble was exactly what I needed.

Dear Reader,

Thank you for reading The Pledge. If you enjoyed this story, please consider leaving a review. Reviews are incredibly important to indie authors.

Thank you!

ACKNOWLEDGEMENTS

We have to start off by thanking Bekky Levesque for introducing us. When she realized she had two friends who were writing manuscripts, she made the introduction and the rest is history. Thank you Bekky! Without you, THE PLEDGE would never have been born.

Joe and Johnny (our real life book boyfriends), thank you for understanding when we choose to write instead of snuggling on the couch. You've had to listen to us talk about our characters as if they were real, and we are lucky to have your unwavering patience and support. We love you!

To our children, thank you for sharing our love of books and reading. We hope one day you're able to follow your dreams and spend every day of your lives doing the things you love.

Thank you to our parents! You have dealt with our reading and writing obsessions since we were small children. You bought our books, pens, papers, and eventually computers. Your support and encouragement gave us the courage to follow our dreams.

To our wonderful beta readers: Amanda Rounsaville, Amber Huber, Bekky Levesque, Dani Fisher, Gail Laughlin, Jen Brandenburg, Kelly Erdman, Laurie Marin, Lisa Graham, Pam Hoehler, Pat Rosner, Rich Sanidad, Tamara Debbaut, Tara Paraska, and Teri Chason—how can we possibly show our gratitude? Thank you for reading the first few drafts and giving us such valuable feedback.

We had an incredible team supporting us along the way. Thank you to Ana Zaun for editing this book and always pushing us to improve our story line. Alexis Durbin, thank you for proofreading. Your attention to detail is awesome. Thanks to Sarah Hansen of Okay Creations for the gorgeous book cover and to our photographer, Vania Stoyanova, for bringing our vision for the cover to life. We would also like to thank our models Jordan Verroi and Fawn Coba. Tamara Debbaut is the creative genius behind our marketing artwork and we appreciate her help more than we can say. Finally, we would like to thank Wordsmith Publicity for planning our cover reveal and book tour.

While we are at it, there are a few bloggers who have been instrumental in sharing our books. Thanks to Candy from Prisoners of Print, Erin from Southern Belle, Jennifer and Theresa from Sassy Divas, Tash from Book Lit Love, Kim from KimberlyFaye Reads, Betsy from Book Nerd Betsy, Liza from I Dare You to Read, and Ethan from One Guy's Guide to Good Reads. A special thanks to Ethan for the laughs and tears as he has reviewed our books!

Laura would like to give a special shout out to Tamara Debbaut for holding her hand through this indie writing experience for the last year. Tamara gives so much of her time supporting, sharing ideas, creating websites and newsletters, and helping with any and every technology question that has ever existed. Thank you for your talent and friendship!

Christine, thank you for taking a chance on this writing partnership with me. Since we began, a day hasn't gone by without our emails or texts! Your hard work, beautiful writing, and dedication to books are an inspiration to me. I can't wait to try out the ropes course together!

Laura, thanks for being the sweet to my sassy, the extrovert to my introvert, and the early bird to my night owl. Opposites attract and I'm so lucky to have gotten to share this journey of writing and self-publishing with you. I can't tell you how much I love learning from you and writing with you as we tackle the book world!

Finally, to anyone reading this right now—you have made our

dreams come true. We are writers thanks to you!

ABOUT THE AUTHORS

Laura Ward is the co-author of *The Pledge*, as well as the author of *Past Heaven* and *Not Yet*. She lives in Maryland with her loud and very loving three children and husband. Laura married her college sweetheart and is endlessly grateful for the support he has given her through all their years together, and especially toward her goal of writing books. When not picking up toy trucks, driving to lacrosse practice, or checking spelling homework, Laura is writing or reading romance novels.

The first thing **Christine Manzari** does when she's getting ready to read a book is to crack the spine in at least five places. She wholeheartedly believes there is no place as comfy as the pages of a well-worn book. She's addicted to buying books, reading books, and writing books. Books, books, books. She also has a weakness for adventure, inappropriate humor, and coke (the caffeine-laden bubbly kind). Christine is from Forest Hill, Maryland where she lives with her husband, three kids, and her library of ugly spine books. Christine is the co-author of *The Pledge*, as well as the author of *Deviation*, *Conviction*, and *Hooked*.

AUTHOR LINKS

Other Titles by Laura Ward:
Not Yet
Past Heaven

Other Titles by Christine Manzari:
Deviation (Sophisticates #1)
Conviction (Sophisticates #2)
Hooked

Keep up to date with Laura Ward via:
Website: www.laurawardauthor.com/
Facebook: www.facebook.com/LauraWardAuthor
Twitter: twitter.com/laurarosnerward
Amazon: www.amazon.com/Laura-Ward/e/B00M8HIOSS
Goodreads: www.goodreads.com/author/show/8328712.Laura_Ward
Newsletter: http://eepurl.com/9O3T
Email: laurawardauthor@yahoo.com

Keep up to date with Christine Manzari via:
Website: www.christinemanzari.com
Facebook: www.facebook.com/ChristineManzari
Twitter: twitter.com/Xenatine
Amazon: www.amazon.com/Christine-Manzari/e/B00EIHIXBE
www.goodreads.com/author/show/7218946.Christine_Manzari
Email: christine@christinemanzari.com

Made in the USA
Middletown, DE
15 December 2024